DOUBLE
OR
NOTHING

CINDY STEEL

Front Cover Design: Melody Jeffries

Editing: Jana Miller at The Writer's Assistant, Jenn Lockwood, and Amy Romney.

ACKNOWLEDGMENTS

It takes a village to raise up a book. And I have a big village to thank for this one.

James, Stetson, and Dawson. You probably won't ever read this, but just in case—you three are my breath of fresh air. Thanks for loving me and picking up the slack when I'm away somewhere in my fictional world.

Lisa. Thanks so much for being willing to talk plot with me for hours. You are the very best, and I couldn't do this without you. Thanks for another one.

Mom. Thank you for reading multiple versions of my books and telling me you love them every time.

Dad. Thanks for reading my books, and I'm so sorry for all the kissing.

Karen. I don't know how I would survive this author stuff without you. You give great advice. You pick me up when I'm down. And you repeatedly talk me off of ledges. I'm so grateful to have found such a great friend in you. You're the best.

My critique group. What times we have had in such a short time of knowing each other. You each have such a gift for writing, and I have learned so much from rubbing shoulders with each of you. Thanks for the lessons, encouragement, and the laughs.

My beta readers. Your feedback and reviews are so critical to my whole process. Thanks for being gentle and loving and telling me when the jokes don't land.

My ARC readers, author friends, and the Bookstagram community. You guys make social media a delightful place to be. You make my author world go around and I'm so grateful to you.

Florida Georgia Line. For singing the song "Dirt." Which seemed like the perfect theme song for this book.

Melody, thank you so much for another beautiful cover in this series.

Jana Miller at The Writer's Assistant. Thanks so much for your kind feedback and for helping me save Logan's character.

Jenn Lockwood. You were amazing! Thanks for all your work cleaning up my manuscript.

Amy Romney. You helped me out so much. Thank you for your generous edits, time, and feedback.

Thank you, readers! Your messages, emails, and excitement mean the world to me. Thank you for allowing my stories to be a small part of your life.

Mom,
There was a short period growing up when I went through a difficult
time, and my self-esteem had taken a hit. During this time, there was
one night where you sat next to me on the couch and reminded me, in
unequivocal terms, of my worth. And my value.
I am forever grateful.

THE INCIDENT

TEN YEARS EARLIER

Tessa

I bent over the kitchen counter and peered into the bowl of light-brown liquid that had definitely not gotten foamy after a five-minute rest.

"Tess, can we please just grab a pizza from the freezer?" my best friend, Kelsey, asked over my shoulder.

"Let's give it another minute," I pleaded. "I got it to work at my house."

Kelsey groaned and began rummaging through her mom's cupboards. "I'm too hungry to waste any more time. I'm turning on the oven."

"The water must not have been hot enough." I felt the bowl, and indeed, it was tepid to the touch. Dejectedly, I stirred the liquid with the wooden spoon, begging it to foam. The failure was a definite blow to my precious fourteen-year-old ego.

I was staying at Kelsey's home for a weekend sleepover. We had just come from watching her brother, Logan, play a home game for the varsity basketball team. He had scored eleven points, had nine rebounds, one steal, and basically helped our small team in Eugene, Idaho to not suck too badly. I knew all of those stats *not* because I was still obsessed with him, but because I cared about our town's success. As children, we used to exchange love notes, and when I say exchange, I mean, as an eight-year-old, I would write gibberish with lots of hearts in note form and hide it under his pillow during sleepovers. Obviously, by the mature age of fourteen, those had stopped. And though I still kept the secret scrapbook full of pictures of Logan, I no longer added to it. However, I did keep that particular secret hidden deep in the recesses of my bedroom. Hidden even from Kelsey. Actually, *especially* from Kelsey.

"So, when do you think your family will be home?"

Kelsey shot me a look, her light brown hair falling into her eyes as she pulled out a pizza pan. "I know what you're really asking, Creeper, and I have no idea. Logan usually hangs out with friends after the game. No more talk about my brother. It's gross."

"I don't like him anymore." Not quite true, but at four years older, Logan might as well have been from another planet. I had a crush, but I knew my place.

"Your feelings sure changed fast from last summer. Okay, we're done with this." Kelsey grabbed the yeast bowl and dumped it down the sink.

"Fine." I made a mental note to attempt pizza dough again later that week. "Last summer was just a joke that got blown out of proportion."

"Liar." She laughed.

I was a little miffed she kept bringing that up. It felt like she was trying to remind me of the most embarrassing thing that had ever happened to me. One summer ago, Kelsey had a group of friends over for a party at the same time Logan had friends over playing basketball. Shirts and skins. Later that night, all the girls were talking about how cute Logan and the other boys were. Then, thinking I was so cool because I knew Logan the best—besides Kelsey, of course—I told my friends, out loud, how much I preferred Logan without his shirt on. He was right behind me. Much laughter ensued from my friends as well as Logan. I avoided him now at all costs, because he loved to tease me about it. Knowing he wasn't home made being here much more relaxing.

"You can go pick the pizza. There's a bunch in the freezer in the laundry room."

"Which freezer?" Kelsey's family had a ranch and a dairy farm. Their home boasted not one full-size freezer, like a normal family, but three.

"Last freezer. No fungus."

"I know." Our opinions on mushrooms would always be drastically different.

I left Kelsey in the kitchen pulling out more cheese to add to our frozen cardboard and walked down the darkened hallway toward the laundry room connected to the garage entry in the back of the house. I walked easily, feeling almost as at home in my best friend's house as my own. The familiarity began gaining ground in my head as I rounded the corner that led to the laundry room. It became a game to me. A challenge. Make it to the freezer and back without turning on any lights.

The laundry room was almost completely black, minus a sliver of outside light from the window. Upon entering, three massive freezers lined the left wall, and straight ahead was a sink and a washer and dryer. Cabinets and a small table littered with missing socks and towels took up the rest of the space. I was halfway into the room, headed toward the last freezer—stealthy as a cat, eye on my target—when a sudden movement directly in front of me disturbed the room. At a glance, it looked like the silhouette of a person facing away from me with two arms raised in the darkness. Two arms raised...taking off a shirt? What? And then a noise. Breathing?

My heart lurched first.

I lurched second.

My feet had tangled up with something in the middle of the floor. Combine that with the over-confident speed of my entry, and I tumbled forward, arms flailing, and gripped the first thing my hands connected with.

Fabric.

On a warm body.

And like my eighth-grade science teacher had taught me just that morning…gravity took me down.

The elastic shorts on the shadowy personage in front of me, which I naturally clutched in my hands to prevent my fall, came down with me. My knees stopped a full descent, along with large hands frantically gripping mine, holding me up but, more importantly, keeping the shorts from sliding down his body any more than they already had. I was splayed forward, my top half in a Superman position, both hands locked on the fabric of the shorts with my knees bent as if in prayer.

I said a few prayers just then.

I prayed to make it all go away. I imagined myself having a redo on what would surely end up being the most mortifying night of my life. How easy it would have been to tamp down the strange and completely idiotic ego trip and turn on the light before entering a darkened room in a house not my own. I prayed that the person who stood before me—facing away from me, thank goodness—was *not* Logan Marten. Even though I knew, without a doubt, that was exactly who it was. I prayed that this had not happened to me, but mostly, I prayed that the light from yonder window wasn't shining on a very firm and taut partial moon before me, inches from my face, my eyeballs searing every detail into my brain.

Three seconds.

That was all it took to land from point A to point B. If point A was a young, naive, bumbling idiot, and Point B was, '*Thanks for the memories, Kels. I'll see myself out. Have a nice life.*'

Two more seconds and Logan had extracted himself from my grip, yanked up his shorts, and moved around me to fumble for the light switch.

My top half plummeted to the ground without Logan's body holding me up. Blinding light broke through the darkness. For several moments, I sat on all fours, frozen in shock.

"Uhhh…hey, Tessa. You alright?"

I saw his butt. I couldn't talk because I had just seen his butt. Naked. In my face. Only half of it, but still. I had pulled down his pants. Of all the times I had commiserated with Kelsey about Cade's second-grade indiscretion, I had never imagined what it might have been like to be the one who had done the pulling. Especially when one did not mean to do the pulling. Visions of me being the actual butt of jokes in the senior boys' locker room had me desperate to try and explain myself to him.

I leaned back on my knees and peered around the room. A crumpled jersey and dirty socks lay in a heap on the floor next to the washer in front of me, where Logan must have been starting a load of laundry. Dang. So far, he had done nothing wrong. I focused on the bulky basketball shoes in the middle of the floor. The one tangible thing where I could place my blame.

"Shoes," I mumbled, gaping at him while he stood there staring at me with no shirt on and muscles. I was desperate to make him understand that this wasn't my fault. Why were there shoes in the middle of the floor? They shouldn't have been in the middle of the floor. But only broken words would come. "Pizza. I…shoes."

His jaw tightened as he peered at me. "You saw my butt, didn't you?"

I nodded miserably.

His cheeks were red, and I didn't think it was because he had just gotten home from a game. He looked like he was nearly ready to keel over with laughter, which thankfully he didn't. He rubbed a hand over his face instead.

"I know you like me with my shirt off, Jailbait, but this is getting a little excessive."

Alright, I deserved the shirt comment. But Jailbait? The second I got home, I would be looking that word up in the dictionary—after I sunk into a speck of dirt on the floor.

"I'm so sorry." The words were barely above a whisper. Heat flamed my cheeks.

"You're alright." He stepped around me again and picked up the shirt and socks he had dropped on the floor (probably when he had stopped my hands from placing him into full-moon territory) and threw them in the washer. He looked over his shoulder and added, "I'm actually gonna finish changing, so you should probably…"

I crawled backward, bug-eyed, before I realized how dumb that looked. I jumped up and twirled around, making my getaway just in time to trip again over the shoes still lying on the floor. It didn't hurt. I was flying high on adrenaline, though my pride shattered as I dashed from the room with Logan's low rumble of laughter following me out. I stopped in the hallway to collapse into a pit of despair for a moment before collecting myself. I would not be mentioning a word about this to Kelsey. Or anybody. Maybe I should write Logan a note and ask him to kindly do the same. I could leave it on his bed like the old—

No.

No more notes. No more Logan. I had been cured of my idiotic crush on him. Like a Band-aid. I ripped him off so fast.

Just like his shorts.

"What took you so long? Where's the pizza?" Kelsey asked when I finally entered the kitchen again, all traces of embarrassment wiped from my face.

I stood, gaping like a fish, when a body approached me from behind. A light hand on my shoulder moved me out of his way. "I've got it." Logan handed Kelsey two frozen pizza boxes and made his way into the sunken family room. "Make enough for me."

Kelsey looked at me with a questioning gaze before busying herself with opening pizza boxes.

"What are you doing home so early? I thought you and your friends would be out celebrating only losing by twenty points tonight."

He wrinkled his nose at his sister. "It was actually only by seventeen points. Maybe you should brush up on those math skills."

"Awww…look at that. Practice really does pay off."

I watched the siblings banter back and forth while Logan plopped onto the couch and turned on the TV. My guess was there would be no chick-flick tonight, but Logan was here. I was here. And I had seen his butt. I waited uncomfortably all night for Logan to mention what had happened. He teased me constantly about the shirt thing. Surely this would be no different. Logan didn't mention anything, though. He didn't tease me at all in front of Kelsey. The rest of our night was spent eating pizza on the couch and the siblings fighting over control of the remote.

Before long, though, he did tease me about it. But just me. To my knowledge, he told nobody else about the incident. The no-shirt thing was the public tease. The butt was for private. Eventually, I stopped being so mortified about the incident and looked forward to Logan teasing me whenever I saw him. With the gap in our ages, I felt grateful we had an inside joke at all. How did the saying go? *No matter what happens, we'll always have the laundry room.*

And the nickname Jailbait, apparently.

1

TESSA

"Those guys keep looking over here."

I followed the direction of Margo's gaze, looking over my shoulder across the dim-lit diner. A group of five men dressed in an impressive array of flannel shirts and dirty jeans were strewn around a table near the bar, laughing at something. Their gazes flicked toward Margo and me.

Yup. They were clearly talking about us.

None of the men looked familiar. And in a town as small as Eugene, that was rare. Though I had been away for a few years, everyone looked like someone I used to know.

"Looks like they're checking you out," I said, smiling at my friend sitting across from me. It had been a year since I had last seen Margo, and her face that had always been naturally pretty was now enhanced by a subtle blend of color and bold strokes. Her brown, pixie-cut bob was striking, and her trendy top looked newly purchased and very much in style.

I hadn't realized our casual get-together would include me sitting next to all *that*. I had envisioned more of a 'let's meet up for a quick dinner after working in the orchard all day' type of girls' night. But I refused to feel dowdy next to her in my t-shirt and black joggers, old running shoes, and my mass of blonde tendrils sticking out of a high ponytail, because honestly, there was very little in my life these days that could embarrass me.

Margo's face colored. "I doubt it. All the guys couldn't keep their eyes off of *you* in high school."

I glanced down and laughed. "What a prize I turned out to be."

Her eyes moved behind my shoulder for a second before landing back on mine.

"Are they still looking over here?" I asked.

"They've already moved on and are now flirting with the waitress."

"Men are so fickle."

I meant that, by the way.

She smiled and took a drink. "So, you're back in Eugene for good?"

"Yup." I picked at the small pizza that sat before me. This place had gone downhill since high school. "Wish I could say I didn't see that coming, but I did."

She laughed. "When will the new office be finished?"

"September 1st."

My older brother, Nate, had done very well with his money since he left home. He had been a physical therapist for the past six years while, at the same time, investing in Las Vegas real estate. His latest idea was to move his family back home and build a physical therapy office in Eugene. After graduating physical therapy school in Boise, I was officially licensed and would begin work at Willow Creek Physical Therapy when it opened its doors in September. Until then, I'd stay busy helping my mom recover from a double knee-replacement surgery, see a couple of at-home patients Nate had set up for me, and work my family's orchard and produce stand. The fact that I was a twenty-four-year-old college graduate now living back at home was an unfortunate reality to my circumstances and one I planned to rectify as soon as my mom's new knees could support her tiny frame.

"How do you like living in Virginia?" I asked Margo. "Do you still live with Holli?"

"It's alright. Holli loves it, but it's too far away from home for me. I might move back this way in a year or so."

We were interrupted by Chad, the thirty-something new owner of The Grub Shack (formerly known for years as the beloved Ranch House Diner). The man was huge, thick-chested, with long, greasy hair pulled up in a macho man bun. His forehead glistened with sweat, his shirt was dotted with oil stains, and he had large, rough hands that seemed more suited to fishing or hunting than manning a kitchen. He usually kept to himself, fixing burgers behind the bar, leaving the customer relations to his waitress, Jen, but as she was currently busy flirting with the table of unidentified men, it seemed he had no choice.

"Here." He plopped a plate of fries unceremoniously down in front of Margo.

Before he could walk away, I couldn't help but needle him a little. "Hey, Chad?"

He stopped, eyes perched on mine warily, his body inching backward. "Yeah?"

"Could you tell me what animals were harmed in the making of this cheese product?" I held up a section of my pizza. At my touch, the orange-and-white sludge broke off in a thick, curdled mass.

He fixed me with his steely gaze. "I already fired you. Do I need to kick you out, too?"

I grinned. "Can you actually fire a volunteer?"

"You absolutely can."

"Come on. You can't deny sales were up the week you were gone."

Chad dipped his face into his shirt and wiped the sweat from his meaty brow. Okay, maybe the stains on his shirt were *not* from oil.

"Restaurant sales were up, but your product cost ate away every cent I would have taken home."

"Quality products are a good investment."

"Nobody's heard of your smoked mozzarella, and nobody wants it on their pizza. We do down-home cooking here. Stuff Grandma would fix."

"Last I heard, *our* grandma grew up in a suburb in Washington, not some backwoods holler in West Virginia."

Did I forget to mention? Chad and I were cousins.

I went on. "I'm thinking specifically about the meatloaf sandwich. There is no way I will believe you if you tell me that was straight cow meat." Idaho roadkill laws were…relaxed at best, and I wouldn't put it past Chad to take advantage of free "filler meat."

"Why do I put up with you?"

"Because I did you a solid, even if you can't appreciate it. I'm back in town now. I can help you."

"I only see that scenario ending with me being arrested on murder charges."

"I think you may be overestimating *your* charm just a bit."

"I appreciate the solid, not the commentary," he said generously.

A few days after I had moved back home, Chad's appendix burst. My mom hadn't had her knee surgery yet, so I filled in at the restaurant with Jen. I had been surprised at how much I enjoyed working there, chatting with all the locals and feeding them food—if you could call Chad's menu food. Don't even get me started on his cake.

"Fries are good," Margo broke in, holding up a crisp fry. It was true. Whatever magic Chad was missing from the rest of his cooking, he hit it perfectly with the fries. Long, thin, and golden to perfection.

Chad pointed to Margo. "You just earned yourself a free refill." At that moment, Chad's beautiful waitress, Jen, sidled in, swathed in tight jeans and a tank top that displayed her size Ds in all their perky perfection. Standing beside Chad, her head barely reached his shoulder.

"You giving my cook a hard time, Blondie?" Jen grinned at me. For a moment, I was blinded by her megawatt smile and the smell of vanilla sunshine.

"Nothing he doesn't deserve."

"Feel free to kick my cousin out if she gives you any trouble," Chad piped in. "She looks sweet, but she has claws."

"Sweet With Claws is my middle name," I said amiably.

"Atta girl." Jen refilled our drinks before making her way toward the bar, only to get stopped by the flirtatious men.

"Do you know who those guys are?" Margo asked Chad, nodding discreetly toward their table. For the record, Chad was still conversing with us, which meant he obviously loved me more than his words let on.

"I've never seen 'em before," Chad said, his eyes on his pretty waitress laughing with the men. "But if I were a betting man, I'd guess they're part of the construction crew coming to build Nate's therapy building."

I scanned the crowd again, searching for a familiar face. "Nate told me it was Chase Riley's crew coming."

Chad shrugged. "You'd know better than me."

"They keep looking over here," I said.

"I've been watching them. If they bother you, let me know. I'll send 'em packing."

That's the thing you had to like about Chad—he acted like he didn't care, but deep down, he had the vibe of a bouncer in a club. He kept a careful watch over his patrons and took a measure of everybody who walked through his door. He was huge and grumpy and intimidating (if you were the sort who wasn't related and therefore got intimidated). As a close relation, I was well aware that his gruff exterior was just a front. Chad definitely had a soft side.

"Although, if they knew you they'd probably be more scared of you than me," he added, a twinkle in his eye before he blinked it away.

I made a face at Chad as he made his retreat. Good-natured laughter and some loud ruckus burst out from the other side of the room, and I stole another quick glance behind me. I didn't necessarily sense trouble from them as much as boredom and some good old-fashioned mischief. The only problem with being bored on a Friday night in a tiny town was that they would probably be looking for something to ease the boredom. By the looks on their faces, I had to wonder if *we* just might be that something.

"Have you dated much since—" Margo broke off her question quickly, fidgeting in her seat and taking a suspiciously long sip of her Diet Pepsi. Almost as if she couldn't believe she had brought it up.

IT.

I had something in my past that had become an *it*. The thing everybody thought they had to dance around when, really, I wanted *it* to either be forgotten completely or shouted from the rooftop. It was the whispers I hated. It had been a year. I had been to therapy. I could handle talking about *it* with an old friend. Now it was just embarrassing—the biggest reason I had been reluctant to come back to Eugene. To the very town where *it* took place.

"A few dates. Nothing serious," I said.

A few actually meant two. Both had been blind dates. Both had been a disaster. I wasn't quite sure how I felt about dating. I had boldly declared to my therapist at our last appointment that I had healed and was ready to start dating again. But that may have been more the fact that I no longer wanted to pay the hefty monthly bill for a therapist, because if I was honest with myself, the thought of getting close to somebody like that again was enough to make me want to get those claws back out and scurry up a tree to hide.

"I'm not opposed to dating," I lied, bent on proving to Margo that I was completely fine to say his name. To give *it* a name. "After Tyler, I just haven't found a guy I trust enough to pursue anything." I laughed, giving my best impression that all was okay on that front.

Margo didn't press for anything else but instead said, "It looks like you might get that date." Her eyes followed something past my shoulder. "One of them just stood up and is looking over at us."

"I'm not the one they've been drooling over all this time," I said. It was true. My back was to their table.

"What do we do?" Margo asked, sitting up straighter, a look of panic dashing across her face.

"You could start with, 'Is your name Google? Because you've got everything I've been searching for.'"

She kicked me under the table. "I'm serious. He's probably coming for you, but just in case. This stuff doesn't happen to me."

"If he asks you out, and you want to go, go. As long as he doesn't give you Ted Bundy vibes."

"Ted Bundy acted like a normal guy," she whispered frantically. "He fooled everybody."

"Alright, bad example. Maybe Godzilla?"

"He could be coming to ask *you* out, you know."

"Nope. This is all you," I said, taking another sip of my water.

"I'm going back to Virginia in three days. He's not going to want me."

"I'm still waiting for the Eugene old-lady gossip channels to die down from the last time I dated and almost married a local boy." Tyler wasn't technically local, but two towns over in Salmon was close enough.

"Wait." Margo leaned across the table, looking past my shoulder and clearly trying not to seem disheartened. "Oh. He's leaving. He wasn't coming over here."

I glanced behind me, and sure enough, I caught the back of a man's head before the door closed. I turned back to Margo, our eyes immediately going to our plates of food. I picked at my pizza. She ate a fry. We both took a drink. The wind had left our sails. I didn't think I had wanted him to come over, but I found myself strangely disappointed. Where there had been anticipation and intrigue only a moment ago, now we were just two girls feeling foolish. I made it a long moment before a snort shot out of my nose. Margo's face broke into a grin, and hushed laughter burst out of us.

"We were so sure he was coming for us," Margo whisper-howled, wiping her eyes with her fingers.

"Do you think he got a closer look and changed his mind?" This made us bend over once more, crouching over our plates of below-average food and wheezing until we were out of breath.

"I knew I should have showered today," I said much louder than I had intended.

"Hey, ladies."

My eyes widened as a voice approached us from behind me. Margo's head popped up from her folded arms on the table, no trace of the mirth that was showing on her face only seconds before.

An average-build man in a red-and-gray plaid shirt with brown hair spilling out of a baseball hat smiled down at us, holding out his hand as he stopped at our table. "I'm Briggs."

His gaze swept over us both but rested on Margo. My cute, innocent friend looked like she was caught in a hunter's snare, eyes darting wildly and hands constantly in motion. She did manage to tell him her name, but hearing the catcalls and 'Yeah, Briggs!' behind us probably didn't help her anxiety. To his credit, Briggs looked embarrassed and rubbed the back of his neck with his hand. As for me, my eyes narrowed as I shifted into full mama-bear mode, sniffing for something foul in the woods.

"We'd like to buy you girls a drink." He motioned toward the guys in the back. It was just like in the movies where the guy at the bar offers to buy the leading lady a drink. I glanced around the dingy room with the perpetually sticky tables, booths with rips in the seats, and old tables and chairs strewn about the room. This movie set needed some work.

I leaned forward. "So, are you the brave one, or did you lose a bet?"

A sheepish smile lit his face. "Brave, though I definitely had some encouragement."

I swished my glass around before tipping it back and draining the liquid inside. Holding up my glass, I turned to Briggs and said, "Great. Another water for me, please. On the rocks."

He looked at my drink and nodded, amused. He looked at Margo. "How about you?"

She smiled, tucking her hair behind her ear. "I'm not feeling very wild tonight." She held up her half-empty glass of soda and shook it. "Diet Pepsi for me, but you don't have to buy it."

Briggs folded his arms across his chest before unfolding them again. "No problem. I'd love to. I'll go grab those drinks and be right back."

He must have given his friends a sign of some sort as he walked away, because that section of the room erupted in cheers that resembled some sort of duck mating call. He returned a minute later with our drinks.

To avoid him standing over us awkwardly, I pushed at the extra chair to my right with my foot. "Have a seat."

Briggs smiled gratefully and sat, passing us our drinks. "Sorry about all that."

"Are you guys just passing through?" Margo asked.

"We're all here for the summer, building the new physical therapy building in town. That's almost all of us. We're just missing one more guy."

So, they *were* Chase's crew.

The two of them conversed lightly while I studied Briggs. The strange thing was…he seemed almost…oblivious to the guys behind me. There was a natural sweetness in his eyes as he flirted with my friend. My mama-bear heart began to settle. He might have come over here as a part of something, but that had taken a side seat once he sat down at this table. My shoot-'em-up vibe began to dissipate, and I broke off a piece of crust on my pizza.

"So, do you both live here?" he asked.

"I'm visiting for a few more days, but Tessa just moved back," Margo said.

Briggs's face fell. "Ah, dang. Maybe we'll have to do something before you leave." He watched her carefully as he cast his line, wondering if she was going to bite.

"Might be fun."

He grinned before looking over at me, his arms folded casually on the table. "Tessa, huh? I know a few guys who might be interested in knowing that."

"Your groupies in the back?" I asked, giving him my sweetest smile.

He had the good sense to look chagrined. "Yeah. Sorry. They're annoying but mostly harmless. Fair warning: more of them might be over here before the night's over."

Two years ago, I would have been flattered by the attention. But now, I looked at that group of guys and felt nothing. Not that I thought they would be serious dating material, but I knew their type. They were the good ol' boys. Rough, rowdy, and probably knew the cops in their town by name, but they had hearts of gold that bled red, white, and blue. Every town had them. Eugene was filled with them. In my other life, they would have been fun to flirt with. But now…I felt nothing.

No pang. No jitters. No excitement. That had all been sucked out of me by Tyler.

I proceeded to sit awkwardly for another few minutes while the two potential lovebirds muddled through weak conversation points before Briggs finally ended my misery and asked her out. They exchanged numbers, and he stood up to leave.

"I'll leave you ladies alone for now."

I had to give him points for not overstaying his welcome. He glanced politely at me again before giving Margo his full smile. As she melted into her seat, even I had to admit it was a pretty great smile. Though, again…nothing. We were silent for ten seconds, both of us pretending to pick at our food while making sure he was out of earshot.

"I feel like I have pit stains. Do I have pit stains?" Margo's eyes briefly flicked to Briggs's table, and she must have felt safe enough to lift her arms for a split second.

I didn't look her in the eye. "Looks great. Totally dry."

"Liar."

"It's fine because he still asked for your number."

"That's never happened to me before." She leaned back in her seat and took a deep breath, as though the entire exchange had exhausted her. "We'll see if we actually go out on that date before I leave."

"He'll take you out. He couldn't stop staring."

"It sounds like you'll be next. Maybe we can double." She motioned toward the table, though I didn't look at them again.

I gave her a noncommittal grunt. It was the best I could do with my conflicting emotions. It had been almost a year, and while I no longer wanted Tyler, I missed *us*. I missed our plans. I missed what could have been. I missed the little apartment in Boise we had rented—the one we chose after only two hours of searching because I told him I loved how the kitchen was set up. How much time had I spent daydreaming about baking cakes and pies and dinners for my new husband in that kitchen? It was all very 1950s in my head, but it felt perfect to me. Our plans. From what I understood, Tyler still had those plans. He just switched out the girl.

Either way, my heart was closed for the foreseeable future. Place any attractive male celebrity in front of me without a shirt on, and I would probably turn and walk away. (Although, to be fair, I'd sneak a quick peek.) But tonight, it felt fun. Just a little. This whole evening suddenly had an air of excitement. Margo had some confidence shining in her eyes, and I felt hope in my heart for the first time in a long time.

Well, maybe not hope, but it was nice to be out of my head for a bit.

Margo cleared her throat. "Um…DEFCON 1? Another guy is headed this way. This time, he's looking at you."

I took a long drink and stifled the urge to laugh. Maybe it was the ice water going down my throat or the idea that somebody was about to be flirting with me, but a little zing of excitement ran through my veins. Maybe I had spoken too soon about not feeling anything. I could finally admit to myself that I *wasn't* interested in dating right now, especially not in Eugene. I wasn't even interested in going on *a date*. But a distraction sounded nice. Those guys looked fun, they could *definitely* handle being brought down a peg or two, and they wouldn't be heartbroken at my rejection. Perhaps that was what my disheartened spirit needed. These guys wanted a turn at bat? I was up for it. Just because I wasn't playing the long game didn't mean I couldn't enjoy striking someone out now and then.

Batter up.

2

LOGAN

I pulled my truck into one of the few remaining parking spots for The Grub Shack and killed the engine. The seatbelt stretched as I leaned forward in my seat, assessing the old building. Other than the name change, it looked much the same as it had twelve years ago—one bad windstorm away from demise. Paint-chipped, brown wooden siding lined the one-level building. The whole site seemed to be leaning to the left. How this place passed inspections was beyond me. In a glance, I could spot at least ten easy fixes to add or change to the outside wall that would improve its appearance.

"Really pulling out all the stops for our date tonight, big boy," Jake said from the passenger seat. He was grinning as a burly man passed in front of us, looking around for witnesses before digging for gold at the seat of his pants.

"I thought you'd appreciate the ambiance of a place this classy, sweetheart."

Jake Evans was the little brother I never knew I always wanted. I was raised in the middle of two sisters, who I loved dearly, but there was something about having an annoying little brother around that did the soul good. For the past seven years, my dad had hired on two cowboys to work the ranch, Jake and Dusty. Even though I had been out of the house by then, we had all bonded during my visits home and the occasional cattle drive I moved heaven and earth to be a part of each summer. When my dad sold the dairy cows two years earlier, Dusty had taken a job on his uncle's ranch in Wyoming, but Jake was still around, taking online classes, running the rodeo circuit, and acting as my dad's right-hand man. With his best friend off in Wyoming, Jake wandered around, looking like a kicked puppy. I couldn't help feeling sorry for him, which was how I found myself inviting him to come and meet my crew for dinner tonight.

Jake and I yanked open our doors and stepped out, our boots kicking up the dust in the dirt parking lot.

At twenty-nine years old, being back in Eugene wouldn't have been my first choice in a summer job, but I had to admit, it felt kinda good to be home. I was back in the land of one stoplight and traffic jams caused only by tractors. Other than the lingering aroma of cow manure, Eugene was a breath of fresh air. I had arrived in town an hour earlier, dumped all my things in the bunkhouse (much to my mother's dismay), called 'Here, boy' to Jake until he jumped into the truck with me, and drove straight to the restaurant.

"Do you ever eat here?" I asked Jake as we meandered toward the front door, which was barely hanging on by the last hinge.

"I don't eat anywhere 'cause your mom's the best cook in the world."

"Suck up."

"But I heard they're under new management."

"I heard that, too," I said.

"Fingers crossed we still get to throw peanuts on the floor." Jake gave a satisfied sigh.

He meant it, too. The more low-down and country a place could get, the more at home he felt. It went well with his long legs, boots, and that confident cowboy swagger. Though he was six years younger than me, the twenty-three-year-old was a few inches north of six feet, pulling ahead of me by a couple of inches, which he never failed to remind me of. The height difference was further accentuated by his black cowboy hat.

"Will you buy me dessert, honey?" Jake asked, peering through the water-stained and dirt-crusted window into the restaurant.

"If you treat me nice."

My phone buzzed before we got to the door. I checked it and typed a quick text back to Chase.

Chase: You guys there?

Me: Yeah. I'm meeting the boys for dinner now.

Chase: Sounds good. I'll bring the fam down over the 4th to check on things. Let me know if you need anything before that.

Me: Will do.

Chase: FYI...fries only at The Ranch House or whatever it's called now. Things are much worse than before.

CHASE HAD SENT a skeleton crew to Eugene to build the physical therapy office he was investing in with his good friend, Nate Robbins. Though, at the last minute, he had gotten tied up in a project he couldn't leave, so he sent me. This was unfortunate because Nate and I had a history that was a bit on the rocky side. But high school was a long time ago.

"What a pansy," Jake said, turning away from where he'd been reading my text thread over my shoulder. "He graduated from Eugene, same as us. We've been training our stomachs our whole lives for this kind of food."

Bile rose in my throat in remembrance. "Mrs. Garber's Friday Lunch Surprise."

"Fish stick burritos."

I did a full-body shiver before putting the phone in my pocket and opening the door to the restaurant. The smell of fried foods, weak alcohol, and cheap cologne hit me in a wave. It took my eyes a second to adjust to the dimly lit room. There was a handful of people and groups scattered throughout the diner, and my very loud crew was lounging around a table near the bar, laughing at something.

Javier noticed us first, standing up to greet us. "Hey, boss. When'd you get here?"

I moved to shake his hand and introduced Jake, who made himself at home, shaking hands all around. Javier was a year younger than me. Tall, dark, curly hair, strong chin, good looking, and told me every day he was gunning for my job. Maybe one day, he would get it. While I loved working with Chase, running my own crew on my own terms would be a dream come true for me. Javier and I didn't always see eye to eye, but we respected the crap out of each other.

"About an hour ago. Have you guys already eaten?"

"Unfortunately." He made a face. "Don't get the meatloaf sandwich. I don't care what they say; there was something not right with it."

"Thanks for the tip." Turning to Jake, I asked, "I'm ordering. What do you want?"

"Surprise me."

The Grub Shack was something of a bar and diner mix. The kind of place you find in a town too small to handle both. The rest of the crew was engrossed in something probably annoying, so I made my way to the bar where a barrel-chested man stood behind the counter. He poured drinks for customers sitting at the counter in a rush, while also manning the stovetop, flipping burgers. I waited for him to take notice I was there and greet me, but he never did.

"Hey, Chad. Good to see you."

The man looked up and stared at me for an uncomfortable amount of time before the light dawned in his eyes. "Hey, Marten. How's it going?"

We stood in the awkward silence of old acquaintances attempting to re-acquaint. Chad was a few years older than me, and he went to state all three years in wrestling. We didn't run in the same circles, but I do remember playing a few pickup games of football with him a time or two. My shoulders still ached thinking about his tackles. Our interaction had probably ended, but I felt a sort of kinship to this man in front of me. Most of the guys my age were married with kids. Some had big hot-shot careers, and my social media was flooded with pictures of suburbia and fancy vacations. It was nice seeing a normal, run-of-the-mill guy with no wife or kids and a decent job.

Guys like us needed more representation in the world.

"Whatcha want?" Chad's grizzly-bear eyes landed on mine impatiently.

My stomach rumbled. I peered closer at the stove. Certainly it *looked* like regular meat. A hamburger was just about the most basic thing to cook. People were usually safe with a hamburger and fries. Right?

A tall, pretty redhead tucked into a tank top and tight jeans breezed past my elbow, coming to stand next to the man. "Chad, we talked about this. You don't speak to the customers. I do." She flashed me a brilliant smile, and I couldn't help but smile back. I liked her already.

"What can I make Chad make for you?"

The beast of a man grumbled but said nothing. My focus wasn't on him anymore but a pair of interested blue eyes. The feeling was mutual.

I took a seat at the counter, my feet sticking to the floor as I stepped. I was once again grateful I had grown up on a farm. Germs didn't scare me.

"What's good here?"

I tried to ask my question quietly, giving the impression I wanted honesty, but Chad looked annoyed for a split second before saying, "Depends on who you ask." He nodded toward a table in the center of the room. "Don't ask the blonde over there." He seemed so offended I instinctively turned around to look. Sitting with her back to me was a woman with slender shoulders and blonde hair in a ponytail. She didn't seem especially scary, but due to my own experience with a certain blonde woman, I was inclined to believe him.

"Focus, Chad." The woman pointed at his burgers, and the man went back to his stovetop. She leaned toward me, her elbows on the counter, giving me ample opportunity to check out more than just her face. I kept my gaze focused on her bright eyes as she whispered, "Everybody likes the fries."

Chad flipped the burgers on the grill. One patty broke in half, and I watched as he used his meaty fingers to squish it back together.

She followed my gaze. "Hot dogs are usually a safe bet since there's little one has to do to make them edible."

"Hot dog and fries it is. And one order of the biggest and grossest thing you guys serve here for my brother. With some fries." Jake wasn't my brother, but he might as well have been, and I couldn't have the lady thinking I was ordering an extra meal for a date.

Grinning, she shouted out an order of a hot dog and a large meatloaf sandwich to Chad before grabbing a cloth and wiping down the bar.

"I don't see a name tag."

"It's Jen." She eyed me critically. "Are you passing through, or…?"

"I grew up here. I live in Boise, but I'm here all summer."

Her eyebrows lifted. "Fresh meat, huh? Eugene could definitely use more of that."

"You don't look familiar. Are you from here?" I was interested in learning her last name. For all I knew, she could have been the little sister of an old high-school friend of mine. Coming back to your hometown after eleven years away was strange. Everything felt familiar but different.

"Just moved here from Salmon." Not a pureblood. Perfect.

I was about to ask her out when her attention became diverted by new customers. When I caught her eye again, I motioned with my hands where I'd be when my food came. She nodded the affirmative, and I made my way over to my crew's table.

Most of the guys had finished eating, their plates pushed aside, and were lounging around the table, brimming with mischief. Some greeted me with nods and waves, but their attention was focused somewhere across the room. I pulled out a chair between Jake and Javier.

"What's going on?"

Briggs pointed at Ronnie, a tall, hefty guy with a beer gut, walking toward our table. He was grinning all the while shaking his head.

"We dared Ronnie to go ask out that blonde over there, and it looks like he got shut down." Briggs grinned. "Before that, she turned down Carl."

My eyes narrowed, scanning the men in my crew. I turned to Javier and asked quietly, "They're not harassing her, are they?"

Javier leaned in on my right side. "No. I've been keeping an eye out. She's been laughing with them all as much as they have. You should hear the zingers she has for the guys when they come back. They're loving it. They're not being gross, just funny."

I looked again toward the blonde with her back to me. Across from her sat a pretty brunette who kept glancing our way. Along with everybody else in this diner, the brunette looked familiar, though I couldn't place the name. Clearly, they were talking about our group behind their hands and darted glances. I relaxed. Chase kept a tight crew. They didn't get too many chances to prove themselves. He expected decent men and honesty, and he usually got it. I trusted these guys, and I even liked them all, but that didn't mean they couldn't get out of hand with a few drinks in a new town.

Ronnie plopped back down in the chair and whistled. "She let me go on and on, and right when I thought she was eating out of my hand..."—Ronnie slammed his hand on the table for effect—"shot down."

"I told you, man," Carl said, bits of crumbs stuck in his Viking beard.

The table laughed.

"Who's next?" Trevor asked.

"How about we leave her alone and talk business?" I said, leaning forward in my seat. I was fine with some harmless flirting, but this felt like some sort of wolfish group hunt. The crew was set to start work on Monday morning, and I had a list of things to go over tonight.

"Aww, it's a game now, boss. She just told me to send the next guy," Ronnie said.

I looked at Briggs. "Did you try your luck?"

He grinned. "I'm taking out her friend. That's what started the whole business."

Just then, the blonde in question turned her head enough for me to get a view of her side profile. My body stilled while I took in the high cheekbones, tan skin, and—though I couldn't see them—fiery green eyes. I bit my lip, holding back a smile that suddenly threatened to tiptoe across my face. As my little sister's best friend, she had practically grown up in my house. Suddenly, Chad's derision made sense. Though it had been almost a year since I'd seen her last, I could well imagine Tessa's take on her cousin's "food." But Jake's silence on the matter of Tessa seemed odd. I turned to look at him, only to find an annoying grin on his face as he sat back in his chair, arms folded and legs crossed, patiently waiting for me to connect a few dots.

"Alright. I'm going in. Gonna get me a hot date for next weekend." Lanky, red-headed Trevor stood up from the table. He looked at Carl. "Seventy-five bucks."

Carl leaned forward and stuck out his hand. "Deal."

I watched as Trevor pretended to mop up beads of sweat off of his forehead before making his way to Tessa's table.

He stood, somewhat awkwardly, next to the pretty pair of friends, but he tried to disguise his nerves with animated gestures, no doubt telling some wild story. Tessa was grinning up at him, laughing at something he said. For a moment, it seemed like she might take Trevor up on whatever he was offering, but then she leaned closer and said something to him before waving him away. Trevor looked stunned. Apparently, he had thought it was going well also, but then he hightailed it back to the table, slinking down in his seat.

"Shut up," he said to his crowd of onlookers.

"What'd she say?" I couldn't help but ask.

Suddenly, he grinned. "She said I was hot. Like a tall Prince Harry."

The rest of the guys snorted while he continued, meeting everybody's gaze theatrically. "But then she said that the thought of one day having a red-headed child was a risk she wasn't willing to take."

Trevor sat back in his chair with a smile on his face. He seemed proud of his rejection and probably grateful it hadn't been worse. The guys laughed and clapped him on the back, each one offering their own sympathies and rejection stories.

"Javier, you up?" Carl asked.

"Not my scene, amigos." Javier's long, graceful fingers picked up his cup, and he took a long drink, taking in the room with calm and collected eyes.

"I bet a hundred bucks Marten can't get a date with the blonde."

My soul groaned inwardly when Jake's strong voice lifted above our group. Instantly, the table quieted, and eight interested pairs of eyes swung my way. My fingers itched to strangle Jake when I took in his knowing grin.

"You're not good for a hundred bucks. I'm buying your dinner tonight."

"I'm good for it. I thought you were being nice. What kind of guy doesn't pay for his date?"

"Consider me no longer nice."

Jake sighed. "And now the image is shattered."

Why, again, did I like this kid?

"Boss always has a date. He has some sort of voodoo charm over women. I wouldn't bet against him," Ronnie stated.

My heart rate slowed, and my fists relaxed as the rest of the men murmured in agreement. I planned to go say hi to Tessa. I would tease her for a minute and then be done. I'd probably see her around because Eugene was a small town. That's even *if* she was here to stay. But this… For some reason, I didn't want to play this game. The last thing I wanted to do was get in the middle of one of Jake's bets. Especially not with a girl so beloved by my family they'd kick me out when I messed up.

Not if…when.

She was not somebody I would date. Or attempt to date. Even if it was a joke. Though the protective big brother in me happened to be glad she was shutting everybody down. Proud, even. It was nice to see she was able to take care of herself.

"Well, she turned down Trevor's pretty face. It might be our best chance to see the great Logan Marten take a fall. Or lose a bet." Carl folded his meaty arms and leaned back in his chair, giving me a smug look.

Once he had an ally, Jake leaned forward in his seat, calculating. "Maybe you're right. Except, she looks way out of his league. There's no way he could get her to say yes."

I knew what Jake was doing. I *knew* it, and his arrogant face made me want to punch something. I also had an interest in seeing if he really was good for a hundred bucks. I had my doubts. I tried one last-ditch effort to get myself out of this.

"I think I've got something going with the waitress."

The group turned toward Jen as she brought out an order to a table, laughing and teasing with every patron she came in contact with, her red hair curled and pulled back in a loose hair tie and flowing freely down her back.

"I'm pretty sure to get anywhere near *that*, you have to go through *that*." Ronnie motioned first toward Jen and then behind us toward Chad.

I turned back toward Jake, who was beaming at me. "Looks like we're back to the *hot blonde*," he said.

"She's closer to your age than mine," I said, giving him a pointed stare.

"I'd just like to see the *great* Logan Marten throw his hat in the ring."

When I didn't move, Jake turned back toward Javier. "You sure you don't want to give it a shot, Javier? You look like someone a girl couldn't say no to."

Javier eyed me as he contemplated Jake's nudging and began to rise from his seat. A flash of heat bubbled up in my chest. Something protective. Something…something. I wasn't marriage material. That idea had been demolished long ago. I had a job to do this summer, then I'd move back to Boise. End of interaction. It was true that I was always open for a date, and I usually didn't have to look too hard. I didn't have a type, beyond a Saturday night, and Tessa wasn't *that*. She was like a little sister. Not only *my* little sister but also Nate's little sister. Our new boss for the summer. And I knew for a fact he would not approve of tonight's activities.

But it was all just a game. A joke. Tessa seemed happy to play along. The opportunity to throw her off her game was too good to pass up. And if I was being honest, I didn't want Javier anywhere near her. He was basically me but with a charming accent. Lethal. I'd take Tessa out on a date, then be done with it.

It's not like the formula was unfamiliar to me.

I pushed Javier back down in his seat and stood up, smacking the back of Jake's laughing head as I did so.

I pointed at Jake. "One hundred bucks, moneybags."

He smiled. "Only if you can get a date. And I happen to have my doubts."

Catcalls and hollering filled the room—this time directed at me. I rolled my eyes and began walking toward the familiar blonde at the table in front of me. I may not have had Javier's smooth accent, but with the exception of Jake, I had something none of these guys had: a history with Tessa. And Tessa's history was riddled with a lovesick crush on somebody.

Me.

3

TESSA

"Here comes another one," Margo whispered, smiling behind her Diet Pepsi.

I resisted the urge to turn around. How many guys were there? I could have sworn all of them had taken a turn, except for the handsome Hispanic with the dark, curly hair. He sat back and seemed so in control, smiling occasionally, but so far hadn't made a move toward us.

"He's really cute. He looks familiar."

I felt his body approach our table and braced myself for a sexy accent. I took a drink of my water, trying to seem nonchalant.

"Hey, Jailbait," a low voice breathed into my ear, immediately sending a bolt of lightning down my spine.

Water didn't exactly spew from my mouth at his words, more like got stuck mid-swallow. Half came up and the other half squeezed painfully down my constricted throat. I began coughing, my body in full reaction mode, searching for oxygen, and it didn't seem to care that it was ruining the whole James-Bond, smooth-talking, shoot-'em-up vibe I had going on.

A strong hand from behind began thumping my back. Blessed air entered my lungs once again. Although, I wasn't sure it was better to be breathing. If I was breathing, then I would have to face the man behind me.

I turned around to meet my fate. Logan Marten stood watching me with an amused expression. For a moment, I was taken aback by how handsome he looked. I had always been a fan of a man in a baseball hat, but the way it slung low across his forehead, mixed with his long lashes…it was almost criminal.

"Well, look what the cat dragged in," I wheezed, definitely not James-Bond style.

He smiled and pulled out a seat, not waiting for an invitation. Glancing at Margo, he stuck out his hand. "I feel like I should know you, but it's been too long. Logan Marten."

She smiled widely. "I remember you now. I'm Margo Jensen. I graduated with Kelsey and Tessa."

His eyebrows raised. "Interesting. Did you know Tessa prefers me without my shirt on?"

My eyes drifted down his chest before I caught myself and yanked them back up—but not before he caught me looking.

Dimple. Just in the right cheek. Only when he grinned. I had forgotten how that made my insides melt like butter. I had also forgotten how to speak.

"I was actually there when she told you." Margo smiled at him.

Okay, I had to get a grip. He had been here for two seconds, and every ounce of control I had was now gone. I needed to gain back my authority in this conversation. I had been commanding the table with every guy that approached me, playing their own game, laughing and smiling. We were all onto each other, but I still had control. The final word. Strike. Strike. Strike. You're out. I had just pitched Logan not a strike, but a ball. I only had three more pitches left.

"I thought Chase Riley was coming to build the office?"

"He got held up in Boise. He sent me and all those broken hearts behind you."

I smiled, feeling myself flush. "I didn't realize you worked for him."

He leaned back in his chair and adjusted his hat. "I'm his partner now. Are you just here for the weekend?"

"I'm here to stay. I'll be working with Nate once the office is built, but until then I'll be running the orchard this summer."

The conversation stilled. Not in boredom, but in anticipation. I glanced behind me. If the group of guys staring at Logan with expectant smiles on their faces meant anything, he would probably be asking me out any second. I kept a saucy look on my face to mask my inner turmoil. For the first time all night, I wasn't sure how to handle myself. To preserve the status quo, I needed to turn him down. I *should* turn him down. If Kelsey's constant commentary on his flavors of the week held any truth, I *had* to turn him down. I wasn't in the mood to be played. Been there, done that.

But he was Logan.

My Logan.

As a child, I had followed him around like a lovesick kitten. The love notes, the spying, the no-shirt comment came into my mind in full remembrance. Then, there was the secret scrapbook that I needed to find and destroy at some point this summer. Not to mention the laundry room. The fact that he was sitting at my table, smiling at me, after all of that was something of a miracle.

But he was Logan.

A womanizing, serial-dating, never-take-any-woman-seriously, attractive man. The most dangerous kind. I didn't want him. Not really. Life had hardened me enough that he was no longer my idealized childhood crush. But he was also someone no longer too old for me. I was no longer jailbait.

Game face.

"So, Tess…"

His voice deepened and dropped off to form the S in my nickname. The word left his mouth in a deep puff of air that hardly moved his lips. Why must he call me Tess? It was my name, but personalized. Loganized. I'd prefer Jailbait.

I had to say no. Stay strong. If for nothing else than to prove something to the male herd behind me.

"How much is the bet?"

Laughter sprang into his eyes. "What do you mean?"

I spoke slower, gaining my edge back. "How much is the bet if I go out with you?"

"Geez, Tess." He held up his hands. "I just got here, but…if you want to go out, I mean…"

"Logan Marten, I'm going to ask you one more time. How much?"

An uncomfortable grin bit his face. "It wasn't my idea. Jake forced my hand. A hundred bucks."

"Jake's here?" I immediately flipped around in my chair, searching our audience for the man in question. A lanky cowboy nearly bursting with mischief met my gaze and raised his glass. I shook my head slowly at him but was unsuccessful at keeping the grin from exploding onto my face. With my best friend happily married and living in Colorado, I had been reluctant to move back to Eugene. Most of my friends had moved away. I was lucky Margo had come home for a family wedding this week. The knowledge of two guys being here, who had played such a prominent part in my youth and summers, shouldn't have filled me with so much joy, but it did.

"You are aware that, by the principle of the thing, there is no way I can or will say yes, right?"

"Aww, come on, Tess. I just thought I'd give you a chance to fulfill your teenage fantasy." He couldn't even get through his sentence before he cut himself off, laughing.

My toes curled. "Are we really going there?"

He gave me a meaningful look. "I think we've *been* there, haven't we?"

I wiped a drop of sweat from my brow.

He leaned closer, stealing a drink from my water. The casual familiarity of that move did nothing to soften me toward him. NOTHING. He took a minute to compose himself before saying seriously, "It's a good chance for us to kill two birds with one stone. I get to take money from Jake, and you get…"—he motioned theatrically across his body—"all this."

I didn't allow my eyes to follow the trail his hand was making across his chest and, instead, pushed at his shoulder. "Be serious. I'm not going out with you."

Cue sad trombone.

"Tess…" His voice was low and sultry as he fingered the bottom of his shirt. "Do I need to take it off?" His eyes lowered seductively, highlighting his dark lashes across his cheek. I could feel my face heating and the laughter ready to burst out of me, but I had to hide it. He was kidding, of course, but I needed to gain composure before I called him out on his bluff.

"Yeah, actually." I leaned back in my chair, arms folded, chin up, leveling him. "Take your shirt off. Right now."

His tongue flicked across his bottom lip as he studied me. "And then you'd go out with me? Or you just want to see me half naked?" He leaned closer, and with his eyebrows raised suggestively, whispered, "Again."

I didn't look at Margo to see her face, but I could guess at her thoughts decoding this conversation.

"Might depend on what's under there. I haven't seen you with your shirt off for quite some time."

"Though probably not for lack of trying, right?"

He made no effort to remove his shirt, and for a long moment, we sat grinning at each other. My mind bounced from a laundry room long ago, to eating late-night bowls of cereal next to him on the couch with Kelsey, to a certain water fight on a trampoline. My foot wouldn't stop fidgeting. I was calm and as still as a statue up top and a dog chasing a squirrel down below. I couldn't stop smiling at him, and I wasn't sure why. Or what I should do. Margo was still there somewhere in my peripheral vision, but I couldn't even break my gaze to check. Logan was crowding every inch of my space.

I was going to do it.

There was no way I could say no to him. I braced myself for all the ribbing I would no doubt get by saying yes, but…it was the crush of my youth, and dang it all, it *was* a teenage fantasy. I was going on a date with Logan Marten.

Enter Jen.

"There you are, handsome." We both turned as the red-headed beauty brought a plate of food and set it in front of Logan. "I thought you were with the construction boys over there."

"I'm saying hi to an old friend." Logan smiled at her.

Old friend.

Nothing like two simple words to ground a person. To remind them of their place—maybe not in society, but their place in Logan Marten's life. He was not wrong. It was a very good reminder.

Jen smiled, tucking a long strand of hair behind her ear before asking, "How do you know this troublemaker?"

I wasn't sure if she was referring to me or Logan, but before I could answer, Logan did, leaning back in his chair, his arms tucked behind his head. "She's my little sister's best friend. She used to leave me love notes and spy on me."

Logan's smile grew wider as he watched me pretend to reel in a fish with my left hand while my right middle finger slowly raised upward.

"Looks like she's still got it bad," Jen teased, her hand on her hip and the hint of a tattoo showing at the top of her shoulder. Jen and I had gotten to know each other during my week of running the restaurant for Chad. It started off a bit rocky, as I figured it would be when another female entered into an alpha's domain, but we ended on a pretty good note.

Logan had his hands on his stomach while he leaned back, two pegs of his chair in the air while he dangled casually. I had the sudden urge to kick the chair to see what would happen. I stole a few fries off of his plate instead. Margo met my gaze across the table.

"I have a lot of questions," she said.

"Get in line."

Margo laughed at the same time our sociable waitress did. Logan's eyes were trained on her pretty face, which, honestly, I had to give him some props for because she had a couple of other attractive features begging to be admired.

Once Jen had left, Logan picked up his hot dog, inspected it curiously, and took a bite. Margo and I watched him on pins and needles.

"Well?" I asked. "How is it?"

Once he swallowed, he said, "It tastes like something my grandma boiled on the stove."

"I guess he's killing it, then. Chad's goal is to make down-home cooking like your grandma used to make."

Logan's eyes widened. "*My* grandma?"

I made a face. "Well, maybe not *your* grandma, but somebody's grandma."

Between bites, he asked, "How's the meatloaf sandwich here?"

"Imagine if badger meat and a cow pie had a baby."

"Perfect. I ordered it for Jake."

We both turned around in time to see Jake taking a big bite of the brown hunk of sludge smashed between two slices of toasted white bread. He dipped it in a pile of ketchup, happily talking with the guys, telling some animated story and gesturing wildly.

"Kelsey never told me you were coming home this summer." I tried to keep the accusatory note out of my voice, but Kelsey and I would have words later.

"And why would Kelsey feel she needed to tell you?"

I didn't like his knowing gaze. "She probably would have called to warn me of the stench coming into town."

He laughed, polishing off a few fries. I reached across the table and stole a few more off of Margo's plate. She glared at me before pulling her plate closer to her. I glanced up to see Logan looking back at his construction friends and giving them some sort of signal, which seemed to give the men a reason to burst out laughing.

He turned back and caught me watching him, all innocence. "So, Tess, what kind of things do you like to do around here?"

Inside, I was waffling. What answer would come flying out of my mouth when he asked?

"I mainly sit at home and read."

"Liar."

Let's see, we could make out. I could have his babies.

"You still like to hike?" he asked.

"Alone. Yeah."

"Things are always better with an old friend." Logan took another bite of his hot dog and gave me a friendly grin.

I wondered again about saying yes. I shouldn't. I know I shouldn't. I didn't want to take part in anybody's games or bets, but this was Logan.

Except, at that moment, the eyes of the man I had been so infatuated with left mine to follow a pair of pretty women passing by our table, scanning their backsides with a quick, efficient gaze before returning to his food. My heart landed in my stomach with a thud. Tyler used to do that, check out other women in the restaurant while he was with me—and apparently, when he was without me, too. I swallowed.

"So, what do you say? Do you want to meet up sometime this week, and we'll see if you can keep up with me on the trail?"

Was hiking a date?

"I'll buy you dinner afterward."

Yup.

Logan oozed confidence. Grinning at me, smooth-talking me, giving hand signals to the guys behind us, all while smiling at Jen when she passed. My heart deflated. There was my answer. I wouldn't put myself in another situation like Tyler. Sweet-talking or not, Logan would be put in his place. Our babies were not meant to be. *Dang you, secret scrapbook.*

"No, thanks. I wouldn't want to have to carry your body up the mountain." Strike one.

Undeterred, he leaned back in his chair, studying me. "I'll split the money with you." Ball two.

"You reek of desperation."

"Wrap it up, Marten!" somebody from the crew called out, laughter breaking out behind us.

I was starting to feel sick. It had been fun with the other guys. We understood each other. Logan was something else entirely. Childhood crushes usually went away. And mine did. I went to college and even got engaged to somebody else. Logan wasn't even on my radar beyond the occasional musings of my childhood. But now, he was sitting in front of me and asking me questions I had always dreamed of him asking, but instead of feeling flattered and sought out, I felt cheap and used. The pawn in some dumb game.

"Ready to go?" I asked Margo.

She nodded, and we stood. I grabbed a few more fries off of Logan's plate. "See you around, Logan. Next time, bring your abs."

He leaned forward. "Wait, what about our date?"

"I hike alone." I couldn't resist my sardonic smile when I added, "If you want somebody to show you around, Jen looks like she might love to." Strike two.

He had the gall to look startled. "But I asked you."

"And I guess I said no to…"—I motioned toward him with my hands—"all that." I smiled at him, though inside I was going to be sick. "See ya." We turned to go.

"Wait. I have a coupon."

I stopped. Hold up.

Foul ball.

For all my emotions, an embarrassed smile began to form across my face. I wiped it clean before turning around.

"What?"

He stood and took a step closer, a smile playing on his lips. The sweet, earthy smell of his cologne went right to my weak heart.

"I don't have it on me, but I do know it says it's good for one date with you anytime."

The umpire called a time-out.

"You don't have it on you?" I cleared my throat and got my head back into the game. "I'm sorry, I'll have to see it before I can accept. How would I know if it's expired or not?"

He rubbed his chin with his hand, studying me. "I don't think eight-year-old Tessa would have put an expiration date on that particular love note." He looked pleased with himself, thinking he had me.

He didn't.

"No coupon, no date. Good to see you, Logan. Sorry about the hundred bucks." I gave him a grin to let him know I wasn't all that sorry and left him standing there, dejected, but with a growing smile on his face. Strike three.

Game over.

Deep down, past the prickly exterior of my current existence, lived a little girl who was delighted that her childhood crush was here for the summer. Somewhere, deep inside, that little girl was scampering through a field of wildflowers at the news. This was the stuff of dreams. Of romance novels. A summer with my long-unrequited crush.

But the heroine in my story had been broken, and the hero looked to be made of the same stuff as the last guy. If my year of expensive therapy had taught me anything, it was that I couldn't throw my self-worth down the drain at the whim of some man. Even if that man was Logan. I remembered the way his eyes moved from my face to check out the women walking by and felt my heart go cold again.

Especially if that man was Logan.

4

TESSA

My feet made a soft, crunching sound on the gravel road as I ran. I kept my focus forward, my gait long, and my body felt strong and steady. The June air was crisp and smelled of fresh-cut hay and a touch of exhaust. The hair I kept high in a ponytail bounced against my shoulders in rhythm with my stride. The stiff cold in my muscles had warmed considerably while the numbness in my bones had spread, making the running feel automatic.

I was three miles into my five-mile run when I rounded the curve in the road that led onto the main street of Eugene—the only street in the whole town boasting a stoplight along with a hardware store, tractor parts store, a grocery store, and the post office.

As I hit the back road that would lead back to my house, I pulled out my phone to check the time. Perfect. 7 a.m. Kelsey had some answering to do. I meant to call last night to quiz her on her silence but needed to process what had happened at the restaurant. Kelsey would have wanted details, and I didn't want her commentary on my interactions with Logan. Had she hinted at Logan coming this summer and I missed it? Was there a code somewhere? I scanned my phone for the last few messages Kelsey had sent me.

I was looking specifically for something that said, *Hey, my idiot brother is going to be in Eugene this summer, same as you. Crazy world, huh?* Or, *Tess, my brother called and wanted your number. He said he's changed his womanizing ways and can only think of you.*

Except, I didn't get any of those. I did get a few of these:

Kelsey: I have this new, weird mole in that crease between my butt cheek and thigh. The borders don't look crazy yet, but I will definitely keep you posted.
Me: You know I love that.

Kelsey: I peed all over myself today because my beloved spouse plastic-wrapped the toilet seat. Any good ideas?
Me: Itching powder in his shaving cream?
Kelsey: Is there real, legit itching powder in the world?
Me: Not sure.

ONE WEEK LATER.

Kelsey: FYI. Itching powder IS a thing and it works.

Kelsey: Cade just informed me that YOU helped him get my car onto cinder blocks. I gave you RIDES to school in that car.
Me: You're breaking up. I can't understand your last message.
Kelsey: UGHHHHH.
Me: On a super-unrelated note, what is Cade's social security number?

She deserved this. I hit number 3 on my phone's favorites list. In Kelsey's world, 7 a.m. on a Saturday was still the middle of the night. My best friend grew up on a farm, but it was sometimes hard to tell. After about seven rings, a groggy voice answered.

"Why is this happening?"

"Good morning, traitor." My voice was cheerful as I took a deep breath, the smell of the hayfield next to me entering my lungs. For the first time all morning, I slowed enough to take in the towering pine-filled mountains in the distance. I felt like doing a happy dance. How anybody could live where there were no mountains was beyond me.

Waking Kelsey up early with a chipper phone call was also a good time.

"I thought we had a no-calls-before-ten-a.m. rule?"

"You poor, loved, married, twin-baby-having best friend of mine. I'm so terribly sorry to disturb you."

"Your words sound nice, but your tone is scary."

"How are you feeling?" She really did sound groggy. I was beginning to feel bad for waking her.

"My stomach doesn't know how to keep food down anymore. It's all throw up, all the time."

"I'm sorry. How's Cade?"

"Taking a few summer classes and an internship and working like a madman, but somehow still finding the energy to switch the salt and sugar jars in my kitchen."

"Ugh, you guys are so weird and in love. It's no wonder you got pregnant. What, do you kiss and make up after every prank now?"

Kelsey laughed, her voice sounding less manly the longer we talked. "It's our new rule. Every prank ends with—"

"No! Stop," I cut her off immediately. "I don't want to know any more than I already do." My cheeks still burned from hearing a few select details of their honeymoon night she had saved for my ears only, as best friends do.

"It beats making a homemade trap to catch a squirrel to put in Cade's locker."

"The times we had."

"Why am I not still asleep right now? I don't remember doing anything to deserve this."

I was starting to feel bad for waking her so early. I hadn't realized the babies were *already* keeping her up at night. "I'm sorry, but I ran into Logan last night."

There was a long silence on the phone.

"Kelsey..." My body had slowed down to a walk. I willed my breathing to settle.

"Ugh. I'm sorry. I found out a few days ago. I just didn't want to get your hopes up."

"Kels, I don't want to date him. I just... A little warning would have been nice. Did you know he's here all summer?"

"I'm sorry. I should have told you. But I swear, it's a new girl every other week, and I know you used to like him, but if he played you at all, I would castrate him. So...I'm trying to save him from that and you from more heartache. I still can't think of Tyler without wanting to stick him, head first, into the back of a cow."

"Now there's a picture."

"I have so many raging hormones with this pregnancy. It's a good thing I'm exhausted all the time, or else I would commit...something. For sure."

I stepped off the road and waved to Betsy May driving by in her long Buick. The older-than-dirt Eugene resident was one of my at-home patients for the summer. She was famous in town for her bug eyes in thick glasses and bright-pink lipstick. But everyone gave her a wide berth when she sat behind the wheel.

"It's all good. I just wanted to give you a hard time."

"I think Chase was involved in some big projects in Boise that kept getting delayed, so he sent Logan at the last minute."

"Don't try and tell me things now, traitor. Too late. I already know all this."

"When did you see him?"

"He was at the restaurant formerly known as The Ranch House last night. I met Margo there for dinner."

"Ew. How is it there? I've heard it took a nosedive ever since—" Kelsey broke off suddenly.

"My cousin took over management? Yeah. Let's not talk about it."

"Did he talk to you?"

I bit my lip and moved into a light jog again. Of course Kelsey would home in on my lack of details and press further. I would have done the same. But for some reason, I didn't want to tell her all the details about last night. I didn't want to tell her about the bet. I didn't want it to get back to Logan that I gave it a thought or, to my shame, a second thought.

"Yeah, for a minute. Then he ogled the waitress."

She let out a sigh. "I hate that he's like this now. Just ignore him. Because if he tries to pull something on you, I swear I will kill him myself."

"Thanks, Rambo. I'll be fine. Jake's here, too."

"Aww, Jake. Why don't you date him?"

"Too many little-brother vibes there to suit me. Any cravings?" I didn't know much about babies or pregnancy, but the cravings thing fascinated me.

"So far, I've lived off of Taco Bell. The thought of eating beef makes me dry heave, but put it in a tortilla and hand it to me through a window, and I'm drooling just thinking about it."

"Sounds amazing. The only thing edible in this entire town is fries. Is Cade there now, or is he studying somewhere?"

"He's currently heading to the store to feed my cravings."

"This early? Wait, you were awake when I called?"

"It was the nausea, okay? I was about ready to roll over and go back to sleep."

"Such a whiner. What's Cade getting you from the store?"

She hesitated. "I'll have no smug health judgments from you. The heart wants what it wants. And Cade's heart desperately wants my stomach full without me puking."

"Ice cream and pickles?"

"Too cliche. Cheetos and hot fudge."

"Together?"

There was a long pause before Kelsey breathed, "Good heavens, I never thought about them together. That sounds amazing. Mostly, though, I just want a ginormous jar of hot fudge that I can shove down my throat."

"Atta girl."

My heart was pacified enough that Kelsey's intentions were honorable that I hung up to let her try and sleep a bit more.

5

LOGAN

Monday morning was my crew's first official day of work on the site. Chase had been down to Eugene a month earlier and had hired a local crew to clear and level the ground as well as do the footing and concrete work. The skeleton crew he sent to Eugene for the summer was not random, though it worked out that none of us had families. We were all hands-on at every stage and each of us had our specialties. Briggs was the framing expert. Javier and Carl oversaw the Sheetrock and texturing. Trevor and Ronnie handled electric and HVAC. Frank Robbins (though retired) was coming in to do the plumbing for us as a favor to Nate. And I was the trim and cabinet guy.

Today, we were framing—one of my favorite parts of the whole process. I loved seeing the design of a plan start to take shape. The office was about 2,000 square feet with a reception and waiting area, a hallway with a large gym on one side, and three patient rooms on the other. The end of the hallway was a staff lounge and meeting room as well as a storage room.

"Hey, boss, someone's here to see you," Briggs said.

I wasn't sure why the first person that came to my head at this news was Tessa Robbins. I was a little startled at how quickly my thoughts went to her. It must have been the residual effects of her rejection the other night. She had no reason to be here, but I couldn't help hoping to see her face as I made my way over in front of the concrete slab to where Travis had pointed.

It wasn't Tessa's face that greeted me. But it wasn't that far off.

A tall, blonde man, who looked as if he'd grown up on a steady diet of protein shakes and pushups, was leaning over, examining the concrete, when I stepped down onto the dirt next to him.

"Nate. How's it going?" I held out my hand and was relieved when he smiled.

"Good, Marten. You?" He gave my hand a firm shake. So far, so good.

"What do you eat, a whole weight room, for breakfast now?"

His eyes narrowed, evaluating me with a quirk of a smile. "Have you even *seen* a weight room since high school?"

I lifted my hands to my still-flat stomach, though I had filled out some since my glory days. "Gotta keep the women at bay so I can get some work done."

His hands dropped into his pockets as he took a step back. "Ah, still stealing women and breaking hearts?"

Okay, maybe he hadn't forgotten everything.

"Only on the weekends."

His mouth lifted at the corners before he had enough small talk. "How are things going here?"

"This is our first day. We've got the outer wall framed. Chase was here a couple of weeks ago, getting it ready. I've got trusses set to be delivered sometime next week. I don't anticipate too many issues coming up this summer."

He nodded. "We never do, though, do we? Listen, I emailed you a change in the blueprint."

Change in the blueprint. The absolute worst words for a contractor to hear. "What is it?"

He looked past me. "I shrunk the gym down and added more space to that back storage room. It might mean an adjustment to the back wall."

Though I cringed on the inside, outwardly, I took it like a man. "Alright, I'll go print it out and have a look."

I asked him a few questions, but the conversation took a steep dive after I exhausted all my knowledge of Nate Robbins. I knew Tessa much better than Nate. Nate was large and intimidating and, while he sounded happily married, definitely hadn't forgotten our run-in in high school.

"Anything...new with you?" The question was big of him. It didn't come out naturally, and I hated to disappoint him. Nothing much was 'new' with me. No kids, no wife, no dog. I still slept a solid eight hours at night and was currently living with my parents.

"Not much. Just living the dream."

He moved closer and pretended to inspect some of the wood. I took that as a sign our conversation was finished.

"I'll be in and out this summer, checking up on things," he called after me.

"Sounds good. We'll be here."

I called out for Briggs to follow me and walked toward the single-wide construction trailer sitting at the edge of the job site. Chase had bought the trailer for a steal, and his wife, Penny, had spent a few months turning it into an office space, which meant ripping out the orange shag carpet, replacing the laminate cupboards in the kitchen with real wood, and putting in two large desks and a printer station for blueprints.

"What's up, boss?" Briggs said, following me up the rickety wooden steps and inside the office.

"There's been a change in the plans."

He groaned.

"You'll have to adjust the back wall. Nate wants to expand the storage room."

"Is this going to be a regular thing with him?" He motioned out the window as Nate got in his truck and pulled away.

What did I know about Nate? He was tall. Athletic. Smart. If he was anything like his sister, a perfectionist. I pulled up the blueprint on my screen. The change wouldn't mess us up too badly. I pushed print.

"Maybe. I'll bring you the new prints in a minute."

Briggs didn't leave right away like I expected him to. Instead, he leaned against the door frame, peering at me. "You sure you don't want to double with me and Margo tonight? I hear you can get anybody to go out with you."

"Shut up." I threw a pencil at him while he skipped out the door, laughing.

I busied myself, returning emails and phone calls, until the noise level outside of the trailer grew. Ronnie was at the center of it all, of course, doing his own special bald, beer-gutted, and hairy imperson-ation of Tessa rejecting our whole crew the night earlier. I watched for a moment longer, briefly entertained, until he began using crude female anatomy expressions to add to his joke. Breaking up the crowd before it went too far, I sent everybody off once again to their jobs, keeping a couple of the guys to help adjust the back wall to match the new set of blueprints.

Being in the construction business my entire adult life, vulgar expressions rolled off of me. I usually left well enough alone, but something about them talking about Tessa had my guard up. It felt disloyal to let them say things like that about the girl who had practi-cally grown up at my house. I planned to treat her just as I did my sister—lots of teasing, a few laughs. The end.

I put in a convincing performance of studying blueprints, hammering nails, making phone calls, and keeping the guys on task for the next thirty minutes, though my thoughts kept inadvertently returning to 'the hot blonde.'

THE BUNKHOUSE HAD a smell to it. You noticed it first when you opened the door and stepped inside. It was a mixture of hay, dust, and wood with a little old-dishes-soaking-in-the-sink aroma. The main floor held a tiny kitchen with a round table and four chairs surrounding it. There was a small bathroom next to the table, and Stitch's bed and things were in the corner on the opposite side of the kitchen. My mom had been disappointed when I moved into the bunkhouse with Stitch, my dad's ranch foreman and retired veterinarian, instead of my old room. She didn't tell me in so many words, but I could see it in her eyes. I'd be sure to visit her plenty in the house, but I was almost thirty, and the thought of moving back in with my parents was more than my pride could endure.

I didn't have a problem, however, making myself at home in their kitchen.

My parents and Stitch were gone for the evening, so I grabbed a frozen pizza and made my way back to the bunkhouse.

My parents adopted Stitch a few years back when his wife of fifty-five years passed away, and he couldn't bear the thought of living in his house without her. They invited him to move into the bunkhouse, and he's been a part of the family ever since. Against the wall next to the doorway was a staircase leading up to the loft, which had enough room for a queen-size bed, a small closet, and my 65-inch TV I couldn't bear to part with for the summer. The last person to stay here with Stitch had been Cade, my brother-in-law, three summers ago when he was putting the moves on my sister. After that, it was turned into a storage space until I moved in. I liked to think Stitch appreciated the company.

When the oven dinged exactly seventeen minutes later, I plopped down on my bed in the loft with half of a stuffed-crust pizza piled on a plate on my chest.

Bon appetit.

I flipped the TV station to the Discovery channel, settling in when I caught the beginning of a documentary on the Amazon Rainforest. I was three slices in when a knock at the door sounded—a knock to an annoying tune of something I couldn't quite place.

Jake.

My first impulse was to hide the pizza, but I knew he would sniff it out in no time. Jake had the appetite of a parched camel. I would have no pizza left by the time he was done here.

"I know you're in here!" The door flung open, smashing into the wall next to it.

I changed the channel to SportsCenter before raising myself off the bed to look down below, only to find a grinning Jake leaning casually against the doorframe.

"Mmm…has someone been cooking?" Jake leaned closer and sniffed the air. "Is Tessa here?"

"If she was, I'd consider it a date, and you'd owe me. Aren't you done for the day?"

Jake moved out of my sight and began rummaging around the kitchen before emerging at the top of the stairs with the other half of my pizza on a plate. He flopped onto the other side of my bed. "What are we watching?"

I eyed him as he took a huge bite. "I miss Dusty."

"Dusty got himself a girlfriend."

I stopped, mid-chew. "Dusty? Since when?"

"I talked to him a few days ago. He told me it's been going on since winter."

"And we're just hearing about it now?"

"Some people are the worst."

Not to be dramatic, because Jake would never admit it, but his right arm had been cut off. He and Dusty had been inseparable for years, even working the same job, going to school together, and running in the same rodeo circuit. I would consider Jake and me something like brothers, but Jake was not here lounging on my bed for any other reason than that he was missing his friend.

That was the only reason I let him stay.

"What are we watching?" Jake asked again, taking a sip of a Coke stolen from my fridge.

"SportsCenter."

Jake looked my way, his brow raised slightly. "Oh. Did you see the big game the other day?"

"No. I've been working."

"Really? Ravens versus Colts? You didn't see it?"

Ravens and Colts? My eyes narrowed as he stretched casually on the bed, eating my pizza. *My* bed. Eating *my* pizza. I shifted my shoulders away from him while casually typing out a Google search for the

Ravens and Colts before I stopped and pocketed my phone once again.

"Nice try."

"What?"

"It's summer, moron. No football."

"I know. I was checking to make sure *you* knew."

I ignored Jake for a while and inhaled a slice of pizza in about the time it took Jake to eat his whole plate. The announcer droned on about games I didn't care about, and I was wishing myself back to the Amazon Rainforest, learning more about tree frogs.

"Wait, shouldn't you be on a date right now?" He snapped his fingers and leaned against the headboard. "Oh, that's right, didn't work out."

"I should punch you in the face for all of that."

"What?"

I scowled at him, unable to take his wide, knowing grin anymore.

"Some people call me The Matchmaker," he said.

"Nobody calls you that."

"I'll bet Cade and Kelsey still thank the heavens for me in their prayers every night."

"A freight train wouldn't have stopped those two from getting together."

"Their pride might have if I hadn't organized a little, now infamous, basketball game. If they don't name one of their kids after me, I'm going to be ticked."

Even I had to admit he might have been right. Though I wasn't there, I had heard more than I cared to about the supposed basketball game that was the nudge my sister and Cade needed to finally get together.

"Well, I have no feelings to admit to anything, so you are welcome to switch the bet to you and the…Tessa, if you're so interested in what she's doing."

I had almost said 'hot blonde' but stopped myself just in time. Not that Tessa wasn't attractive. She was very attra—(throat clearing)—she looked fine for a little-sister type. Which was exactly what she was. No longer jailbait but still justifiably terrifying and somebody I would never truly consider dating. Jen was more my type—out for a good time. I just had to work up the nerve to ask her out with her pet grizzly bear sniffing around behind her shoulder.

"I think you're just sore she rejected you. I guess childhood crushes only last for so long."

"How did you know about that?" I had been surprised the other night to discover Jake knew anything about Tessa's crush.

"Who doesn't know about that? Kelsey used to make fun of her all the time."

Great. Thanks for that, Kels. I moved my attention back to the TV and said the worst thing I could have said to Jake. "She had to say no. If we had been alone, she wouldn't have rejected me."

Jake's ears alighted, and I suddenly wondered how my night alone eating pizza and watching the nature channel had ended with me here: with Jake nudging me toward the edge of a cliff, on the precipice of something terrible brewing in his head.

"Oh, really? So, if we drove out to her place tomorrow after work and you asked her out, she'd say yes?"

"That's what I'm saying." There I go, egging him on because my stupid pride demanded it.

He considered me while I focused on the TV, my leg twitching.

"Double or nothing."

I sighed. "Let's just leave it alone."

"So, you *don't* think she'd go out with you?"

"I'm gonna kick your a—"

"Double or nothing," he pressed again.

I ran a hand through my hair so I didn't punch Jake's laughing face. He would never let this go.

"Fine. But you'll have to prove you're good for two hundred bucks. I don't believe it."

The way he whipped out his wallet, producing two crisp one-hundred-dollar bills made me push him off the bed in one swift movement.

"You planned this."

"I've got a feeling about you two."

"Don't talk about feelings while you're in my bedroom."

He made himself too comfortable once again on my bed, arms folded behind his head. "You sure caved fast."

"Don't misread my interest. I'll go on one date with her, and then I'll be getting a wad of cash from you in return. End of interaction. And then you're going to stay out of my life." I fixed him with my fiercest stare.

And like a cat who just ensnared the fat, stupid mouse, Jake smiled.

6

TESSA

"Okay, Betsy, lift that leg." I held onto her frail elbow while she grumbled at me. Her wrinkled and manicured hand held onto the living room wall and a dining room chair to balance as she attempted to do what I had asked. Her foot barely left the ground.

"Betsy," I asked. "Have you been doing the exercises I gave you over the weekend?"

Silence.

"Betsy." My voice came out in a warning tone.

"I didn't have the time."

The beloved 87-year-old firecracker resident lifted her haughty chin and stared out her window, willfully ignoring me. Her white hair was washed, curled, preened, and perfumed. And her thin red lips pressed together in a pout. Her big eyes, magnified by a thick set of lenses, were narrowed.

"Betsy, we've got to get your leg stronger, and we can't do that if you don't work with me."

Nothing.

I ground my teeth as I tried for another angle. "Betsy, Nate is going to come check on you in a few weeks. Don't you want to show him how much you've improved since your fall?"

She huffed. "Nate would never yell at me."

"I'm sorry, Betsy. Let's try again. I didn't mean to yell." I hadn't even raised my voice, but no sense getting the woman fired up. My eyes flicked to the clock again before I yanked them back. "Can you do a couple more lifts for me? Then, we'll take a break."

The woman still ignored me. I glanced at her clock on the wall. I had only been here fifteen minutes and had another forty-five to fill. What does one do with a willfully disobedient elderly lady? I was strongly beginning to suspect that Nate passed Betsy May off to me on purpose. Since he moved back to Eugene a couple of weeks ago, he had begun an in-home patient care service until the new building was up and running. Word of a physical therapist in town spread like wildfire, and Nate began pushing a few of his patients onto me. So far, Betsy had been much more interested in chatting and had done few to none of the exercises I left for her.

It wasn't like she didn't know me. She had lived down the road from my family my entire life. Most of the time, she was an eccentrically sweet old lady who occasionally ran into things with her car.

"Come on, Betsy. Bill Rogers will probably be at the Fourth of July Festival in a few weeks. I've seen the way he looks at you. Don't you want to get better for him?" Old Bill had to have been pushing ninety, but he still looked handsome as ever in his polyester track suit and a full head of silky white hair.

She didn't move. Dang, I could have sworn I saw the two of them canoodling in her car the other day.

"I think you two would make really cute babies," I prodded.

A smile broke out across her face as she finally glared over at me. "I liked you much better when you were the snot-nosed girl with the wild hair, snatching peaches off of my tree."

"That could be arranged. Your tree grows the best peaches in all of Eugene."

I sent Nate a text after I left Betsy May's to head home and start working in the orchard.

Me: Betsy May was a delight to work with. She always did what she was told and didn't ever complain or get mad at all.
Nate: Bring her cookies next time.

There was something about Betsy May's appointment that was bothering me. I *liked* Betsy May. We had always had a fun relationship. But *that* was not fun for me. I generally liked people. I could be charming, fun, and sarcastic as needed, but I was beginning to learn that *dealing* with people was much different than interacting with people.

Nate was the opposite. His casual, everyday conversation was nothing to write home about, but he was a natural at *dealing* with people. He had the patience of a saint. I knew this because during PT school, I did a clinical rotation in Las Vegas, working with him in his office. His manner of talking to patients was full of clucking noises, sympathetic nods, and gentle coaxing. I sat in the same room, observing him, and tried not to claw at the walls. I would clench my fists tight and plaster a fake smile on my face instead of shouting at each patient to stop being so lazy. *Do your exercises! You can walk the three feet without keeling over, I promise. Bend your leg. Stop the whining!*

Maybe Nate was smart to ease me into an official position at Willow Creek with a few house calls. I clearly needed to rub shoulders with him before I offended every person we knew and loved in Eugene.

"ACCORDING TO MY CHARTS, Mom, you're about a week ahead of schedule as to where you should be with your flexibility and mobility. You're a rock star. Keep it up." I had returned from Betsy May's in time to run through some exercises with my very best patient. It had been two weeks since her double knee-replacement surgery, and she was doing well, but the recovery was not going fast enough for her. We had finished her physical therapy for the day, and she was heading back to bed for a nap. The strong medication they had given her made her mind groggy and her body exhausted. It was strange seeing my mom, who had always been so active, stuck in bed so much throughout the day. I got her settled, refilled her water, and then gave her a hug.

"Such a sweet little liar." She leaned back on the pillow before closing her eyes. "Now, fan and noise machine, please."

"Yes, your highness. Call me when you need me." I turned on both and headed toward the door.

"Nate and Anna and the kids are coming by sometime today. Will you call me when they get here?"

"Yeah. What are they coming over for?"

"Nate wanted to check on me."

"Is he planning to poach my best patient?"

Mom smiled and pulled up her blanket. "Nothing like that. They haven't stopped by in a while. He's been busy with his own patients and checking out the construction site."

My thoughts took a turn when I began to imagine my brother and Logan working together before I yanked myself back on track.

"Sounds good."

Outside, the early-June sun shone brightly. A cool summer breeze fluttered the base of my tank top as I strode across the yard in my work jeans and my hair tucked away in my hat. I yanked open the door of the large, metal greenhouse and stepped inside. The heated moisture felt dense against my skin. Tomorrow, we were opening our fruit stand for the first time this summer. With it being only June, we were reduced to selling whatever crops we had grown in our greenhouse. Rows of strawberry and raspberry plants filled the large structure. A few years ago, my dad realized, after apples and peaches in August and September, our number-one-selling crops were our strawberries and raspberries. Our supplies were limited, so he built a greenhouse to supply the buyers all season long with fresh, sweet berries. Now we'd be opening up our berries to the public.

I pulled out a large crate and began picking red strawberries off their vine, sampling a few in the process. I filled pint after pint, wiping the sweat dripping from my face from the humidity with the bottom of my tank top. Country music poured from the speakers on my phone as I sunk into an easy rhythm. Pick, pick, eat, pick, pick, eat. Out the window, Dad was headed toward the orchard with his hedge trimmer. He wore overalls, rubber boots, and his waterproof polyester gardener hat. It looked like a bucket turned upside down with string connecting both sides below his jaw. He had worn that hat outside for as long as I could remember. He moved in and out of my eyesight among the trees, and I sat transfixed like I always did when I looked at the orchard.

I couldn't believe it had been a year ago. I hadn't had the luxury to avoid the orchard. I wouldn't be much help to my dad if I didn't weed and spray and prune. I was grateful most of the trees in the orchard were apples and wouldn't be ready to pick until closer to August. I hated that I wanted to steer clear of the place I used to love more than any other part of our property. Kelsey and I spent much of our life as children in and out of those trees. With low limbs, we would climb to the top, eat apples, and talk about boys. At thirteen, I had whispered to Kelsey from those trees the horrifying secret that I had started my period the day before, to which Kelsey grabbed my hand and told me she had started two weeks earlier but had been too embarrassed to tell me. The long line of grass between the trees served as an impromptu bowling alley, cartwheel lane, and, on occasion, a make-believe wedding.

And then, one day, a real wedding.

The opening of the greenhouse door snapped me off the trail my thoughts were on. I watched, grateful for a distraction but also curious, as Logan and Jake ducked under the low door frame and stepped inside. They both wore jeans and t-shirts, though Jake's pants were much tighter, and they both had smiles on their faces that screamed trouble. And fun. But mostly trouble. And even as I grew wary, the tiniest thrill shot through me.

The day was suddenly looking up.

7

LOGAN

J ake had insisted he needed to come along. When I had told him to take a hike, he said the bet would be off if I didn't let him come. He needed to see it with his own eyes. There had been a look brimming on his face that I hadn't wanted to examine, so I rolled my eyes and agreed to it. Hopefully, Tessa would just turn me down again, and we'd be done with this whole mess I'd gotten myself into with my big mouth.

"Did your GPS take you to the wrong house again?" Tessa asked as she watched us approach, her eyes sparkling.

The greenhouse was huge. Once inside, I guessed it was almost as big as my dad's shop. Vines of fruits and vegetables lined the walls and rows in between. An old cherrywood desk littered with packets of seeds and tools served as an island in the middle of the room. Tessa sat in one of two old computer chairs, then attempted to open a drawer. I could tell our arrival had flustered her, and so watching the drawer stick and refuse to open as she yanked it several times only resulted in me trying to hide my smile.

"Try kicking it," I offered.

"That's usually my next move."

I ambled around the desk and squatted down next to her, my arm brushing her leg. She rolled back a few inches, allowing me closer access to the rogue drawer. It suddenly felt very strange being in her space so casually. I wasn't sure if the smell of citrus was from something growing in this greenhouse or her, but either way, I was too close to her for comfort.

I shook the door, leaning further down to open the cabinet door under the drawer, and jiggled a few things before giving it one strong tug. The drawer glided open.

Her mouth dropped. "How did you do that?"

I looked up at her as I sat back on my haunches. "A magician doesn't share his secrets."

She opened and closed the drawer once more, marveling at the smooth glide back and forth. "How good are you at fixing printers?"

I made my way around the desk before sitting on the other chair, propping my feet up on the island. "I'm a construction guy, not an IT guy. Don't look at me like that. And no, I don't fix chairs either."

She bounced up and down. "It's just so squeaky."

"No."

She opened her newly fixed drawer again and pulled out a pair of black gardening gloves. "Fine. Go away. I'm done with you, then."

"Oh, we're not done. We've got something to settle first." I glanced over at Jake across the room, leaning against the door, who was all smiles under his black cowboy hat but had been strangely silent so far.

"What?"

"Jake extended the bet. Which means *you* get another chance to go out with me." Might as well just spell it out. Tessa would never agree to this if she thought it was still for a bet. And I needed Tessa *not* to agree to this, but I had to play it up a bit for Jake.

"Are you sure you can handle another rejection?"

I held back a smile. "Come on, Tess." I motioned toward Jake with my head. "This isn't about us. This is about that redneck cowboy over there. Picture this: you and me eating a nice steak dinner on Jake's dime." Actually, that didn't sound horrible.

She laughed. "That thought is really tempting, but it's still a no from me."

"Wow. That rolled right off your tongue. Don't you want to take him down? I'll split the money with you."

"The more I say it, the easier it becomes," she said, her eyes sparkling.

"The Tessa from three years ago would have jumped at the offer. I *know* Tessa from *ten* years ago would have." I shouldn't have brought that up, but I had a feeling she would blush and I was right.

"Tessa from today isn't interested in the arrogant flirt you've become." She leaned forward and pushed my legs off the island. My body jolted forward as my feet hit the ground with a thud.

I laughed, though it seemed hollow in my ears as I leaned forward in my seat. "What about that coupon?"

"I'm going to need to see it before I can accept it."

"I can have it here in ten minutes."

"I think you're bluffing," she insisted.

I held up my hand, inspecting my nails in the light. "I'm also reminded of a certain love note..."

She fought off a smile.

I continued, confident she would be turning me down, which for some reason made me a bit reckless. The attractive way she bit her lip at my teasing had nothing to do with me enjoying myself. "One that professed an undying love and devotion and pledging herself to marry me if I ever ask her."

"I was eight."

"I mean...it's practically written in stone."

"Erasable pencil."

"Same thing."

She glanced down, pulling on her gloves while I took notice of the light spattering of freckles on her cheeks. "Yeah, I've been thinking about that—"

My eyebrows raised. "Really?"

"The past ten seconds."

"Ah."

"And I don't think it's going to work out."

"Well, maybe if you go on one date with me, you'll see what a handsome, upstanding guy I am."

"I don't think getting girls to go on *one* date with you is the problem here," she said sweetly.

Oof. Direct hit. "So, you can see why it was a big blow to my ego when the girl who's loved me the longest rejected me in front of all the guys."

I glanced at Jake and felt my stomach drop. Somewhere in the middle of our exchange, Jake the Snake had been released. He watched us with a wide, calculating grin, his arms folded and looking deeply entertained. This had to end now.

"Hey." I waved my hand in front of Jake's face. Slowly, his eyes focused on me.

"You alright?"

He pursed his lips, his eyes flicking over to Tessa and then back at me. He opened his mouth to say something before shutting it again. Something must have resolved in his brain, because a look of satisfaction planted itself on his face.

"I've got a working theory I need to test." He walked backward toward the door, rubbing the imaginary whiskers on his chin. Tessa and I were rooted to our spots on the floor, on high alert.

"What?" Tessa asked.

When he reached the handle, he stopped, staring at us until Tessa and I were glancing at each other uneasily. Satisfied with whatever he saw, he smiled. "Go on about your business." Giving us each a look, he added, "Whatever that may be. And I'll be right back." He muttered a few more unintelligible things before exiting the greenhouse. We watched from the window as he started up his old truck and pulled away.

"Looks like your ride left you," she said.

"I'm not sure I want him to come back, either." He had left me in Tessa's lair. Alone. Well done, Jake. If that was his plan all along, he had surprised me. It lacked a certain finesse. But something in me knew he would be back which explained the cold feeling of dread that washed over me.

Tessa recruited me to help pick raspberries. When she realized I was eating more than I was saving she smacked my arms with her gloves and shooed me over to a chair. I grinned, stealing a few out of her bucket before she could stop me.

Tires crunched ominously on the gravel outside. Tessa stood beside me as we peered out the window. A brand-new, slick, black Chevy Silverado with a Duramax Diesel engine and a lift was parked out front. After admiring the truck for a long moment, I nearly sat back down before the door opened and Jake stepped down from the truck.

Our mouths dropped open.

"What in the...?" Tessa started, her voice trailing off. My thoughts exactly.

We stepped outside and crept cautiously toward Jake and his extra-wide smile.

"Are the cops on their way?" I asked.

"I think I outran 'em."

"Whose truck is this?" I asked as I approached the glistening beast before me. It was the truck of every man's dreams right in front of me, and I couldn't figure out why it was here.

Jake stood back from the truck, watching me. "I've had it for a few months. It's my first time driving it."

I stared at him in horror. "Why?"

"It was a birthday present from Daddy." Though he still smiled, he spat the last word out somewhat bitterly for an eternal optimist like Jake.

I knew some passing bits about Jake's family life. In a town as small as Eugene, you couldn't hide much, even if you wanted to. Jake's dad had struck it big as a professional bull rider. I hardly remembered him living here. Soon after he made it big, he divorced his wife and left her and Jake. I hadn't realized there was any contact between them at all.

"How does it drive?" I asked.

Jake grinned. "Not bad, if you're into the kind of truck that starts up when you first turn the key, or a gas gauge that shows you how much gas is left, or if you like driving with a windshield that isn't cracked a thousand different ways—which I don't."

"Why aren't you driving it?" Tessa asked.

"I don't want it."

Slowly, Tessa and I shifted to stare at him. A sucker punch to the gut would have surprised me less.

"You don't *want* it?" I asked again, slowly.

Jake folded his arms and leaned back against his door, enjoying the theatrics. "Nope."

There was an undercurrent of mischief running in his eyes. I felt the pull but immediately had my guard up. He was up to something. Other than giving one of us his truck out of the kindness of his heart (not likely), I was coming up empty.

"Something wrong with a truck that's been the Diesel Course truck of the year for four years in a row?" I asked, my voice sounding hoarse.

He grinned. "Yeah. My dad gave it to me. I'd rather take this thing out to a minefield and have it explode before driving it."

"So…why did you bring it here?" Tessa asked, giving the snake a cautious poke with her stick.

At that question, Jake rubbed his hands together with glee. Too much glee. If glee were a candy, he had a sackful. "I want to see if I'm right about something."

"What?" I crossed my arms in front of my body.

For the record, this was where my stomach began its mad descent into mayhem.

Jake held his hands up in between us. "There's something here. Do you feel it?"

We stared at him, blinking.

I found my voice first. "Is that what that is? I feel it, too. Every time Tessa looks at me, it's like she's one fantasy away from yanking my shirt off."

She glowered up at me. "And then you wake up."

"That's always the worst part."

Jake went on, breaking into our rhythm of teasing jabs. "That's what I mean. Logan should have no reason on this green earth to refuse Tessa. And Tessa, you've crushed on him your whole life."

Tessa's face colored with his statement, and I jumped in to put a stop to whatever was in Jake's head.

"Listen, Jake. Tessa's great, alright? But I'm not looking for anything like that. I like my life how it is. Lots of dates, lots of *fun*, and no ball and chain around my neck. No offense, Tess." There, that ought to do it.

Jake only smiled and looked at Tessa. "And you?"

She folded her arms across her chest. "First of all, that crush was when I was eight." She waited a long moment for my coughing to subside. "It was short-lived. Kid stuff. I have no interest in dating a player—ever again."

I was dismayed to see the spark in Jake's eyes had been lit by our confessions, not dimmed in the slightest.

"Classic denial. Just as I thought."

"Jake. What's going on?" I asked, my eyes caressing his behemoth of a truck once again.

"I have a little bet in mind for the two of you—if you're interested."

I waited for him to continue, my body clenched tight. One never knew what would come out of his mouth. It had something to do with his new truck, and I couldn't for the life of me figure out what it would be.

"Spit it out," I said.

Jake clasped his hands together, looking at us both with barely restrained glee. "I'll bet you two my truck that you'll fall in love with each other by the end of the summer."

Gobsmacked silence stretched out between the three of us for the space of many seconds.

"What?" Tessa and I asked at the same time.

Jake grinned. "See? Already, you're finishing each other's sentences."

"You can't bet an $80,000 truck," I sputtered.

Jake's jaw tightened. "I already have a truck."

"You don't have a truck. You have a dented tin can on its last leg."

"Bought and paid for by the sweat of my own brow. I have no need for my dad's bribery toy. I'm not joking when I say that I have fantasies about blowing it up."

"Sounds like *you're* the one who needs a girlfriend," I said.

"Jake…" Tessa began before she trailed off, at a loss for words.

"So, we get the truck if we fall in love?" I asked, a smile growing on my face. Maybe I was the marrying type.

"Nope. That's too easy." Jake shook his head, looking us both in the eye. "You get the truck if you *don't* fall in love."

8

TESSA

My head hurt. I didn't understand how I had gone from innocently picking raspberries in the greenhouse to being propositioned for one of Jake's schemes.

"If you want us to fall in love, why are you betting the truck *against* it?" I asked.

"Because you've got to work for it. I'm going to put you through the dating wringer. If I'm right—and I think I am—I keep the truck until I can haul it to a minefield. If I'm wrong and you two can swear to me and yourselves you aren't in love by the end of summer, you keep the truck. You can sell it and split the profit."

"What if we fall in love a week later, after we get the truck?" Logan asked, an impish smile forming. That dimple making a fine appearance. I would not be deterred.

"Then you owe me an $80,000 truck. And a thank-you note."

"What are the stipulations?" I asked. This was crazy. *Jake* was crazy. There was no way I was going through with this bet. But I had to know how Jake was going to spin things—it was a sickness.

"I'll have a list of rules for you two to follow. Basically, it goes like this: you have to go on a date of my choosing once a week. You have to hold hands whenever possible during your dates. You have to kiss at least once—and it has to be a good one."

"You're kind of taking the magic out of Tessa's and my imaginary relationship, don't you think?"

Jake smiled. "Just setting myself up for an advantage. It's a nice truck, after all."

"That you *should* be keeping, Jake," I couldn't help but add. When I thought of Jake, smiles and sunshine came to mind. Betting. Cowboy. Impish. A big tease. When I looked at him now, I still saw that, but underneath the sunshine, there was a hint of sadness. Defiance.

He looked at us both sternly. "This is the last time I'm going to say this. I will never keep this truck. I don't want the money from the truck. I don't want a damn thing from my dad."

Pensive silence stretched between us before I broke it.

"I just got out of a small-town relationship disaster," I said, rubbing my foot in the dirt. "I have no desire to be the talk of the town again, only to have it end." I nodded toward Logan. "This time with a well-known serial dater."

Logan gave me an annoyed look, but before he could say anything, Jake continued, "The dates don't have to be public. I'll get creative."

"You being creative is the main problem I see presented here," Logan said.

"Just think, I've got a 100% success rate on love matches."

"If you're meaning Kelsey and Cade, that was not you," I said.

"They needed a big push. And...."—he pointed toward himself—"big push."

"So let me get this straight," Logan said. "We hang out all summer, pretend to date—"

"You're not pretending anything," Jake cut in. "You will be dating this summer. It's just more controlled. Meaning, you have rules to follow, or else the bet is off."

"What if I want to date other girls over the summer? And Tessa other guys?"

Jake paused, looking over us both before he shrugged. "I can't force you to not date anybody else. But every Saturday night will already be tied up. You can work it out however you want, I guess, with the exception of one date a week of my choosing."

"So, when summer is over and we've followed all your cryptic rules, and we still claim to be only friends, you'll give us your truck, free and clear? And we either share it or sell it and split the money?" Logan asked.

"Once you win the truck, what you do with it is your business. But it will belong to both of you, fifty-fifty."

"But if we fall in love, we get nothing?" Logan folded his arms.

Jake rolled his eyes and looked at me. "It might be tough to put up with him all summer, Tessa. I forgot what an idiot he is."

I nodded. "I agree."

"What?"

Putting his arm around Logan's shoulder, he said, "Let me paint you a picture, Bill Shakespeare. You get the thing money can't buy, which is love. You won't want the truck once you have that."

Logan grinned, shrugging him off. "No offense to Tessa here, or to the Hallmark Channel, or any other woman, but I highly doubt that."

"The more he opens his mouth, the more I'm sure I have nothing to worry about," I said to Jake.

"It will take a good woman to whip him into shape. You up for it?"

"Nope. But forty thousand bucks sounds pretty nice."

While Logan walked around the truck, drooling, I looked at Jake. "You need to sleep on this. What you're offering is certifiably crazy."

"I have never been more sure of anything. So, you guys up for this? Please say yes. I've got my heart in this now."

Logan's eyes were already on mine when I looked up at him.

"Give us a minute to talk it over," he said and motioned me toward the side of the house.

"Take your time," Jake called after us cheerfully.

Once out of Jake's earshot, I leaned against the white wood siding. Logan stood facing me, his muscly arms folded directly at eye level.

"What are you thinking, Jailbait?"

"What are *you* thinking?" I parroted, hands on my hips.

"Jake needs his head checked."

"I don't feel right about doing this, do you?"

"No. But I'd rather win it and sell it than see that thing blown up somewhere."

I blinked up at him, suddenly blindsided by the thought that I was on the side of my house, having a secret conversation with Logan Marten. Alone. It seemed so intimate, like something from a dream long ago.

"Here's what I'm thinking. We're both here this summer. All of our friends are gone. This will at least give us something to do," he said. "Jake's obviously bored, and if he wants to play this game with us, fine by me. I could definitely use forty thousand bucks."

My eyes narrowed, taking in his confident posture, a little affronted I was so easily unlovable to him. "So sure your heart's safe from me?"

"My heart's on lockdown, but you're welcome to any other part of my body."

I folded my arms. "Stop it."

He smiled. "Tess. This is what I do. I date pretty girls and send them packing. I was born for this."

DEAR DIARY,

Logan Marten called me pretty. He has also turned into an arrogant, shallow moron. XOXO

GAME FACE, Tess.

"Enjoy leaving a trail of tears in your wake?"

"No tears, because they're all like me—in it for a good time." He studied me. "You're the wild card here, and we both know it. I blush every time I take my shirt off."

"You think of me without your shirt on?"

"Remembering all those nice things you said about me to your friends…"

"Shut up."

His smile faded while his face grew more serious. "Listen, I don't date women to hurt them, and I don't want to do that to you. My family would murder me. Kelsey would dig up my grave and murder me a second time. So, before we go any further with this, I need to know, can you handle it?"

For a brief moment, I caught a flash of something real in his eyes. Something deep and soft. It was rare to see it beneath the teasing he seemed to hide behind. Practically living at Kelsey's house as a child and teenager, I had known a different side of Logan—the farm boy side of him. The one who worked alongside his dad, giving me tractor rides. The one who played basketball in the backyard with Kelsey and me. The Logan who used to pick us up from school dances and listen as we talked about boys. The one who found out about my crush on him and, instead of leaving it alone and awkward, teased me mercilessly about it. I remember once when I was six or seven and I scraped my leg at their house. It was bleeding, and I started crying. Logan sat beside me on the porch, cleaned my scrape, and put a Band-Aid on it for me while telling me jokes to make me laugh. The Logan who, to my knowledge, never said a word to anybody about what had happened between us in the laundry room.

The Logan who stood across from me now had to still be that man, but he didn't look or act like him. He was different. Jaded somehow. This was where things got risky. As long as he stayed the shallow flirt, I would be fine. The player I could handle. Not a problem.

It was the man underneath that scared me.

Truth was, I knew this was a dangerous plan. I was deeply attracted to Logan Marten. I couldn't turn off something so ingrained inside of me, even with my history with Tyler. But the difference between this me and the me from ten years ago was that I no longer wanted him. I could be attracted to him, but I didn't want him. I didn't want anybody like him ever again. And that was a very liberating feeling. You know what I did want? Forty thousand dollars in the bank for a down payment on a house—and maybe a quick trip to Europe. I could do this.

"I can handle this. You forget, I almost married a guy like you, and I didn't especially like how that turned out. I'll be fine."

He stilled. "A guy like me?"

It needed no explanation, so I gave him none. "Yup."

He bounced on the balls of his feet with both hands in his pockets, his playful mask carefully back into place. "What if Jake makes us go swimming and I have to prance around in front of you without a shirt on?"

"I'll be sure to gouge my eyes out before we go."

The grin that tiptoed across his face did nothing to my insides.

As far as I could tell, this could go one of three ways.

One: Logan keeps our dates light and funny. No deep thoughts. Neither of us falls in love. We hang out as friends, fulfill Jake's rules, and win a truck, therefore winning me forty grand for a down payment on a house.

Two: Logan and I break all barriers and fall in love, forfeiting a truck for our happily ever after. Extremely unlikely, but still a possibility if Jake's intuition is correct. (It isn't.)

Three: I date Logan this summer, and all my teenage hormonal angst is re-awakened. I pretend it's not there, even when it is. I fall in love, and he has no idea. My heart shatters into a thousand quiet pieces. We win a truck.

I should also add a quick fourth version because crazier things have happened in the world.

Four: Logan falls madly in love with me. I resist because I will not be played again. We win a truck.

"So…" I began. "Worst-case scenario, we both fall madly in love. Best case scenario, we stay friends, have someone to hang out with for three months, and walk away with a pile of cash at the end of summer."

"That's what I'm seeing. I don't know if there's a downside to this arrangement. We could keep the truck and pretend like we're divorced. It can spend one week with you and one with me?"

He lifted hopeful eyes in my direction. I laughed. "Maybe we can keep it for a week or two before selling it, just to play out all your truck fantasies first."

His eyebrows shot up, eyes full of laughter. "All of them?"

"Ew. Not in a truck shared by me."

"It could *be* you."

A thrill raced up my spine at his insinuation. I tamped it back down where it belonged. "Not in this lifetime."

He smirked. "Sounds like we're on the same page, then."

"So, we good?"

"I guess so." He held out his hand toward me. I eyed it like a pit bull on a leash. After a brief hesitation, I shook it. His handshake was warm and firm, with just the right amount of pressure. We released contact almost immediately.

"I was thinking we should put a few rules in place and have a check-in every week, just to make sure..." he trailed off, clearing his throat.

"Make sure of what?" Spell it out, Logan. Spell. It. Out.

"To make sure neither of us is..." He trailed off, his hand motioning in a circle as if he expected me to fill in the blanks.

"I'm not interested in you." I was almost certain.

"Tell that to the stack of 'marry me' notes I've got buried in my closet."

He wasn't going to embarrass me. His hits couldn't touch me because my humiliation cup in this town had runneth over.

I leaned closer, hands on my hips. "I think that you keeping them all says more about adult you than eight-year-old me."

He gave me a look. "Eight? Come on now, Tess. You were older than that."

My cheeks heated, but I kept going. "What? Do you read them every night before you fall asleep?"

"I'm not a psycho. They're neatly stacked in my hope chest." His sardonic grin did nothing to my insides except make me want to punch him, even as he draped an arm across my shoulders and pulled me in for a hug, friendly-like. And that was how I knew my heart was safe from Logan Marten. Forty thousand dollars was a much more sure thing to bet on.

"What happens when I can't resist your charm and I fall in love

with you?" The words came out as sarcastic as I meant it, but my trai-
torous stomach did a little flip as I said them.

"I guess I'll try harder to not be so adorable. Might be dang near
impossible."

"What if it's you falling for me?"

This time, the light from his smile hit his brown eyes. "Same plan
for you, then. Stop being so adorable."

As we walked back toward Jake, I allowed the wave of anticipation
to flutter through my stomach without giving it much space in my
mind. It was only a side effect from grade-school longing. If I didn't
acknowledge the hit, it never happened.

"We'll do it," Logan said to Jake.

Jake jumped down from the tailgate of the ostentatious truck, his
smile growing wide as he appraised us both. "You guys playing for the
truck or for love?"

"Truck," we both stated.

"Famous last words." Jake laughed, reaching inside his truck door
for a yellow-lined notepad. "If I could get you two to sign this."

"Kind of official for you, isn't it?" Logan asked.

"Like you said, it's an $80,000 truck. And if my suspicions are
correct, lines may get blurred this summer. I want to make sure we
each remember exactly what we're playing for."

Jake climbed up into his truck, searching for a pen, leaving Logan
and me facing each other. My gaze flitted everywhere, taking in his
low-slung jeans and t-shirt, his tan arms bulging out of the sleeves.

"My eyes are up here, Tess."

His eyes were also laughing at me when I glanced up at him, but I
tried my best to pay him no heed.

Jake handed me the document. Logan sidled closer to me, peering
over my shoulder at the words.

I squinted closer, trying to make out Jake's handwriting. "Sorry, did
you get a five-year-old to write this?"

"I figure it could only help my cause if nobody can read it but me."

Jake removed the notepad from my hands and read the paper aloud.

. . .

THE BET:

Logan Marten and Tessa Robbins will do the following:

Go on one date per week, beginning now and ending August 31st. The first date will begin the first Saturday after this document is signed.

Jake will be in charge of the date each week, unless otherwise specified. Logan and Tessa must attend each date unless sick or dying. Dates will be non-public whenever possible.

They must hold hands whenever possible during their dates.

One kiss must be performed this summer, and it has to be a good one. Logan, you know what I mean. I don't want to watch, so it's on the honor system, and if you lie, you will burn in truck hell.

One overnight mountain hike and campout at the end of the summer.

If by the end of the term, both parties can still honestly say they are not in love with each other, they will win the Chevy Silverado with a Duramax engine and a lift (hereafter known as "the truck") which they will share evenly and/or sell to split the cost. If something happens to the truck (accident, act of God, discovery of a minefield, lightning strike, etc), the bet will be forfeited automatically, and no obligation will be held on Jake's end, AKA...no suing Jake.

If one party does not want to continue with the agreement, all parties must agree to end the arrangement.

My eyes raked back up, skimming over the kiss clause once again, wondering if there was a way to back out that wouldn't incriminate me. But to admit that now was to admit to something I wasn't willing to. *Game face, Tess.*

I was a means to an end for him.

He was a means to an end for me.

If we went on a few dates and shared a kiss at the end of the summer, it wasn't a big deal.

The end.

· · ·

WE SIGNED THE PAPERS. Our first date was in three days. Jake would be letting us know what we were doing soon.

My brother and his family showed up a few minutes later. The three of us still stood by the monstrosity, talking, when Nate's tiny Ford F150 pulled into the yard next to it. I made a beeline for the doors to see my nieces. I gave Nate and Anna each a quick side hug before two tornados with stringy blonde hair and dirty faces descended on me, jumping into my arms and on my back. From the corner of my eye, I saw Logan shake Nate's hand and introduce Jake, but with a quick wave to me, they left soon after.

My mind buzzed with noise as we walked up the porch steps and into the house. Ideas of Logan and me filtered in and out, painting pictures of what might be, memories of what had been, and the anticipation of what was to come. I reminded myself sternly that the old Logan wasn't around much these days. This was the new Logan. Cheap Logan. The dollar-store version of Logan. I was not going to fall for him. He was in no shape to fall in love with. This summer with Logan would give me something fun to do. He was still a friend. We'd keep things light, get our money, and then be done. There was no denying it was strange, though. This was the weirdest thing I had ever done—and I grew up helping Kelsey make homemade traps to catch creatures of all kinds and sizes to put in Cade's locker.

9

LOGAN

Jake: You are both cordially invited to your first date as a real-life dating couple.
Date: This Saturday. 6:00 p.m.
Where: Coordinates will be sent to your phones a half hour before you leave.
Dress: Something that can get dirty.
What: More instructions to follow.

Tessa: So basically, you've told us nothing except how to dress?
Jake: I feel, even now, I've said too much.

So far, even with Nate's changes, we were still on schedule with the physical therapy office. We were nearly finished with framing, and I hadn't heard from Nate in two whole glorious days. Which was surprising after the curious greeting I received when he found me in his sister's company the other night. That had been really bad timing. Not that I had anything to be ashamed of. I was only about to secretly date his little sister to win a truck. Not unusual at all. We were both adults. I wasn't afraid of Nate. I just didn't want to tick him off while working for him. That was all. What Tessa and I chose to do was our business. I'd just prefer to never have him find out.

Either way, since we were still on schedule, Saturdays were spent on the ranch, helping my dad. Of course, had I known we would be picking rocks, I would have called Nate up myself to discuss some changes I thought he might like. The sun shone down on the hay field as my dad drove his old farm truck back and forth along the rows, stopping every time we spotted any rocks. Jake and I sat with our legs hanging off the back of the truck, gripping the side for dear life as my dad took a tight turn—again.

"Sorry!" he called from the open window, the big grin on his face giving away his true feelings.

He stopped the truck when he spotted a substantial boulder and waited patiently in the cool cab while Jake and I trudged toward it with the sun beating down on our faces.

"What would my dad have done if I wasn't here?" I asked Jake as we both bent to secure our grip around the rock.

"We wouldn't have been picking rocks today, that's for sure." Jake and I grunted as we hefted the rock up on three and waddled back toward the pickup, tossing it in the back.

"How's that cushy ride over there?" I asked my dad, wiping sweat off of my brow with the hem of my shirt.

"I think I'll turn the AC down a bit. It's getting a touch chilly."

I wasn't a farmer. Growing up, I knew it wasn't something I wanted to do forever. And with the dairy farm, it always seemed like we were one train wreck away from bottoming out. Though my dad always pulled us through, some years had been more nip and tuck than others. Construction was dependent enough on the weather; I didn't want to throw cattle and horses and crops into the mix. All that to say, since I knew it wasn't forever, coming home to work the ranch had been fun so far. Rubbing shoulders with my dad, driving tractors, fixing fences, even riding in the back of the truck, picking rocks, brought back the best taste of my childhood. The parts that a person could easily forget if they weren't careful.

"You ready for your date tonight, Romeo?" Jake looked over at me with raised eyebrows as we sat next to each other on the open tailgate while my dad hot-rodded us all over the field.

"Why are you doing this, Jake?" I turned on him.

"I have a feeling."

"She's Kelsey's best friend. We're familiar with each other, alright, but that doesn't mean there's something there. It's only been a few years since I could even check her out legally."

"I've heard you call her Jailbait. Doesn't that imply you've been checking her out for a while now?"

It implied my embarrassment from accidentally getting de-pantsed by a fourteen-year-old girl when I was eighteen. It had been uncomfortable and weird, and the thought of anybody walking in on that, as innocently as it had happened, left me with the word *jailbait*. I teased her to soften the moment so neither of us died of embarrassment. Simple as that. The nickname stuck, but there had been nothing vulgar in my meaning. But I couldn't have said any of that to Jake without divulging the laundry room incident.

"It's not for any reason you're thinking of. She's always been a little sister to me. End of story."

"Well, she seems about the right age now. What is she? Twenty-five?"

She would turn twenty-five in November. I blamed Kelsey for me having that knowledge, though I kept it to myself. And I hadn't been checking her out in a way that meant I wanted to date her. More like, checking her out in a way that meant I noticed she was definitely not tiny, annoying Tessa anymore.

She was tan-and-curvy-in-all-the-right-places, annoying Tessa now.

"Are you really wanting to give away your truck?" Before he could put up a fuss at me for double-checking again, I bulldozed forward. "I know we signed your stupid paper, but it's not too late to forget about it. I don't think Tessa would mind. It's crazy."

"I don't care about the truck. I promise."

"You could sell it and use the money for something."

Jake was silent for a good ten seconds, which was about nine seconds longer than he was usually silent. But when he finally answered, what he said surprised me. "You probably don't know any of this, but when I was a senior, I was in the state championship rodeo finals in Boise."

"I knew you went. Bulls?"

"Broncs. My mom had told me that my dad was in Boise that night for some big conference. He lives in Texas, so it was really random that it happened to be over the same weekend. I hadn't seen him in a few years, at that point. Anyway, after it was all over, I figured he had been in the stands watching, and I told myself I'd play nice and go talk to him afterward. Well, turned out, after his conference, he went and got drunk with some of his buddies and never made it."

The truck hit a sharp bump in the field, both of our bodies jolting forward. My hands gripped the side of the truck to keep my balance, but also to give them something to do when they really wanted to throttle something. Jake was as good as a brother to me, and the fact that his own dad couldn't even make it to his son's state championship in the very sport he made his living off of was nothing short of appalling.

Jake continued, "So when I tell you the money means nothing to me, I mean it. I don't want anything to do with it except see the look on his face when I tell him I gave it away."

The truck stopped, and we jumped off and collected a few small piles of rocks. This time, my dad came out to help, claiming he was getting too cold in the truck. Amid teasing and laughter, the three of us loaded a few more armfuls of never-ending rocks into the truck.

"I'm sorry I wasn't there," I told Jake when we were moving again.

He looked confused. "Huh?"

"At state. Watching you. I should have been there."

He made a face. "Don't worry about it. I don't want you to feel bad. I want you to stop making a big deal about the truck."

Smiling, I shook my head. "What did you place?"

"Didn't place, but thanks for bringing *that* up."

I chuckled, and we rode in silence for a long moment.

"You know who did show up, though?" He spoke in a low tone as he looked at me. His eyes were a touch shinier than usual, and he glanced away quickly.

"Who?"

He lifted his right hand and, without looking behind him, pointed his thumb back toward my dad.

He didn't say any more, and I strongly suspected it was because he couldn't. And then, suddenly, I couldn't. When my dad stopped again, we both popped off the truck with the speed of a jackrabbit, neither of us looking at each other.

I PULLED into Tessa's driveway and parked at the same time my phone buzzed in my pocket.

Jake: Have fun tonight. Hold her hand. Treat her right. She's a good one.

SOMETHING WARRED INSIDE of me as I stared at my phone. No matter what way I looked at it, how many times I tried to talk Jake out of it, he was determined to put his truck on the line. Determined to see this bet through. The whole thing was crazy. I didn't want to get in the middle of Jake's daddy issues. I was not going to fall in love with Tessa Robbins. I wasn't interested in any sort of long game. There had been a time in my life where that had been different, but now? I was happy how things were. I had good friends. A house in Boise. I liked my schedule. Dating was enjoyable with no pressure and everything being new and exciting. Some of us weren't meant to live a life of kids and family and little league.

Hearing about my dad with Jake that afternoon had only reinforced my thoughts. My dad was special. One of the good ones. He had seamlessly embraced Jake into our family...working the ranch, Saturday

morning breakfasts, basketball competitions, and cattle drives...
because he spotted a void in Jake, a deep wound in his otherwise bright
life. I couldn't imagine ever influencing another person in that way. I
didn't have his goodness or his wisdom. And I had no desire to hold
that much power. I came from a great family. I was lucky, I knew that.
I had a whole crew of men who came from all walks of life, each with
battle wounds from the people they loved. Scars. It was terrifying,
really. There were so many ways to wreck a life. Lying. Cheating.
Belittling. Misleading. Secrets. Innocent people completely at your
imperfect mercy.

Your whole life...obliterated.

Just then, Tessa came out of the greenhouse, her hair pulled up in a
ponytail, cutoff shorts hitting her mid-thigh. I forced my gaze upward
to her red t-shirt and the soft smile on her face as she spotted me.

My phone buzzed again, reminding me of Jake's unopened
message.

I didn't want Tessa to be caught in anything where I could hurt her.
Because I did care about her. Her teenage crush on me was the one
thing keeping me up at night. The fact that she had liked me for so long
only added to my list of worries that she'd get hurt. Jake thought me
teasing Tessa was a sign I had some sort of secret crush. Really, she
was just fun to tease. It had become a game between us over the years,
a safe way to acknowledge the awkward moments between us without
delving too deep. The attractive flush on her cheeks of late had simply
been a bonus.

But she had her own history now, with '*guys like me,*' as she had
put it. She seemed as equally resolved to keep me at arm's length as I
did her. Maybe that was the key. I'd follow the same motto I'd used for
dating the past few years. Keep them laughing. Keep them blushing.
Then get the heck out. I couldn't change Jake's mind. Tessa knew my
stance, and she was still on board.

Me: I know she's a good one. And your plan is crazy.
Jake: Don't go for that kiss too soon. Make her work for it.
Me: Shut up

I opened my door, the squeak reminding me I had not been gifted a new $80,000 truck from my dad, and stepped out to help Tessa put away the last few boxes. And then, when the time was right, we would be having our first check-in where I would ask her very nicely to go burn those shorts.

"Hey, Jailbait," I called when I entered the greenhouse with a box half full of fresh strawberries.

"I need a name for you if you insist on calling me Jailbait."

"Hot stuff, big muscles, good looking...that's what I usually go by."

"Yes, but I'm not your mom."

"You're hilarious. You about ready?"

"I guess." She looked down at her outfit. "Do you know what we're doing?" My eyes followed hers and landed on her legs again before yanking them back up.

"Jake sent coordinates, and it looks like we're hiking."

"Is that Logan Marten?"

We both glanced over to see Tessa's dad walking toward us. I grinned and stepped forward to shake his hand. He had come from the orchard, wearing his overalls and a shade hat. You had to like Frank. He was one of my dad's best friends, and anytime the two of them were in the same room, you'd find them in some corner, shooting the breeze, swapping stories about farming. Frank had a quiet demeanor. He wasn't a big talker unless you hit on exactly three subjects: trees, produce, and golf. Lucky for me, I knew a little about all three.

"How are you, Frank?"

"Busy. Where you at on the office building?"

"It's going alright. A couple more days and we should be done framing. Once we pass inspection, we'll be ready for you." Nate had Frank coming out of retirement to do the plumbing for the new office.

He nodded, wiping sweat from his eyes. "Me and Nancy are going to look at it tonight. You do fast work."

"I've got a good crew."

"Did Tessa offer you a piece of hot-fudge cake? She made it last night. I'm not one to dole out compliments, but I went back for seconds," he teased, smiling over at Tessa.

"She actually just offered to bring me a big piece with some ice cream."

"Did I?" She looked a mixture of amused and annoyed, which suited her greatly. I just hoped that was a mixture that would bring me cake.

"Hey, Logan, since you're here, maybe I could pick your brain for a minute," Frank said, as he motioned me toward the wrap-around porch.

The two-story white farmhouse had seen better days. Two of the five front steps leading up to the porch were hanging on by a couple of nails, one stair had a foot-sized hole in it, and the railing posts surrounding the porch needed more nails and a bucket of paint. As Frank walked me up the stairs, I couldn't help noticing the porch was in desperate need of new wood planks.

"I'm sick of tripping on this porch every morning when I come outside. I wish I had time to do it, but every spare ounce of my time this summer will be spent in the orchard. Would this be something you could help me with? In the evenings and your down time, of course. And that's only if your dad hasn't already called dibs on your weekends."

I squatted down, checking out the flooring. "Gotta be honest, I'd rather do this than fall asleep driving a tractor. This is redwood, right?"

He nodded. "We have the original stain we used in the garage. Could you change out the rotting wood and stain it to match?"

I shook my head. "It wouldn't look even. The stain you have out here has been weathered. If you want it all to match, you'd have to sand the whole porch and re-stain."

He sighed as he mulled it over. "Dream crusher. That's what I thought you'd probably say."

I smiled and looked over at Tessa, who was listening to our conversation like a rabbit before something scared it away.

"Your porch rails are pretty standard. I think those would be easy enough to find to replace the broken. The stairs are an easy fix. The biggest hassle would be sanding and re-staining the flooring."

"Is this a project you'd be interested in?"

I hesitated. I really didn't have much time. Between the office job and helping my dad on Saturdays, I would have to squeeze it in after work. I scanned the porch once more, assessing to the best of my ability the price and amount of work.

I should have said no. I didn't have the time. Jake was already getting a lot out of us this summer, and I didn't want to add seeing Tessa every day to his list. But he was my dad's best friend. I remember one particularly warm spring when our fields had flooded, and Frank had spent two days helping us sandbag around our house to keep the water out. So, instead of telling Frank no, I found myself saying, "Yeah. I can do that. I'll stop by whenever I can over the next few weeks, as long as you're not in a hurry."

In my peripheral vision, Tessa moved like she was about to say something but stopped herself. She opened her mouth again, moved forward a bit, and stopped. I raised my eyebrows to her in question and enjoyed her speechless face. I definitely wanted to take the job now. For work purposes. It would be fine. I'd be working and she'd be working. No need to make it a thing.

Frank shrugged. "Whenever you get to it will be fine. I'm just happy to not have to do it myself."

"Most of my Saturdays are tied up with the ranch, so an hour or two after work is probably the best I can do."

Tessa disappeared while Frank and I discussed the details. All the while, my mind was reeling. Jake couldn't have planned it better if he had tried. Instead of a date once a week, I'd be seeing Tessa every day for a good part of the summer. It'd be fine, though. Tessa and I had a good understanding of what we were doing—a good, eighty-thousand-dollar understanding.

Frank headed back toward the orchard at the same time the front door squeaked open, and Tessa walked out, holding a bowl of hot-fudge cake and vanilla ice cream.

My eyes drifted down to the piece of cake that was hot enough to cause the ice cream to pool at the edges. She'd even put a handful of fresh raspberries on top.

She pushed it toward me, a teasing gleam in her eyes. "Eat it. I dare you."

I took the bowl. She watched as I filled a large spoonful dripping with warm cake, soft ice cream, and extra hot fudge on the top and took a bite. And then my eyes rolled to the back of my head.

I took another bite as fast as I could. "I'm not scared of you."

She moved to sit on one of the chairs on the porch. I followed behind, inhaling another bite. I only had two more bites left and was already wondering how I could beg her for another slice without sounding needy.

"Should we set up a few rules for our dates?" I asked. "To keep you in line?"

Just as I knew it would, the look she gave me made that whole comment worth it.

"Rules so we don't fall in love? Like what?"

My eyes drifted briefly to her legs, and I wanted to ask her not to wear those shorts again, but I couldn't figure out a way to say it without her chopping my head off.

"I've got one. No more offering me treats." I pointed to my nearly empty bowl and added, "Because THIS makes me want to haul you off to see the preacher right now."

I smiled, enjoying the light flush my words brought to her cheeks. *Rein it in, Marten.*

"If you recall, I didn't offer any of this to you."

"How about we keep things light between us?" I said. "Easy conversations. No deep thoughts. You keep your secrets, and I'll keep mine. We're just a couple friends having a good time without getting emotionally invested."

"Is this the speech you give all your women before you go on a date?"

"I usually don't have to speak this much at all."

She elbowed me in the arm. "Why are you so scared to get emotionally invested? Isn't that just basic friend stuff?"

"I've found that I'm a real sweetheart beneath the chiseled physique, and I can't risk you seeing that. It would compromise our whole mission."

She shook her head, trying not to laugh.

"You got anything for me?" I asked.

Tessa hesitated, tucking a loose strand of hair behind her ear before she said, "No more of your cologne."

I met her gaze, very interested. "Really? What does my cologne do to you?"

She didn't look directly at me. "Wear it or don't, but just know… you'll be walking a fine line."

I laughed, suddenly feeling high as a kite, though I wasn't sure why. "We can't have that." I peered into my now empty bowl. "You being here is the only thing stopping me from licking this bowl clean like a cat. What do you put in this stuff?"

"Butter and sugar."

"One more scoop?" I asked her hopefully.

"Didn't you just make a rule about no treats?"

I grinned and held out my empty bowl toward her. "Rule starts in ten minutes."

She shook her head, grabbing the bowl from my hands and moving toward the house. "Nope. Not before hiking."

"Killjoy."

10

TESSA

fter a quick ten-minute drive, Logan parked his truck at the base of a small mountain chain that was dry and covered in sagebrush except for the top, which was dusted with a large crop of green pine trees.

As we made our way toward the trailhead, our phones buzzed simultaneously with a text from Jake, just checking in to make sure we were following *all* of the rules.

Wink, wink.

We were both silent before Logan muttered, "Freaking Jake," under his breath. He grabbed my hand and held it as we began the easy climb. I tried to be casual. Easy. Breezy. It was part of the bet. Not a big deal. He readjusted his grip slightly, the contact making my breath shift and leaving me unable to forget *who* was holding my hand. It was fine. Friends held hands all the time. Small children held hands on their way into school. I held Betsy May's hand the other day while she mumbled mean things about me under her breath.

DEAR DIARY,
I'm holding Logan Marten's hand. I don't like him like that, but I

wanted to let you know that it happened. Just like we imagined. Although, I didn't expect it to be so sweaty. It's almost ninety degrees out here.

XOXO

"WE PROBABLY DON'T *HAVE* to hold hands," I said, fighting off the growing awareness between us. "It's not like he can see us."

It felt intimate in the most innocent way possible. And there was no good reason why it should have felt that way. They were hands. The things that opened doors, held burritos, and gave high-fives. Not sexy. But when we passed another couple coming down on the trail and Logan tugged me closer to his side so they could pass, it all felt so sexy. And a tiny bit possessive. Like I was his.

Yikes. Maybe Jake *was* a brilliant, conniving wizard.

"I figured you could check this off your bucket list, too." He gave me a teasing grin.

I needed to calm the heck down. I had to stop over-thinking everything.

This was dollar-menu Logan. He was a quick, easy, fun snack but not what you really wanted. Not that he was any sort of actual *snack* to me, but…you know. To be fair, he didn't seem like cheap Logan earlier with my dad. What was it about Logan shaking my dad's hand that had my insides melt like an ice cream cone on a hot day? Why did I find it so attractive? Was it because, for a split second, he had gone from an annoying guy who teased to a manly man with a firm grip who knew his way around power tools? He had gone from a childhood crush to a man right before my eyes. Showing respect and kindness to my dad was the icing on the cake.

Unfortunately, it had been short-lived because for the first ten minutes of our hike, I was subjected to Logan's replay of the infamous laundry-room scene, a detailed summary of my love notes as a kid, and constant teasing. Every time I tried to steer the conversation to something real or—heaven forbid—new, he would crack off another joke. Deflection was definitely his angle in our weird little dating game, but it was already getting old. I knew we had an agreement about not going deep, but even a simple conversation about something meaningless sounded great to me.

I pulled my hand from his. That was enough. Points for trying. I bent down and picked up a rock to hold instead. Jake's rules said we had to hold hands *if possible*. "Sorry, I can't hold your hand right now. I really want to look at this rock."

Logan grinned and picked up a rock of his own. "Don't trust yourself, Jailbait?"

"What's your favorite color?"

Logan looked over at me confused. "Why?"

"Because if you think for one second that I'm going to hike any more of this mountain with you teasing me about the laundry room or the tiny crush I had on you when I was a kid—"

"Teenager."

Pushing at his shoulder, I continued, "You need some new material."

"Hmm. Do you remember that time I overheard you tell all your friends and my sister that you preferred me without my shirt on?"

I scowled at him. Another blatant deflection.

"See? I've got plenty of material," he said, dodging my hands attempting strangulation.

"Logan. What's your favorite color?"

"We aren't supposed to be progressing our relationship, remember?"

"Exactly. That's why we're talking about colors."

He made a face and ran his hand through his hair. "Green."

I let out a nice, calming breath. "Just tell me one dumb thing about yourself that isn't a joke or a flirt."

He thought that over for a minute before he said, "My pinky toe points outward. It's pretty gross. I'll show it to you if you ask nicely."

I pushed him off the trail and felt some satisfaction when he stumbled into a tree. Needing some space before I pitched him over the edge of the small canyon to our left, I picked up my pace to a light jog.

"Come on, Tess," he called out after me, drawing out the S sound in my name, which usually did something to me, but this time, I kept jogging. I knew what he was doing, and honestly, I could appreciate it, but I wasn't asking for his secrets, just simple conversation. Stuff you'd discuss with the mailman. Three months of the same jokes and stories at my expense seemed like torture.

Torture wrapped up in a handsome package of teasing brown eyes and muscly forearms.

Heavy footsteps sounded behind me. "Alright, I'll say whatever you want as long as you cut the running. I'm not used to the elevation here yet."

Instead of pointing out that I was also still adjusting to the elevation, I held my tongue and slowed to a walk. The trail widened, and he fell back into step beside me.

"What do you want to be when you grow up?" I asked. Logan was nearly thirty. I knew he was already grown up, but I couldn't help nettle him a little.

"Retired."

"Logan."

He sighed. "I am grown up. The same thing I'm doing now. I love my job."

He seemed almost defensive with his answer, which took me by surprise. Silence stretched out before us, so much so that I could hear Logan's breathing start to rattle as we began our quarter-mile rocky incline.

A minute passed before Logan asked, "What about you?"

"Physical therapist," I said automatically. So far, this was going great.

"If this is supposed to be a getting-to-know-you game, we both suck at it," he said.

My foot slipped on an unstable rock, and before I could stop myself, I went down onto my knees. A warm hand gripped underneath my upper arm and pulled me up.

"You alright?"

"Yup."

A scattering of pine trees and quaking aspens was our view as we kept marching forward on our hike. I was determined to make Logan talk to me, though I wasn't quite sure what about his answers were so annoying. Maybe it was the fact that we had a line drawn between us. We couldn't push things very far. Maybe it was the fact that we had been more like acquaintances. Other than a shared love for his sister, I was beginning to realize that we didn't know each other much at all. But this dry silence? The shallow answers? Hang Jake's bet. I couldn't do it.

But then again...cracking him might only make me more vulnerable.

My legs itched to run up the mountain and get rid of the restless energy I felt between us. I had to find a happy medium, where we talked enough to satisfy my need for more, but with no feelings.

"What are your plans for the truck money?" Logan asked. Perfect. The money. That was a great way to keep us on topic.

"I will definitely be taking a trip to Europe. And then, after that, I might try to use it for a down payment on a house—if I don't feel too bad about taking Jake's dad's guilt money."

Logan nodded. "It's crazy, isn't it?"

"What about you? Saving up for a penthouse?"

He wrinkled his nose in my direction, which was not cute at all. "Nah, I'm not sure what I'll do with it exactly." He looked like he wanted to say more, so I waited. "I've got a list a mile long of house projects I still need to do. I could always use it on that. Or maybe start my own construction business. I don't know, maybe I'll join you on your Europe trip." He raised his eyebrows, and I hated the twinge of pleasure that coursed through me.

"Great. You and your muscles can carry our luggage."

"Shirtless? You'd like that, wouldn't you? Skeevy little perv—"

"Stop." I held my hand up. "New rule. You can't quote *The Office*, or I will absolutely fall in love with you. Guaranteed."

For the slightest second, he looked taken aback by my confession before nodding. "Good to know."

"Beach or mountains?" I asked over my shoulder. The trail had narrowed, and Logan had dropped a pace or two behind me and looked like he was having trouble controlling his breathing. I slowed my stride a tad.

"Couch."

"You regretting that bowl of cake, Rocky?"

"I think I need to tie my shoe."

I turned around as he buckled over, hands on his thighs, gaze fixed on the ground, and looking pained.

"Your laces look fine to me."

"Trust me, they're about to come undone. It's too dangerous to go on with…shoelaces like this," he wheezed.

I laughed and pulled my water bottle out of my backpack and took a swig.

"How did you get to be such a gazelle?"

He stood tall once again, grabbing the water bottle from my hand and taking a long drink.

"Did you not bring water?"

He scoffed. "I don't need water."

I yanked it out of his hands after I let him have one more sip. He looked like he needed it. "Great, I'll just have this back, then."

I waited while he put on a good show of adjusting his perfectly laced double knots before we trudged up the last quarter mile of the mountain.

We arrived at the top without much fanfare. Stopping to catch our breath, we soaked in the clean smell of pine and aspen trees. Since there was an easier trail even closer to my house, I had never hiked this particular side of the mountain before.

Logan checked the coordinates on his phone. "Looks like we need to move toward the river a hundred feet or so."

We arrived at a muddy section of dirt that looked like it was an overflow from the stream. Deep footprints and animal tracks in the mud were filled with pockets of water, leaving the whole area one big mud bath.

Things began clicking into place in my head at about the same time Logan pulled down an envelope nailed to a tree that read, *Logan and Tessa.*

"This seems ominous," Logan said, ripping it open and looking at the contents. He snorted in laughter before shaking his head, thrusting the letter into my hands.

HEY, lovebirds.

For your first date, I thought something special was in order. A getting-to-know-you game!

It's pretty simple, really. You begin by standing ten feet apart in the mud pit. In this envelope are two lists of questions. One for Tessa, and one for Logan. You get the question wrong, you get mud thrown on you —and vice versa. ALSO, Logan, you have to stand there and take it like a man. If you dodge the throw, Tessa gets to mud-wash you.

If both of you answer less than five correct, it's a mud fight.

Make sure you hold hands coming back down the mountain.

Can't wait to hear all about your first date!

Love,

Jake

"A MUD FIGHT WITH A GIRL?"

In ten seconds flat, Logan had kicked off his shoes, peeled off his socks, and rolled up his joggers to mid-calf.

When he stepped into the murky water, mud squelching under his feet, there was a sweet boyishness about him. Unguarded. It was familiar to me, a lifetime of seeing him under my watchful gaze growing up. Something pinched at my heart before I swatted it away, regaining focus. It really was too bad I was going to murder him at this game. Not to be creepy, but I knew everything about Logan. I stripped myself of my shoes and t-shirt, revealing a coral tank top underneath.

"That's enough stripping out of you." Logan was standing ramrod straight across the mud pit, watching me warily as I adjusted my tank top.

"And we've got to talk about those shorts," he continued. "I vote any shorts worn by either of us this summer have to be knee length."

I bristled at his ordering me around. "I will wear whatever I want."

"I'm just saying, it might be a good idea to dress down for our dates. Just to help keep us both safe."

I stepped into the cool water. It felt good after our hike. "Listen, Marten. What I wear is my business and my business alone. If what I choose to wear is going to derail your plans for a new truck, then maybe you have no business betting Jake anything."

He lifted his hands up, as if he were placating a toddler. "Listen, I'm not trying to be a jerk. I'm trying to keep our heads on straight. I'm fully aware you can wear whatever you want, and the problem is me. I'm just asking as a guy who will be fake-dating a hot blonde—as all the guys at work call you—try and help me out."

I scooped up a handful of mud, watching it ooze out of my hands, thinking about what it would feel like to hit him directly in the face.

"Tess."

I looked up at him then. His eyes were pleading, and he seemed legitimately worried about my clothing choices.

I grinned and scooped up another handful of mud. "I think I'm going to enjoy this."

He sighed and nodded toward me. "Ladies first."

I pulled Jake's list of questions out of my pocket and laughed as I read the first one. "Which statement is true? In high school, Tessa helped Cade prank Kelsey by putting her car on cinderblocks. Or… In high school, Tessa opened Kelsey's locker for Cade so he could put a garter snake inside."

Logan rubbed his chin, deep in thought. "If I recall, amid the long list of misdemeanors from those two, both of those happened to Kels…" His voice trailed off while he studied me. "Cinderblocks seems the obvious answer, but I'm worried about it being so obvious. How do you feel about snakes?"

I gave him my best poker face.

"Snakes."

A smile broke across my lips as I bent over and added more mud to my hand, preparing to throw.

"Snakes is the lie! That's what I was going to say!" He threw his hands up, trying to prevent what was coming.

"Too late, Marten." I let the mud fly. The image of watching it splat across his gray t-shirt was supremely satisfying.

We went back and forth, trading questions. Jake had a mix of salty and sweet, TV or books, places we'd traveled, and would-you-rather questions. So far, the one speck of mud I had on my shirt had been my own fault, slipping a little with my last throw. It was getting to be sad, really. Logan looked ridiculous, even as he grinned and pretended to welcome the onslaught.

"This isn't fair. You've been obsessed with me for years," Logan said, laughing and dodging out of the way when I threw another handful at him.

"Stop whining. You're up."

Logan read over his question silently, keeping a tight game face, but I thought I heard a soft, "Freaking Jake" before he shook his head to begin his question. "If given the chance to watch a game of football on TV or the nature channel, what would I pick?"

I hesitated for the first time since we started. It felt like a trick. Logan seemed annoyed by the question, but he could also have been trying to confuse me. Logan had played whatever sport he could in high school and was naturally gifted at each one. The nature thing didn't fit. I had to go with my gut.

"Sports."

"This stays between us, Jailbait."

Cold, wet mud came flying at me, splatting all over my tank top and gushing over my neck and down my front. My mouth dropped. "What? You love sports."

"I like to *play* sports. I don't love watching them on TV." I gaped at him, and he only smiled, a hint of red appearing on his cheeks. "What? Didn't know I was so in tune with nature?"

"For someone 'so in tune with nature,' you sure complained the whole way up this tiny hill."

"I think I missed a spot." He flung another handful in my direction, which I dodged easily.

"Stop embarrassing yourself."

He folded his arms with a playful glare. "You're up."

I began reading the last question. "Once, when Tessa and Kelsey were having a sleepover at your house and your sister was mad at you for something, they either A - dipped your—".

I stopped reading immediately, darting a nervous glance toward Logan.

He had grown very still, a dangerous gleam growing on his face as he watched me carefully. "Oh don't stop now. You were just getting to the good part."

I was going to kill Jake. And Kelsey. It was clear Jake had called her to get some ideas for questions, and this was her way of getting back at me for not telling her I was going out with her brother.

"Let's just be done. We'll call it a tie." I pleaded, laughing a little too loud. I was going for breezy, but it definitely came out deranged with a side of guilt.

He studied me for a long moment before bending over and grabbing a handful of mud. "I'll be finding out what's on that paper either way, but if I have to wrestle it from your hands, it will only make things worse for you."

The thought of wrestling Logan Marten sparked another emotion that I quickly swatted away. When I hesitated, he took a step toward me, a faint trace of amusement in his expression.

I swallowed while my heart raced erratically. Finally I raised the paper upward and began to read, inching backward as I did so. "They either A - dipped your toothbrush in the toilet, or B - used it to brush your dog's teeth."

I dropped the paper and took off running—laughing like a hysterical lunatic with each step. A handful of mud splattered across my back as I sprinted toward the trail. Toward freedom. I'd run all the way home if I had to.

"I had a great time, Logan. Thanks!" I yelled over my shoulder.

Any other day, I could have beaten Logan in a race with my hands tied behind my back. But he had determination and pride on his side and I soon felt arms around my waist and a warm body at my back. I tried to get away, but I was laughing too hard to put up much of a fight. Logan was laughing too, while spouting mild obscenities my way, but his grip was strong. He tried to pull my squirming body back toward the mud pit, but I had turned into a messy tangle of claws and limbs. Finally, he picked me up and threw me over his shoulder like a sack of grain.

"You didn't even guess which one. That's cheating." I pounded against his back. My pathetic defense tactics did nothing to stop his movement. He was out for blood.

"Don't care. Either way, you deserve this."

"Logan, don't."

He walked me across the mud, oblivious to my squeals, and into the thickest part of the wet, marshy sludge, dropping me softly into the center.

Water and wet dirt oozed down my back and into my shorts. I lay stunned for a minute before swiping my leg at an arrogant Logan standing above me, arms folded and thoroughly enjoying himself. My leg connected with his, but he stepped over me easily.

"Nice try."

I picked up a scoop of mud and flung it toward him. He dodged it and tossed another handful at me. Mud flew between us, both of us laughing too hard to be much of a threat. When he slipped and fell to his knees, I didn't hesitate and rubbed my mud-filled hands all over his hair, down his cheeks, and onto his neck. It was a triumphant move, bold and empowering, until he grabbed me once more and carried me past the mud and dropped me unceremoniously into the freezing-cold creek.

Later, when we stepped onto the trail to head back down the mountain, the sun was nearly level with the horizon, a splash of orange and pink showing off in the sky. Our shoes were squeaky, and our clothes were drenched with water and mud when Logan gently pushed me several feet away from him.

"New rule, Jailbait. You stay over there. Five feet between us whenever possible. Especially after a mud fight."

I had a grin on my face that refused to go away. "It didn't have to be a mud fight. We could have ended that much more civilly."

"If you think my revenge is complete, think again, Tessa Robbins."

"You're pretty obsessed with your toothbrush."

His dimple appeared for a brief second before Logan kicked a rock with his shoe. "I'm going to kill my sister."

"You and me both."

The night had grown cool, or perhaps that was because we were both drenched. Jake, in all his foresight and planning, had failed to provide towels. I would probably have some wicked blisters on my toes from my feet rubbing against the sand that had refused to come off when we washed our feet in the water. Our conversations hadn't been ground-breaking, and I had never been dirtier, but Logan's smile was real as we made our way down the mountain. And I couldn't help but think Jake had done a decent job breaking the ice for our first date.

Later that night, as I was getting into bed, my phone buzzed on my nightstand.

Logan: First check-in, Jailbait. Did my confession about the nature channel woo you senseless?

Me: No. It was all that wheezing up the mountain that sealed the deal for me.

Logan: It's all that sugar you crammed into me.

Me: I've been feeling bad about your toothbrush. Why don't you let me get another one for you?

Logan: You're not allowed within 50 yards of my toothbrush.

11

TESSA

The phone call I was expecting came much earlier than anticipated.

I had gotten out of bed the next morning to do some stretches before my long run when my phone rang. My brow furrowed until I saw who it was. I had a grin on my face when I answered, even though I knew what was coming.

"Hello?"

"You're dating my brother this whole summer, and you didn't tell me?! I had to hear about it from JAKE?" Kelsey exploded into the phone.

I stood next to the wall, balancing myself as I stretched my thigh. "Am I dreaming? You do know it's 5:30 in the morning, right?"

"You know what they say. Paybacks are a beast."

I grinned. "Is that what they say?"

"Either way, I had to set my alarm for this, and I haven't set my alarm for months. Were you still sleeping? Did I wake you up?" Her voice sounded giddy and hopeful.

"Aww, sorry to disappoint. I'm up early to go running. Just about ready to leave."

"Of course you are," she said. "Now tell me what's going on."

"First of all, the toothbrush thing. That was *your* idea."

"I know, but I was mad at you, and it felt appropriate. What happened? Was he mad? No, actually, first explain the whole dating thing. Jake was pretty quiet about it."

I began breaking it all down for her, probably like I should have done a week earlier. I didn't like keeping her out of the loop, but her feelings had always been clear regarding me liking Logan. When I was done explaining, she sighed. "Holy crap."

"Yeah." I sat down on the floor to stretch my hamstrings.

"I can't believe Jake's giving away his truck like that."

"We both tried to talk him out of it, but he's pretty set."

There was a pause on the line before Kelsey said, "So, how are you handling it all? With my brother?"

"Fine. We had a good talk before we said yes to Jake. He's not looking to get serious, and I don't want anybody not serious. So, we're keeping things light and breezy."

After a beat, Kelsey repeated, "Light and breezy? What does that mean?"

What did that mean? "It's just… We're just..."

"'Cause you're still going on dates and stuff, right?"

"Yeah."

"You're in so much trouble. Don't say I didn't warn you when this goes bad."

"I almost married a Logan, Kels, remember? I don't want him, I promise."

She made a noise that sounded like disbelief. "But he hasn't always been this way. You know that. And you were obsessed with him for a really long time."

"Not with this Logan." My mind went briefly to me holding his hand the night before, and the laughter in his voice, and the strength in his arms when he picked me up and dumped me into the stream, before I pushed those thoughts away. Physical attraction was different than actually liking somebody. "We're going to check in with each other every week to make sure we're both still on track."

"That's really messed up."

"The more I try to explain it, the worse it sounds."

"I just don't want you to bite off more than you can chew, that's all. I hope, at the end of this thing, you're exactly where you want to be. To be clear, I'm against the whole idea, but a part of me is really hoping you're the one to help him change, because having you as a sister-in-law would be a dream. Cade would be terrified, but I would love it."

I was surprised that Kelsey seemed to be on board with the possibility of me and Logan. It wasn't going to happen, but still...my heart seemed to lighten at the idea. Ugh. Go away, bad thought. "Don't worry. I'm being careful, and so far, things are going just as planned."

"IT IS SO *HOT* OUT HERE!" Pause. "I could really go for some lemonade or maybe some pie or something." Pause. "Or cake?"

Logan's voice carried from the porch all the way across the driveway to where I was sitting with my feet propped up on the fruit table. The book in my lap and my feet on the table probably gave an impression that the day had been a lazy one. Not so. I had been run ragged all day with orders and people. I had sent my dad back to the greenhouse twice to pick the rest of our ripe berries. Now, I was finally enjoying a moment of peace in the last few minutes we were open—or trying to.

"My mouth. It feels like cotton. I can hardly swallow. If it was my last day on earth, do you know what I would want? Lemonade. Or cake. Or pie." Pause. "Maybe all three."

The smile I was holding back finally broke across my face. I sighed and put my book down. Logan had shown up just after 5 p.m., wearing his toolbelt, his baseball hat, and an empty stomach, apparently. I dropped my feet from the table and stood, turning to face Logan, who was kneeling on our front porch, shooting nails into the new floorboards. His toned arms bulging out of a white t-shirt had me giving him an appreciative second glance. I strode across the driveway and up the porch before he turned with a sparkle in his eyes as he heard me approach.

"Oh, hey, Tessa. I didn't know you were out here."

I laughed. "I'm only doing this to shut you up, even though it goes against YOUR rules. If any cars come while I'm gone, take all their money."

His low chuckle met my ears as the screen door slammed shut behind me. As was my habit every time I entered the house during work hours, I ran upstairs to check on my mom. She was getting stronger every day but had been frustrated with her lack of progress.

"Mom, everything alright? Do you need anything?" I stopped short when I saw her standing up, coming out of the bathroom, bent over her walker, walking like a ninety-five-year-old as opposed to the usually vibrant woman in her mid-fifties that she really was.

"Hey, you're supposed to call me if you need the bathroom."

She looked up at me proudly. "Consider yourself off the hook from bathroom duty from now on."

"Good job. Look at how good you're doing." I channeled my best Nate impression and clucked and cooed over her steps.

Her eyes narrowed as she shook her head. I should have known I couldn't fool my mom. "Yes. It's only been three weeks, and look, I can go to the bathroom all by myself."

"Well, most people don't have both of their legs sawed open and their parts replaced. You're doing great. You hungry?"

"I'm still working on the lunch you brought me earlier. Is your dad watching the fruit stand?"

My cheeks colored slightly for no good reason at all. "No, Logan is. He's here working on the porch and guilted me into getting him some treats, so I snuck in here to check on you."

I backed out of the room when her expression turned to intrigue before she could press me for anything else.

"Get back here, Tessa Robbins! I need more details."

"Bye, Mom, good chat." At the moment, having a semi-invalid mother definitely had its perks. I wasn't *opposed* to talking with my mother about things, but given my current situation, where would I even begin?

In the kitchen, I searched for a can of frozen lemonade concentrate in the freezer and mixed it with water because...I don't know, I seemed like the type of person who makes lemonade when a boy talks about being thirsty—not to impress him, but because it sounded good. I grabbed a paper plate and filled it with four raspberry-lemon bars I had made yesterday. As annoying as raspberries were to pick and take care of, they were my absolute favorite fruit to eat. I popped one in my mouth, grabbed the lemonade, paper cups, and the treats, and walked back outside.

Logan stood and stretched his back when I approached him. I handed him his plate of goodies and glass of lemonade, gave a small bow, and started for the stairs.

He blocked my exit by kicking his leg out in front of me. "Wait a minute. Where are you going?"

"I'm at a good part in my book."

"No way. If your dad catches me being lazy by myself, I'll get fired. If I'm on break, you have to be the one forcing me to stop."

"Forcing you to stop?"

He only smiled and motioned me toward the porch swing, settling down next to me with a sigh.

Dear Diary,

Logan Marten's warm body is pressed up against my side. And we're swinging on the porch together, and it's freaking adorable. But don't worry, my heart is still safe.

XOXO

WE SAT in silence for a few moments while Logan inhaled his treats.

"What do you put in this?"

"I like to think the special ingredient is love."

Logan halted just as he was about to take another bite. His eyes flicked over to me as mine widened in horror. I had meant that as a joke. My mom always used to tell us her food tasted better because of that extra dash of love she mixed in. It was out of my mouth before I could think about what I was saying.

"I didn't... I..." Words were not coming fast enough.

He raised his eyebrows as he watched me struggle to talk myself out of whatever I'd just gotten myself into.

"It was just a joke," I finally sputtered.

He shook his head and sent a mild threat my way. "If I'm fifty pounds heavier and in love with you by the end of summer, Jailbait, you're gonna be in big trouble."

I hid my smile while I processed *that*.

He took another bite. "Why don't you sell these at your stand?"

I shrugged. "I'm not sure people want to buy treats when they're here for healthy produce."

"You're around fruits and veggies all day long, and that doesn't seem to stop you. This is two days in a row I've been here, and you've had a different dessert each night."

A flush heated my cheeks. I had definitely *not* been baking more because I knew Logan would be around. "Baking is a stress reliever for me."

"What are you stressed about?"

Logan was back to eating. He had started out with four and was now on his last bar, and he didn't seem to realize he had broken one of our cardinal rules with his question.

Suddenly, all I could feel was his warm body pressed against mine as we rocked together. He felt like a friend. Even with the bet, being with him felt easy. Comfortable. A warning bell began to ring deep in the recesses of my mind. I almost told the bell to shut up, but after giving it thought, I thanked the bell for its wisdom. Being casual friends with Logan was fine, but I had to set the boundaries. I still needed to make it through this summer with my whole heart. Though I was proud of Logan's question, I had to shut it down.

"Wouldn't you like to know."

Logan gave me half of a smile and polished off his last square.

"Anyway, you could just start small. A different treat every day and see how it goes. It might give people recipe ideas for the fruit they're buying."

I glanced at our two saggy, beat-up old tables, trying to imagine selling my baked goods on them. I loved feeding people my own food, but asking somebody to pay money for simple homemade goodies was something else entirely.

He wasn't deterred. Sitting up, he turned toward me. "I'm serious. You like baking. This is a great showcase for the products you're selling."

When I only stared at him, he slunk back in his chair. "It's Business 101."

I remained silent as the moment seemed to pass, but I couldn't help but think about his idea. Baking soothed me. It made me happy. It made me forget. I loved watching people as they ate something I'd created. The idea of it certainly held weight in my head, and it wouldn't have been a horrible thing for my waistline to get rid of some of the treats I made.

"You could try it one time and see how it goes. No skin off your nose either way."

"I'll think about it."

12

LOGAN

There was a movement outside of the construction trailer window. Out of habit, I glanced up in time to see the flash of Trevor's blue t-shirt as he passed by. I flexed my hands at my desk where I sat in front of the computer wishing I was outside working. I'd have a great view of the parking lot out of the office. I forced myself to finish the email I had been working on for the past twenty minutes until I glanced out the window yet again, this time with no movement drawing my eye.

"What are you watching for?" Javier's smooth accent broke into the quiet of the trailer. He stood on the opposite side from me, printing off the mockup cabinet designs I had worked up for him to look at. Nothing like being called out over things that should have never happened.

"Nothing." I cleared my throat and picked up the phone. I guess now was as good a time as any to put in that order for the tile I wouldn't need for another two months.

Javier furrowed his brow at me before glancing back out the window, trying to discover whatever it was I was looking for, before turning his attention back to the printer.

I'd been biting back a smile most of the morning, which had gotten awkward when Javier had asked me *twice* what was so funny. The first time was easy enough to pass off, but the second had gotten his curiosity up, and now he had just caught me again. I needed one of those shock collars people use to keep dogs in a yard, only this time to keep my head focused where it needed to be.

It had been evident that Jake had been plotting with the devil himself when we arrived at the coordinates for our date this past Saturday night. I didn't have to take us too far. We ended up back at my dad's shop where a huge box and a pile of parts had been dumped on the concrete floor. A note, kindly left by Jake, had informed us that we'd be putting together a foosball table he had bought for himself and hadn't wanted to set up. I saw a bit of the Robbins Family type-A tendency come out while Tessa slogged through the pile of parts. The activity had been her worst nightmare, but I ended up having a great time. Refusing to look at the manual for the sole purpose of driving Tessa crazy was not the only reason, but it had definitely helped. My dad's shop hadn't seen a broom in a long while, if ever, and she kept escaping to sweep or organize something.

Our goal had been to make a table. And a table we made. Though there were definitely one or two raised voices (Tessa's), quite a bit of laughing (both of us), a handful of curse words (Tessa, surprisingly), and several tears that were blinked back (both of us).

Getting tools thrown at me by Tessa? A bonus.

Five mysterious leftover parts? A fun gift for Jake.

The foosball players put in backward? Priceless.

As per the instructions from Jake, once we made the table, we had to play a game in which the loser had to perform one favor for the winner. Hence the reason for my staring out the window, waiting for her to arrive.

She had lost.

I pulled myself together, attempting to return some emails and make a few calls on some orders before heading back into the framed office to help run electrical wire with Trevor. Frank Robbins had already come and gone, roughing in the plumbing, and Ronnie had finished the HVAC last week.

I was up in the rafters, pulling a home run wire from one end of the office to the electric box, when she pulled up. My crew and I were used to cars coming and going and slowing down to peep in on our project, so the guys went right on working, running wire and hanging outlet boxes. I had a fantastic birds-eye view of the woman walking into the office, and I couldn't help but stare.

"Hey! It's Tessa," Ronnie called out, immediately gaining the attention of my men. "Did you change your mind about our date?"

Tessa grinned at him behind her sunglasses as she approached. "You'll be the first to know if I do."

"Hold on just a minute." Trevor slid down from the ladder he had been standing on while wiring lights, landing with a thump on the floor. "*Him*? I'm the hot Prince Harry, remember?"

She was wearing jeans and a t-shirt today. Simple. Though she always looked beautiful, it shouldn't have been an outfit that caught a man's eye, but I couldn't look away. And I didn't want to let her see me just yet. I was completely fine with watching her tease and laugh with all the guys she would never be interested in while holding a gigantic plate of lemon-raspberry bars.

Enter Javier.

"I don't think we've been properly introduced," he said, charm oozing from his lips as he made his way toward Tessa. She shook his hand, which he promptly kissed just before he shot me a look up in the rafters.

"Tessa Robbins," she said, staring up at Javier.

Breathless. Did her voice sound breathless?

Javier made a big point of looking toward the parking lot before giving me another calculated look.

"Oh... You here to see Marten?" He pointed up at me. "The boss has had his paws on the window with his tail wagging all afternoon. Now I know why." I detected a smile underneath his expression that I wanted to scrape off with a knife.

He did *not* know why. I shot him a look that was full of swear words, but he only bit back a chuckle.

Tessa turned and looked up to where Javier had pointed and smiled when she saw me. With her sunglasses, her bright smile, and her blonde hair up high in a ponytail, she looked like a perfect summer day.

I pasted a smile on my face. Either way, I had created this. I had to see it through. And so did Tessa. "Hey, Tess," I said as I maneuvered my way down to the ground. "What brings you here?"

She motioned to the plate in her hand. "Oh, I was just in the neighborhood and thought I'd swing by with some treats."

My eyes narrowed, well aware that every guy in the room had stopped working and was staring at us. "Why is that?"

She grinned impishly at me. "No reason."

Folding my arms, I waited for her to crack while trying not to smile.

"You sure?" I baited.

We stood at a face-off, staring at each other. Finally, her eyes widened as though she had just remembered something.

"Oh, that's right." She turned to Ronnie, who stood salivating at the treats, and handed him the plate while she dug into her pocket and pulled out a piece of paper.

She then proceeded to read our script with a mock monotone voice and stumbling over her words.

"I brought these treats to show my appreciation for the hunk of man named"—she squinted at the paper—"Logan? Marten? Yeah. Anyway, to show my appreciation for the most amazing date I have ever been privileged to go on."

"But wait, I thought you had turned me down for a date." I breezed through my memorized script with a passion for the craft.

She stared at me with an innocent expression on her face for a long moment before I glared at her. "Oh right. Yes, but once I left the diner I realized that I couldn't say no to THE Logan Marten."

By this time, the guys had caught on to what we were doing and had begun to clap amid much cackling and insults thrown my way—except for Ronnie, who had made a hefty dent in the plate of lemon-raspberry bars. Tessa bowed.

"Alright, everyone except for Ronnie can take one lemon-raspberry bar and then get back to work." When Javier reached toward the plate, I slapped his hand away. "Nope. Not you either."

Tessa grabbed the plate and held it out to Javier, grinning. "You can take two."

It took some convincing to get the guys back to work, but when everyone else was occupied, I pulled Tessa down the framed hallway with me.

"You want the grand tour, you dirty rat?" I asked.

"Dirty rat? I said everything I was supposed to say."

I wasn't sure why my arm was around her shoulders, but since we were playing up the crowd behind us, I kept it there. That was the only reason.

"Reading the paper was a nice touch, Jailbait."

"You can't imagine I was ever going to say those cheesy lines on my own."

I grinned. "It was even better than I imagined." The only thing I wanted for winning the game was for Tessa to find a way to let the guys know I did, in fact, get that date. I had a reputation to uphold. Tessa hadn't wanted anything public, but since none of these guys were local, I convinced her they'd be safe.

"Is this the gym?" Tessa asked, stopping at the entrance of a large room.

"Yeah."

She stepped inside. "So, this is where Betsy May will yell at me and refuse to do her leg lifts. Now I can imagine it all perfectly."

I nodded, pointing to the far corner of the room. "Yup, and there will be stairs on that wall for Preacher Douglass to whine about going up." I didn't know any of her other patients, but she had told me plenty about Betsy May and Preacher Douglass.

She smiled. "Perfect."

I prodded her along, showing her the rest of the rooms, the space feeling magnified without walls but also intimate without the guys as close.

I was about to turn us around when we got to the storage closet, but she stopped suddenly. Two sample cabinets sat on the floor. I had brought them in to show Nate the different stains he could pick from. They were striped with different tones of brown and black. I had built the cabinets years ago for an earlier project Chase and I had tackled and ended up keeping them for visual aids.

"You're doing the cabinets, right?"

"Yeah."

She sunk to her knees and touched them. "You know how to make this stuff?"

I eyed her warily, though I found myself inching closer to her.

"Yeah," I said again.

"That's amazing. They're beautiful."

"Those are…pretty old. I… There are lots of other styles I can do now." My head began to sweat. *Get it together, Marten.*

"I'd love to watch you do this sometime." She stopped touching the cabinets long enough to look up at me and say, "I think it's fascinating. What an awesome skill to have."

I fingered the collar at my neck. Things were getting too personal now. Time to put an end to this cozy little tour.

"Well, Jailbait, as much as I'd love to hang out here with you, my men would revolt—unless you brought us something to eat every day. Think of the advertising for your business."

"Or they could just come to my fruit stand." She stood up and dusted off her jeans.

The thought of my men knowing where Tessa lived didn't sit right with me. Not because I thought they'd try anything inappropriate, but because I just didn't like them…knowing where she lived.

We walked back down the hallway to the sound of hammering and the guys laughing about something—and probably eating all my treats. Though, that was okay. I'd be stopping by to work on the porch, and I would grab some then. Suddenly, an idea came to me that I should have shut down before it had room to grow.

Instead, I found myself saying, "You know, Jailbait, one way to really seal the deal with these guys is if you were to give your amazing date a kiss on the cheek before you go." Her head shot toward me, and I couldn't help the grin.

"Killing two birds with one stone?"

"Huh?"

"Jake's kiss for this summer?"

I looked at her like she was crazy. Because she *was* crazy. I may have been a glutton for punishment, but even if I went down in flames at the end of this summer, I would be kissing Tessa Robbins.

"If you think you're getting out of Jake's stipulation with just a kiss on my cheek, you're in for a big surprise."

Tessa didn't look at me then, and a slight flush rose on her neck and cheeks. I needed to stop. Now. But first...

"Enough distracting me, woman. Give your man a kiss."

She shook her head at me before rolling her eyes and rising up on her tiptoes. Her hand pressed against my chest, and her perfumed lips were on my cheek at the exact moment my men began catcalling and Nate walked into the building.

"So, the Fourth of July is Tessa's mom's thing. She spends days leading up to it baking, cleaning, and preparing all the food, setting up tables and chairs, and organizing the sound system, on top of everything else."

I nodded on the phone while Kelsey talked, and I rummaged through the refrigerator at my parents' home for something to eat. I had pulled a long shift at work and then another two hours working on Frank's front porch. My back hurt from bending over. I was annoyed at Nate for walking in on me and Tessa earlier that day, and as much as I loved my sister, this conversation was over for me about ten minutes ago.

"So you have to help her out," Kelsey was saying.

"Wait, what?" I asked.

"Tessa. Her dad is busy and very dense at what exactly it takes to pull off this big of a party. I'm serious when I tell you that Tessa's mom does almost all of it. And she's laid up and can hardly move right now."

"I get that, but what does any of this have to do with me?" I finally decided on a ham sandwich and started pulling out all the fixings.

"Umm...because you're DATING her. The fourth is next week. Cade and I are coming home on Wednesday, and I'll be over as much as I can, helping her bake and stuff, but she'll need help getting tables and chairs set up, lawn mowed..."

"Wait, did you say you'll be helping her *bake*?"

"Yes. Shut up. Cade likes my cooking."

"He's grown a tolerance to it for survival. But the rest of us haven't had your cooking in years. You might kill us."

"Zip it. Anyway, we'll be there to help, but trust me, she'll need muscle. Well, actually, in that case, I'll send a message to Jake. Maybe we can use you as an errand boy."

"Smart alec," I muttered as I slathered some bread with mayo and mustard.

"Just please tell me that you'll offer to help. I know you'll see Tessa this week."

I made a noncommittal grunt.

"And promise me whatever this bet thing is, you won't mess with my friend. I think you know exactly what I'll do to you if I catch wind of anything."

Sisters were the worst. That was a fact. Why they always thought they had to jump into my business was beyond me.

"If I say yes, does that mean I can hang up now?"

"Yes, but don't cry. I'll see you next week."

"Sounds good. Take care of Bob and Willie for me."

"Ugh. Between your redneck names and Cade's baseball names, our kids are going to be on talk shows, blaming everything on us."

I hung up the phone and debated taking my dinner back to the bunkhouse but decided to step into the family room. The sunken family room held probably fifty pictures strewn around the walls in frames. It had been years since I had really studied the images. On my way to the couch, one photo caught my eye. It was a grainy picture of me, Kelsey, and Tessa. It looked like I was around nine, which put the girls at about five years old. I was on our concrete patio, holding our new kittens.

The girls were on both sides of me, and when the camera snapped, Kelsey was looking down at the fur balls in my lap with a big smile on her face. Tessa had a look of pure adoration, but when I looked closer, her gaze was on me, not the cats.

I was playing Jake's game this summer. How could we not with an eighty-thousand-dollar truck on the line? The problem was how easy Tessa was to be with. She was cool and funny and dorky in the most appealing way possible, and it was easy to get caught up in it all. In her. But the fact of the matter was, I was not marriage material. I wasn't even boyfriend material. She had crushed on me her whole life, and the last thing I wanted to do was break her heart with this stupid game.

13

TESSA

I sat on the front porch swing, waiting for Logan to pick me up, wearing cute white capris and a flowy, navy top. This was the first time I had somewhat dressed up for Logan. And it wasn't even really for Logan. It was for the nice people in the restaurant we would be sitting at soon enough. Mom had run the fruit stand today while my dad used me for manual labor, thinning fruit trees all afternoon. My shoulders were stiff from the work, but it was nothing compared to the dull ache in my lower back. The hard porch swing made an uncomfortable seat, and I sunk down lower to ease the pressure.

The sun cast a happy glow about the farm, but my mood slowly darkened the longer I sat on the porch. There was no cloud of dust in the air telling me Logan was headed up the gravel driveway and no text on my phone explaining why he was now seven minutes late. Though both of our previous dates had ended up being fun, I wasn't sure I was in the mood for more flat conversation while trying to pull out just enough of the real Logan so I wouldn't kill him.

Now, he was working at my house nearly every evening, and while we had great fun teasing and tossing mild insults back and forth, I was beginning to feel restless. Where we should have been more like friends, in many ways, he still felt like a stranger. He held back so much. It was like anticipating eating a really delicious club sandwich with so many flavors and layers but then being handed a plain ham-and-cheese on white Wonder bread. Logan definitely had the potential of a club sandwich, but he wasn't bringing it to the table.

I mean…which was good because we had an agreement. I'm just saying that I'd like a *bite* of a really good sandwich. Not the whole thing.

I checked the time again. Jake needed to add a clause in the agreement that said every minute Logan was late for our dates, I got a thousand dollars extra from the truck sale. I bet that would get him here on time.

I probably wasn't being fair. He was only nine minutes late now.

No. Nine was unacceptable. Five was okay. That was…traffic—a tractor broke down or cows on the road.

I picked at the salted-caramel-and-chocolate brownie I had saved him, left over from my offering at the fruit stand today. I hated to admit he was right, but people were excited about the treats. I'd even received a few special requests and had one or two customers stop by for the sole reason of seeing what I had made that day. It was almost embarrassing that I hadn't thought about doing this sooner. It was something my family had never done, so I never considered it.

TEN minutes now.

Nothing like having your date forget all about you. I cracked my knuckles and took a large bite out of the brownie. My stomach was nearly ready to claw its way out of my insides. We still had a forty-five-minute drive into Salmon. Jake wanted us to have a fancy dinner, but since I had stipulations of not wanting to be seen by anybody local, Jake had reserved us a spot at The Sassy Heifer, a local fancy steak restaurant in Salmon. It wasn't throwing mud or assembling furniture, so it naturally sounded amazing to me, and it was the *only* reason I was still rooted to my spot on the uncomfortable porch swing.

TWELVE minutes. I was going to kill him.

The front screen door squeaked open, and I turned to watch my mom hobble out with only her cane.

"I thought you'd be gone by now." She took a few steps out onto the porch before sinking onto the rocker next to the swing.

"I was supposed to be." My trained eye took in the movement in her legs as she sat. "You're looking good. Look at how far you can bend your legs."

She sighed and looked down. "Well, I might be showing off a tad for you. It hurts really bad."

I breathed a laugh. "Relax them, then. You don't want to pull anything."

She sighed and straightened her legs back out, leaning back against the bench. "When is this all going to be over?"

"Look how far you've come. Two weeks ago, you could hardly move anywhere by yourself. Now, you've scaled the stairs, manned the fruit stand, and made it outside without any help."

"I'm a medical marvel," she said dryly. She sighed and straightened up in her seat, pushing a strand of blonde hair behind her ear. "Alright, enough whining from me. I've been hearing from your dad that Logan Marten's taken you out every week since you got home. I swear I might as well be living in another country stuck back in my bedroom. You're helping me do leg lifts every couple of hours. Couldn't you have mentioned to your dear old mom that the boy you've been in love with forever has been asking you out?"

I snorted. "It's nothing. Trust me. That was a long time ago. Logan's nice, but I'm not interested. This is just about two people passing time together over the summer."

She peered at me, arms folded, leaning back on the bench. "Why aren't you interested?"

"He goes through women as often as a stick of gum." Even as I said it, I cringed inside, judging him so completely. But still, if what one hears from his own occasionally overly dramatic sister is true, I was probably not too far off.

"Since when?" Huh. I thought that was relatively common knowledge.

"Since...I don't know. A few years ago."

"Do you know all this as a fact?"

"Straight from Kelsey's lips."

"Hmm."

"I think I'm too deep for him these days."

My mom adjusted her position. "Maybe he just needs help drawing it out."

Nope. I didn't need a ton of depth from Logan Marten. Just enough to not drive myself crazy on our dates. What I really needed was forty thousand dollars in the bank. Did that seem shallow to anybody else?

Finally, a cloud of dust by way of an old, red Ford F250 marked its path on our driveway. I half expected him to honk for me to meet him at the truck, but his door creaked open, and Logan stepped out. My heart sunk. Should I make a rule about wearing tight t-shirts that show off biceps made from working construction? No. Why punish us both? A throb from my back reminded me that I should not have been ogling the man who was *twenty-two minutes* late to pick me up.

"Depth is overrated, Tess," Mom whispered as Logan spotted us and began making his way toward the porch.

"Quiet, you."

Her deep, rich chuckle was a temporary balm to my back ache.

"Hey, Nancy. How are you? Is your physical therapist taking good care of you?" Logan leapt up the steps and leaned in close to give my mom a hug. Mom's face showed nothing but delight as she maneuvered herself to have the range to hug him back.

Mom looked at me. "Eh, she could use some softening up."

He nodded empathetically, eyes shining. "She's kind of mean, isn't she?"

"Feed her chocolate and baked goods, and her claws will usually retract."

"That's good to know."

"Alright, that's enough, you two." I stood up slowly, bending over to stretch out my back before brushing past Logan and heading toward his truck. "Let's get this over with."

"Tessa!" Mom exclaimed after me.

"Now, that's the attitude I want from the women I date," Logan quipped, opening my door from behind me.

"He can handle it, Mom," I yelled out before Logan shut me inside of his truck. He and my mom exchanged a few words I couldn't hear before he slid in the driver's side of his truck and began backing out of my driveway.

"You are twenty-two minutes late picking me up." I placed the half-eaten chocolate brownie on his lap before I folded my arms, leaned back against the seat, and simmered, daring him to test me. On a scale of one to ten, I was at a hearty twenty-two with how much I didn't care about my attitude so far that night. Maybe I should have canceled. Then, I remembered, Jake didn't allow cancellations unless we were sick or dying. Though my back did feel like it was trying to kill me.

"Actually, sunshine, I'm eight minutes early. Did you eat half of my brownie?" He looked almost delighted at this fact for some reason.

My smug expression didn't fall exactly, but it dropped a little. "What? No, you aren't. 7:00. And you're lucky I saved you half. I'm starving."

"Check your message from Jake again, because he said 7:30." He took a large bite of the brownie, saw there were a few morsels left in his hand and tossed the rest into his mouth, groaning with pleasure.

I wanted to scoff out loud to him. I should be confident in my time. No way was Logan right. Was he, though? Why did I not have any recollection of a 7:30 start time? I grabbed my phone and pulled up Jake's last message to us both.

> **Jake: Hey, lovebirds. Since I can't trust you with tools (really that was surprising, Logan), your next date is a hot night out in public—in Salmon, Tessa, don't freak out. A nice dinner at The Sassy Heifer. Dress up, eat out on Logan's dime (Tessa, I recommend the steak), and nobody should know you there. Logan will pick you up at 7:30.**

I put the phone back in my purse, not willing or able to look at Logan yet. This news didn't fill me with relief as one might have expected upon hearing the fact that her obnoxious date hadn't forgotten about her, as originally implied.

No.

I was still annoyed at him. Almost like it was his fault I hadn't read the text correctly. I knew it wasn't right to feel this way, but I couldn't help my thought process. Emotions were a complicated business.

"Anything you want to say to me?" Logan's low drawl and self-satisfied smile stretched out between us.

"Your truck could use an upgrade." I smiled at him.

He shook his head. "I'm working on it, but this bet is proving much more difficult than I first imagined."

"Hmm, that's weird. I'm having no issues at all, and I find you perfectly annoying."

He snorted. "You're kind of mean tonight."

"So, do your other girls just fall all over you for the whole week you date them?" A slight flinch to his body had the visual effect of him taking a hit, though he recovered quickly.

"Something like that. But they say thank you when I pick them up early, and they reserve their murderous intent for when I end it."

I pasted a smile on my face. "I'm sorry I doubted your ability to tell time."

"Aww, that's sweet."

We drove in semi-awkward silence. Though I had said the apologetic words, we both knew it wasn't an apology. The thought made me feel hollow inside, even though I didn't want to feel bad. I wanted the throbbing in my back to go away, and then maybe I could concentrate on a more well-crafted apology. I should have taken some over-the-counter drugs, but I hadn't thought I needed them.

Poor Logan. I think I needed them.

We pulled up to The Sassy Heifer, both of us sighing audibly with relief to be done with the car ride. The place was busy on a Saturday night. Logan drove around, looking for a spot in the overflow gravel parking lot. I had hunched over, trying to stretch my back once again, when a shiny, red Mazda caught my eye.

"Stop."

Logan jerked visibly at my outburst, immediately pressing on the brakes. "What?"

"That's Tyler's car."

He leaned closer to me while he squinted out the window. "Which one?"

"The red Mazda."

He narrowed in on me. "You were going to marry a guy who drives a Mazda?"

"Shut up."

"Are you sure that's his?"

"Yes, there's a Ragnar sticker on the back of it."

"What's a Ragnar?"

"It's a big 200-mile relay race with teams. We ran one a couple years ago."

He looked at me in disbelief for a couple seconds before shaking his head. "Who are you people?"

I stared at the Mazda. I really didn't think I could handle seeing him and his fiancée out on a date tonight. I'd have to play nice, and I was not in the mood to play nice.

"I don't want to go in there."

He stared back at the restaurant. "Okayyy."

We pulled back out onto Main Street with Logan leaning forward, peering from side to side and telling me food options as he spotted them.

"Fast food, fast food, pizza. Alright, I'm going to interject. Let's not do pizza tonight. I've had too much pizza in my life, period, but especially lately. Can we not?"

"No pizza, period," I mimicked before I tensed.

Period.

PERIOD.

Oh my gosh.

Ohhhhh my gosh.

As Logan drawled on, realization dawned on me like a bird smacking into a clean window. The back ache, the hunger, the intense desire to snap my date's face off. I was on my period. I usually got cramps, but every once in a while, it would switch to a deep-set backache. It wasn't often, and I had completely missed the warning signs. My back always hurt after thinning fruit, and I hadn't given a thought to my time of the month.

Suddenly, I felt much more in tune with my body. Aware of things I hadn't thought of while being a huge jerk toward my date. I discreetly leaned forward as far as I could and glanced downward to make sure my white pants were okay. White pants. WHITE! On day one! I'm not saying that leaking on the truck seat of the biggest crush of my childhood would be the worst thing in the world, but I wasn't *not* saying it. We had a long summer to go for Logan to have any more embarrassing material between us.

I needed medication and tampons—pronto.

We reached the edge of town, and he pulled a quick U-turn on the two-lane road.

"Anything look good?" he asked.

"The grocery store?"

He looked at me like I was crazy. "You a big fan of their deli section or something?"

"I need to make a stop there really quick."

"Okay. Do you want to go after we eat?"

"No, now—if that's alright," I added. There may have been leakage on his truck seat. Being nicer to him at this moment could only help me.

He pulled into the grocery store parking lot and parked. I opened the door and slid/backed out carefully like a five-year-old child might slide out of a pickup so I could check out the seat. My heart stopped racing. The seat was fine. Now, I only cursed myself for not bringing a jacket to tie around my waist, because I had no idea how the pants had fared during the trip.

Logan rounded the truck the same time as me, apparently coming inside. I briefly debated the merits of whether it was better for him to *watch* me walk inside or have him in the store with me. No, he could come inside. I would just make sure to walk behind him and then shoo him to the candy aisle while I made my purchase and ran to the bath-room. It was foolproof.

Except, Logan was *not* foolproof.

We reached the doorway and found the sliding doors out of order. I made my way to the outer door first and yanked it open, hoping to usher him inside, only to feel the heat of his body behind me as his hand hit higher on the door than mine, holding it open.

"Go ahead, Jailbait."

"No, you go. I've got it." I turned back to smile at him. All of my insides were twisting together like snakes.

His brow furrowed. "What? You're in front of me. Just go."

"I was here first. I'll be the gentleman—gentlewoman."

I was making it weird, but I couldn't stop. I could feel *things happening*, but I had no idea the damage. I had so many things to do in this store, and I couldn't waste any more time. First thing was to grab a box of tampons then run as fast as I could, without bouncing, to the register. I would buy it and then move swiftly, yet cautiously, to the bathroom—after I located it in the store. Which was probably down some shady hallway with an employees-only back-room door next to a forklift and some storage boxes. Note to self: always bring a light jacket with you, even if it is currently 95 degrees outside. Also, never wear white pants, even if they are *so cute*.

He stared at me, bemused, looking like he wanted to argue further. Thankfully, he played my game and stepped around me, entering through the doorway before me. "Alright. I'm just used to going out with Jake, and he insists on me opening all his doors."

Even in my predicament, a laugh bubbled out of me at the image.

Once inside the store, walking side by side, I scoured the signs, searching for the words 'feminine hygiene.' But first, I needed to distract Logan.

"Listen, why don't you go pick out some candy or something? I'll be right back."

He searched my eyes, a hint of amusement on his face. "You trying to get rid of me?"

"No. I just remember how much you love candy."

He gave me a pointed look while I sent subliminal messages into his brain to suddenly need candy.

"Listen, Tess, I can pick out tampons as good as any guy who has sisters."

I stopped short, my shoulders drooped, and caught a glimpse of his smile before my hands covered my face.

"Are you serious?"

"Go get 'em, Jailbait. Don't be embarrassed. What else do you want? Chips? Chocolate? I know how this works."

Heat rushed to my cheeks. I couldn't believe I had been so dense to *not* realize this was happening and that Logan was being a gentleman about the whole thing, even after the way I'd treated him. With my humiliation level at an all-time high, I mumbled, "Chocolate."

He bowed and dutifully turned, and I hightailed it out of there. I found tampons in aisle seven, next to the cat food. I grabbed the first box I could find that had the word 'super' on it and jogged stiffly toward the end of the aisle, looking for an employee or a sign above that told me where the bathroom was. Forget about buying it first, this was an emergency. I was in luck. Some smart person had placed the bathroom in the same aisle as the feminine product section. A small sign on a black door twenty yards up read: *Employee bathroom only.*

Not today, Satan.

Today, the bathroom read: *Employee and girl-in-white-pants bathroom only.*

I had already ripped the side of the box open like an animal in my desperation, grateful the grocery store seemed quite empty for a Saturday night. My sight was set on the door in front of me, now only ten paces away, sandwiched between the cheese and lunch meat. I was so close. I reached the end of the aisle and kept going, not slowing down for anything.

Except when I plowed into a warm body with long, light-brown hair who stepped out in front of me.

Bodies and tampons went flying.

My landing was surprisingly soft, but the body beneath me grunted as her head and sharp points of her body slapped against the cold hard floor beneath us.

Horrified, I crawled off the woman, my mouth gaping and my humiliation shattering into a thousand pieces.

"I'm so sorry. I'm so sorry," I whispered frantically. "Are you okay?" She was still sprawled out on the floor, her hair-covered face turned away from me, when another voice from behind me called out to her, sending sudden chills down my spine.

"Cam? You okay?!"

I stopped. My heart, my brain, my emotions. Everything stopped. For a second, I was washed in an array of colorless memories. Visions of holding hands, movie dates, talks of the future, and the back of his head as he walked away from me.

Tyler.

Which meant that the body not moving beneath me was Camille—the woman he left me standing at the altar for.

14

LOGAN

Two sisters.

One older. One younger.

I'd been the victim of PMS one week out of every month for my whole teenage life, which was why—when I made my way toward the aisle in the back that circles the entire store with my arms full of candy bars, M&Ms, chocolate-covered pretzels, and sour gummy worms—I was in search of the chip aisle for something salty.

I wished Tessa would have just told me. For some reason, it rankled that I hadn't given her the impression she could trust me with something like that. But then again, when *could* I have given her that impression? I'd been deliberately keeping things light between us—surface level only.

There was a couple walking a few yards ahead of me, though I didn't pay much attention. The guy stopped to look at a deal at the end of the aisle while his girlfriend kept moving forward—until a hundred-and-thirty-pound blonde left tackle came firing out of nowhere and took the other girl down.

It took me a moment to realize what had happened. Then, I saw the white pants and the blue shirt.

Tessa.

TESSA.

The takedown had been something my high school football coach would have given his signature impressed eyebrow raise over. Direct hit. Even the exploding box of tampons reminded me of the fireworks after our home team scored a point. Tessa's face was white as the man approached her. She scrambled off the limp body with a look of such terrible dread that alarm bells began going off in my mind. The three were not awkwardly dusting themselves off and going on their merry way, laughing about the mishap. There was tightness and lingering and what looked like a sorry attempt at small talk.

Then, I knew exactly who they were. Apparently, they had finished their dinner at The Sassy Heifer. I bent down and picked up a tampon by my foot.

I didn't have much of a heart, at least not for women beyond my mother and sisters. No, that had been destroyed long ago. But something *familiar* began banging in my chest. My stomach tied into knots while my thoughts warred against themselves. Tessa and I weren't really dating. She could take care of herself. I knew this. It had all happened a year ago. I had to play this right. For her. But for some reason, playing this right failed to coincide with my first instinct, which was to shove this tampon up his—

Tessa's desperate eyes found mine, and before I could second-guess what I was about to do, I stepped forward and wrapped my arm around her shoulder, pulling her snug against my side. Protective. Like a boyfriend might do. Or a brother. Tessa molded to me, leaning against me for support.

"You alright?" I asked her, my eyes roaming over her face for any signs of injury.

"Yeah," she breathed, looking miserably toward the couple who were darting glances at us.

"Are you okay?" I looked at the other woman, who was rubbing her head, clearly nursing a battle wound. "Can we do something for you?"

The woman smiled brightly at Tessa, each rub on her head making more of her hair stand up due to static. "No, it's no problem. I'll be fine. It's been...nice...to see you again." Her voice tried hard to be sincere but fell flat.

My gaze fell onto Tyler, who eyed me with curiosity before sticking his hand out and introducing himself.

His handshake was the stuff of sissies—cold and limp, and though he gave the impression he could be suave and cocky in the right setting, this encounter with Tessa had visibly shaken him. It must have been the big-brother instinct I had toward Tessa that made me want to throttle him, and with his body type resembling a toothpick, I didn't think I'd have any trouble teaching him a lesson. Extremely aware of the beautiful blonde curling into the side of my body, I condensed all of my rage into the twitch of my finger. If this were an old western, I'd have been the first to shoot.

His eyes flitted to Tessa. "Hi, Tessa."

I heard her intake of breath, and I was about to cut our visit short when she leaned forward with a timid smile.

"Hey, Tyler." She looked toward Camille. "I'm so sorry for running into you like that, Camille. And for knocking you over. I'm mortified."

My arm skimmed around her waist, sliding the tampon into her left pocket before hooking my thumb in her belt loop. After a moment, I felt her right arm slide around my back.

"It's okay. It's kind of funny, really," Camille said, smiling almost shyly, wringing her hands as she glanced up at Tyler.

"Were you playing a game or something?" Tyler asked, his eyes on my arm around Tessa, before inching closer to Camille.

"Scavenger hunt," Tessa said automatically.

There was a silence. Everybody's gaze fell onto the ground where the tampons lay scattered on the floor. The fact that I was nearing thirty, Tessa almost twenty-five, and we were still playing games teenagers played on dates for high school dances didn't seem to hold anybody up. It was the tampons that were going to give us away.

"And you guys helped us out! Our instructions were to grab a box of tampons and tackle somebody to the ground. We won."

Tough crowd. Joke did not land. Tessa gave my waist a squeeze.

"How've you been, Tess?" Tyler's voice broke into the silence.

I shifted, ready to remove us from this scene, when Tessa said in a soft tone that she's never used on me, "I'm good. I hear you have some news."

Tyler and Camille reddened slightly. "Yeah, we're getting married next month."

"I'm happy for you guys."

They were all talking so calmly, if a bit stiff and awkward, but Tessa seemed almost earnest. Where was the fight? The scratching and hair pulling and punching? Guys would have settled this much differently.

When there was a pause in the awkward conversation, I broke in, my hands on Tessa's shoulders. "Well, it was nice to meet you both. I'd better get this little linebacker home." The group disbanded slowly with nods and small waves.

Pointing to Camille, I couldn't help one tiny parting shot. "You might want to put some ice on that. Okay, see you guys later."

Once they turned the corner down the aisle, I gave Tessa a light push toward the restrooms and then went in search of more chocolate.

15

TESSA

The white pants made it through the crisis unscathed.

My pride did not.

Logan opened the truck door for me and, with his hand on my elbow, helped me inside. He put my purse on my lap and a shopping bag filled with an *absurd* amount of sugar at my feet. With the tiniest hint of a smile, he broke open the bottle of pills, checked the label, and handed me two, our eyes clashing for a moment before I looked away. He leaned forward, rummaged through the plastic sack, his elbow resting lightly on my knee, until he found a water bottle, twisted the cap, and handed it to me.

Every part of me wanted to resist. I didn't want to have to take pills to make the throbbing in my back go away—the root cause of my humiliation tonight—but my dignity had already been shattered. By the time Logan had closed the door and made it around to the other side, the pills had been swallowed, and my face was sufficiently hidden behind my hands.

The truck burst to life at the turn of Logan's key, but we didn't move. He turned down the radio.

"You doing alright?"

I made no attempt to answer.

"Come on, Tess. It wasn't that bad."

I peeked out from behind my hands and scowled at him.

He let out a low chuckle. "Okay, it was pretty bad, but you survived it. You did good."

I slunk back into the seat, my head on the headrest. "I have never been so humiliated in my life."

Logan nodded, and we sat there in silence, my mind replaying the entire grocery-store scene a thousand different ways.

"I don't know who you ticked off upstairs for the timing involved in something like that—ow." He flinched away from my whack to his arm.

I moaned as I leaned forward and rested my head on the dashboard, my arms hugging my face.

Logan sighed. "Did I ever tell you my most embarrassing moment?"

"No."

"It was my freshman year. We were coming back from a field trip, and I fell off the bus."

My head lifted from its spot on the dash. "You *fell* off the bus?"

"Right off. Tripped on the first stair. All I remember is my head slamming into the railing while my legs got twisted somewhere behind me. I landed in a heap on the sidewalk."

I tried to hide the smile behind my hand.

"Are you enjoying my pain, Jailbait?"

"Is that all you've got? I could run circles around your embarrassing moment."

"I'm not done."

"Do tell."

"I stood up, laughed about it like a man to everybody who saw, and just as I was turning to walk away, I ran smack into a pole."

A smile burst across my face. My night hadn't been forgotten, but it felt nice to have a reason to smile and commiserate with someone. With Logan.

He continued, "I had this massive purple bruise on my forehead for a week. To add insult to injury, my ninth-grade love, Samantha Benson, saw the whole thing and laughed."

My smile began to fade at that. Warm fingers found my neck and began to rub gently.

"It was an accident, Tess." His low voice swept over me like that feeling you get when you're cold and you step into a hot shower. "You can be sorry for running into her. But that's it. That's all you have to be sorry for. And her pain will fade a lot quicker than what they did to you."

His fingers moved to my hair where I felt a light tug. I moved my head to look at him.

"Alright?"

"Alright."

He took the truck out of park and began making his way toward the street. "And for what it's worth, that tackle was a thing of beauty."

I didn't want to smile. I shouldn't have smiled. I should have demanded Logan take me home and drowned myself in a pint of ice cream. But a hint of a smile crept onto my face anyway.

"Do you want to go back to that cow place now?"

I sighed. "No. I kind of want to blow off Jake's date and do our own thing."

He looked interested. "Blow off an overly fancy restaurant with less-than-stellar reviews? Yes, please. What are you thinking?"

I thought for a minute. What kind of food would make this night better? "A big, fatty hamburger with fries handed to me through a window."

Logan looked like he might cry from happiness.

We ended up parked out by the Salmon River, sitting on the tailgate of his truck, shoulders touching, sharing fries and eating oversized hamburgers in the dark. I even splurged and ordered a Pepsi. The full-sugar kind, not diet. Diet was for days when I was on top of things. But after today…it was a loaded cowboy burger with barbecue sauce and an onion ring on top, a large waffle fry with fry sauce, and a Pepsi—large.

The food in my belly, the drink in my cup, and the medicine

working its way through my bloodstream had done wonders in settling my nerves—as well as the man sitting beside me.

"I don't mean to tell you your business," Logan said, his mouth full of his "Sunrise Burger" with egg yolk dripping down his face, "but if it were me, I'd stick one waffle fry on that burger for more texture. You won't go back."

"Are you a foodie now?"

He wiped his face with a napkin before continuing. "It's your fault. One of the guys brought in some brownies to work the other day. I had one bite and had to throw the rest away. I also used the words salted caramel for the first time in my life."

I smiled and glanced down at the burger I was currently eating like an ape, with barbecue sauce dripping down my hands and face. "Well, this burger needs nothing else. I'm trying to find the right word to describe how good it tastes."

"How about really good?"

"That's pathetic."

"Perfect?"

"Still not right."

"How can anything be better than perfect?"

I thought for a moment. "It's too sterile. There's not enough warmth in the word. This burger is messy, and big, and with the onion rings...it's a rule breaker. It's not perfect. It's better than perfect."

"That's all the words I got."

"It needs more syllables. The level of how good this burger is, mixed with how crappy my night has been, means the word has to be...something amazing. But not amazing. That's too generic."

He rolled his eyes, leaning over to take a swig of my Pepsi. "Nobody talks like that."

"Sure they do."

"Nobody normal. Like the word magnificent. Who actually uses that word?"

"Lots of people use it."

"When's the last time you used it in a sentence?"

"This burger is magnificent." My eyes and mouth widened with excitement. "You've found the perfect word."

"Nope. You sound pretentious."

"It sounds like a word that waits for the right time. Like when the most perfect piece of food in existence makes its way onto my plate. This burger deserves me stepping up my language game."

I took another bite, my mouth full of hamburger and barbecue sauce and onion rings in all of their magnificent glory, when Logan suddenly nudged my arm with his elbow. "I thought we talked about this."

"What?" The word came out muffled and slow as I was careful to say it and not spray it.

"Being too cute. You gotta stop."

My mouth was currently bulging out like a chipmunk gathering nuts for the winter. I didn't look at him. I went over the steps in my head of how one chews and swallows and did so with careful exactness.

We finished our dinner around dusk. The sky was an orange haze due to several wildfires a hundred miles to the west. The water reflected the reddish-yellow hues, giving the air around us an orange glow. Technically, my night had been a disaster, but now with that all behind me, for the first time, being with Logan didn't feel like we were checking off items on Jake's date list. We'd gone rogue, and now the night seemed brimming with possibilities. I suspected Logan wasn't ready to be done either, because he jumped off the truck to open the passenger door and pulled out the bag of treats.

"In case we're not done eating your feelings," he said as he flung the bag between us before jumping up next to me once again. "Chocolate or candy?"

"Why is there an 'or' in that question?"

He dumped a handful of both into my lap. "I like the way you think."

Eventually, we lay back on the tailgate of his truck, pointing out stars that would peep in and out of the sky from behind the hazy wall. The night felt strange. Nice, but unusual. Logan was a muted version of his usual flirtatious self, and as much as I craved a moment like this, I wasn't sure what to do with it, especially under our dating guidelines.

He cleared his throat and lay on his back, looking up at the sky. "Can I ask you something?"

I shrugged and popped a handful of Skittles into my mouth. "Sure."

"What all went down on your wedding day? I heard the gist of it from Kelsey a while back, but while I was meeting the man himself, it kinda hit me how little I actually knew."

"You were there."

"You remember that?"

He was one of the faces in the crowd that I remembered. Looking out in the audience before my life changed, I had found Logan's curious eyes burning into mine.

"This has already been one of the most embarrassing nights of my life, thank you very much. I'm not exactly dying to go into the details of the other one."

"Really? The *most* embarrassing?"

"Yup."

"You're telling me, out of all the embarrassing nights in your past —I'm thinking specifically teenage years and a particular laundry room—a light tackle of your ex-fiance's mistress is the worst?"

I leaned over and smacked a laughing Logan against his stomach. His hand gripped my wrist to stop another attack.

"We agreed to never speak of that, therefore it does not exist to me."

"I didn't agree to anything. And it most certainly exists in my mind."

"You're the worst," I said, pulling my hand away.

"I've always wondered. Why did you come barreling into the laundry room in the dark?"

A soft laugh escaped me as I thought about that night, reliving the awkwardness. "I was trying to see if I could make it all the way there and back without turning on any lights."

A deep rumble escaped his chest. "A perfect storm."

I waited a beat before I asked him something I had always

wondered. "Why didn't you ever tell anybody? I thought for sure I'd be the laughingstock of the entire basketball team."

"I felt bad for you. And a little for myself." He broke off to laugh and pinch the bridge of his nose. A grin etched its way onto my mouth while I waited for him to continue. "You were fourteen. I couldn't tell anybody that story. Out of context, I'd be thrown in jail."

"You started calling me Jailbait."

"Only when nobody else was around."

The night settled to the sounds of the rushing water and the chirping of nature. The scent of both the mountains and fields combined with the crisp summer evening had me filling my lungs with air just for the sheer pleasure of it.

I moved the candy off of my lap with a heavy sigh. "All right, I'm done with sugar."

He dropped a bag of sour gummy worms on my stomach. "You better just eat slower. This is the only thing keeping us from holding hands."

I made a face. "How about you keep eating with your right hand. That should be enough."

He sighed and dropped another piece of chocolate in his mouth. "Don't let it be said I never took one for the team."

The grooves on the tailgate were starting to jab into my back, so I adjusted my position slightly, which brought my shoulders pressed more firmly against his. Finally, I got up enough courage to relieve my conscience. "I'm sorry I was a jerk earlier tonight. Thanks for being so nice."

"Don't apologize to me. Poor Cami's the one nursing a killer goose egg right now."

I shook my head but really didn't want to start thinking about Camille and Tyler again. "But I am sorry for how I acted."

"You're alright," he said softly, nudging my arm with his elbow. "So, your ex-loverboy looked like a tool."

I laughed because Tyler had looked the exact opposite of a tool. He was clean cut, wore jeans and a t-shirt, and was holding the hand of his cute girlfriend. He could have been your friendly neighborhood grocer taking bags to your car. Any old lady seeing them in a store would pat their cheeks and gush over their general cuteness.

"They actually seemed kind of sweet together."

He turned to look at me. "You definitely dodged a bullet."

When I didn't say anything, he asked, "How'd you two meet?"

"I thought we were keeping things light?"

"We are. I just want to know everything."

I laughed and tried to ignore the tingling sensation crawling up my spine at his words.

DEAR DIARY,

I am lying on the tailgate of Logan's truck in the dark, and he's acting sweet and genuine and it feels dangerous, and I don't have the heart to wish for Fake Logan to come back.

XOXO

I TURNED my head to look at him. "If I tell you mine, are you going to tell me yours?"

"I don't have anything."

I scoffed because we both knew that was a lie.

"Just tell me the basics. You don't have to go into detail."

I sighed. I didn't have to tell him anything. It wasn't like he was pounding at my door with all of his secrets. And he seemed full of them, guarded and wary of going past his surface. I would give him the basics, as requested. The kind of thing I would tell my mailman or the person checking me out at the grocery store—because getting jilted at the altar is totally the kind of thing you bring up to people like that.

"We met at the gym."

Logan snorted. "That guy?"

I poked at his foot. "He wasn't going for bulk, just keeping healthy. He's a runner, too."

I couldn't see it, but I *knew* he was laughing. His body tensed like he was holding back a sneeze. I continued, not knowing why I was feeling defensive for Tyler's sake. "Anyway, he asked me out, and we started dating, and then got engaged, and then, yada, yada, yada, we were getting married up until five minutes before we said I do."

"Wow. That was...basic."

"You asked. I delivered."

"Those yada, yada, yadas seem pretty loaded, Kramer."

I smiled at his *Seinfeld* reference. I didn't know what to do with *this* Logan. This Logan was the one I was most wary of. The one who could carry on a conversation and be interested and thoughtful. He was pressing me for answers and information, and it didn't seem to match up to the Logan I'd been dating under Jake's watchful eye. Maybe that was the trigger. Jake hadn't been a part of this date. We had rules and check-ins that kept us safe from each other. We had some controlled fun and then marked the date off of Jake's list. But now, I found myself wanting to divulge all. Wanting to go deeper with Logan. To see what might happen.

"You really want to hear this?"

"I really do."

16

TESSA

It was hotter than the blazes in Eugene last June. To make matters worse, our air conditioning had gone out that morning, the same time my bedroom upstairs was crammed with women—my mom and sister, Kelsey, half-dressed bridesmaids, and a charcuterie board filled with snacks we were all too hot to eat. The record 102 degrees was threatening to make most of us keel over dead. Kelsey had been reduced to holding a towel and wiping away moisture secreted from any visible part of my body, while I was being primped and teased and stuffed into my dress.

Later, out in the orchard, my poor dad looked like a flushed turkey stuffed unnaturally into a blue suit, his cherry face glistening with sweat. My mom kept fanning herself with the wedding itinerary. The scent of my mother-in-law's jasmine perfume sprinkled throughout the orchard threatened to overpower the apples as we stood in wait for the ceremony to begin.

Tyler's family were big potato farmers from Salmon. Growing up, I had heard of his family. The Wittenhouse's owned the potato factory where farmers from all around sold their potatoes. I knew Tyler's type well—the town golden boy. Handsome, popular, and athletic. He had blond hair and a charming grin that could curl your toes. Every girl loved him. We dated during my second year of physical therapy school before he asked me to marry him.

I don't remember feeling nervous that day. There were so many things to get done; I spent the morning answering a million questions about where to put this, and what color went here, and did I like this or that. I didn't really give much thought to the ceremony itself. I hadn't felt a need to worry about it because, well, what was there to worry about? A nice, handsome guy had picked me, I was in love, and I said yes. Wasn't that how all love stories went?

There was a problem with the microphone. Dad had already walked me down the rose-petal-covered aisle. Tyler had given me a tight smile as I took his outstretched hand. I had chosen not to wear a veil—much to my mother's dismay—but gah, it wasn't 1980. I wanted to see every inflection on Tyler's face as we pledged our lives together. Tyler's clammy, cold hands were unusual, especially given the heat, but my attention was soon arrested by Preacher Douglass. He was a cowboy if I ever saw one. Even when he was marrying somebody, he still wore dark jeans and a button-down shirt stretched to the max with a bolo tie cinched at his neck. He pulled the microphone stand closer to himself and opened his mouth to begin the ceremony when a loud screech shrieked through the orchard filled with a hundred of our closest friends and family. The entire crowd jerked as if shot, putting their hands up to their ears to muffle the sound.

After that, the microphone went dead. Tyler attempted a light-hearted fumble with the cords before turning back toward the audience with a shrug of his shoulders. He had never been much of a handyman. Soon, helpful family members and friends in dark suits shuffled toward the podium and began bungling with cords and the microphone.

It was fine. These things happened. A little bump in the ceremony would be something we would laugh about later. Kelsey's and my childhood was filled with *bumps* that we laughed our guts out at now. The humor was lacking in Tyler's eyes. In fact, he looked a little green. My fiancé was going to puke. It must have been the heat. Even in the shade of the orchard, there wasn't a stitch of breeze in the air.

"Are you okay?" I whispered.

He blinked at me and seemed confused by the question.

I asked him again, and this time, he startled out of wherever his thoughts had gone. He smiled weakly at me and squeezed my hand once before mumbling, "I'll be back."

He pulled away from me and made his way down the aisle, across the road, and disappeared into my parents' white, two-story farmhouse.

The mind could be an amazing tool when one was trying to suspend reality. As I watched the back of my fiance's head walk down the aisle away from me, the idea that he had suddenly developed a strong desire to find some tools was the only option I could come up with that made sense. Or actually, no. He was going to grab the old karaoke machine from the basement and switch it out. It wouldn't be perfect, but it would elevate Preacher Douglass's soft voice loud enough for the crowd to hear. Relief filled my body. He was getting the karaoke machine. We had discovered it a few nights earlier in the basement. Kelsey and I had spent many years of our childhood annoying the household by singing our own renditions of pop songs on the radio.

I glanced back at my best friend and, catching her confused gaze, I whispered, "Karaoke machine."

A small smile lifted her face, though the concern in her eyes remained. I looked around the audience, worry etched on many of the faces staring back at me. Oh no, they thought...

"He's going to grab the karaoke machine." I smiled brightly at them all, wanting to laugh, but I couldn't because of the pit that suddenly appeared in my stomach.

"Testing. Testing."

My uncle Lance's voice rang strong throughout the orchard. I turned back toward the preacher and smiled with relief. We needed to get this show moving. Except now, I was missing a fiancé. I looked back toward the house, waiting for the door to swing open with a sandy-haired charmer holding a karaoke machine striding out.

He said he'd be back.

There was a shuffling that came next. The men in suits who had come to rescue the microphone made their way back to their seats. My mom stood up from the front row, meeting my eye, and let me know through gestures that she was going to go find Tyler. To let him know the microphone was now working.

Was he in the bathroom?

I had no idea where I was supposed to look. Faces of people I loved and had known forever looked back at me. Some offered me curious smiles. Most were full of sympathetic nods and pitiful glances. A low hum began in the crowd as some began whispering. A tap on my shoulder had me turning to Preacher Douglass.

"Do you know where yer feller went?" His voice boomed throughout the orchard, the audience doing a collective jerk of their shoulders at the volume. Preacher Douglass's face reddened as his big, shaking paw clicked the off button. I was rooted to the spot, wide-eyed and tense, suddenly feeling like I wanted to throw up or run away. Or both. I summoned all the strength in my possession to smile meekly at the sweet, bumbling preacher man.

I braved a look toward the house, and my stomach dropped. My mom stood on the porch, motioning for me to come to the house. I couldn't see the look on her face from the orchard, but judging by her body language…it wasn't about the karaoke machine.

Swallowing, I turned back to Preacher Douglass. "I'll go find out."

My eyes burned in my sockets as I gingerly took a step down the aisle without a husband on my arm. I made the mistake of glancing at my brother, Nate, sitting with his wife and two kids, looking as if he were about to commit a murder. I stopped looking people in the eye after that. Instead, I put a placid smile on my face, as though we had forgotten something and would be back in a minute.

There was a good explanation for this. I'd hear Tyler out, marry him, and then murder him. In that order. I was nearly to the house now, my mom's flushed face in my view. At this point, all emotion fled. I was numb to everything, my body kicking into survival mode.

Walking up the stairs, the lace from my dress got caught under my shoe. My shaking fingers were grateful for something to do when I lifted the front of my dress like a princess walking up the stairs.

I couldn't bring myself to ask my mom what was wrong and was about to push past her when she stopped me, taking my left hand in hers.

Willing myself not to cry, I stared straight ahead at the screen door on the porch.

"He wants to talk to you." Mom's voice, usually sunny and optimistic, was none of those things.

I nodded numbly and moved past her.

"I'll be waiting right out here, Tess." My hand felt a light squeeze before she let me go.

Tyler was sitting on the couch when I opened the screen door and stepped inside. He was leaning forward, elbows on his knees, face in his hands, staring at the floor. When the door closed, he looked up at me.

I knew right then that there would not be a wedding. That was not the body language of a happy groom skipping to the altar.

But the heart wants what it wants. And currently, mine wanted a husband. It wanted to walk down the aisle to the wedding march, waving happily at my friends and family. It wanted to make itself sick on cake. It wanted to dance and kiss and gaze happily into Tyler's blue eyes. It wanted Kelsey's bridesmaid speech. A romantic night in a fancy hotel room. It didn't want to go outside and tell the group of people who had taken the day off of work, flown in from other states, and spent the past two days helping to decorate and set up the orchard that it was all for naught.

"What's going on?" Though I had many thundering emotions warring in my head, my voice came out quiet. Skittish.

Tyler put his face in his hands and looked down at the floor again. He didn't move for a long moment, while what felt like a thousand flying daggers buried themselves into my heart. Finally, he looked up at me.

"I can't do this."

I looked at his face, pain etched all the way from his eyes to the tautness of his mouth, and wondered when I was going to wake up from this nightmare. Things like this didn't happen to real people. It was for the movies. He had once loved me enough to think he could do this. He loved me enough to invite his closest family and friends to our wedding. His old college buddies were groomsmen. So why was he sitting on a couch, alone, instead of holding my hand in front of the preacher?

"What do you mean? It's our wedding day, Tyler." Maybe he needed a reminder.

"I know. And I'm sorry. I thought I could, but…" His voice broke off as he swallowed.

"Everybody we know is outside. What are you doing? You were fine at the rehearsal yesterday. What happened today?"

He sighed, putting his face back down in his hands. He didn't even have the decency to look me in the eyes. And then his soft voice intruded into my thoughts, changing everything.

"I'm in love with somebody else. I'm so sorry, Tessa. I…thought I could get over it. But I can't. I didn't mean to hurt you. I didn't mean for this to happen. I do love you, Tessa, but…I can't marry you."

His voice was muffled from his hands while I stood there in numbed silence. The only sound was the fan oscillating in the corner of the room, blowing at the skirt of my dress. A fly buzzed around my face. My limbs were stiff. Shock clung to every corner of my body.

"You were cheating on me?"

Silence.

"Tyler."

"Yes. I'm sorry. It just happened."

"It just happened," I repeated his words. "Nothing *just* happens. Things happen because you allow them to happen."

"We worked on a few houses together at work. We didn't mean for it to happen."

I tensed. "At work?" I knew most of the people in his office. "Who is it?"

He hesitated before saying, "Camille."

I sucked in a breath. Camille was my favorite at his office. Brunette and beautiful, she always had a friendly smile. She'd go out of her way to chat with me. *Camille*? A normal person might have been worried about Tyler working with her. She was striking, but her natural, friendly way put everyone at ease. She would always refer to us as a couple. When she was annoyed with Tyler over something work related and was relaying the story to me, she would always refer to him as '*your dang fiancé.*' Camille? Really?

It felt like a sucker punch right in the gut. And to make matters worse, Camille was out there right now, watching this all play out. Was she happy? Joyful? Embarrassed? Excited to finally get her man?

My man.

"I'm so sorry." He was looking at me now, his blond hair disheveled. To his credit, regret showed on every part of him. His eyes shone with unshed tears. Concern. Worry. All the appropriate emotions for a man jilting his bride on their wedding day. But I didn't care, because the relief that was now dripping from his body trumped all his concern. The pity in his eyes fueled a sudden anger inside of me.

"She's in the audience, you know."

"I know," he said.

"She was always really nice to me. Was it fake?"

"No. She liked you, too. She feels awful."

I nodded numbly. "Yeah. I'm sure she does."

He eyed me warily but said nothing.

"How long?"

Swallowing, he glanced away. "A few months."

My knees nearly buckled beneath me. Tyler and I had only dated for eight months. We had been engaged for three of those. Which meant…

"The whole time we were engaged, you were seeing her?"

"Not the whole time."

"Explain to me your thought process when we were picking out invitations and rings and tuxedos. What were you planning to do? Was waiting until the last possible second your master plan?"

"No!" He stood up from the couch. "We tried to stop seeing each other. We knew it was wrong, but things just happened."

"Stop saying that! Things do not JUST HAPPEN. You LET them happen. You chose her and were playing me."

"I'm sorry, Tess! I'm so sorry."

It was done. Over. In the space of three minutes, my wedding dress had been reduced to a costume. A hundred guests waited for us out front. Perhaps they were more clued in on what was going on than I had been. They all probably knew by now. A groom taking off during the ceremony was a definite red flag.

"I'm going to go change. You're going to go tell everybody the wedding is off. I'm sure my dad and brother will want to chat." I shouldn't have felt the twinge of glee at the panicked look in his eyes at the mention of my dad and Nate, who were both well over six feet. He deserved all of it. If he slinked out of here without a black eye, it would be a true miracle. And I didn't care.

"Tell Camille I said hi."

I flew past him, went up the stairs to my room, and flung myself down onto my bed, covering my face with my pillow and doing my very best to block out the past eight months.

———

LOGAN WAS quiet after I finished my story. I had nothing else to say, so I waited in the silence. The sound of the river floating lazily next to us left me feeling deceptively calm. Or maybe it was retelling the whole story from my perspective to new ears. Ears belonging to someone who *wasn't* being paid to help me dissect all the associated emotions.

His voice was a husky rumble when he spoke. "When I figured out who he was at the store, I had very vivid thoughts on where I could shove one of your tampons, but I played nice because you were playing nice. Now, I'm wishing I could do it all over again. I know just the spot…"

A soft laugh escaped me. "Telling Camille that she should put some ice on that was good enough for me."

He made a noise somewhere between a grunt and a sigh. "That all really sucks, Tess."

"I'm over it. I've dealt with this for over a year. I promise, I'm okay. Seeing Tyler tonight was actually good for me, I think." Trying to lighten the mood, I looked over at him and added, "That tackle really brought things full circle."

Sometime during my story, we had both turned toward each other, our arms bent beneath our heads for pillows, curled on our sides. He didn't laugh at my joke, but he watched me, instead, with hooded eyes. When he spoke again, his words were soft and seemed controlled, like he was afraid to give too much but was determined to say something.

"You had a good family life growing up. Good parents. Which is ideal, you know, but it can make it easy to be naive going into relationships sometimes." He jerked his hand between us. "Not that being naive is a bad thing necessarily, it can just…make it hard to see the warning signs."

"Yes." I leaned forward, my thoughts animated with validation all of a sudden. "Looking back, there were so many times with Tyler where I should have questioned his actions. Anybody else probably would have, but I never did."

My breathing slowed, and I willed my limbs to not make any sudden movements. I didn't want to break the mood. I was a walking contradiction, ignoring the warning sign flashing in my mind. For the good of the bet, we should have stopped the conversation right there. It was too dangerous. Too cozy. I had told him too much. It was exactly what Jake would have wanted to happen.

But Jake hadn't been a part of this date, and I wasn't ready for him to make an appearance.

"Is that what happened to you? Were you too naive?" I sucked in a breath, waiting for him to shut this down.

There was a long pause before he said, "Yeah. The untold tragic tale of a lucky childhood."

"Your parents are awesome."

"I know."

I knew he was finished, even as I hoped for more. He had given me a crumb into his past. The tiniest gift ever. But I wanted to guard it and keep it safe because I knew the admission had cost him something. So, I held out my fist. He stared at me, confusion wrinkled in his brow.

"Here's to hugging our parents more, being less naive, and making better choices." I waved my fist in front of him expectantly.

A smile swept across his face even while he shook his head. He held out his hand, but instead of bumping my fist, he held it in his palm. "I never knew how weird you were, Jailbait. You know, other than the love notes and the laundry room."

I moved in closer to push against his hand. Teasing. But he kept his hold on me a moment longer than necessary. The ever-evolving mood between us had changed once again, and prickles of awareness began spilling out across my body. His eyes were almost hidden from me in the dark, but I felt them everywhere, igniting fires across my body. I wanted him to kiss me, I realized. It was happening just as I had predicted—the worst-case scenario playing out before my very eyes.

He blinked, his body giving the tiniest jerk like he was awakening from a dream. He released me, sat up, and ran a hand through his hair.

"I'd better get you home, Jailbait. Or else Jake will have the shotgun out."

17

TESSA

"It's been forty-eight hours. Are we to the point where we can laugh about you tackling Camille, yet?" Kelsey asked over the phone on Monday afternoon. "Because I could be there if you are..."

"No," I said, adding the last cup of flour to the mixer. I had gotten most of my work done earlier this afternoon. My mom was covering the produce stand, so I snuck into the kitchen to relieve some stress.

"Are you sure?"

"Kels, I *smashed* into her with a huge box of tampons that went flying. NO."

There was a long, suspicious silence on her end. I patiently waited for her to catch her breath.

"Sorry. I was...about to sneeze."

"I hate you. How are my favorite twins doing?" I asked, changing the subject while turning the KitchenAid on.

"I had my four-month check up this morning, and everything looks great. And I finally don't feel like puking all day."

I laughed. "Have you guys picked names yet?"

Kelsey groaned. "None that we can agree on. He's convinced he wants Dodger for one and Hank for the other."

"Wait. Dodger, like his horse on your dad's farm?"

"Dodger like The Dodgers and Hank like Hank Aaron. Baseball stuff."

I smiled while I prepared the raspberry filling. "Oh. And you don't want Dodger and Hank?"

"Would you?"

I laughed. "I'm still holding out hope that the technician read the ultrasound wrong and they're really girls with an extra finger or something."

"Don't curse the ultrasound. I'm finally accepting the fact that I'll be a boy mom and outnumbered by two more mini-Cades."

This time, it was her turn to change the subject. "Are you baking something? I don't know the sound personally, but I'm gonna guess I just heard a mixer."

"I'm impressed by your Martha Stewart detection skills."

"Which one of your patients drove you to the kitchen today?"

"I'm always in the kitchen," I said automatically. But in truth, it had been Preacher Douglass. He was the nicest man in the world, if a little clumsy, but try and get him to do a few exercises, and a world war breaks out.

"When's your next date with my brother?" Kelsey asked.

"It's on Thursday this week. At the bonfire and fugitive game Jake's planning with everybody coming home for the Fourth."

"Oh yeah, Cade mentioned something like that. So, you guys will be on a date there? I thought you wanted to keep it quiet."

"It will be quiet. We have to pair up for the fugitive game, and it will be dark."

A long silence ensued. "So, you'll be alone in the dark with my brother?"

"Sounds like it." I did not appreciate the tone of her voice.

"And this will be one month since you guys started this dating thing?"

"Yuuup."

"Which is at least two weeks longer than anybody I've heard of him dating in years?"

"I can't confirm or deny that."

I heard the smile in her voice over the phone. "I wasn't a fan of all this at first, but I may be changing my tune. I think Jake really might be some sort of genius."

"We're just friends," I protested, though I couldn't stop my own tiny smile from lighting my face.

"I'm guessing Jake definitely put in some sort of friends-with-benefits clause."

"Gotta go, tell Cade hi for me." I laughed as I ended the call to the sound of her squealing and turned off the mixer. The fact that Kelsey didn't seem as against the idea of Logan and me as a couple relieved me, and I wasn't sure why.

I took the dough out five minutes before it was done kneading in the KitchenAid. With rolled-up sleeves, I used my hands to finish the job. It felt therapeutic to me, pounding and pushing the dough on the counter. Therapeutic with just enough busy work to allow my mind to wander.

Seeing Tyler the other night had thrown me in a way I hadn't been expecting. I hadn't seen him since the wedding. As much as I might have wanted to erase him from my life, it took work to fully disband the blending of two lives. After the fallout, we communicated by text about moving our things out of the apartment we had rented together, making sure to go at separate times. There had been light contact about random things that had filled our lives for the past eight months together. Things like:

Tyler: I have your sweatshirt. Where do you want me to put it?
Me: Mailbox. Thanks.

He had ripped me from his life. Cold and impersonal. We had been polite but terse toward each other. Other than the shocked words I'd spoken to him on our wedding day, every other thought and feeling had been stuffed so far down to a place only my therapist could pull out of me.

At the wedding, when I found everything out, I imagined him and Camille sneaking around his office, making out in coat closets and on top of desks (thank you, romantic comedies). But seeing them together, I guessed it wasn't like that at all. They weren't bad people. There had been true sorrow and guilt in Tyler's eyes on our wedding day. They made mistakes—huge mistakes. I certainly wasn't justifying them, but did we all have to suffer for the rest of our lives? I didn't have to hold onto this darkness. This grudge. Even months later, when I had claimed to be over it, there was still a weight there, pulling me down even as I marched forward with my life, guns blazing.

I had been holding onto something that was no longer mine. No matter what happened to get us to this point, he wasn't mine. Even more…I no longer wanted him. Not in the way that I had told myself for the past year, out of spite or hurt. Not in the way I talked it through with my therapist. Even after a whole year of trying to erase Tyler's impact on my life, deep down there had been a part of me still waiting for him. Waiting for him to admit that he had made a mistake. Waiting for him to come running back to me. Holding onto him in a way that never allowed me to turn the page on a chapter that was finished.

Tyler was now a guy I used to know.

Watching Tyler and Camille stand there together, their incredulous glances back and forth, his hand on her shoulder and looking very much like a couple, had been therapeutic in a way. He wasn't mine. They were happy together. He wasn't going to be crawling back to me with his tail between his legs. And I was fine with that. More than fine, actually. That night had given me closure on something that had been holding me back in my life.

And that was the kind of knowledge that could set a person free.

THE NEXT MORNING, I opened the front door at 6 a.m. to head out for a run and was surprised to find Nate on the porch. He was dressed in running clothes with a blue sweatband around his head. He looked out of place. He also looked like he had been waiting for me.

This was new.

"Um, hey," I said, stepping out onto the porch. "You're going to get beat up in this neighborhood with a sweatband like that."

"Don't be jealous." He smiled at me, his blond hair catching the sun so bright it began burning my retinas. "You up for a run?"

My eyes narrowed even as I bumped against his shoulder. "Why do I feel like this is a calculated encounter?"

He gave an exaggerated gasp. "What? I'm here to exercise and thought I'd come drag your lazy butt out of bed."

I laughed while doing a few quick stretches. There was a six-year difference between Nate and me. Growing up, it seemed like we were always a stage or two off. By the time I was five or six and wanted to go build dirt forts or hunt bugs, he had passed that stage and was into shooting hoops with his friends. By the time I got old enough to shoot hoops decently, he was eighteen and leaving home. I had no real complaints—he had been a good brother, and I have lots of good memories—but it wasn't until my residency at his office in Vegas that we had really bonded. As adults, we were finally on a more level playing field and had been able to truly connect.

Most importantly, I learned exactly how Type A he really was, so I spent much of my free time at the office in Vegas, turning product labels around backward, moving papers off kilter on his desk, and putting the scissors in his drawer where the (gasp) stapler belonged.

We spent the first two miles of our run talking about the new office. Correction: *Nate* spent the first two miles talking about the new office.

"And then I thought we could get a Jacuzzi sometime in that back room? For some water therapy."

"Yeah. Sounds good." I concentrated on my breathing. Nate's legs were longer than mine, and it was throwing my pace off.

"And then maybe a giraffe for the storage room. And I think a tiny kite room might be perfect for the little patients."

"Hmm. Okay."

"TESSA."

I jolted. "What?"

"You're not listening to anything I'm saying."

"I was down with the giraffe idea."

"What's going on?"

We turned off of Main Street and onto a back road through the fields. "Honestly, the building itself doesn't interest me that much. It's yours. I'm just working there."

He was quiet for a minute. I was hoping he was being quiet because running with me was too tiring for him, but one glance at his relaxed face and that thought was extinguished. He hardly looked winded. Logan would have passed out by now. Not that I'd ever run with Logan, but we'd hiked, so...

"Do you want it to be yours too?"

I stumbled over a rock and almost fell before I caught myself. Did I want that?

I had some savings, but it had significantly lessened after I bought my car. I had never really considered getting money from Jake's truck, but now I allowed my mind to go there.

He continued, "I never meant for you *not* to have a part ownership in this. I just knew you didn't have the kind of money to invest yet. You're fresh out of PT school, who does?"

"I don't," I said. "But I do have...a few things in the works. Can I think on it?"

"Sure."

He waited until the last mile before he brought up Logan, which was about four miles longer than I thought it would take.

"What's going on with you and Logan Marten?"

I gave him a sidelong glance. "Why?"

"Just curious."

"You act like he's a stranger to me, but he's honestly like another brother." Ew. That was a lie. "I practically lived at his house growing up."

"Are you dating him?"

"We're hanging out this summer to pass the time." I kept my voice even and light so he wouldn't suspect a thing.

"That kiss last week looked like maybe you were something."

I worked hard to keep the smile off my face. "That was all just a joke."

"Even I know you used to have a creepy scrapbook with his face all over it. You're not fooling me."

My stomach dropped. "What? How did you know that?"

He started to laugh. "You left it out on your bed once, and I leafed through it."

"Oh my gosh." I upped my pace to leave him in the dust before he grabbed my arm, laughing, and pulled me back.

"It just confirmed what I already knew about you. You're a freak."

"Do not tell anybody about that."

"I knew this kind of knowledge would come in handy one day."

I glowered at him.

He chuckled. "I'm not worried at all about you. I want to make sure *he* knows who he's hanging out with."

"We're just friends."

"Mom and Dad tell me you've gone on a few dates."

"It's nothing."

"He's got quite the reputation."

"Are you still mad about high school? You know he didn't really steal your girlfriend. She came on to him *after* you broke up with her."

He gave me the side-eye as we both picked up our pace with our childhood house in sight. "What? How did you know about that?"

"Just assume everybody knows everything in this town."

He rolled his eyes. "I'm not still mad about anything." He flashed me his ring. "Happily married. This is about you. If he's changed and different from what I hear about him, great. If you really are just friends and passing time this summer, fine. But you liked him a lot at one point, and your bright-red face right now gives me that same impression. I'm telling you to use caution, that's all." He pointed toward our childhood home, now only a hundred yards away. "First one to the house wins."

We took off sprinting, laughing, and holding each other's arms back in our effort to win. When we finally collapsed onto the porch swing, I was gratified to see a few drops of sweat beading on his forehead.

"So far, this all seems like a pretty civil ultimatum. Aren't you supposed to tell me to stop seeing him or else?"

"Nah, I don't like you that much." He nudged my arm as I leaned my head against the back of the swing, lungs burning and needing to stretch, but no longer wanting to move. "If he hurts you, then I'll kill him, but until then, it's your call."

18

LOGAN

The smell of wood and smoke filled the air as I parked the four-wheeler next to a sea of trucks behind my parents' house. It was July 3rd. As was tradition, many old friends had come home for Eugene's Fourth of July celebration.

Jake had prepared a blast from the past with all of our friends. First up, dinner and a bonfire while we waited for the sun to go down. Afterward, he organized a game of *fugitive*. A small crowd of people gathered around the bonfire. Jake had sent me to the house to grab a handful of camp chairs and the bag of hot dogs I'd been tasked to bring. I tried refusing to allow my eyes to search out for one face in particular, but they scanned the crowd anyway. Tessa wasn't here yet.

Disappointment and relief washed over me, and I hated myself for both emotions.

"Hey, Marten." My boss, Chase Riley, saw me approach the bonfire and made his way over to me. He had the build of a football player and the easy manner of somebody who liked people. He talked as friendly to a banker investing in a construction project as he did to the lowliest framer on his payroll. He was a great boss.

I shook his hand. "Hey. You been out to the site yet?"

"Just came from there. Looks good. Moving along quicker than I thought it would. Has Nate been any trouble?" He adjusted the baseball hat on his head, giving me the tiniest hint of his thinning brown hair before he covered it up.

"No. No trouble." Nate hadn't even brought up seeing me with Tessa a couple weeks ago at the site. He hadn't been any trouble, which had surprised me.

Chase's brow furrowed. "Really? He told me he had you add a few more electrical outlets. Hadn't you already started to Sheetrock?"

I mentally punched myself. He meant *work Nate*, not *Tessa's brother, Nate*. "Oh, that. Yeah, we figured it out." It took a whole day, and we had to redo a completed wall of Sheetrock, but we ran a few extra outlets for Tessa's perfectionist brother.

Chase looked at me like something amused him. "How are you liking being back in Eugene?"

I shifted uncomfortably. "It's alright."

He stared at me for a long moment before his lips lifted at the corners. "From what I hear, it's been better than alright."

My body froze. Abort. Abort.

Before I could reply, we were joined by Cade and Kelsey and a few others. I stopped looking Chase in the eye. The next few minutes passed by in a blur of familiar faces. My body felt on autopilot as I laughed, and shook hands, and slapped shoulders with old friends. I think I even re-hashed a few stories, but so far, the night felt like an opening act at a concert. Second-rate. The music you had to politely wait through before the headliner took the stage.

I was in the middle of a conversation with my brother-in-law, Cade, and my sister when a familiar truck pulled up.

My first instinct was to run to her, which scared the crap out of me, so I forced my body to stay where it was. Kelsey squealed and ran forward to greet her friend, leaving me alone with Cade.

I tried to not stare. Cade was talking, and I focused on his face for as long as possible before my eyes darted another glance at Tessa. It was just for a second before I brought them back to our conversation, but Cade saw.

He looked at me and back at Tessa with great interest brimming on his face. "Down, boy. She's coming."

Immediately, I deflated. Freaking Jake. Did *everybody* know about Tessa's and my arrangement? With some effort, I wiped the excited-puppy-dog look from my face.

Cade chuckled. "I'll bet if you ask real nice, she'll give you a treat."

I scowled at him. "It's not like that."

He nodded sardonically. "I know. You don't look like a man who's been whipped at all."

We looked toward the girls, now walking toward us. Tessa's gaze lifted to meet mine, her soft eyes holding me captive.

"Logan."

I looked at Cade but was surprised to find his expression was serious.

"It's a good look for you," he said simply.

Tessa wore jeans and a simple black t-shirt. Her hair was in a pony-tail. She smiled at me as she made her way closer. The crowd became blurred as my focus narrowed.

I was attracted to Tessa Robbins. I could admit that much. Any man would be. That wasn't the problem here—well, not the biggest problem, anyway. For the first time in years, I found myself wanting to tell a woman things. Specific things. The other day at work, I picked up my phone *three* different times, wanting to text her something, and every time, I stopped myself. I went to her house yesterday to work on the porch, and instead of working, I spent my time helping her trim the yard and setting up tables and chairs for their neighborhood get-together on the 4th. Things a boyfriend would do. The word escaped from my consciousness like it was dripping with venom.

I needed to backtrack. We had to keep things light this summer. I was the one who had put the rules into place. *Me.* It was *my* job to keep us in check. Tessa was still very much a wild card. The queen of mixed signals. And I was afraid that if I failed to enforce our rules, there would be nothing holding me together anymore.

But did she have to be so dang likable?

"Hey, Tess," I greeted, giving her a casual nod. Because that was how I felt right now. *Casual.*

Her eyes trailed down my body briefly and back up while I told myself the heat I felt was from the fire blazing several feet in front of us.

"You clean up pretty good, Marten," she said.

I felt the eyes of the group on me, as if waiting for something. Well, they weren't going to get it.

"Thanks," I said, shoving my hands in my pockets where they belonged.

The girls immediately began talking a mile a minute about pregnancy cravings, Cade's pranks, and old inside jokes.

"Should I just pick my wife up from your house in a few days when it's time to go home?" Cade asked Tessa.

Tessa grinned at him. "Look, Kels, your husband is learning so fast."

I studied Cade for a moment. I wasn't sure if it was vet school or being married to my sister, but something about him felt different to me. He still dressed like he always did. His baseball hat still covered up his frumpy brown hair, but he looked different somehow. Older? More mature? I couldn't put my finger on it.

Soon, we were surrounded by familiar faces—some I hadn't seen for years. Old friends from school and softball summers sat in lawn chairs scattered around the large flames. The sun had lowered in the sky, casting long shadows across the farm.

Jake, the instigator of it all, sat in the middle of the group, laughing, joking, and throwing mild shade at everyone. I didn't understand how he could get this ragtag group of friends and acquaintances of all ages together, but I could see how people would come to just be near Jake.

A black truck rumbled to a stop behind us, and we all turned and watched as Dusty stepped out. His black cowboy hat, jeans, and timid smile was a welcome sight for sore eyes. But none were sorer than Jake's. With a whoop, he ran over to his best friend and jumped into his waiting arms.

"Who's the girl?" Tessa whispered to me. The entire group of friends was all captivated, no longer by Dusty and Jake, but by a pretty, black-haired pixie with glasses that got out of the passenger side of the truck and made her way over to the boys. Dusty was laughing at something Jake had said while he reached over and casually draped his arm over the girl's shoulders.

"You don't know?

"What?"

"Dusty's got a girlfriend."

"What?" she gasped, assessing the brunette settling into Dusty's side. "How come I didn't know this?"

"You're not as popular as me, I guess."

"Hasn't he only been gone a year?" she asked.

"Just over a year." I was mildly impressed. "Pretty fast work for Dusty."

She raised her eyebrows at me. "If he moved by your standards, he'd already be working his way through girl number five by now."

I gave her a light nudge. "You're telling me. I've been stuck on one girl for a whole month now. It can't be good for me."

The smile that escaped her lips shot a heat wave through my entire body. That's right, Marten. Flirt *more* with the girl you're trying to not think about.

"Is this your girlfriend, Dust?" came a cheeky question from someone behind me.

Dusty's face widened into an easy smile. "She is, so don't get any ideas." To the group, he said, "Everyone, this is Lucy."

Lucy blushed slightly at the attention but smiled sweetly to everyone, leaning into Dusty's side.

The rest of our time at the bonfire was spent with me trying to resist a close proximity to Tessa, to then being unable to help myself, to quickly whispering in her ear a joke that I knew she'd laugh at. I had given myself a strict no-touching rule for the rest of the night but couldn't help the accidental leaning into her shoulder, or brushing up against her arm, or nudging her leg. There was a disconnect somewhere between my body and my brain. So, I would move to a different spot and force myself to talk to other people before the pattern would start all over again.

The evening wore on. It wouldn't be long now before the four-wheelers would start up and the field games would begin. After the hot dogs and s'mores, we all stood, casually mingling in small groups, talking and catching up. Kelsey had complained quietly about her back pinching in one spot as she shifted uncomfortably. Cade stood on the other side of her, talking to Chase, and without skipping a beat in his conversation, his hand dropped to her back and began rubbing at just the right spot, as if he'd done it a hundred times before.

I knew right then what it was that felt different about him. I had finally put my finger on it. Cade had always had this easy, fun-loving way about him. He had that still, but gone was his restlessness. His impatience. He was settled. At peace. He had the girl he'd loved since childhood in his arms.

The big brother in me was glad to see my sister so happy, but something unsettling clanged around inside of me as I watched them. Since my relationship with Valerie had imploded all those years ago, I had shut out people. Women. A protective layer of bubble wrap had grown around my heart. I had some good friends, but beyond watching a game on TV and golfing on the weekends, talking about jobs and the weather, things never ran too deep. Watching Cade with my sister, I realized it was his connection to her that had me entranced. It wasn't the touching. It was the feeling of knowing just *where* to touch. It was the vulnerability of showing another person where something hurt.

There had been a moment after Tessa had told me about Tyler where I wanted to give her something. The feeling had startled me, but I had been so far out of practice with real connection I couldn't have begun to scrounge up what she was asking for. Things were buried too deep. It went against all of our rules. And for the first time since Jake put this whole bet thing into play, I resented it.

As the twilight dissolved into darkness, we put out the fire and meandered toward the barn where the four-wheelers were waiting. I made my way to Tessa's side as we pulled away from the group.

"Have you been practicing for this, Marten?" Tessa asked, leaving her stupid, lonely hand dangling at her side. "I better tell you now. I will leave you in the dust if you hold me back."

"Are you asking if I've been running on purpose? It's like you don't even know me at all."

She laughed. "You and Kelsey are the same person."

"I bet you haven't kissed Kelsey before."

Instantly, her head swiveled around, making sure nobody was close enough to hear that remark. I didn't quite understand why I was being flirtatious when I had just told myself I had to stop. It was something I couldn't seem to turn off, even if I really needed to.

"That doesn't count, Marten," she said. "I used to kiss my grandma on her cheek all the time."

"Was I better than your grandma? As far as cheek kisses go?"

She shrugged. "Eh. You were a little sweaty. She usually fed me dry cookies and smelled like peppermint. I'd say she was a solid eight, and you were maybe a seven."

I laughed, bumping the side of her arm in the dark. "Well, we can't have that."

What was I doing?

The past few years, I had been happy with what I had chosen for my life. Plenty of fun. No drama. No wife. No drama. Did I say that already? I could make my own decisions. If I wanted to go on vacation for a month, I didn't have to run it by anybody besides my work. I made my own money and spent it how I wanted. I could go out with the guys every night of the week if I wanted to. I met lots of cool women, keeping things to one or two dates. I'd go to work every day, and then I'd come home to an empty house every night and do it all again the next week.

Empty house.

I was hoping that phrase still sounded good after a summer in the company of Tessa Robbins.

19

TESSA

"Alright, everyone shut up!"

The excited chatter in the field lulled to a quiet buzz, thanks to Jake's good-natured shouting. He stood in the bed of his old pickup truck, speaking to the rest of us who were watching him from the ground. The full moon had come out for the game to give us just enough light. A breeze carrying the scent of freshly baled hay lifted the wisps of hair off my face. Kelsey and Cade stood next to Logan and me in the dark, Kelsey's four-month-pregnant belly protruding adorably. Cade had his arm wrapped casually around his wife's shoulders.

There was nobody happier for my best friend than me. But looking at her and her life with Cade—the vet schooling, the teaching job, living in Colorado, and the babies on the way—their life had so much meaning. Their future together was brimming with opportunity and excitement. I suddenly ached for how much seemed to be missing in mine.

I was locked in a weird game where I won a prize if I *didn't* fall in love. I was back to dating a player, somebody who saw me as a means to an end. This time, it was forty thousand dollars. I was not innocent in these games either, but I was starting to wonder if I had bitten off more than I could chew. The past few days, I had begun to sense a shift in myself. It was happening just as I had feared. Logan's facade was fading just enough for him to wheedle his way into my heart. I would be the only one hurt at the end of this summer. And yet…here I stood.

"Everyone remember how to play *fugitive*?"

There were murmurs of 'yes' in the crowd, but Jake explained the rules briefly anyway.

"There are fifteen fugitives, two cops, and one guard." Jake pointed toward Kelsey and her bulging belly. "Kelsey has been nominated to stand guard so she's not diving through ditches and climbing fences in her delicate condition."

A few whistles and shouts rang out in the crowd. A few of the guys clapped a grinning Cade on the back. I watched Kelsey, waiting for the hormonal firecracker to protest. And the lady did not disappoint.

"Hey! What? Who nominated me? I don't need to stand guard. I'm not that far along."

Jake made a face. "I'm not stepping into the middle of this. Cade, control your woman."

"Control my *what*? Have you ever met my wife?" Cade quickly pulled her into a bear hug from behind, covering her mouth with his hand before saying to Jake, "Keep her as a guard and I'll take one for the team."

"From the looks of you two disgusting lovebirds, I think you'll be fine."

When Kelsey finally wrangled her mouth free from his hand, Cade turned her to face him and dropped a kiss on her lips. When he finally allowed Kelsey to break free, she was all smiles, hiding her face in Cade's laughing chest.

I bit my lip, smiling, craving a love like that so badly it almost hurt to look at it.

"Alright, as for the rest of you, Layne and Frank will drive us out and drop us off in a pasture two miles away before they jump onto a four-wheeler and become our cops for the night."

Logan's dad and my dad grinned at us while they revved up their high-powered four-wheelers.

"The object of the game," Jake continued, "is to make your way back to Marten's barn without being caught by a cop. Once there, if you make it, the flag will be somewhere along the front side of the barn. If Kelsey tags you, you're out. If you are caught by the cops in a field, you're out. You're welcome to dive through ditches, and we have permission to use the hay fields surrounding us within a one-mile radius, but beyond that, you may get shot. Stay out of the corn field, and if you step into any potato field, it's an automatic out, and…" he continued dramatically, "you may be shot."

At that, we climbed into the backs of pickup trucks. Logan followed behind and sat next to me on the floorboard. He originally left a few inches of space between us, but as more people climbed in, eventually the whole side of his body pressed against mine. I became extremely aware of every bump in the road that would cause his body to attach to mine like a BandAid. He'd been playing the crowd all night, laughing with friends, but anytime he wasn't physically near me, his eyes had always found mine.

We were dumped in the middle of a stubbled hay field with only the stars and moon to guide our steps. Layne informed us we would have a five-minute head start to scatter and hide before the four-wheelers came hunting.

Jake gave us both a pat on the back. "Well, you two, good luck out here. Don't forget to hold hands. Sure would hate for you to get lost in the dark." Then, he ran off with the rest of the crowd, scattering down to groups of two or three, leaving Logan and me by ourselves.

"Alone in the dark. About time Jake has a good idea."

I turned toward him. "What are we supposed to do out here in the dark all by ourselves?"

"I'd rather not talk about it, but I'd be happy to show you." He folded his arms and smirked at me.

I hesitated, my eyes dropping to his lips for a split second before blinking me out of my stupor. This Logan wasn't quite what I had in mind tonight.

"I didn't know you enjoyed stargazing so much." I began walking in the field toward the house. We needed to be running, but I thought I'd give Logan a chance to warm up.

"Is that what the kids are calling it these days?"

I shook my head and pushed at his arm.

"See any rocks around, Jailbait?"

"Rocks?" I looked around at my feet but it was too dark. I'd need to get on my knees and do some digging. "No."

"I knew we shouldn't have picked them all out of this field." Logan sighed and held out his hand toward me. I pushed back the smile threatening to escape and took it—allowing myself a sweet moment immersed in the feel of his large hand wrapped around mine.

He was silent as we made our way across the hay field, a contemplative air between us. Then, he cleared his throat. "Aren't you a runner, woman? Why are we still walking?"

"You sound like you might be better off walking. Those are some wheezy breaths you got there."

"You're slowing down for me? That sounds almost like you care."

"Kelsey would kill me if I left her brother to die out here. Well, she wouldn't *kill* me, but maybe a stern lecture before we hit up the movies or something."

This was all good. Fun. Felt more like ourselves. Until Logan stumbled over a rock and went flying into a large patch of mud made from water leaking out of the ditch.

I froze in shock. Then, the sight of Logan in a muddy puddle was almost more than my heart could take. His elbows had stopped his face from smashing into the wet mud, but he would be spending a miserable run back to the house in heavy, wet clothes.

"Hey, I should warn you, the field is bumpy. Lots of mouse holes," I couldn't help but add.

Slowly, he rolled over so he was on his back, holding his shoulder. The mud had missed his face and head, but now it was everywhere else.

"You alright?"

"Ow," came his muffled groan.

"Get up," I said, my ears perched in alert as I scanned the fields, hearing the sounds of a distant four-wheeler creeping closer. "We have to move."

"I don't think I can."

"Are you serious?" The urgency in his voice caused my amusement to come to a stop. I leaned toward him but without taking a step closer, just in case.

His right hand massaged his left shoulder. "This is the shoulder I hurt in high school. I think it's jammed. I can't move it."

The four-wheeler was getting close enough that they would soon be able to see us in their spotlight. We were sitting ducks. The only place we could hide and still stand a chance was *in* the ditch, not above it.

"They're getting closer. We need to do something, unless you wanna just call it. We can get caught, if you want." Even as I said the words, it made me a tiny bit sad. We had barely begun the game, and I wanted to steal the flag from Kelsey so I could rub it in her face forever. But those thoughts were petty and selfish. There was a man down. I needed to help. If he needed my strength to hold him up the rest of the game, so be it. If wrapping his arms around my shoulders and leaning his sexy body against mine was going to save him, then I would suck it up and do it.

He took a deep breath and shook his head, nobly insisting we finish this game. My goodness. He really was hurt. Big, tough Logan had gotten himself injured in a little game of fugitive.

"Help me up, and then we can hide in the ditch. I don't think I can crawl there."

Closing the distance between us, I took the hand he had offered. Wait a minute. The *left* hand. The hand with the supposed hurt shoulder. But I realized too late. In a move so swift and sudden, he yanked me to the ground. Only, it wasn't ground I hit but a warm, solid Logan. Instantly, he moved, rolling me over onto my back, the weight of his body on top of mine as his face leaned closer, victorious in the moonlight.

"I KNEW it," I said.

"You didn't know it."

"I thought it at first."

"I should be in Hollywood with that performance."

I rolled my eyes and tried to squirm out from under him, but he held me firm. My whole body erupted in sparks. Fissures. Cracks. Feelings. I couldn't get a full breath, but that was probably due to the 200-pound body lounging comfortably on top of me.

He shifted slightly, taking a bit of the weight off before he leaned over me. The cold ditch water seeped into my clothes, and my hair was squished into the mud, but all I could see was Logan's shadowy eyes raking over my face. He lifted a dirty hand and brushed my hair across my forehead.

"There's been something on my mind the past few days, Jailbait." He swallowed. "Might be a good time to get it out of the way."

Get it out of the way.

I didn't have time to decide how I felt about those words. He was so close. His voice was husky and caused the hair on my arms to stand rigid. All coherent thoughts were nowhere to be found. This would be the end of the game for me. A month ago, when we had made the bet, it was *this* moment that I knew, deep down, would be my downfall. Logan's kiss. The kiss for the bet. The final nail in my coffin of love and denial. To Logan, it was still a game.

His head dropped down, millimeters from my lips, before he hesitated, pulling back to watch me. He was waiting for me, I realized, to give him some signal of permission.

I knew what I had to do. What my heart needed me to do. I was going to win this bet. And in order to win, I had to play the game. But I feared I would also be losing the bet. It was only the first week of July. My heart still had a month and a half to resist. I had to resist. I knew all of this but still couldn't help myself when my head lifted up a fraction, feeling the hint of Logan's lips on mine. A whisper of a touch. Logan sighed and moved closer to me, to fill in the gap, to—

I splatted my mud-filled hands on top of Logan's head. A guttural noise came from the back of his throat, and a tiny part of me appreciated the fact that, for one shining moment, I had taken control. The splash from the mud ricocheted onto my face and arms. I dropped my hands, suddenly nervous about what I had done. Logan stilled. His fiery eyes burned into mine, and a wicked smile unfurled across his lips. Pulling back, he adjusted his position so he sat on top of my legs, his hands holding mine hostage above my head. He leaned forward again as mud and water dripped down the side of his face and onto my cheeks.

"Interesting way to play this, Tess," he whispered. "I've still got the advantage, but now, I'm out for revenge."

He hovered over my face, studying me. My body had gone numb. His weight pressed upon me. Though I knew he would move if I insisted, I was suddenly interested in playing this out. I was right where I had always dreamed of being. I had moved my chess piece without knowing the rules, and now I waited for his next move. My heart would probably be broken either way. Maybe it was okay to let myself have my moment. I wanted it too much. I would piece my heart back together tomorrow.

"Any last words before I get even?" he asked.

"I'm not scared of you." I wasn't scared. Scared was not the right word. I was terrified.

"Good to know."

This time, when he touched his lips against mine, they stayed. He lingered there, giving me time to resist. When I didn't, I felt the full blessed lips of Logan Marten on mine.

For exactly two seconds.

Muffled laughter and shuffling feet were heard in the distance, moving closer. Logan's head lifted, and our bodies stilled, listening for where the noises were coming from, which was hard to hear over my ragged breath.

"They're coming this way." Logan rolled off of me, scooped a handful of mud in his hands, and before I could stop him, he rubbed it into my hair and up the back of my neck. "Now we're even. Follow me. Don't stand up."

I hardly had time to react to the muddy sludge now sliding down the back of my shirt before he motioned me forward. With both of us on our knees, we maneuvered over the ditch bank and into the water. If we were standing, the ditch water would come to our waist. On our knees, it splashed around our chests as the soft dirt squished beneath us. This all seemed so familiar. This was two times now that dirt and mud had played a role in our date night.

I stood, scanning the ditch bank, trying to find an easy spot to crawl out and onto the other side, when Logan pulled me back into the water.

"Company's coming." He sank back to his knees, tugging me down with him, the water slapping against our chests. He moved us behind a patch of overgrown weeds lining the ditch bank. "Shhh." He nodded toward the outline of what looked like Chase and Penny Riley and Nate and Anna about thirty yards away, maneuvering through the water. Squeals of quiet laughter and splashing sounded through the night.

A four-wheeler engine revved suddenly, and a bright spotlight shone into the ditch, illuminating the two pairs of fugitives between us and the road. Logan snaked his arm against my waist and pulled us deeper into the water and against the ditch wall, just beyond the reach of the light.

Good-natured laughter and ribbing ensued down the way from us as the fugitives climbed out of the ditch onto the other side, walking toward Layne Marten who was busy throwing down smack talk and bragging about his big catch.

Logan grinned down at me. "Aww, look at that. My dad almost caught us."

"So did Nate. Let's go. Your dad's distracted."

"Let's wait 'em out for a minute," Logan said. "If we try to climb out of the ditch right now, they'll see us."

With my back pressed against his stomach and his arms tight around my waist, Logan pulled us farther out of the path of the four-wheeler light. I tried very hard not to think about all the bugs and parasites that were probably crawling all over me and focused on the steel bands wrapped across my body.

The spotlight flashed along the ditch, moving the length of the water in front of us, back and forth, searching. The light tapered off where we were hidden, tucked away in the shadows of weeds. Finally, the light shut off, leaving us in eerie darkness once more. The four-wheeler didn't move or turn on, and we were very much aware that Layne Marten was still out there, ears perched, waiting for any sound to alert him in the darkness. The voices of my brother and his friends, the caught fugitives, were muffled as they made their way toward the house, talking and laughing, no longer in need of keeping quiet.

"Are you scared of my brother?" I asked. The thought made me smile.

He slowly turned me to face him. The moonlight caught his eyes and I drew in a breath. There was a soft look to his gaze, no longer teasing. *This* was the Logan I had come here to see tonight. He had made an appearance at the river the week before and I couldn't get him out of my mind. A thrill of anticipation shot up my spine. He moved us both until my back pressed against the dirt wall of the ditch, his face a mere two inches from mine.

"No." He swallowed and looked away as though he were wrestling with something. When he turned back to me, his voice was low and caused goosebumps to scatter across my skin. "I'm scared of myself."

This time, he didn't ask for permission. His mouth that found mine came direct, without hesitation, as if we had been underwater and I was the burst of air he needed. My body stilled upon contact. I didn't know what this all meant. Emotions were a risky business when a bet was involved. He had been teasing about this kiss for a while now, but this didn't seem like a joke. It didn't *feel* like teasing, the way his hands landed in my hair and on my waist, tugging me closer. It didn't *feel* like teasing, the way his body pressed into mine, warm and possessive.

A feeling of hope swirled in and out of my consciousness and began to burn in my chest. The feeling had pricked at my heart for a while now, but I had always pushed it away, aware of the danger. Now, hope began to trickle its way out of my chest and into my fingertips as I traced his strong jaw and wound my fingers through the hair at the nape of his neck. Even though I understood the risk, hope had begun to soften my edges. My head called out in protest, reminding me of things I tried to forget, while my arms settled over his shoulders, pulling him tight against me. If his dad found us now, I would die a thousand deaths, but even that thought couldn't pull me from the fog my brain was currently lost in.

With every dip of his head, every touch of his fingers, my head shouted at me, *He's a player! He's a player! He's a player!* His hot mouth slid against mine, nudging my willing lips open. *He's playing you!* I pressed up against his body, the water splashing between us, making too much noise, both of us not caring. He pulled back to look at me, his shadowy eyes roaming over my face in the darkness. *This is just a game to him! A bet!* I cradled his face in my hands as his insatiable mouth captured mine once more.

Shut up, head.

I don't care.

20

LOGAN

I gripped my hand tight around Tessa's as we ran through the hay field. Our bodies were soaked, making running in our jeans a horrible affair. The weight of my wet pants threatened to expose a lot more than I wanted to.

Apparently, that was the theme for the night.

I noticed Tessa seemed to be having the same difficulty, one of her hands gripped onto mine with the other desperately trying to keep her pants up. Was it appropriate to strip down to one's underwear? With my boxers and Tessa's underwear, it would be basically the same as a swimsuit.

But at the same time...*not* a swimsuit.

I had no notion of time. No way of knowing if the flag had already been captured or if we were going to be strolling in half an hour late amid Jake's annoying, all-knowing eye. My dad had left the ditch eventually, starting up his four-wheeler and moving toward the house, scanning the fields, leaving us the perfect opportunity to remove ourselves from the water. Except, it took me another ten minutes before I even thought about moving. Another five to stop kissing her. And, well...we were late.

The four-wheelers were easy to spot in the dark, even if one couldn't hear the roar of their engines. Both four-wheelers stood guard at the edge of the field closest to the house, moving back and forth, scanning their lights across the dark. I picked up my pace, realizing now, for the first time, that Tessa was probably slowing her stride so I could keep up.

Running in wet jeans had to be the worst form of torture.

One of the worst forms of torture.

Crap.

Tessa stopped suddenly and pointed toward the house, a half mile away now. "I've been watching. There's a dark spot right to the side of your parents' house, where the four-wheelers never go. What is that? Could we sneak in through there?"

I followed her gaze. "That's the bull pen."

"The bull pen?"

"Yeah. A big, mean, hairy bull with horns on his head and a couple of his girlfriends live in there. You're welcome to prance through his house in the dark, but I won't be joining you."

"Chicken."

I was definitely that.

"I think our best bet might be to sneak through the fruit trees in front of the house," I said. "Anywhere else, the cops will spot us for sure. We need places to hide."

"Can't we circle around to the back of your property and surprise them from behind?"

"Those are all potato fields behind our house and to the side."

"What's your dad doing with potato fields?"

"He sold the dairy cows and didn't need as much hay, so he rented some of his land to McMillian Farms to plant potatoes," I said.

"Those punks knew there was no way for us to go behind the house."

"Yup." I motioned to the fruit trees. "What do you think?"

She tightened her hold on my hand. "Sure."

I took a deep breath and braced myself to begin running again. "Try to keep up, Robbins."

She looked over at me. "You want to race?"

"No. Please don't go very fast."

Her soft laughter draped over me like a blanket fresh out of the dryer. I swallowed. We began running again, one of our hands clasped together and holding up our pants with the other. The hand-holding thing was unnecessary. Even Jake would understand. It seemed dumb to do it while running, but I wouldn't be the first to pull away. It was too dark to find a rock to hold. Besides, once you started holding hands with someone, it got awkward to stop. It was easier to keep doing it. To keep torturing yourself.

Crap.

We ran toward the trees, getting into a habit of dropping to an army crawl every time a spotlight flashed our way. I thought we had been caught a hundred times, but no ruckus was ever made about two fugitives running in the dark. The spotlights were swinging back the way they came about every fifteen seconds. We'd run, then we'd drop.

We were back to running again. Tessa stumbled, and my hand gripped hers tightly until she righted herself, then we were back at it. See? That was why we were holding hands. Too dangerous out here not to.

"I should probably warn you about the mouse holes in this field," I said.

"Can it, Marten."

I ran with a stupid smile on my face for a good thirty seconds before catching myself.

I remembered a time as a teenager when my older sister was on some new diet and kept repeating the phrase, "A little tastes the same as a lot," every time she ate anything unhealthy. The phrase had stuck with me for some reason, and now, with every step I took, the words repeated itself.

All lies.

I thought a lot would taste MUCH better than a little.

"Get down." Tessa pulled my hand, and we dropped onto our stomachs as the spotlight swept the area.

We were fifty yards from the trees now, the moonlight illuminating our pathway. The four-wheelers came together and the riders began conversing, leaving a dark gap in the trees. For a dark, shining moment, our pathway was clear.

"Let's go." We pulled each other up, a bit clumsily, and took off again, our pants dragging in the dirt.

"It's probably a good thing you're not running behind me. You'd enjoy this view too much." It was a dumb thing to say. I was surprised she laughed at it. She was definitely getting sick of me bringing up anything from our past, but when her embarrassed smile lit her face, I may as well have won the lottery.

I hadn't planned on kissing Tessa tonight. I mean, sure, I'd *thought* about it, but I thought I had talked myself out of it. When Jake said there had to be a kiss this summer, I had intended on something quick and sweet—a proper ending for a fun summer with a friend. Then, I'd go on my merry way. That kiss had *not* been a proper ending with a friend. *Now,* it would be an awkward middle with an…unclassified blonde female.

But I hadn't wanted to stop.

For the first time in a long while, I found myself beginning to *care* about something. Someone. I'd been going out of my mind at the bonfire before she arrived because I had needed to see her. Only her. I wanted her eyes to light up when I teased her and to hear whatever zinger she'd respond with.

In just a few short weeks, she had taken a needle and begun popping all of the bubble wrap I had so carefully wound around my heart. It happened so subtly at first. One or two pops. Seeing her again, the bet, the teasing back and forth…it was right up my alley. Pop. Pop. Then, I was hanging out on her porch, watching her blush, eating her food. A comfortable easiness between us. Pop. Pop. Then, it was the date in Salmon. The grocery store. The way her arm clung to my waist, depending on me to keep her upright. The soft lilt of her voice when she told me about Tyler. Her vulnerability. The way I wished I could let myself do the same. The way I had wanted to kiss her right then. Not for a bet. For me.

Pop. Pop. Pop.

The front porch. Her sun-tanned legs and teasing smile. And then, tonight at the bonfire. Where there had been too much and not enough space between us. Where I made up stupid things to tell her so I could lean close and whisper in her ear. Where everything collided with a kiss and a woman that was unlike any other for me. Years of layers and resistance were threatening to collapse. I had worked so hard to keep myself guarded. To shut people out. Rejecting them first to keep myself safe.

But Tessa Robbins was a hard one to resist.

We were off once more. A twig snapped beneath my foot as we ran full speed. By the time the cop had turned his four-wheeler around and came prowling over to where we had last been, we were safely tucked away behind a large apple tree. We ducked low into the weeds and grasses while the light passed above our heads.

"Now, we just need to outsmart your sister," Tessa said, her gaze locked onto the barn. We couldn't see Kelsey, but she had to have been out there. "Where do you think she's hiding?"

I scanned the area. "My guess is she's to the side of the barn. Close access to the door, but out of sight."

"I think one of us needs to distract her," Tessa said.

"Do you see Cade anywhere? We could probably bribe him to take care of that."

"I don't see him, actually." Tessa squinted into the dark toward the group. "I wouldn't put it past him to already be distracting her."

If that was true, I was beginning to think my brother-in-law had the right idea. We were so close to the end. So close to being discovered. We were on our knees on the other side of the tree, facing the house. The group of caught fugitives was under the porch light, draped in lawn chairs on the grass, laughing and carrying on. Kelsey and Cade were probably making out by the barn. Nobody cared anymore. I didn't care anymore.

"How many do you count over there?" she whispered.

"At least eleven or so. Not sure. We might be the only ones left."

"I say we make a run for it." Tessa turned toward me as she stood up, carefully keeping herself in the shadow of the tree. I followed suit, leaning in close, wanting to feel her close by but not wanting to admit it out loud. Bumping, jostling, and nudging were things that happened in the dark. I was getting greedy now.

She peered up at me. "You good with running? I'm starting to not care. I just want to get out of these clothes."

My mouth opened, but words failed me and I could only blink like the hormonal boy I was coming out of a daydream. She gave a soft laugh. "What's with you tonight? Well, I'm going for it."

Me too.

"Hold up, Tess." I grabbed her hand before I could think anything through and pulled her back toward me. If I was going down in flames tonight, I was going to light myself up like a blazing inferno. She looked at me in question. I was questioning myself as well, but I couldn't find it in me to stop. "I don't know if I'm ready for our night to be over just yet."

She looked down as my fingers tugged the bottom of her shirt, pulling her the last few inches to me. "Do we need to have another check-in?"

I smiled, my arms making themselves at home around her waist, and brought up the bet, which was the quickest way to put a boundary between us while still being able to get close to her again. "Jake said it had to be good. I can't, in good conscience, let us leave here without making sure I covered my bases. The one earlier was just so messy and…"

HOT.

She nodded softly, her hands on my shoulders. "It was really bad."

I nuzzled my face closer, my forehead on hers. "I'm going to kiss you again, Jailbait. But you aren't allowed to read anything into it. I'm doing a thorough job of this bet for Jake's sake. Alright? We're getting this all out of our system, and then we won't need to do it anymore. Got it?"

"Yeah."

She had barely gotten the word out before I kissed her. An explosion of warm sweetness filled my mouth. She clung to me, her hands in my hair, giving back as good as I gave. My hands followed suit with my adolescent-boy vibe. They were everywhere—at least, everywhere that wouldn't get me shot by her dad. Or Nate. They were both still out there somewhere, after all. She was my little sister's best friend. But that was the thing when a man started kissing somebody they used to know. Somebody who used to have very clear lines drawn around them. Kid-sister lines. Too-young lines. Jailbait lines. Things were starting to blur, starting to—

"Well, ain't this a nice turn of events?"

Jake's voice broke into my dream like the sound of my niece playing her school recorder. Horrifying. Grating. Tessa and I pulled apart somewhat sheepishly. Jake was leaning against the next apple tree over, arms folded, and staring at us with a self-satisfied smile on his face.

"It's not what it looks like," I began.

"Oh, I think it's exactly what it looks like."

"Just fulfilling the bet," I declared, cringing as Tessa wrapped her arms around herself at my words.

He took a loud bite of an apple. "So, there won't be any more kissing now that you've got it over with?"

I met Tessa's gaze as I was suddenly unsure of what to say. Her face gave me no clues, so I said, "Yup."

Jake laughed, rubbing his hands with glee. "It's hard being right all the time."

The four-wheelers revved their engines and began making their way toward us. Toward the noise. Freaking Jake.

"I'm so overjoyed right now I'll even take one for the team." Jake motioned for us to make a run for it. "The flag's inside the barn. Cade and Kelsey are on the left side, but I haven't seen any activity over there for a while. I didn't know I'd find it right here."

"Shut up, Jake." I automatically grabbed Tessa's hand before dropping it like fire. Without sparing me a glance, she took a step away from me and grabbed a rock to hold onto. I did the same, feeling like a first-class jerk as I did so.

We made a run for it at about the same time Jake turned toward the four-wheelers closing in and walked out with his hands in the air, dramatic to the end.

And when I said *we made a run for it*, I should have said, *Tessa made a run for it*. I was somewhere between a hobble and a punk kid pulling up his pants at every step. She reached the barn before me and yanked open the door. The flag was sitting on the old milk tank. Was it really that easy? Tessa grabbed the flag, and we walked back outside.

We turned the corner to the dark side of the barn where closer inspection revealed a sleeping Cade and Kelsey, sitting on a hay bale, holding hands, with their heads resting against the barn, clearly not giving a hoot about anything this game had to offer.

Just like I predicted. Nobody cared.

We should have never gotten out of that ditch.

Me: Check-in time, Jailbait.

Tess: I'm not sure you can be trusted.

Me: What on earth do you mean?

Tessa: I think you know.

Me: First up, no more running. Especially on a date with me. It will kill you one day.

Tessa: That jaunt back to your barn? It felt more like a brisk walk to me.

Me: You wound me, woman. You got anything?

Tessa: No more kissing?

Me: What's with the question mark?

Tessa: Typo?

Me: Interesting.

Tessa:

Me: I'm leaving for the cattle drive in two days, Jailbait. Stay out of trouble.

Tessa: Have fun.

21

TESSA

"I want out," I told Jake over the phone two days later.

"Who is this?"

"You heard me, Jake."

Jake sighed. I heard a low rumble in the background. It sounded like he was on a tractor. "What do you mean you want out?"

"It means I don't want to play this game anymore."

"It's not a game. It's a bet."

I shoved a piece of warm cookie into my mouth before scooping the fresh cookies off of the pan and onto a cooling rack. "Betting is a game. A stupid, dumb game. And I knew it was a stupid game when I agreed to it. And boys are dumb."

"Those sound like the words of somebody in love," he said, sounding very pleased with himself.

"Jake."

"Give me a half hour, and I'll meet you out at your pond."

"Why the pond?"

"My work is done for the day. If I have to go girl-talk with you, my consolation prize is that I'm fishing at the same time."

I went ahead and shoved another bite into my mouth, letting the warm chocolate make me feel better. "Why do I put up with you?"

"My mom calls me a sweetie-pie."

"Ew. See you in a few."

I BROUGHT MY FISHING POLE, too. It took me five minutes of rummaging around the basement storage room to find the pole, only to spend another five minutes untangling the line from three other poles that hadn't been used in a decade.

It felt weird having a Saturday night without seeing Logan. Jake had counted our date from Thursday since the rest of the weekend we'd both be with our families over the Fourth of July. My family had hosted our annual neighborhood get-together, where Logan had made an appearance along with a hundred of our closest neighbors and family. Though he had been friendly, he had also been noticeably distant, which led to an impressive internal freak-out on the part of yours truly. Hence me calling Jake in a panic.

I had dragged two camp chairs to the pond. I sat in one while waiting for Jake and enticing the fish with a half-mauled worm skewered on the hook. My foot jiggled restlessly. I should have called Kelsey. She was used to my confessionals, but it was weird talking to her about her brother. Anyway, it was too late now. Here I was, waiting for a known prankster and self-proclaimed matchmaker to listen as I bared my soul.

"Caught anything yet?"

Jake settled into the chair beside me. He was wearing a t-shirt, basketball shorts, boots, and a cowboy hat and looking as at home with himself as I had ever seen him before.

"Not yet. You might be disappointed in the fishing tonight. I'm pretty sure it's been years since this pond was last stocked."

"Joke's on you because I always leave disappointed when I'm fishing."

Jake readied his pole and cast his line. When I said nothing else, he looked over at me. I averted my gaze and focused steadily on the pond. Jake cleared his throat expectantly.

"Girl-talk starts now. You have five minutes."

I drew in a big breath, trying to sort all my emotions into something I could tell Jake without dying of embarrassment. "I like Logan. I knew I had the potential to like him again going into this stupid bet, but I hoped that the fact that I got dumped by a player would cure me. Apparently, I'm a glutton for punishment. I don't want to like him, but I can't seem to help it." I searched around for something I could bury my burning face in but found nothing.

"It was that kiss I interrupted, wasn't it?"

My first thought went to the kiss in the water—the one I hadn't been able to stop thinking about—until I remembered that Jake hadn't seen that one. Nobody saw it. But he did see the one in the trees. "Shut up."

Jake rubbed his hands together with glee. "My evil plan worked."

I bumped his shoulder with mine. "Only half of it. Can you call off the bet?"

He held up his hands. "I can't call off the bet. Especially with that truck on the line."

"You're not normal, by the way. Who puts that much on the line for a bet? It's crazy."

"Because I have eyes. Trust me, there's no way he's walking away this summer with that truck. Mark my words."

A thrill rose up inside of me before I squashed it back down to reality. "I think you're underestimating how much money that is for him. He could start his own business."

Jake shook his head. "He could start his own business anytime, with or without the truck money. He's just scared. He needs a push and a reason to date somebody real."

"Real?"

"He hasn't dated anybody with the intention of settling down for a few years now."

"Why is that?"

Jake pulled a weed growing next to him. "Not sure. I think it was a girl. A long time ago. He hasn't told me anything, but it's just a feeling I have from a few things he's said."

"We could still win your truck, you know. I'm not pretending he has any sort of feelings for me, other than as casual friends. You sure you don't want to change the bet? Take the truck off the table."

He grew quiet. "I already have a truck I love."

"You have an old bucket of rust."

"I hate to break it to you, kid, but all shiny things rust eventually."

I looked out at the pond and the shimmering orange moon's reflection on the water. Somewhere in the distance, a frog croaked. "Are you proving to your dad you don't need his money?"

Jake leaned forward, checking the drag on his line. "I'm proving it to myself."

I picked absently at the weeds near my feet. My heart burst with sadness for this endearing friend of mine. Wounds in people are often buried so deep you don't realize they're there. Jake's were buried under his humor and constant movements. His shiny eyes and zest for life were unmatched, but I ached for the little boy who'd had his heart broken by a selfish father who couldn't see his son's worth. I grabbed his arm, leaned in close, and squeezed.

"I love your guts, Jake."

"Settle down, woman." He flinched away from me. "You've already called dibs on a man." He leaned forward. "Alright. Let's break this down. You like Logan, but you don't want to be a part of the bet anymore, right?"

"Right."

"Why?"

I lifted my downcast eyes to study a ripple in the pond. "I don't want to date him like this."

"But you *do* want to date him."

I clenched my trembling fingers. Admitting something like this to Jake was a risk. Admitting it to myself was an even bigger risk. It went against everything I stood for when I moved back to Eugene.

"Yes."

"What? A little louder for the people in the back." Jake leaned closer to me, his hand cupping his ear. "Did you say you want to *date* Logan Marten?"

A smile broke across my face as I pushed him away. "Shut up."

He leaned back with his hands clasped behind his neck. "It really is hard being right all the time."

"Ugh. This is so complicated." I reeled in my line and checked that my waterlogged and puffy worm was still attached, then threw it out again.

"It's actually not complicated at all."

I thought of Logan's history, my past, his reputation, the truck, our agreement to keep things light, and my humongous crush on a man so close yet so far away from me. "Actually, it's a little complicated."

"Not if we break it down."

"How?"

"Do you know what I was doing yesterday morning? Before the Fourth of July party? One day after your make-out session in the trees?"

"We did not make out." *That time.*

"I was fixing fences with Layne and Logan out at Willow Creek. Logan smashed his thumb three times with his hammer."

I stared at him, confused and also concerned for Logan's thumb.

Jake leaned in closer. "*Three. Times.* Do you know what he does for a living? His mind was not on fixing fences, I'll tell you that."

I tried to wipe away any trace of my smile before he could see it, but Jake saw it.

"We've got to get under his skin. Operation Logan Crack."

"What?"

"Logan Crack."

I stared at him, horrified. Did Logan tell him? How many other people knew I saw...that?

"You know...we're going to crack the tight shell that is Logan," he said.

"Oh." I sighed, sinking back down into my chair, my cheeks flushed.

Jake set his fishing pole on the ground and stood up, pacing. "We've got to play this subtle. We can't be obvious about it, or he'll know something's up. He's like one of those wild cats that show up to the farm. They come sniffing around for some easy food every now and then, but they'll bolt the second you open the door."

"Yeah, for some reason, that explanation did not clear anything up. What are we doing?" My stomach took a dive. The mischievous look in Jake's eye was back, and it was never a comforting sight.

"You guys have been doing this dating thing for over a month now, which is about three weeks longer than he's dated anybody in years. He's bound to be getting a little twitchy. He'd be long gone by now, but he's here for the next month and a half."

"For the truck," I said, dejected.

"For the appearance of wanting the truck. If I had my guess, the next six weeks is where the real Logan will start showing up. But it's up to you to help him get there."

The real Logan. I liked the sound of that.

"So, what do I do?"

Jake sat back in his chair and looked up at the sky "Hold on. Let me think. I feel an idea brewing, but I need to sort it out first."

"Is this the mind of an evil genius at work?"

"Yup. Now hush."

While Jake's mind was churning, I slunk down in my chair. What did I really want out of this? I had thought that by calling off the bet, Logan would be free to date me without the pressure. But would he? Was the bet the only thing keeping him around? No. I refused to believe that could be completely true. Our growing friendship was real. Our teasing and laughter was real. I just wanted more. But was it more real than the thought of a forty-thousand-dollar payout at the end of summer?

"Alright, I've got it," Jake said, sitting forward in his chair. "We go half-court press. It's not just one thing; it's a bunch of tiny things. Keep going along with what you've been doing. Whatever stupid plan you've put into place to keep the feelings out. Do it all…mostly. The key is mostly. You've got to leave something dangling in front of him."

"Ew."

"You know what I mean."

"I really don't."

"I'm going to make myself scarce. I'll put Logan in charge of a few of the dates. He'll probably relax if I'm not telling him his business all the time."

I glowered at him. "We'd all probably relax if that was the case."

He grinned. "But nobody would be dating."

"Okay, so Logan's planning some dates now. Is that all?"

"It's your job to show a few cards. You're still in this bet, but you're on my side now." He gave me a pointed look. "Which you always were, but now you're admitting it."

I couldn't really argue with that.

"You'll need to make sure your flirting game is top notch."

"Flirting game?"

"Yup. You know what to do."

I eyed him. "He would definitely know something's up if I *flirted* with him."

He looked at me, mouth gaping. "Are you kidding me right now?"

"No."

He bit his knuckle, holding back a smile. "All you have to do is open your mouth and say something to him and it will come out flirty."

I scoffed. "No, it doesn't."

He covered his face with his hand, laughing. "Why do you think I did this bet with you two?" He laughed for a good ten seconds before he stopped himself. "You know what? You're right. Forget I said anything. Just keep on…doing your thing."

I glared at him. Interacting with Logan had always felt more like teasing than some suggestive flirt. It hadn't been a conscious thing, but *now* I'd probably be very self-conscious about it.

He continued, "You can't be obvious about this or else he'll know something's up. Bake him food, hang out with him on your porch, flirt, leave a little trail of sweets for him to nibble on. And then, when he's close to the door, yank it open, toss him inside the house, and lock it."

My nose wrinkled in distaste. "We can't lose with a plan like that."

"It's foolproof." He waited until I met his gaze, which had turned serious. "Logan and I leave for the cattle drive tomorrow morning. You have one week to figure out your move. Go get him, Tess."

Me: How's your thumb?
Logan: What? Who told you?
Me: I'll give you one guess.
Logan: Freaking Jake.

22

LOGAN

We arrived home sore, tired, and dirty from the cattle drive on Friday night. My legs felt permanently bowed after being in a saddle for five days straight. Was there an easier way to move the cattle without driving them ourselves with horses? Yes. Was the cattle drive such a part of our summers for the past thirty years that we would kill my dad if he ever stooped to modernizing this part of our summer? Yes. There were some summers I had to miss the cattle drive, jobs I couldn't get out of, but most of the time, I'd give my left kidney to get myself there.

Spending four days riding horses and moving cattle through fields, sagebrush, and mountains with my dad, Jake, and my adopted grandpa, Stitch, would have been the highlight of anybody's year. Things went well, besides the fact that Stitch still served his "famous" campfire beans, insisting we all liked them. We didn't. And the fact that Jake kept giving me winks and knowing glances anytime the mention of a girl was brought up—which was a lot. By the end of the ride, Stitch and my dad knew I was casually seeing Tessa. They didn't know the details, thank goodness, but they already knew too much.

The time apart from Tessa Robbins should have been good for me. An opportunity to re-train my brain into not wanting to see her.

Instead, I went through withdrawals. There were plenty of ways to keep my mind occupied on a cattle drive. My eyes were constantly looking ahead, watching for danger or cows to break from the group while trying to breathe with all the dust. Busy. Like a real cowboy. But dang if there wasn't a lot of time just sitting in a saddle, wondering what Tessa would look like on a horse, thinking about her riding in front of me on Dodger, her head on my chest and my arms wrapped around her. I didn't want Jake to be right, EVER, but lines *were* starting to feel blurred, just like he had predicted—which was my fault. The kisses during the fugitive game played on my mind far more often than they should have. It didn't make sense. I had kissed plenty of girls. And usually, by the time we kissed, I was ready to move on.

Tessa was becoming a craving. My drug of choice. A very dangerous little addiction.

I pulled up to her driveway on Saturday evening. I'd spent most of the day in my dad's shop, building cabinets and attempting to catch up after being gone for a week. But really, I spent most of the day re-cutting and re-measuring wood a dozen times because I couldn't keep my mind focused on my job. I knew where I wanted to be, but I forced myself to stay and work until the last second.

She was helping a customer when I pulled up to her driveway. She wore her denim cutoff shorts and a loose white t-shirt tucked casually in the front. She had kicked off her flip-flops and was laughing with the woman as she helped load the produce into her car. She didn't look my way, though she had to have heard my truck arrive. When the woman backed out of the driveway, I gave myself a stern pep talk before getting out of my truck.

Our eyes found each other across the driveway. I allowed myself to walk closer to her as long as I promised to keep things civil. The last time I saw Tessa, we'd kissed twice. My body definitely remembered that. I stopped with a respectable three feet between us.

"Hey, Jailbait," I forced myself to say. The nickname was a good reminder of boundaries.

Her hands fell to her hips, her eyes flashing. "Is that any way to greet your date for the summer?"

I swallowed and held out my hand. "The last time, you broke too many rules. I'm terrified to see how you'd greet me now."

If she noticed my hand left hanging, waiting to be shaken, she ignored it. "*I* broke too many rules?"

I paused, my head tilted, considering her. "*We?*"

"I think that was all *you.*"

I bit my lip, but my sheepish smile couldn't be contained. "I definitely remember a *we.*"

She shook my hand then, a smile forming on her lips and an attractive flush rising on her cheeks. There was something different about her today that I couldn't put my finger on. She always looked beautiful, but today I couldn't look away. Once she released me, I shoved my hands into my pockets. I had only meant to tease her, but instead, I flirted like a lovesick teenager, and now it was almost impossible to wipe the grin off my face.

She didn't move and I watched with growing alarm as her gaze traveled casually down my body. I stiffened and looked down at my clothes. A little wrinkly but that was nothing unusual. Then her gaze traveled back up, just as slowly, lighting a match inside of me everywhere her eyes touched. And she didn't miss an inch. She looked at me then, with an air of defiance. There seemed to be a short circuit in my airwaves and I could only gape after her. What in the he—

"You must have remembered how to ride a horse," she said, turning back to the tables and consolidating the leftover fruit into some empty cardboard boxes. Casually. As if she hadn't just ravished me with her eyes.

"Barely," I choked out. "Need help with this?"

"Sure," she said as I moved in beside her, making sure not to touch her. My body couldn't take that after what I had just witnessed.

"What's going on for tonight?" she asked after we had cleaned up the tables and headed toward the house.

"Well, that's the thing. Normally, I would have planned an amazing date, flown you to Italy or the beach...the whole bit. But Jake forgot to tell me I was in charge of date night until I was driving over here. So, I'm not sure. Any ideas?"

We lingered on the porch for a moment until she dropped onto the swing, and I sat in the rocking chair. I hadn't sat down all day and couldn't help the sigh that escaped my lips.

"You look exhausted. When did you guys get back home?"

My eyes closed on their own accord as I laid my head against the rocker. "We limped home last night, just before ten."

"Limped?"

"It felt like it. I hadn't been in a saddle since last year's cattle drive."

"How was it?"

"The best."

"Kelsey always loved it, too. I'm a little miffed that I've never been invited."

I opened one eye. "I've never seen you on a horse before."

"I've been on one exactly two times. I'm basically a pro."

Now, both eyes shot open. "You've been best friends with my sister your whole life and haven't mastered riding horses yet?"

She tucked her hair behind her ear. "We made a deal: I didn't have to ride horses with her, and she didn't have to run with me, unless we wanted to."

It was her hair. That's what was different. She wore it down today. I hadn't seen it down all summer. It was always up in a ponytail. Which I also liked. It was very Tessa. With her joggers on most of the time, hanging out with her at the fruit stand felt like we could break out into a light run at any time. Wearing her hair softly draped around her shoulders today seemed…suspicious.

"Do you wear a cowboy hat on the cattle drive?" she suddenly asked.

"Nah. Just my baseball hat and a bandana when it gets dusty."

When she didn't say anything, I chuckled. "Sorry to disappoint your cowboy fantasy."

"Baseball hat works, too."

It was the way she said it that had me looking at her. Her eyes flitted over to mine, and the slowest, sexiest smile crawled onto her mouth that sent my heart rate sky high.

"Do we need a safe word, Jailbait? If you're imagining me on a horse without a shirt on, you're in big trouble," I warned.

"With a little dirt and some sweat running down your chest right about..." She reached a finger out toward me, her face brimming with amusement. My body tightened. Holy crap. She wasn't stopping.

My hand flew out to block her finger and I pushed it away, lightly. "Skeevy little perv," I mumbled, with a little too much heat.

"*The Office.*" She pointed at me, trying not to laugh. "Stop quoting it!"

My eyes narrowed. "What's going on?"

She was all innocence, suddenly leaning back in her swing and closing her eyes. Not looking at me. "What do you mean?"

I was unsure of how to put into words the tangible things she had actually done. Checked me out? I had also done my fair share of checking her out this summer. Flirt? I had flirted plenty with her. I peered at her again, which was easier to do with her eyes closed. Tessa's blonde tresses were draped around her shoulders like a beacon to my hands which wanted to bury themselves in the softness. My legs twitched while I shoved my hands in my pockets. Watching her made me feel like I wanted to run a half marathon. For the record, I had never once experienced that feeling. Tessa was definitely up to something and whatever it was it seemed to be working.

I leaned back in the chair and closed my eyes, feigning exhaustion. I was tired, but I was also one step away from either kissing her or hyperventilating. "What was the treat today?"

"Raspberry-lemon bars."

I swallowed, my mouth instantly watering and not just for the dessert. Maybe it was just a coincidence she made my favorite treat on the day I got back after not seeing her for a week, but again, it felt...pointed.

"Any left?"

"I know your first rule was no treats between us, so I didn't save you one, but I made a little plate for you to take to Stitch in the bunkhouse."

"About time you start following the rules around here. And that's cute you think I'm going to share with Stitch."

"How are the cabinets coming?" she asked. I peeked an eye open and saw she was now watching me again. A vision of us sitting together on our own front porch one day came out of nowhere, slamming into my brain before I could push it away.

"Good. I've got a good start."

"I'll have to come see them sometime."

I cleared my throat and found myself agreeing. "Catch me up on Betsy May. Has she fired you yet?"

"She swore at me during our last session, but then she patted my head and gave me a cookie on my way out. So...I think we're making headway."

"You should give all that up and be the next Little Debbie. You can package your mini cakes and sell them."

She laughed, leaning back into the swing. "I'd love that."

"Jailbait Cakes."

"No."

"Jailbait Bakes."

She kicked my foot with hers. "No Jailbait stuff."

"You're right. That's just for me."

We both stopped our gentle sways at the same time, our knees pressing against each other. Let me be clear, I didn't move away because I was done rocking. I wasn't sure of her excuse. We spent the rest of the evening talking on the porch. The summer sun had been set for almost two hours by the time I forced myself to leave.

The next couple of weeks, I kept myself busy. I was everywhere, but never anywhere too long. No real reason. I was busy at work, busy at home building cabinets, busy helping out on the farm, and most afternoons, "busy" with Frank Robbins' front porch. I wasn't sure what was happening to me, beyond feeling skittish anytime I thought about a certain blonde, which was a disconcerting amount of time.

We had gotten into an easy rhythm since my coming to work on the porch. After the fruit stand closed, I'd help her take the leftover produce into the greenhouse. Then, she'd feed me whatever she'd saved for me that day. She tried to make me think what she gave me was the day's leftovers, but I had heard her, on several occasions, quietly turn away someone who asked about the daily treat. She told them she had sold out, but I hadn't gone a day without a treat. The rest of our evening usually passed with conversation and teasing on her porch. Sometimes she'd hand me a tool. Sometimes she'd touch my leg. Or tug at my hat. Or swat at my arm when she'd reached her limit to my teasing.

I arrived at her home each day, terrified that she would be outside to watch me work and terrified that she wouldn't. I wasn't sure if Frank needed his railing touched up with paint or his porch sanded four times over, but I found it neighborly to go the extra mile.

A person could notice a great deal about someone while watching them not-so-discreetly from the porch. Tessa laughed a lot with people. Her friendly manner and sarcasm endeared her to everyone. Her back usually began to ache at the end of a long day of leaning over the short tables. She'd bend and twist when she thought nobody was watching.

She kept half of the fruit on the ground in boxes and would refill the tables as needed. That was another thing. I could have sworn the tables were set up closer to the orchard when the summer had started. Now, they were a stone's throw from the front porch—the front porch I worked on every evening.

She twirled her hair a lot while she read, although she rarely picked up her book when I was around. By the time I showed up after 5 p.m. each day, her flip-flops were kicked off. She wore her denim cutoffs a lot.

I sent a silent apology to her shorts. I had nothing but good things to say about them now.

As much as I tried to keep my distance, I couldn't kick her off her own porch when she came to sit by me while I was sanding, claiming she needed some shade.

If I had a necktie, this was the moment I would pull it loose from around my neck and gasp for breath. The air on the porch felt stifling. Which was crazy because the house sat on fifty acres of some of the prettiest farmland and rolling hills Eugene had to offer.

—————

It was Saturday night.

According to my plans, Tessa and I should have been watching a movie together in Salmon right now. A movie date. Darkness and popcorn with Tessa Robbins next to me.

No thank you.

It sounded like a good idea when I bought the tickets. My emotions were a regular ping-pong match.

A summer cold in the form of a scratchy throat and a runny nose, two days earlier, had me calling in sick for our date—the first time all summer one of us had canceled. No matter that I felt almost completely fine now. It was just to be safe. I sniffed for good measure. Yup. Couldn't be too careful.

It was dark outside the windows of my dad's dusty shop. I had brought many of my own tools and supplies for the cabinets from Boise, but I used a few things of my dad's as well. It had taken me about half a day to clean and sweep the floors and move his junk scattered across the concrete to make room for my lumber. I was making cabinets for the storage room in the back of the office as well as two bathrooms. Over the past couple of weeks, I had cut and measured and sanded, producing two long cabinet boxes for the storage room and two small pieces for the bathrooms.

I loved this part of the job. This time of night. It was quiet. Jake had gone home. My parents were in the house, watching a rerun of an old western. Stitch had been asleep for an hour. It was just me out here. I rarely got to make cabinets anymore because we were so busy with other jobs we had to hire it out. I had enough of the right equipment to make them, but not enough of anything for mass production. That was one of the main reasons I told Chase I could do this job in Eugene. The office building was our only focus here, which meant I could do the woodwork.

There was still more to be done, but I had a decent start. At work, we were putting up the doors and trim this week; painting and flooring would go next. I still had plenty of time to finish. I glowered at the stack of maple wood piled on the floor. For some reason, I had ordered extra material. It had been an oversight, an accident. I kept telling myself that, which was probably why I was a mixture of excitement and dread as I pulled out a large sheet and began cutting. I had figured out the dimensions weeks ago. I almost threw the paper away once or twice, but each time, I stopped myself.

I wasn't a man of grand gestures. This wasn't the time or the place for any bold statement. We had a bet to win, even though the thought of upgrading from my old F250 had been giving my conscience a run for its money lately.

I swore at myself even as I sanded down the cut wood.

Tessa's reaction to this might be more than I could take. I stopped once and forced myself to work on the doors for the office cabinets before swearing and starting again.

I could always back out. I didn't have to give this to her. She had no idea it was coming. No harm, no foul. My mom could probably use it for something. Those were the things I told myself as I glued and nailed and measured. The thought of Tessa's reaction if I brought this to her both terrified and spurred me on.

I swore again.

The bright-orange glow from the shop windows lit up the night for hours.

23

TESSA

Operation Logan Crack was in full swing.

Jake had said to be subtle, but I felt as subtle as a foghorn in a library. If I moved the fruit tables any closer to the porch, I'd be sitting in his lap. The flirting had come to me much easier than I thought. It had been fun to rile him a little. I had straightened my stupid hair five times in the last two weeks. I had to admit, I did enjoy Logan's double-take and the goosebumps that flooded my body at his gaze. I couldn't bake his favorite treats every day, but they made the lineup more often than not. Through all of this, I still wasn't sure the effect it had on him. He had always been charming, but we were definitely feeling more like friends. He still wasn't a revolving door of emotions, but we had conversations that were fun and interesting, and more often than not, our nights were spent talking on the porch.

The fruit stand was nearly closed for the day when one more truck pulled into the drive. I grinned as Chad parked and made his way over to me, his beard longer than I remembered.

"Hey, Chad."

"Hey, Pipsqueak." He stood in front of my tables, his eyes flitting back and forth between all the produce left for the day.

"This all you have left?"

I raised my eyebrows. "What do you need?"

He let out a sigh and folded his beefy arms across his chest, almost defiantly. "Well, everybody coming into my restaurant has been telling me I need to get your recipe for chocolate cake. Apparently, dry and tasteless isn't a thing that sells in my restaurant."

A smile lit across my face. "Oh, really? So, you're coming to *me* for product advice?"

"Don't make this a thing."

"A thing?" I propped my feet up on the table. "I'm just curious what the people have said about my baking. The thing you were so disgusted by when I tried to help you a couple months back."

"Just let me taste something. Do you have any cake?"

"Wait, who's been telling you about my cake?"

He sighed. "Most of the little old ladies who come in, Logan Marten, Jake Evans…probably all the people you pay to tell me. Do you have any cake?" he asked again. My brain was only thinking about one name. Logan was telling Chad about my cake?

I thanked my lucky stars I had made chocolate cake slices the night before to sell today. I make a layered round cake and cut individual slices, wrapping each in plastic wrap to sell. They had always sold very well.

I grabbed the last one available from the cooler. "That'll be five bucks."

His eyes widened. "Five bucks a slice? Are you kidding me?"

"Don't make me raise it to six."

A reluctant smile slipped onto his face as he pulled out his wallet, because deep down, he loved me. He slapped a ten on the table, unwrapped the cake, and took a large bite.

I watched with feigned disinterest, though I was dying inside. It had been sitting out the whole day. Fingers crossed the half pound of butter in the frosting was just enough to keep it from drying out.

He gave me no sign of anything while he chewed. He took another bite.

We made eye contact before he finally groaned and shoved another piece into his mouth. He swore. "You have no idea how much I wanted this to be horrible."

I lifted my hands triumphantly in the air.

"Would you want to make me a couple cakes to try out in the restaurant next week? I'd pay you."

"Did that hurt? I feel like it hurt you to say that."

"Don't make me ask Aunt Nancy for this recipe."

I scoffed. "It's not my mom's recipe. It's mine."

"You came up with it?"

"It's a mixture of three different recipes I've tweaked and added to over the years."

He made a snort that sounded like he was mildly impressed before he asked, "That was your last slice?"

I hesitated. Logan's slice was still in the cooler. Chad was good for business, but Logan loved my cake...

"No. Sorry. Last piece. I could make you a cake for free next week to test it out," I offered, because I was pathetic.

Chad rolled his eyes. "I'm paying you for anything you bring me," he said, walking backward toward the driveway. "Friends and family will run you right out of business if you're not careful."

"Are we friends?" I called out excitedly.

"Family," he shouted back, getting into his truck. "I didn't choose this. I'll figure out the details and legal stuff and get back to you."

I laughed and waved him off, feeling flattered and happy and excited and like I wanted to share this news with Logan.

Like I would a boyfriend.

I WALKED outside the next morning just after 7 a.m. to begin organizing and filling up the tables with produce. The front door slammed shut behind me while I made my way down the front steps, my feet coming to a halt on the last stair when I noticed I wasn't alone outside. My hand perched on the rail, my eyes wide, and my mouth open.

Logan's truck was parked near the old tables, and he looked as though he had just finished unloading a wooden structure that towered over him by at least three feet. He was dressed for work in jeans and a t-shirt, steel-toed boots, and his baseball hat, his light-brown hair sticking out of the bottom. At the sound of the front door, his head snapped over to me, and his shoulders seemed to sink, even as he turned back and continued pulling out of his truck another piece that looked the same size as the first. He grunted under the weight as he lifted and edged it next to the first piece. My brows furrowed as I made my way over to greet him. To my surprise, he turned back to face me, holding his hands out in front of him almost defensively.

"Now don't read into this, alright? I had some extra material. That's all this is. I promise."

He immediately turned back around and busied himself, pushing the two sides of the structure together, making one long table with a thin pillar in each corner, holding up a large wooden sign that ran the length of the table. Logan snapped something together before lurching back from the table at my approach.

My heart hammered in my chest as I reached the structure, running my fingers along the wood. It was even more beautiful close up. The table had been stained a perfect medium brown, the wood rustic and sturdy, about ten feet long and four feet wide.

"I thought if you had a higher table, it wouldn't hurt your back as much. I think you can probably get everything you sell most days onto this." He trailed off, meeting my gaze for an instant before ducking behind the table, a drill turning on as he attached the two pieces together.

I stepped back so I could read the wooden sign over my head. FRESH PRODUCE was written in a bold red with hand-painted letters. I could envision the table stacked with rows of colorful berries and fresh-picked carrots and peppers and tomatoes, the treat of the day going on the sides.

The drilling stopped, and there was movement behind me again. Logan pulled a few round apple crates out of the back of his truck and dropped them unceremoniously on the ground at my feet. He began inching backward toward his truck.

"Don't look at me like that. My dad had some crates laying around. He wasn't using them. They'd work good for your apples. Or you can not use them. Whatever you want." He threw his hands up in the air again. "I know you have the apple barrel, but if you wanted some on your table, this would work. Or if you don't even want to use the table, again, no big deal. It was just some extra wood I had laying around."

His hand was on his truck, looking like a man who wanted to be far away, yet the handle remained latched. He watched me, waiting for my reaction with what looked like both dread and boyish apprehension.

And my heart exploded.

I concentrated on his eyes while I walked toward him slowly, like I was approaching a jumpy baby bird with a broken wing. He held his hands out, warding off my advance, but I would not be stopped. And I wasn't buying his excuses.

"I had extra time, Jailbait. It wasn't a big deal."

Two more steps until I could feel the heat from his body. One more until I felt him. I nudged closer, pushing through his wall of armor and teasing to land somewhere in the gooey center. My arms found their home around his waist, and I squeezed, the smile and elation inside finally bursting free. Tears welled, but I pushed them back. If he was terrified of praise and a smile, a blubbering female would definitely send him running. After several long moments, his arms lifted and pressed me tight against his chest.

"This is why I was trying to sneak over here early. It's really not a big deal." The words he spoke were muffled against my hair. Soft puffs of heat landed on my scalp causing my breath to hitch.

I lifted myself against him, my lips touching his ear as I spoke. "It *is* a big deal."

"No, it's not," he said, even as he pulled me closer.

"It's magnificent."

He drew back to look at me. A smile lit his features, and it was growing wider by the second, even as he shook his head. "Pretty high praise for a little old table."

"It's not little or old, and I mean it. It's the nicest thing anyone's ever done for me. Thank you, Logan."

"I'm glad you're not reading into any of this, Tessa Robbins." His hands trailed slowly up and down my arms, his eyes wary yet sparking fire into mine.

"I'm not," I said, breathless. "You obviously have lots of free time."

"*Lots* of free time."

"And tons of scraps."

"Tons."

"So, of course you would have to make me the most beautiful fruit stand I've ever seen."

His eyes landed on my lips before he swallowed and released me, backing away completely.

"Check-in time," he said, yanking his door open. "No more hugs."

A smile lit my face as I watched him climb in his truck. "I object."

He shot me an exasperated look before he bit back a grin, shook his head, and peeled out of my driveway.

He was gone as fast as he arrived, though his exit was much louder than his entrance as he raced away. When he was gone, I examined every crevice of wood he had pieced together, sanded, and stained.

For me.

24

TESSA

"Little late to be taking a nap."

My eyelids fluttered. I hadn't even heard the truck enter the drive. I had cleaned up from the fruit stand earlier, and instead of going inside to wait for Logan to pick me up for our date, I made my way into the orchard instead, throwing down a blanket and lying on the grass between the trees.

"What time is it?" I asked, turning to watch Logan approach.

"Late. Sorry. I got held up talking with Nate. I sent you a text though."

"I fell asleep," I said.

The melancholic sense of the orchard felt different the moment he lay down next to me, his arm brushing past mine briefly before he moved it, settling in. The space became alive, the air thumping, the hairs on my arms…charged.

"Have you heard from Jake?" I asked. "I thought he said he would plan this one?" We usually heard from Jake by Saturday afternoon, but the airwaves today had been silent. I wasn't sure why I hadn't texted and asked, but the fact that Logan showed up anyway was better than any date Jake could have planned.

"Jake's been dating a girl from Challis the past couple of weeks. He's been pretty scarce. I'm guessing he forgot."

"He's dating somebody? Have you met her?"

"Nope, but he was gone last weekend and now this weekend."

"Hmm. So, what do you want to do?" I asked, my elation at his being here kicking up about five thousand notches.

"I'm trying to figure out what it is you're looking at. The stars aren't out yet."

"They'll be here soon. How was work today? Has my brother been a pain?" The '*How was work?*' question made it seem like we were an old married couple, and I loved it.

"He's as bossy as you but a lot harder on the eyes."

I pressed my lips together, trying to hold back a smile. "What's he been complaining about now?"

"He's not complaining so much as he can't make up his mind on any of the colors or fixtures for the cabinets. He should have given me his picks a week ago, but I talked to him today, and he's still analyzing the best color scheme." He held his hands up in the air like a choke-hold, pretending to throttle him.

I laughed. "I'm sorry. He asked me for ideas, but I was no help."

"It's fine. All part of the job." He gave me a pointed look. "He does bring a pretty intense big-brother energy to the site."

"Really?"

"Yeah, I'm scared to accidentally bring up your name for fear of my head getting chopped off." He nudged me in the arm. "How was work for you today, honey?"

I grinned. "Some guy dropped off this amazing fruit stand this morning, and then I was busy taking compliments for it all day long. Really overshadowed the brownies I made today."

His head shot up. "The caramel ones?"

"Yup."

"Any left?"

"Chad was right. Friends and family will run you right out of business."

"I didn't teach you to sell today's baked goods tomorrow."

"I already have a plate with your name on it."

He lay back down and sighed. "You're playing fast and loose with my heart, Jailbait."

I eyed him. "I thought that was under lock and key?"

He said nothing. But I detected a smile playing on his lips as he moved his arms behind his head and stared up at the sky.

"You left your drill here," I said, suddenly feeling the need to put my armor on. "So, I knew you'd be back to get it."

"I did?"

"Yeah." I fingered the hem of my shirt as I stared through the trees. A slight breeze had picked up, causing the branches overhead to flutter.

I felt him look at me, but it was only when his low voice said, "Tess," that I looked over at him.

I raised my eyebrows in question, surprised by the intensity in his gaze.

"I'm not here for the drill."

I blinked. And then…tingles erupted inside my body, flowing like lava into every limb. I turned my face from his in an effort to hide the growing smile threatening to divulge all my secrets.

Logan cleared his throat and asked, "Are you excited to work with your brother?"

I took a deep breath to re-center myself before answering. "It's been nice having Nate back in town again. We've been running together in the mornings a couple days a week."

"I can't believe there are two of you in the world."

I kicked at his foot.

"You didn't answer my question, though. Are you excited to work with him?"

"Yeah. I'll learn a lot from him. He's a very good physical therapist."

"You are too, though, right?"

"I don't know," I said honestly.

He shifted next to me. "Why do you say that?"

I took a deep breath, debating saying it out loud, but ultimately, I wanted the thoughts I'd been thinking all summer off of my chest. "It's something I didn't discover until I was too far into the program to back out. I was good on paper. I like people. I like helping people. But I didn't realize until I started actually working with patients that I get frustrated too easily. I usually want to bash my head in by the end of a session."

He was quiet, so I continued, "But I figure about 20 percent of the time, people are really lovely, and trying hard, and the job is good. So, I'll be alright. It's good job security, I guess—working for family."

"I'm not sure 20 percent job satisfaction is good enough, " he said, frowning.

"What are your numbers?" I asked him.

"Probably the same, only in reverse. Every job has some sort of crap associated with it, but most of what I do is enjoyable."

"What's the stuff you don't like?"

"The bigger we get as a company, the less time I have to do what I love. More paperwork, more employees, more managing, but less actual building. I got into the business because I loved to work with my hands, but I'm on the phone and computer more now than I was back in the early days."

"Would you want a smaller company then?"

"Yeah. Maybe," he said, his voice far away.

"How are the cabinets coming?"

"Good. Almost finished—once Nate gets me his stain choice."

"Have you liked being back in Eugene?" This question seemed loaded, though I didn't examine why.

He adjusted the bill of his hat. "Yeah, surprisingly. It's been a good diversion. I've liked having one project to devote our entire group of guys to. We rarely have to hire out or use subs. It's been awesome."

I wasn't sure how I felt about the word diversion, but I didn't let myself dwell.

"Are you thinking of starting your own construction business one day?"

"That was always my plan," he said. "And then Chase approached me about partnering with him and I hadn't given it much thought until lately."

We both sighed. I moved my arms behind my head for a pillow.

"So...what *are* you doing out here?" he asked, motioning around the orchard.

"Being overly dramatic."

"Nothing new, then, huh?"

I pushed him while he laughed.

"Okay, seriously, why are you out here?"

"Can you smell the apples?"

"Yeah." He looked at me with his brows furrowed.

"I bet that's nice."

He pointed up to the trees. "You can't smell that?"

"All I can smell is my ex-future-mother-in-law's jasmine perfume. I hate the smell of jasmine, by the way. Sometimes I can smell the cologne Tyler was wearing when he bolted past me to ditch out on our wedding. I can see the whole town of Eugene staring at me with pity in their eyes. That's all I can see and smell when I'm here now. Which sucks because this used to be my favorite place."

He was quiet. Contemplative. "Then why are you out here?"

Why, indeed. As a kid, I spent hours roaming the grassy aisles between the apple and peach trees. The earthy smell of grass and dirt and fruit was the scent of my childhood. The place where I went to think, or take a walk, or be alone. The orchard had always been mine. And now, it was tainted.

"I saw a therapist for a while after it ended with Tyler, and she told me I needed to allow myself to feel everything. To feel all the emotions of that day. I had a habit of trying to skate past it all. You know, just trying to make everything okay without really feeling it. I've been working on doing that here." I held out my hands and motioned around us. "This is the exact place I stood when I was about to get married."

He twisted, moving his head around, taking in the view with new awareness. "Are you...wishing Tyler back?"

"No." I let out a soft laugh. "But seeing him a few weeks ago helped me move past it all. It was all for the best. I guess I'm just trying to make peace with all the bad memories so I can love this place again."

"Is that how it works?"

"Doesn't seem to be. I've been trying for a while now."

I looked at Logan, waiting for him to gracefully make his exit. I didn't really think men loved to talk about weddings they had no part in. He surprised me, though, when he put his arms behind his head and settled in.

"What was the hardest part of that day for you?"

A light breeze floated through the trees, lifting the hair at my forehead. Nobody had ever asked me that question before. There were lots of little moments that I kept remembering. The inquisitive silence in the audience. Walking down the aisle to a pale and sweaty groom. The nervous twitches. Tyler fingering his cufflink and loosening his tie as though it were strangling him. The cold touch of his hands as they left mine to walk down the aisle alone.

"Honestly, it was the humiliation of it all. I know I shouldn't care that much. Everyone's over it, but it hurts to think about. At the time, I was too naive to realize what was happening, even when it was right in front of me. But now, looking back, I can remember everybody's faces. Kelsey, my brother, my parents, Betsy May, Preacher Douglass…you. Everybody knew, and I stood there, smiling and explaining to everyone that my groom was off to get the karaoke machine." I laughed bitterly.

I could have heard a pin drop, and that was saying something with the crickets making a racket all around us. Finally, he said, "That sucks."

"It does suck," I agreed. "Thanks for not telling me you're sorry."

"I'm not sorry."

I looked at him then, but he stared straight ahead.

"I mean, I'm sorry you went through that, but I'm not sorry it ended."

I pounded my feelings back down into their cage in my heart. Was it just me, or was Logan a good listener? My resolve had been cracked open by my confessions, and now all I wanted to do was keep talking.

"I'm not the first person to get cheated on. It happens all the time. I'm not even the first person to get left at the altar. All the movies I

used to love are full of scenes like that. But you know what I've realized? I was in Camille's story."

I felt his movement on the blanket as he turned to look at me.

"In the movies, you always root for the one who broke up the
wedding. The one who got her guy in the end. The camera never goes
back to the one left standing. The one who had no idea what was
coming. I was the villain in my own story. It just sucked that I found
that out on my wedding day."

"No. You weren't. *They* were the villains. I think we all take a turn
being somebody's hero and somebody's villain." Logan paused. For a
few moments, we lay staring up at the rustling leaves. For the first time
this whole summer, I detected the faintest scent of sweet Honeycrisp
apples. A smell so delicious I could almost taste it.

"He was a jackass to do what he did. And I'm not just talking about
it all going down on your wedding day. You were never the bad guy.
And with the embarrassment stuff...it fades. It sucks, but it fades.
You'll get married to the right guy next time, and it will be forgotten."

"Can I ask you something?"

He hesitated. "My instinct tells me to say no."

"Who was your villian? Why are you scared to date anybody
longer than a week?"

"Can I say no?"

"If you feel good about me baring my soul to you twice now, and I
get nothing in return...sure."

"Great. Have a good night." He started to roll over to get on his
knees when I reached out and grabbed his arm, pulling him back down
by me.

"All those big muscles are a disguise. Inside, you're a little baby
chicken."

"That's where you're wrong. I'm a big chicken. My muscles are
only there to look pretty."

"The only way I'll get over my embarrassment is if you tell me
something, too."

He bit his lip, his right dimple showing off just for me. "So, it's all
on me now, is it?"

"What's a secret boyfriend for, if not for that." I froze at my word that had slipped out. He was not my boyfriend. Never mind that we went on a date every weekend and hung out most afternoons while he fixed the porch, *and* he had built me a fruit stand. We were dating casually for a bet, but that didn't make us an item. Thankfully, Logan didn't stop to tease. It almost seemed like he hadn't thought the label abnormal.

He let out a loud, exaggerated sigh. "What happens in this orchard, stays in this orchard. Got it?"

"Tell that to the one hundred guests at my wedding a year ago."

He made a sympathetic face. "Fair point."

"Say it. I promise I won't bite."

"Well, dang, I don't want to say it now."

"Logan…"

"Fine."

25

LOGAN

"Y ou probably don't remember any of this, but a few years after I graduated high school, I was dating a girl."

"Valerie?"

I raised my head and looked at her, incredulous. "What? How did you—"

"Kelsey made a crocheted-doll thing in our home economics class in high school. She thought it looked like Valerie, so we did a bunch of pretend voodoo stuff to it."

"You two are terrifying together. Poor Cade."

"I wouldn't feel too sorry for him. Did Valerie have a birthmark on her cheek?"

"Yeah, why?"

"The voodoo doll did, too. I was never sure if she really had one, or if Kelsey had stabbed her face too many times."

I covered my face in my hands and groaned, unsuccessfully trying to cover my laughter.

"Anyway, go on."

Tessa took a deep breath and adjusted her body, staring up at the sky peeking through the trees. I did the same. The sky had darkened enough that the stars began to twinkle above us. They were alright in their grandiose canvas, but I found the view somewhat lacking that night compared to what was lying beside me.

"I haven't told anybody this, so I'll need you to keep it that way." I sat up, reached over, grabbed her hand, and shook it firmly. "You are now sworn to silence."

"Just say it."

I settled back down. I knew that once I started talking, it would be hard to stop. There was just something about Tessa's easy manner. And for a guy not used to talking about this at all, the idea of not stopping was terrifying.

"We had been dating for about five months or so," I began. "I was young, an idiot, and all in. I had this plan for my life all figured out. I was going to have some big-shot career, get married to a hot girl, have the nice truck, the big vacations. All of it. We started dating, and she seemed to fit the mold."

"Hold on." Tessa held up her hand. "I'm putting together a puzzle named Logan. Weren't you voted most likely to succeed in high school?"

I had been opening my mouth to say something else before her comment stunned me. "How'd you know that?"

"I remember random things sometimes."

"Like how many moles I have on my abs?"

"Shut up." She gave me a push, and I was grateful she couldn't see my sloppy grin.

"It takes a long time to tell you a story," I said.

"Sorry. Go on."

"The mood is shot now, but anyway, I was a pre-med student, planning to become some sort of doctor. Now, if you had asked me which kind of doctor, I couldn't have told you a thing. The deepest thought I had ever had about my career choice was the paycheck. Anyway, about two semesters in, I'm taking all kinds of horrible classes like genetics, and biochemistry, and biology, and I was drowning. I hated it all. I pushed through because my girlfriend kept bragging to her friends that I was going to be a doctor. And that required a white lab coat."

"Doesn't a mortician wear a white lab coat, too?"

I paused, biting back a smile before shaking my head. "Yes. It's all very tragic. Anyway, it was the anatomy and physiology class that nearly broke me. I hated all the classes but was trying to convince myself I'd love the actual career. Except, the classes kept getting worse. About that same time, a buddy of mine was finishing his basement and asked if I'd help him. So I did, and doing the work felt like such a relief to me. I'd only ever known my dad's 'farmer' way of fixing stuff, which was either to throw some duct tape on it or hammer in a few nails. But my buddy taught me how to frame and drywall, and suddenly, I was watching how-to videos and building shelves and entertainment centers. Finally, there was something I could do that made sense. And when I was done, I had a finished product. I fell in love with the whole idea of building things. Houses, bookshelves, cabinets. Everything. A couple weeks later, I changed my major to construction management, switched out of my classes, and started doing well in school."

"I love that," she whispered.

"Anyway, back to Valerie. This is the part nobody knows. We'd been dating for about six months or so, and I took her to a nice restaurant one night and proposed."

I stopped talking for a minute, suddenly lost in the memories of that night. I had been so ready. I had saved for months. We had been ring shopping once, just casual browsing, nothing serious, but she had fallen in love with this one-carat, princess-cut diamond. I took on a few extra side jobs building shelves and doing tile work for customers to pay for the ring. I remember Val had gotten upset with me a few times because I'd been pulling a lot of nights and weekends. But like an idiot, I smiled on the inside and couldn't wait to surprise her with the diamond.

"She said no?" Tessa ventured softly.

I nodded. "She didn't just say no. She took everything I believed about myself and our relationship and smashed it into the ground. She said I wasn't marriage material. And that I hadn't been truthful about who I was when we first got together. There was no way I was going to make enough for her needs by working construction. When she thought

I was going to be a doctor, she'd been picking out baby names, but now, she told me that she had only wanted a good time. I was completely blindsided by her rejection. So, I get what you mean about losing trust in people."

"People suck."

"Yeah."

"I had no idea."

"That was the general idea. I was too mortified to let anybody know I had put my heart on the line like that and to have her basically laugh in my face. It was easier to tell everybody we broke up and leave it at that."

"And after that, you just..." she prodded.

"I dove into my schoolwork, trying to forget it all. I laid low, and after a month or two of moping, I tried dating again, but every woman looked like Valerie to me. And I got...bitter. So, I decided if I wasn't marriage material, fine. Being on my own sounded easier anyway. Girls became a Saturday night. If anybody began acting serious, I would cut 'em loose."

"Yikes."

"It sounds meaner than it was. I wasn't making a habit out of dating girls who would want much more from me."

"What happens when you turn fifty and you can't get the hot young things anymore?"

"I've been working on my golf game."

A laugh bubbled out of her throat. The birds in the trees began to combine with the crickets to create a soft melody around us.

"So, the past couple of months must have been torture for you." She turned to look at me. "Unless you've been seeing other girls on the side, I guess."

"With all the tackling exes, and fixing porches, and making out in ditches, I haven't had time for anything else."

She laughed softly, and my heart rate spiked, remembering the ditch. "Me neither."

"I've just..." I began, wondering why I was still talking but not

being able to stop—just like I feared. "I've been this guy for so long…
I don't know. It's hard to let go of that."

"Do you want to be different?"

I tensed, feeling myself close inward. Here we go. It wasn't what
Val *did* as much as how it affected me. I had never known rejection
like that. By someone who had claimed to love me. My rose-colored
glass had shattered. Which was probably a good thing. I had been too
naïve. Too stupid. And yet…my shoulder was now pressed up against
Tessa Robbins. Thinking things about her that I had no business thinking. Telling her things I had no business telling her. We weren't really
dating. But that statement was starting to sound hollow.

"I didn't come here thinking I did. But lately…yeah. I've been
thinking about it." I nudged her with my arm. She drew in a breath and
then didn't move a muscle. My arm still rested against hers—she
hadn't moved it away. I was a broken water faucet. I couldn't turn it
off, and I needed to turn this thing off. Do something else. I was either
going to kiss her or tell her more things I shouldn't say, and I couldn't
afford to do that. I couldn't make sense of my thoughts when we were
lying together like this. So…I made a flash decision to change the
course of the night.

I stood up abruptly. "Stay here. I'll be back." I took off running
toward my truck.

26

TESSA

"I'll be back." The exact words Tyler had uttered when he stumbled down the aisle and headed toward my house on our wedding day. He never came back. I was working through that emotion when Logan's truck fired up and his headlights beamed into the orchard, illuminating the trees before me with a harsh circle of light. When had it become so dark? I waited for the truck to back up. For Logan to leave. I had pushed too hard. I had asked too much of him.

The sprinklers in the grass beside me gurgled loudly before popping up and out of the ground. I gasped as a stream of cold water blasted my body. Squealing, I jumped up and made to run toward the house when I smashed into Logan, his hands holding my arms.

"Did you do that?" I asked, trying to move past him, but he held me firm.

"Yeah."

He took a step closer, our bodies touching, and he began to walk me slowly backward to the orchard. The maneuver was *not* hot at all.

"Fun fact about me: I hate being cold, so…" I began.

The water hit us in waves from all sides, a shock to the system with each spray. My hands pushed against his wet shirt while he held me tight. It brought back a memory from three years earlier. He and Cade had heard about Kelsey's and my summer ritual of sleeping out on the trampoline and had completely drenched us with buckets of water. A water fight had ensued, and since Cade was there for Kelsey, it was kind of like Logan was there for me. The memory was now a kaleidoscope of moments bleeding into each other, where I couldn't tell the first from the last. His arms lifting me on his shoulder like a sack of flour, laughing together, me on his back. Both of us dripping wet. Much like now. Outwardly, I had to protest, but whatever plan he had, I was all in.

I complained loudly the entire way, but he paid me little heed beyond an occasional grin. He stopped in the middle of two rows of apple trees, the cold water blasting us on a rhythm now.

"Wow, that is cold," he said.

"Right? You butt. Let me go." There was no heat to my words, and my mouth was shivering. He stepped closer, wrapping his arms around me fully, our chests pressed together.

"Your problem is that you're stuck on the last memories you had here. You need different ones. Better ones to override the bad."

"I'm concerned about your definition of better."

"Shhh. Listen."

Over the sound of the sprinklers, a commercial blasted from Logan's truck.

"Now, don't get your hopes up for the rest of our dates. I don't dance. But I'm willing to make the exception here. I found some random playlist called Party Animal Dance Music. I have no idea what's coming. We dance to the next three songs, whatever style, and then call it a night." He pierced me with a weighted gaze as he added, "Then, we never speak of this to anyone."

"Why the sprinklers, though?"

He made a sound of impatient disbelief. "It's the rain."

"The what?"

He sighed. "Dancing in the rain. We don't have rain, so I had to make it myself."

I was loving where this was going, but I still found myself confused. "So, you're making this more romantic? With the fake rain?"

He stilled, his eyes peering into mine warily. "No. I'm stamping the memory into your brain with the cold water. If it was just dancing, it wouldn't erase the past. Do you know anything about overriding bad memories?"

My head fell onto his chest while I grinned and tried to collect myself. Already the blast of the water had turned my body numb. We were both soaked, and I was glad I had chosen to wear a blue shirt and not the white one I had debated over. I wanted to cry for the cuteness of it all. The sweetness. And the earnest-but-reserved look in Logan's eyes as he studied me.

"Party Animal Dance Music. This is making it sound like you *are* a dancer," I said, smiling up at him.

"It's not *my* playlist. Although, I am starting to feel a little nervous about it."

We faced each other, and I shivered, waiting for the Botox commercial to end.

The familiar lively tune of "Cotton-Eye Joe" suddenly blasted into the orchard. Logan looked horrified before pulling away from me to make a run for his truck.

"No!" I grabbed his arm and pulled him back to me, laughing. "No changing! You *have* to dance to this."

His shoulders dropped, but only for a second, before he grabbed my hand and began twirling me in front of him, my hair flying out in long strands like the swing ride at the county fair. Drops of water flew off my body. He spun me until I was dizzy and out of breath before pulling me close with his left hand and his right grabbing mine as our moves became exaggerated and extremely country.

"YMCA" rolled in seamlessly next, and before I knew what he was doing, he picked me up and, in some hot, manly way, maneuvered my body so I was sitting on his shoulders. His hands were on my legs while I clung to his head for dear life as we pranced around the orchard shouting the lyrics at the top of our lungs. I felt an overwhelming sense of relief that my parents were out to dinner with friends tonight. The last song began as I slid down from Logan's shoulders. We were both

panting and grinning and teasing before we noticed that the third song
was not like the others.

Our laughter faded. Logan's brow furrowed as the slow, steel-guitar
entry began filling the orchard with a mood that was equally sobering
as it was sweet. Suddenly, I was all hands and limbs, shy and unsure as
to why somebody's idea of party music was really a sweet country
song called "Dirt." Logan's gaze flicked to mine, watching me carefully. His body stood rigid, as if he was unsure of what to do as well. I
was guessing there was a reason he had chosen party songs—to keep
us from having a moment like this. Resolve flashed on his face. He
stepped into my space, grabbing my left hand with his right while his
other hand held my waist. Proper. The way a groom would dance with
his mother at his wedding. Three Bibles could have fit nicely
between us.

"Bak, bak, bak," I couldn't help but crow.

Logan glared at me. "Rule breaker." He lasted a stubborn twenty
more seconds into the song before he dropped my hand.

"That way sucks," he mumbled.

He drew me against his body, clasping his hands together behind
my back. He felt rigid, as though he was keeping himself in careful
check. My arms went immediately around his shoulders. The cold had
been forgotten about two songs ago, my body long since numb.
Though he was drenched under the same cold water I was, unlike
mine, his body emitted warmth. A full-body shiver came over me as
the heat from his body began to thaw the ice from mine. I lifted my
head to look at him when he immediately pushed my head back down
against his chest.

"Nope. You aren't allowed to look at me like that," he murmured.

"Like what?" I asked with my face squished against his body while
the song crooned on about the important things in life.

"With big Bambi eyes and this song...no. You can't look at me. We
have rules."

A grin lit my face, and I didn't try to hold it back. It didn't matter.
He couldn't see it anyway. His grip on my head had softened to something more like a caress, though I didn't look up at him again. He held

me now like a hug—one arm around me with the other at my head, methodically running his fingers through my hair. He didn't kiss me. He didn't cradle my face like in the ditch. He wouldn't even look at me. But for once, he wasn't teasing. He wasn't flirting. And his reaction hinted at things he wouldn't while he tucked me close and held me as we swayed back and forth to a really good song.

Even when another song began to play, this time sounding like another true party song, he didn't release me. I began to suspect it was because he didn't know what to do with me. He was scared of what he *could* do with me. I had no idea if my attempts at half-court press had been noticed by Logan, but they felt huge to me. My heart was out there for the taking, and I felt like I was in limbo, waiting to see if he would reach out. We had only a couple more dates until the end of our summer. The overnight camping trip to the hot springs. And then it was up to Logan. I was about to lift my head to play another card when his body tightened.

He released me as the words to the music became more prominent. I met his confused gaze with my own questioning glance. He was listening for something. So, I did too. What was this song? It seemed so familiar, but I couldn't put my finger on it just…

Realization dawned on us at the exact same time. With squeals and wheezy laughter, we took off running toward the truck, Logan ahead of me, my hands at his back, pushing him forward to stop what was coming next.

We were too late.

We reached the truck at the same time the chorus of Nelly's "Hot in Herre" blasted out in booming decibels. Logan stopped suddenly, causing me to run into him. He turned and, with a wicked gleam in his eye, began lifting up the hem of his shirt.

"Alright, *one* more song."

I protested loudly and pushed his body toward his truck while he laughed and turned off the music.

All in all, it had been a pretty magical night in the orchard. Watching Logan play a fake banjo to the tune of "Cotton Eye Joe", the feel of my legs on his shoulders, his hands on my shins, and our slow-dancing to "Dirt" would play out in my dreams for a long time to come. But the part of the night that I lost sleep over had happened before the dancing. Logan had confided in me. He had given me a piece of himself he couldn't take away.

Logan: I swear I said four dances. You owe me a dance. My song choice.
Me: You said three. Nice try.
Logan: How are those memories tonight?
Me: Much better, thank you.
Logan: Well I have a new favorite song now.
Me: Cotton Eye Joe?
Logan: You know me so well.

I went to sleep all smiles. Logan was a better player in this game than I gave him credit for. I only hoped we were playing for the same thing.

27

LOGAN

"I got one."

I looked next to me on the dock in time to see Jake reel in a decent-sized rainbow trout. He pulled it in and yanked it out of the water, landing it behind him. The fish fought for life, gasping for breath, flopping every which way, while we watched it slowly suffocate.

"You gonna eat that?" I asked Jake from my camp chair next to him. I wasn't sure how he had convinced me to wake up early on a Sunday to go fishing, but here I was, at a reservoir ten minutes from my house, sitting on a dock, holding a fishing pole in the hot sun, trying to evade Jake's questions.

"Chad told me he'd buy anything I caught." Jake grinned over at me, his cowboy hat gleaming in the sun. "Fingers crossed he grinds it up into some sort of meat patty and makes it a special."

Before I could appropriately respond, he said, "Hey, speaking of *special…*"

"Stop," I warned, adjusting my line.

"I just want to get the low-down on you and Tessa. Man to man."

I eyed Jake, fishing in his basketball shorts, flannel shirt, and full cowboy gear, and had to object. "I'm not sure what you are."

Jake grabbed the lifeless fish and carefully removed his hook before tossing it in a cooler. "You spend all your extra time at her house, so naturally, I'm curious as to whether or not I'll be handing over the keys to a very fancy truck soon."

"I'm fixing her dad's porch."

"Yeah. And you've almost built an entire office building during the same amount of time." He shot me a look bursting with such obnoxious satisfaction my fingers itched to throw him in the lake.

But it wasn't my time on the porch the past week that had my thoughts flip-flopping around like the fish that might one day see the inside of Chad's meat grinder. If I could have known the words that would run from my mouth last night, I would have left my drill there. Merry Christmas, Frank. It's all yours. Sure beats baring my soul to your nosy, bratty, delight of a daughter. I had told her things nobody needed to know. Things she had no business knowing when this was all supposed to be fake. A bet. We had an arrangement. But I couldn't deny that I felt lighter than I had in months—years, even.

Though, I could no longer look her in the eyes.

It didn't take a genius to know that, somewhere in our summer (looking at you, ditch), her loyalties to the truck and the $40,000 had been compromised. I wasn't sure what it was about that night that caused the sudden shift from our easy-breezy summer with rules and boundaries to dancing in an orchard, spilling my guts, and hanging out not ONCE but SIX times a week.

And I liked it. FLIP.

Any guy would. But she was from my hometown. Kelsey informed me, in no uncertain terms, that she would cut off a *very* important body part of mine if I hurt her friend. Tessa was so embroiled in my family's life that there was no coming back from dating her. It was too hard to let somebody I cared about trust me when I didn't even trust myself. I knew this going into the bet, but Tessa had assured me she was fine to do this. She knew where I stood. I was beginning to think she was a liar. FLOP.

There was a reason for the sprinklers last night. I needed a cold dose of reality. The song choices had been unfortunate, but none so much as the last one. The slow dance. You could deny a lot of things when dancing around like an idiot. Sharing a laugh. It was when you were holding the girl in your arms while words were flying around that made a man think about putting down roots, and setting up house, and kids, and things he had no business thinking about. That was when you knew you were in trouble. Thoughts like that had been blown up with Valerie. Or so I had thought. FLIP.

"Cat got your tongue, Romeo?" Jake's voice cut into my thoughts.

I cleared my throat and checked my line. Still nothing. Fishing was dumb. "We're just friends."

"I just find it surprising you haven't asked out any other girls this whole summer. That seemed an important clause for you to put into our agreement." He raised his eyebrows at me while I stared at him, slightly dumbfounded.

"Maybe I have."

He snorted. "Just give me something, man. Do you like her?"

I shook my head. "Should we paint each other's nails and swap friendship bracelets first?"

"You know I don't have the cuticles for nail polish. Answer."

Sighing, I said, "Yeah, I like her. Who wouldn't? But I'm not looking for anything serious."

I got Jake to pull a ceasefire on his questions, and we left for home soon after. I needed a nap. A weaker man might have thought this was about the money. The truck. It wasn't at all. I hadn't wanted Jake to thrust his stupid bet in my face. I didn't care about the money or the truck. Not at the expense of Jake. It felt dirty and had from the start. Jake had his own issues he needed to work out. I didn't need his dad's guilt money either. It only complicated things. HE complicated things, starting with the night at The Grub Shack. He had forced my hand. Tessa was going to get hurt, and I hated that. She'd already had one huge heartbreak in her life, and now I was going to do it to her all over again.

Who would be the guy to fix her new memories of the orchard? FLOP.

Maybe if I hadn't met Val, I'd be different. Maybe Tessa wouldn't scare me. But I *had* met Val. And Tessa had met Tyler—a man she had trusted and thought she loved. And he had destroyed her. Who was to think I'd be any different?

Jake's bet saved me here. He had given me my perfect out. I could date other girls. It was stipulated in the contract. I *should* date other girls. This *thing* this summer wasn't going to affect me. I was set. I didn't need the white picket fence or a stubborn baker-slash-physical-therapist woman coming into my life and thinking I was something else, only to be disappointed.

You know those people who aren't afraid to take what they want? The guy who takes the last slice of pizza everybody was eyeing awkwardly? The friend who calls dibs for the master bedroom in a rental house shared with other people? The guy who cuts the line? Those people who take the best of everything at the expense of everyone else? While I find them to be mostly annoying, I had to admit, they were also a little inspiring in how they lived their lives. They must have this sense, deep down, that they deserve the best. I had always been a middle guy. I'd happily take the unobtrusive room in the basement, claim I was too full for the last slice, and I'd ignore the line cutter. Always playing it safe. Low risk and low reward was my game.

I tried to think of one word good enough to describe Tessa, but it was impossible. There wasn't just one word. She was a feeling. She was all the words together. Magnetic. Radiant. Funny. Beautiful. She was storm clouds and rain and the best summer day. She was pink toenail polish and a ponytail. She was cutoff shorts and a teasing eyebrow. A porch swing after a long day. A large Pepsi, not diet. She was soft and prickly. Salty and Sweet. The best combo. She was perfect. No. That word *was* too sterile.

Damnit…she was magnificent.

FLIP.

But Tessa was also high risk.

Even though it felt wrong in every limb of my body, and my heart began to beat in that you're-making-a-huge-mistake way, I had to do something. It was getting hard to breathe. Tessa was stifling the life out of me. I wasn't right for Tessa. She didn't need me. She may have thought she wanted me, but she didn't *need* me. I had to stick to the plan. And for some reason I couldn't quite define, I picked up my phone and dialed a number.

FLOP.

"LOGAN!"

My eyes fluttered open. It was later that afternoon and I had been taking a nap in the bunkhouse. From the sounds of the booming racket going on downstairs, Stitch had decided to take a nap as well.

"Logan."

"Yeah?" My eyes focused on my dad peering over at me from the top of the stairs.

"I need some help checking a few cows at Willow Creek."

I swung my legs out of bed and stood, stretching my arms. "Don't you dang farmers ever rest? It's Sunday."

Dad laughed. "Getting soft from that cushy Monday-through-Friday job, are you?"

"I used to think of you before I took a nap every Sunday in Boise, but now I hardly give you a thought at all." I grinned at my dad's appreciative chuckle as I followed him down the stairs.

"We rest on Sunday, but the cows don't sleep, and neither do we."

"I could have sworn I saw you resting pretty deeply at church this morning."

"I was in deep contemplation of the spirit."

We settled into my dad's old, beat-up, white farm truck, him at the wheel and me attempting to make space for myself amid the spattering of hay, grain sacks, baling twine, saw, and a half-dozen loose tools flung around the passenger seat and floorboards.

"If you worked for me, I would fire you for your treatment of tools."

"I'm finally getting 'em broke in."

Our easy banter carried us through part of the five-mile drive toward the sprawling pastureland at the base of Willow Creek Summit

—my dad's pride and joy and the place Kelsey got married three years earlier. It was only with one mile to go in our drive that I began to suspect ulterior motives on my dad's part to trap me in a vehicle with him. Honestly, I grew up here, but what does 'check the cows' even mean? His fingers took turns flexing and relaxing on the wheel, and he shifted in his seat and rubbed his neck, glancing my way every so often. By the time he cleared his throat, I was looking around for an escape hatch but saw none—at least none I was willing to attempt while going my dad's signature forty miles an hour. This wasn't a drive to check the cattle. This was an ambush. A planned attack.

"Listen, Logan, I know on paper you're too old to need your dad, alright? You're a grown man, and your life is your business, and I mean to respect that. But there are times I wish I still had my dad around to talk to, so I'm gonna say my piece. Do with it what you will."

I braced myself for what was to come. My dad loved me, sure as rain, but I sensed a disappointment behind his coming words, and for some reason, that thought gutted me.

Growing up, we had always gotten along fairly well. My dad was a guy who kept his relationships above all else. But as I grew older, ready to leave the nest, I became more of a stubborn mule than a decent son. I began thinking myself more experienced and knowledge-able in the world. Thinking I knew better about everything. My dad began hearing earfuls from me about the millions of different ways to make life on the farm easier and more technologically advanced, if only he'd listen. I could build him this or that. He could buy this machine, and it would cut our manual labor in half. Perhaps some of that was true, but now I realized that a man had to go about the world his own way. On his own terms. It took me some time to realize that my dad wasn't necessarily after ease and comfort. He was after falling into bed each night with a weary body from his labors and a clear conscience from his efforts.

I understood that now.

Perhaps it was because I understood the sleepless nights that could come from an uneasy conscience.

He cleared his throat again. "Now, I don't know what exactly is going on, but it doesn't take an idiot to know you have something cooking with Jake. And it involves Tessa."

I didn't say anything. I didn't have to. My dad kept right on going, even as he parked in front of the gate to the pasture.

He looked over at me. "Am I right?"

I gripped my pants, holding back my fingers that were itching to open the door and make a run for it. "Yeah."

"Why the games? You do know you're old enough to settle down, right?"

You're not marriage material.

You were just a good time.

Even now, six years later, those words still ruled over me, drove me into turning my life into a sick, self-fulfilling prophecy.

"I think we both know that I'm not good enough for Tessa Robbins, Dad."

What was that burning behind my eyes? I said the words, and now I had the feeling like I wanted to get in the fetal position and suck my thumb. I bit my lip hard enough to give the sensation in my eyes the middle finger.

When my dad laughed, really laughed, he held nothing back. His head flew backward, and a big, gusty howl came flying out.

I breathed out a scoff, shaking my head in amazement.

He slapped his leg, and dust went flying. "Of course you're not good enough for her. She's a delight. I especially appreciate how she doesn't seem to put up with much of your crap."

I could do nothing but nod and agree, though it hurt a little.

He stopped laughing and looked at me, a softer gleam settling in his eyes. "You're not good enough for her, just like I wasn't good enough for your mom. But somehow, she still wanted *me*. Imperfect as I am. Some of us are lucky to know an upgrade when we see one."

I knew Tessa was an upgrade. I could pretend this whole summer, thinking she was too young for me, too much like a sister, too…everything. But it all came down to one thing: I wasn't worthy of Tessa Robbins. Not by a long shot.

"You want to know the secret of life for men like us, son? And this is a secret that will cut through all the bull crap."

I wasn't sure, but he waited until I nodded before he continued. "Find a good woman. And when you find her, marry her. And after you marry her, get out of her way. Because she'll be the best thing to ever happen to you, and that will do more good for your life than all the money and all the *trucks* in the world." I looked at him in some version of alarm and amusement that our bet had been figured out, but he wasn't finished. "If Tessa's that woman, grab ahold of her, and don't be an idiot."

Now, it was my turn to rub at my neck.

Then, my dad surprised me. I thought he was done, winding down. From experience, I knew that both of us could only take an emotional pep talk for so long before we couldn't look each other in the eye for a week.

"And Logan? You're not a player—or whatever the kids say these days. Not really. Not deep down. That was never who you were. I'm not sure what happened the few years after you left, but I imagine it had something to do with a woman. Maybe you got scared?"

My gaze was stuck, zoned in on the handle of the jockey box, even as I felt his eyes on me. I couldn't blink, couldn't move. I could only stare at the handle while trying to keep the heat burning the back of my eyes from turning into liquid.

"I know I give you a hard time, son. It's always been our way. The teasing." He paused and seemed to be gathering his thoughts. "But truthfully, I love you so much. You know that? You're the best son I could have asked for. If your mom and I need you for something, you come at the drop of a hat. You've got an army of friends who'd do anything for you. You work hard, and it shows. You're good to your sisters. I'm so proud of the man you are. Of you. Nobody's perfect, alright? Everyone makes mistakes, and that includes you. But that doesn't mean you are any less deserving of a happy life. Own up to your mistakes. Do better. Be better. You're worthy of happiness, Logan. And if that includes a woman you love, go get her."

Somewhere in the middle of the speech I would remember for the rest of my life, I released the pain from my eyes. It got too hard trying to hold it all in.

It got too hard trying to hold it all *back*.

There were holes and cracks in my armor that filled immediately at his words, like a brick load on my soul had been lightened. I hadn't realized that so much of what I needed was going to come from my dad. Hadn't seen that coming. That even after going down a path that was never something he would have wanted for me, he was still proud of me. Still loved me. He had never stopped. When were you too old to need your dad?

Suddenly, we were two grown men, wiping tears in a dirty old truck on our way to check cattle. What was it about these farm trucks? And for the record, I did see my dad brush back a few tears, though if I brought it up, he would surely tell me he was swatting at a fly.

"You got all that, son?"

I gave him a weak salute. "Yes, sir."

He opened the door to exit but turned back to me. "And just so we're clear. I still like her a lot better than you, and if you hurt that little girl, there are a thousand places on my ranch I can bury a body that not a soul will ever know about."

I nodded slowly, a small smile returning to my face. "I think that's pretty clear."

"Good. Enough of this. Let's go check those cows."

ONCE, on a family trip when I was a kid, we stopped at this hot spring in eastern Idaho. They had made an Olympic-size swimming pool out of the spring and, with it, added an enticing high dive. Naturally, as a cocky fifteen-year-old boy in a family of girls, I signed the waiver, got my wristband, and ran the steps all the way to the top. I strode across the large platform, chest puffed out, to peer over the edge.

Panic assailed me.

My hand clung to the railing. I felt dizzy as my eyes adjusted to the height. My family members were tiny specks in the pool, waving at me and calling excitedly for me to jump. To let go. I got ahold of myself, parroted around, and cried wolf several times. Each time thinking I would jump. Each time stopping just before I let myself. My high-dive career eventually ended before it began, and I was asked to either, 'Jump for the love of all that was holy,' or kindly see myself back down so that the braver among the crowd could take their turn. I walked down, my breath coming in easier with each step that brought me closer to the ground.

I'd been stuck on the high dive for years, prancing about, showing off how high I was, enjoying the view, putting on a good show, but, in the end, too afraid to jump. The longer I stayed up there, the more comfortable I became. After a while, the people on the ground knew I was never going to jump, and so they stopped expecting me to. They stopped watching. They went on with their lives. I stopped having expectations for myself, and everybody else followed suit.

Now, somebody else had joined me at the high dive, holding my hand, willing to jump with me.

If only I could let myself go.

I'd once opened up the most vulnerable part of myself to somebody I thought I had loved and had been rejected. So I had resigned myself to a life of bachelorhood. I would be the fun uncle who takes his nieces and nephews on trips and hangs out with them. Maybe when I hit forty or forty-five, I'd marry a divorcee with a few kids mostly grown. Hopefully, I'd look pretty good as a second choice. And maybe they'd be fine to settle for me. Less risk that way.

Except, now I found myself wanting to take a risk all over again. To jump. This time, the reward was exponentially higher. Settling with someone years later down the road wasn't enough for me anymore. I was tired of playing a low-risk game. I'd been happily playing cards with a deck of only ten and under. But now, I found myself wanting a queen.

And there was one person to blame for it all.

Freaking Jake.

28

TESSA

*D**ear Diary,***
   I'm going on a camping trip with Logan Marten.
LOGAN MARTEN. ALONE. That is all.
XOXO

IT WAS ONLY seven in the morning, and I had already run three miles and been packed since 6 a.m. I couldn't help it. I was a morning person. I'd woken up earlier than usual and had extra energy to burn off. Sitting on the porch, my large backpack was next to me, stuffed with food for a day and a half, my tiny pop-up tent big enough for one, a sleeping bag, a blanket, first-aid kit, swimming suit, and…okay…a tube of mascara. My foot moved to the rhythm of the sprinklers on the next field over, and the morning smelled like fresh dew and grass. What a lovely time to be alive.

A beat-up truck pulled into the driveway, but to my surprise, it was Jake, not Logan. He had never seen us off on a date before, but since our summer was rapidly winding down, and this was the last big date before the end of the bet, it was only natural he would attempt some manipulation before we left.

"Hey, Jake-y," I called from my position draped on the porch swing. "You coming along as our third wheel?"

Jake shuddered, slamming the old tank's door shut and making his way toward me. "I would rather climb into a car with Betsy May behind the wheel."

"Poor Betsy May."

He took the steps two at a time until he hit the porch, where he leaned against the railing, considering me.

"You ready for this?"

Instantly, my heart pounded. The way he said it seemed so ominous. So final. Like this date was what would decide everything. I couldn't have that.

"Sure. I love camping."

"That's not all you love."

I shot him a look. "You ready to give away an eighty-thousand-dollar truck?"

For a second, he looked taken aback, but he covered it up quickly. "If you guys walk away with a truck after this, then Logan really is an idiot and doesn't deserve you."

A surprised blush touched my cheeks at his sweetness. Jake met my eyes and smiled. He held his hand out to mine, wanting me to give him knuckles. Which I did.

"Full-court press?" he asked.

I shook my head. "Nope. Just Tessa press."

His eyebrows shot up in delight.

WHY DO I SAY THESE THINGS?

"Come on, I didn't mean it like that. Just...it's all on him now."

He nodded his approval. "I think Logan will be happy with your plan."

"Shut it."

With a wistful smile, he said, "My kids are growing up so fast."

"How are things going with your girlfriend?" I held my hands up in a ceasefire when he glared at me. "That explains why we haven't seen you around too much lately."

"Giving you two space was all part of the master plan. My hot girl-friend was a bonus. We'll see how long I can fool her."

"She's lucky to have you, Jake. If this thing with Logan goes south, maybe *I'll* start chasing you."

He slid his hands down his plaid shirt and jean-clad body. "You couldn't handle all this, trust me."

I checked my watch. This time, Logan was actually five whole minutes late. I would be sure to rub it in his face. I wore lightweight running pants—the slick kind with pockets—old tennis shoes, and a t-shirt with my sweatshirt tied around my waist. Maybe I should grab my hat? The mountains where the hot pools were was an hour drive north of Eugene. I had hiked them with my family when I was a teenager, and I remembered it snowing in August. Nothing stuck, except the memory and the desire to bring a wide variety of clothing so I didn't freeze.

"You all packed?"

I kicked at the oversized backpack at my feet. "Yup."

"It gets cold up there. You got extra clothes? Tent? Sleeping bag?"

"Yes, Dad. I have a sleeping bag, a tent, and I'm wearing a few layers right now."

He nodded. This exchange seemed weird. Jake was out of sorts today. I wasn't sure why he was here, unless to give me a pep talk or gauge my reaction to see if he would be giving away a truck in the near future.

"What are your parents selling at the stand today?" Jake asked innocently.

I eyed him. Or maybe he was here because of his humongous sweet tooth. "Slices of my chocolate cake."

Jake made a sound that seemed almost pained. "Have I ever told you that, out of all the chocolate cakes in the world, yours is my very favorite? It's better than my mom's."

"Really? Do you tell your mom that?"

He scoffed. "Of course."

"Liar."

Big, puppy-dog eyes pleaded into mine.

"Alright, you big baby. I'll go grab you one. I need to get my hat anyway."

Logan was outside talking to Jake in my driveway when I stepped back onto the porch, the screen door slamming shut behind me. Both men turned and took me in as I made my way over to them. Logan was dressed in gray joggers and a light-green hoodie. His hair was stuffed beneath a baseball hat, and his eyes were on me. Long lashes hid eyes that were dark and mysterious, but they did nothing to quell the zing of nerves shooting straight down my body when I met his gaze.

"Hey, Jailbait."

"Hey." I meant to say something more teasing, to make fun of him for being late or at least be a little flirty, but my soft, breathless answer matched his, and words became nonexistent. For a moment, we just stood there, smiling.

"I'll just take this cake and get out of your hair." Jake had a wide grin on his face and motioned toward the two slices of cake I had in my hands. "Are both of those for me?"

I glanced down and opened my mouth to say something sarcastic, something funny to camouflage my heart and the fact that I definitely brought a slice for Logan, but all words failed me once again. My hands holding the cake slices automatically extended toward them both. Jake grabbed his and had already begun unwrapping it by the time Logan took his slice, his fingers brushing against my palm. I risked a glance up at him.

He was smiling, his eyes crinkly and warm. "I thought I had to work on the porch for a slice of cake. I didn't know you'd give me one for just showing up."

"Don't get used to it," I said.

"Too late."

A loud and obnoxious throat clearing broke into the mood. "I'll just be on my way..." Jake began backing away from us, looking extremely satisfied with the fruits of his labor.

"Bye, Jake," I called, finally finding my voice as he stepped into his truck—the old, beat-up, tin-can truck, mind you. Not the fancy one he had no desire to drive around under our noses.

Well played, Jake.

———

Silver Moon Hot Springs had three levels of hot pools, each located at varying miles up the mountain trail. We passed by the first two, which were separated by half a mile and each packed with people. Logan's eyes and sweat-drenched forehead begged me to let us stop, but I couldn't do it. I didn't want to camp with so many people around. The campsites surrounding the hot pools were littered with tents, and children, and loud teenagers. The hike to the third—much more remote —lake was another mile and a half, almost straight up the mountain. As much as I loved children, there would be none up there, and it was a more secluded mountain setting I was craving.

"Look at how beautiful that lake is, Jailbait. I think it's our duty to stop and appreciate it."

"Where? There is no room for us in this inn, Marten."

"You are a cruel woman."

"To the top."

I started to lead us up the mountain but before I could make it one step, he fell in beside me and grabbed my hand. The move was so casual and smooth, it threw me off guard.

I eyed our hands, keeping careful feelings of elation far away from my face. "You expecting me to pull you up this mountain, Marten?"

He motioned to the trail in front of us. "Look at all those rocks, Jailbait. This is for our safety."

Looking ahead to the steep terrain, I took note of how completely un-rocky the path was. Dirt crusted, sure, but very few rocks. "You are so right. Should we find a walking stick instead?"

He scoffed. "Walking stick? You can't trust a walking stick to protect you. You need somebody with muscles."

"Shoot. I should have asked Jake to come along, then."

He shot me an exasperated look while he tugged me closer. "Don't make me put my arm around you, because I will," he threatened.

"I knew I would end up carrying you up this mountain." He tickled the side of my stomach until I said I was sorry. For the record, I was *not* sorry.

I held hands with Logan Marten the rest of the way up the mountain. In a very non-friends sort of way. My heart was nearly bursting—also in a *non-friends* sort of way. When we finally arrived, it was as spectacular as I had remembered.

We stopped at the empty third pool, appreciating the beauty. Logan's sweat-drenched face looked as if he would appreciate a quick dip, but I made him keep moving. I wanted to set up our camp and get organized first, and I knew I wouldn't be able to relax and enjoy the hot spring until we did so. It was another quarter-mile walk on a flat trail until the thicket of trees spread out enough that we could pitch our tents.

Between the drive to the base, a pit-stop for lunch, and the hike, we had arrived at the hot springs just before 6 p.m. I wanted to be sitting in the pool in time to watch the sunset.

The camp was empty, except for a large bear box. I had figured it would be less crowded than the other two equally striking hot pools, but I hadn't planned on quite so much solitude. I'd been imagining other campers nearby with tents and fire pits, sharing polite nods. Perhaps more would be coming. Sunset was a popular time.

"Do you want to eat dinner real quick?" Logan asked, inhaling a granola bar.

"I'll wait until after the hot pools. You can do whatever. I'm going to set up my tent and change into my swimsuit."

He nodded before shoving the last bite in his mouth, and began rummaging through his pack.

I rummaged through mine, too.

And then I kept rummaging. Searching for something that didn't seem to be there.

In a panic, I dumped my backpack out on the ground. My swimsuit, shorts, underwear, towel, mascara, and extra sports bra all piled into a heap while I searched needlessly for my missing tent. Missing TENT. Yeah, I didn't think it got stuck between my extra pair of underwear and my shorts, but since I KNOW I packed it, my search begged to be thorough. I came up empty.

Logan had his tent set up in about five seconds. He then threw his backpack inside the small, pitched, triangle shape and turned to face me.

"What's that look for?"

I closed my gaping mouth and blinked. My mouth opened again, but nothing came out.

"What's wrong?" Logan asked again.

"I don't have my tent."

His gaze landed on the backpack I was gripping in panic and the spillage of my stuff on the ground. "You didn't pack it?"

"I packed it."

"Then, why isn't it here?"

"I don't know."

There was a beat of silence before I met his eyes. Mirth, hidden behind dark lashes, looked back at me. My fingers clenched even while my heart spiked.

"I packed it."

"Did you, though?" He stared down at me, arms folded and eyebrows raised, enjoying himself immensely.

"I wouldn't have spent an hour last night in my garage, searching for my brother's old musty backpack-sized tent, okay? I packed it." Suddenly, a thought so blinding in its truth and so deceitful in its nature came to my mind. I gasped, my hands covering my mouth.

"Jake."

"Jake what?"

"Jake did this."

"Listen, Tess, we can't blame Jake for you wanting to snuggle with me tonight."

I jumped to my feet. "This morning. He asked me to grab him a piece of cake, and like an idiot, I left him alone on the porch with my bags."

Logan gave a disbelieving laugh. "You gotta love Jake."

"No. I really don't."

He sighed dramatically. "Well, I'm going to feel bad, all tucked away in my cozy tent while you're roughing it in the outdoors, but what can you do?"

I folded my arms. "You can be the gentleman and let me have the tent, maybe?"

He made a face. "I get cold at night."

"Logan…"

"Should we head to the hot spring? Looks like you're done setting up."

I was starting to panic. Logan was teasing, but my anxiety levels were not. "Let me get something straight. I do not do the outdoors in bear country, okay? Either you switch me, or I'm crawling in there with you."

"You and your fourteen-year-old self would love that, wouldn't you?"

"Logan!"

Actually, me and my twenty-four-year-old self would love it, but the less he knew the better. He thought I had done this on purpose. I was going to kill Jake. Or kiss him. On the cheek. Depending on how things played out.

"It's not often I hold all the power. Let me live in this for a minute."

"I'm going to kill Jake."

"I might buy him lunch. So, let me get this straight." Logan had his hand on his chin, looking deep in thought. "You don't have a tent. Correct?"

I gave him an exasperated look.

"Interesting. Do you have a sleeping bag?"

"Yes."

"Pajamas? Or did you 'forget' those, too?"

I pushed a grinning Logan and was gratified when I saw him nearly tumble to the ground.

"Alright, we can figure out logistics later. How about you go in your tent and change, and I'll go into mine."

"Logan!" I stamped my foot while the embarrassed laughter I tried so hard to hold back finally sputtered out.

He threw my bag inside and gave me a soft push toward his tent. "Get changed. You're doing a good job living up to your name, Jailbait."

29

TESSA

My black one-piece was your basic halter-style bathing suit with a pretty scallop design around the chest. I threw on a pair of black, nylon swimming shorts that hit me mid-thigh for the walk down the trail. As I adjusted the ponytail on my head, I looked around Logan's tent. It was a long triangle shape with silver, reflective material inside, supposedly to keep in body heat. It was built for one person to survive in the wild. I supposed it would be roomy enough for two adults to squeeze in here, but with Logan's broad shoulders, there was no way *not* to be touching. I swallowed.

And okay, a small part of me was relieved that I wouldn't be spending the night outdoors alone in a tiny tent. There were bears and all kinds of wild animals out here. For some reason, being with somebody made it less nerve-wracking. That is, assuming Logan let me sleep in here with him.

SLEEP.

Logan slipped in after me, changed into his suit, and quickly returned wearing red board shorts and flashing a pair of abs I could wash my clothes on.

"Freaking Jake must have stolen my Speedo."

I laughed as we fell into step on the trail toward the hot spring. "Why are you walking like that? Did you get hurt?"

He shook his head. "Nah, just stiff. Some hot taskmaster forced me on a death march."

"Such a little baby."

"I kept trying to be naughty enough for a spanking, but it never worked."

The worn dirt pathway was only wide enough for two in certain spots. A quarter of a mile later, towering green pine trees ahead of us formed a U-shaped cocoon encasing a large pool of crystal-blue water that steamed toward the sky. The side of the pool without trees opened up to the sprawling valley of mountains and hills beneath us. Cascading shades of greens and yellows and blues worked together below to orchestrate a view that could take someone's breath away. I glanced up at Logan, who had stopped his walk and simply studied the scene before him.

"Anything you want to say to me now?" I asked, breathing in the earthy scent of pines and dirt.

He looked over at me and smiled. And my heart stopped. Dropped. Then it rolled into my stomach and back again. I couldn't look away. This was Logan. The real Logan. The relaxed, sweet, and teasing Logan. His eyes held no guile or pretension. Only excitement, appreciation, and a softness I could lose sleep over.

A splash in the water broke both of us out of our trance. We moved forward once again, zeroing in on the large pool of smooth natural rock. A large, bearded man sat alone on the far side, his bundled-up towel lying nearby. He waved a friendly hello as we approached from the opposite end.

"How y'all doin'? I'm Pete."

We both smiled his way, though I was a smidge disappointed he appeared to be a talker.

"I'm Logan. This is Tessa," Logan said, holding my hand steady while I stepped into the steaming water behind him.

"What brings you two here?" the man called. He looked like a younger version of Santa Claus, with a brown, scraggly beard that hid any idea of how old he was. He could have been anywhere in the mid-thirties to mid-fifties range, I guessed. He had a light Southern accent. The olive-green stocking cap on his head looked like it had seen a few years. His cheeks were rosy, and he had a hairy potbelly and a jolly countenance about him. "Anniversary?"

We settled down next to each other, finding a smooth place to sit with a decent backrest in the water, facing the man, though he was a good six yards away.

"Nah, just a date," Logan said, his shoulder brushing against mine. "What about you?"

"I'm here to see it all." He stretched his arms out wide, motioning all around him. "My wife and I are camped at the lower spring. She's down with a cold, so I ran up here to see it all real quick. We travel full time in our RV, and this is the best hot spring I've ever seen." He motioned at the view. "Harmony's gonna be so ticked she missed this."

My ears perked up. "Full-time travelers? That sounds fun. How do you do that?"

"By selling our house in suburbia and moving into an RV. We camp outside whenever we can and live off the land."

"What did you do before traveling?" Logan asked, putting his arm around my shoulder and pulling me close in a move so swift and smooth I risked a glance at him. Other than a small twitch of his lips, he kept his focus on Pete.

"I worked for a company in Louisville." Ahh, that explained the accent.

"Do you have kids?" I asked, wondering how a whole family would live squished into an RV long term.

"Nope. We want 'em, but so far, they haven't come au naturel, which is important to us." He took a scoop of the water and held it in front of his face, watching it fall in a tiny stream into the water.

"What do you do for work now?" Logan asked.

"Well, when you live off the land, your expenses are already cut in half. But the wife's been working hard burning through the money we got from selling our house." He burst into a rollicking fit of mirth, his belly bouncing as he did so.

We both laughed politely.

"Nah. I'm kidding. Well, mostly kidding. We have a YouTube channel teaching others how to live off the land. What berries to eat. Hunting tips. Au naturel, you know? Pretty soon, we're gonna be so far off the grid the government won't be able to find us. That's the goal, anyway."

Cue awkward silence.

We chatted with Pete for a while before he said, "Well, it's been nice talking with you both, but I better get back to my better half."

And then, he stood up.

The '*Nice to meet you*' forming on my lips died instantly. It was no longer nice to meet him. He stood before us, naked as the day he was born, before turning around, a tanned ham speckled with black hair on full display as he bent forward to climb the rocks out of the hot spring.

Logan tensed beside me, but we both watched, captivated and horrified but unable to look away even as the man bent over once again to grab his towel.

The hand from the arm around my shoulders fell in front of my eyes, blocking the view. I leaned into his body that was shaking from holding in a silent laugh.

The seconds turned into years. I wasn't trying to peek, but I couldn't help but make sure the man was leaving. He certainly took his time drying off, even checking his phone for messages, bending and twisting every which way before sliding on a pair of cargo cutoff army shorts that looked straight from the '90s.

He turned to us, waving. "Have fun, you two!"

"Nice to meet you!" Logan called cheerfully, as the man exited his stage.

We gave it a hearty ten seconds to make sure he had gone before we both lost it. Logan leaned forward, his high-pitched, wheezy laughter making me laugh even as my hands covered my face in horror.

"So much naked," Logan said.

"So much...everything," I gasped, looking around the pool like it was a petri dish full of herpes. "If he is living off the land, does that make this his bathtub?"

"Au naturel."

I groaned, and peered into the water. "How hot does this run? Does it kill...naked things?"

"I'm sure there has been worse done in this pool." He grinned over at me, putting his arm back around my shoulder and pulling me close again. I found no fault with this plan and leaned my head on his chest.

"Question for you," Logan said.

"Yeah?"

"The backside. I have to know...who wore it better? Me or him?"

I slapped my hand against the water, spraying him while he attempted to block my attack.

"What? I figured you were the best person to ask."

I pulled away just enough to launch myself at him, using the momentum from my body weight and the strength of my humongous biceps to push him into the water. It took Logan all of two seconds before he had untangled himself from my attempts at a light drowning and tossed me into the deep end.

I came out of the water wiping my eyes, pushing back my hair, and seeking revenge. Logan stood waiting for me calmly, arms folded, his construction biceps carved out of stone as his eyes trailed down my entire body and back up again. I forced myself to keep moving toward him, to see this to the end. Somehow, Logan Marten would get dunked in this pool before we left. When I was only one foot away, his hands reached down and fingered the waistband of his shorts, and when he began to tug them downward, I stopped abruptly.

"What are you doing?"

"I feel like I'm overdressed now."

He grinned, and before I could react, he slid an arm around my waist, pulling me to him, effectively changing the feel of our game. But revenge was still very much on my mind. I acted like I was closing in for a hug but pushed him backward instead. This time, he fell, but he took me down with him. Water crashed over my head for the second time in thirty seconds. We scrambled up for air, the movement of the water pulling us back down. I was laughing too hard to stand. Then, his hands were helping me up, gripped lightly under my elbow. Then, they were turning me, tugging me closer. On my shoulders and in my neck and in my hair. The heat from his body warmed my skin as he closed the last of the gap between us. Then, I couldn't feel his hands anymore. His lips had taken over.

VOICES in the woods broke us apart. Warm light filtered through the trees. The sunset would probably be making its spectacular appearance soon. We both stumbled to our spot looking out over the mountain view. My lips felt swollen in the best way. I glanced at Logan when we sat down, and he smiled at me while his hand snaked through his hair.

A group of women broke through the clearing. There were about five of them, in their late twenties to mid-thirties, all loud talkers and wearing bathing suits and tennis shoes. By the time they had made their way to us, Logan and I sat casually, our hands to ourselves, with a couple of inches between us. I was trying to keep my heart from leaping out of my chest. Logan had just kissed me. We'd long since fulfilled any requirements for Jake's ridiculous bet, but he was still kissing me. And his kiss felt like something. It wasn't the type of kiss you give somebody when you were planning to trade them in for a truck in a few days.

"Logan?"

We turned to see Jen, the waitress who worked for Chad, step into the pool, wearing the tiniest green-and-white-striped bikini I had ever seen. Her long, auburn hair was in a high ponytail, freckles dotted all over her face and neck beautifully, and her cleavage was…busty and perfect. She waded over toward Logan, and her eyes brightened when she saw me.

"Hey, Blondie. How'd you drag him up this mountain? He told me he wasn't into hiking."

I swallowed, immediately feeling the mood shift at Jen's presence.

It could have been the way Logan's body stiffened beside me as she approached.

"Wait, are you guys together?" Her eyes flitted back and forth between us.

There was an awkward pause. Logan and I shared a glance, but neither of us said anything. Who asks that? Logan opened his mouth to say something, but I beat him to it. "No, we're just...here."

We're just here? I meant to say that we were on a date, but then I remembered not wanting anybody from Eugene to know I was seeing Logan in any capacity. In the last-second scramble inside my brain, 'We're just here,' leaked out.

Logan relaxed, and I wondered what he was going to say. Could I have said anything else? It was true. We were on a date. Just a date, like he had told Naked Pete, but somehow that didn't seem like quite enough. *Well, we just kissed, Jen. Definitely on the verge of a full-blown make-out session before your troop got here. And we've been flirting the past couple weeks like it's our job, but there is also a huge bet on the line, and we really haven't talked about our feelings yet.* Too complicated. Maybe a date was all we could have said.

"Oh good," Jen's voice tinkled loudly, beaming at Logan. "Then I hope we're still on for next week, handsome."

"You have a date next week?" a leggy brunette called out behind Jen. "You never told me that! I thought all the men in your town were dried up."

Jen laughed. "He asked me out last Sunday." She smiled at Logan and me, motioning toward her friend with her head. "That's my cousin, Cheryl, and those are some of my old friends from Salmon."

Jen made quick introductions, but when she got very little out of me and Logan, she waved us off. I could only stare as she jetted to her side of the pool with her friends, her backside as perfectly sculpted as the front, and left us drowning in her wake.

Left *me* drowning.

Logan's face was carved stone as he stared listlessly out at the valley below, his jaw clenched. I inched away from him. He had a date with Jen next week. He had called her a week ago and asked her on a date.

A week ago.

Sunday. The dance in the orchard had been Saturday night.

Sunday. I nodded before I realized I was doing it, trying to convince myself that my feelings weren't valid. I had no right to feelings when, technically, Logan hadn't done anything wrong. He was allowed to date while we snuck around, trying to avoid liking each other.

What was Jake thinking? He had presented the bet, in my mind, as if I couldn't lose. Either way, I get to hang out with somebody fun all summer, then fall in love, or get a fancy new truck. I could pay off student loans with that money. Put a down payment on a house. All cheery and good.

NO. Not cheery and not good.

Childhood infatuation aside, we had shared things. I had told him hard things, and he had listened to me. Comforted me. Like a boyfriend would do. He told me about Valerie. Our kiss five minutes earlier wasn't something you just did on a whim. Well, not me anyway. Maybe that's exactly what Logan did on all his dates. There was no more denying it. I had been falling all summer long, each day a little more, like a drop in the bucket. I thought things might have changed for him as well. It wasn't a game to me. Not anymore.

My greatest fear of the whole summer had just come true.

I was in love with Logan Marten, and he had played me.

Well done, Marten.

If I didn't know how I felt about Tessa before this, watching her face fall at Jen's words clinched the deal. A punch to the gut by Mike Tyson would have hurt less. A man who thought higher of himself would have probably been angry at Jen. But I was not a man who thought highly of myself. This was all my fault. Jen was just being Jen, and I—like always—was just being a complete idiot.

Tessa's shoulders were unbending as she made a beeline on the trail in front of me to our tents. I swallowed. Tent. Since Jen's confessional, I couldn't look at Tessa. I didn't want to see what I'd done to her in her eyes. Her jaw was clenched, and the second we'd seen enough of the sunset, she stood up and climbed out of the water. I had begun to follow her but got waylaid by Jen's gaggle of girlfriends.

"What time are you picking me up on Tuesday?" Jen asked, all smiles, not noticing Tessa practically running up the trail. Or maybe just not caring?

I stepped out of the pool, smiling tightly while wrapping my towel around my waist. "Actually, Jen. I don't think that's going to work out."

Her painted eyebrows lifted before her eyes found Tessa, growing smaller in the distance. "Oh? I'm sorry, did I step my foot in something? I honestly thought you two were just friends."

"Not your fault," I said, stepping into my shoes. "I just can't go out with you." The circle of estrogen grew to a hushed silence, their eyes bouncing between Jen and me like a ping-pong match. A pack of wolves had nothing on this crowd. Good for Jen. Bad for me.

"Well, I'll see you around, Jen. Sorry again. It was nice to meet you all."

"Goodnight, Logan," Jen called to my back as I hit the trail after Tessa.

"Tess, wait up."

She kept walking, her back ramrod straight. I waited to try again until we had reached our tent.

"Tess, I'm really sorry about that. I—"

"You didn't do anything wrong." She turned to face me, her disheartened eyes contradicting everything she said.

I folded my arms and stood my ground, hating myself for the hurt in her eyes. "Really? Because I think I screwed up big time."

Her shoulders jerked into a quick shrug. "According to Jake, you can ask out anybody you want. You can date, kiss whatever girl you happen to be with, and then you can win a truck at the end of the summer. Pretty sweet deal."

"Is that what you think I've been doing?"

"I don't know. I don't really care, I guess. I knew better than to agree to this stupid bet with a player."

I swallowed back the retort rising in my throat. I deserved it. "I broke off the date, Tess. I don't want to go. I never really wanted to go."

She held her hands up while she shook her head. "No, please. Don't break anything off on my account. I've been played one too many times by guys like you, and I'm sick of it."

"Guys like me?"

She nodded, finally meeting my eyes.

"I wasn't playing you, Tess." I made a move toward her, but she lurched backward three steps, holding her hands outward.

"No. Stop. Fine, I'll be honest. I felt stuff…for you. Okay? I thought we had connected, taken this big step forward. But the day after the orchard, you asked another girl out on a date. So, obviously, we were in different places."

"We're not in different places," I stated, heart pounding at my confession.

She stared at me, the hurt in her eyes turning to anger. "You asked her out last week. Last WEEK. That sounds like different places to me." She turned and yanked at the zipper on my tent. "You were kissing me twenty minutes ago, and you have a date with another girl in a few days."

"*Had* a date. And it was dumb. I got scared, and I'm sorry. I don't like Jen."

"Quick to change your mind, but I guess that's pretty on brand with you."

I jerked back like I'd been scalded. "Hold on a minute, where do you come off judging me like I'm some womanizing jerk? I used to go on a lot of dates, yeah, but that's not a crime. I wasn't using anybody or stringing anybody along—"

She held up her hands to stop my words. "Look, it's fine. I'm not angry, I promise. I knew the bet, but I don't want to do this anymore. Forget about Jen, but if your solution when things get scary is to run off with the first girl you can find, I don't want any part of this. Next week, we get our truck from Jake, and then we can be done."

Done.

She turned around, her movements jerky and stiff as she crawled in the tent. "I'm only sleeping in here because I'd rather *not* get eaten by a bear tonight, ok? I'm changing really quick, so don't come in."

I blew out a frustrated breath as I waited outside the tent. In a matter of twenty minutes everything that could have gone wrong had gone wrong. And it was all my fault. I had been a different person when I asked Jen out a week ago, terrified of a pint-sized blonde who had weaseled her way into my life and turned my world upside down.

All summer long I had been stumbling before it finally felt like I had caught my footing this past week. And now, I'd managed to trip myself hard and fast, right over a cliff. I may have felt like a changed man, but that didn't mean there wouldn't be consequences to my previous actions.

I rubbed my hands over my face as I paced the ground outside the tent. It was marketed as a two-man life tent. Which was laughable. It packed snug and tight in a backpack and was meant to keep a person alive in below-freezing temperatures. It could keep a kitten alive in the Arctic, but one idiot male and an angry female, plus luggage, was questionable. It would be hard to not touch her in general, but also, logistically speaking, we would practically have to be cuddling for us both to fit. I had more I needed to say to Tessa, more I wanted to explain, but she was ticked at the moment and rightfully so. I'd wait for a good opening to talk and take it, but if none came until morning, I could wait. I deserved to wait. Besides, no offense to all the relationship counselors out there, but going to bed angry, when I was this attracted to the girl literally millimeters away from me and my wandering hands, would probably be for the best.

If I were a gentleman, I would have volunteered to sleep outside. But deep down, I was also scared of getting eaten by a bear, so when Tessa gave me the all-clear, I crawled inside.

The tiny bit of light left from the sunset had faded, so Tessa had my lantern on and was already wrapped in her sleeping bag, taking up a good three-fourths of the four-foot-wide tent. She was facing the tent wall, her head burrowed under her fluffy sleeping bag, the top of her blonde hair all I could make out.

I was soaking wet, but it didn't seem like she was going to be spying on me, so I changed and dried off as quickly as I could, kneeling awkwardly in one square foot of space. Because the tent ceiling was so low, I had to lie down on my sleeping bag to pull on my boxers and pants, which meant lying halfway on top of Tessa as well while I yanked them on.

"Ow." Tessa scooted farther against the wall.

"Sorry, Jailbait, but I gotta have more than two inches."

"Why are you even changing? I thought you'd be back in the pool with Jen by now."

I took a deep breath, trying to keep my cool. She was hurting, and I had done that. *Me.* I had messed up big time. I had zero interest in Jen. *I* knew that, but Tessa did not. I was fine with giving her time, but she was throwing accusations at me like she personally knew me to be some sort of man-whore. Like she had expected all along for me to be cheating on her—or whatever we were. It was...aggravating.

"Can we talk, Tess?" I finally asked, keeping my tone neutral.

She didn't say anything.

I reached into my duffel bag and dumped a sackful of granola bars and sandwiches between us. "You don't have to talk to me right now, but you do need to eat. I've got to put this stuff in the bear box before we go to sleep." I should have done that as soon as we got to camp, but since learning I would be sharing one tent with Tessa, my mind, under-standably, had been otherwise engaged. She didn't move, didn't say a word. So, I sat there for a moment, wondering what to do with this livid woman who really needed to eat the peanut butter sandwich I held in my hands inside a flimsy nylon tent deep in bear country. It was then that I realized I would much rather have *some* reaction than none at all.

"You ready to eat, Princess?"

There was a moment of silence before her head turned toward me, her murderous eyes throwing darts in my direction. "Princess?"

I lifted my chin and held her stare because her murder eyes only scared me a little bit. "It seems fitting with how you're acting right now."

Well done, Marten. *That* statement definitely got a reaction. "How *I'm* acting, Fabio?"

"Yup. I want to talk to you."

She stared at me for a long, incredulous moment before she sat up in her bed, her legs brushing against mine. "Okay, go ahead." She said the words in a way that a serial killer might offer their victim a chance to plead their case just before slitting their throat.

"First up." I tossed her a sandwich. It landed on her lap where she stared at it like it was laced with cyanide. "You need to eat. We've got to put this food away."

She threw it back. "I'm not hungry."

"I'm not talking to you on an empty stomach. I've learned that lesson, believe me."

"Well, I don't eat when I'm angry."

"I thought you weren't angry."

"I'm not. I was stating a fact."

My lips twitched. Hers did not. I could feel my body tighten with annoyance.

I opened my sandwich and took a large bite. The smell of peanut butter immediately filled the air. She glowered at me before lying back down, facing the wall again.

"Mmm. This is good."

"Great, peanut butter. The bears will love that," she said, still not looking at me.

I took another bite and moaned. "This might be the best PB&J I've ever had."

"Did your mom make it for you?"

I smiled, holding back a laugh. "No, she said I had to do it myself."

There was an almost imperceptible shake of her head. She was a stubborn thing. I finished my sandwich, making a big, annoying production out of it before taking a swig of water from my water bottle.

"Last chance to eat," I said, gathering up the food scattered between us.

She didn't answer. I grabbed my phone and used it as a flashlight as I made my way to the bear box, deposited our food, and crawled back inside the tent. I turned off the lantern and settled into my sleeping bag, facing away from Tessa. I was very aware that if I moved one inch, our backs would be pressed together. I didn't want to make her uncomfortable or push her too far, so I held firm in not allowing my back to touch hers. I had imagined this night going differently. Not that I expected anything to happen, but from our time in the hot spring,

I had definitely imagined more cuddling. The happy kind. Not the kind where if I relaxed a fraction of an inch, I might lose a limb.

Like a little boy pulling pigtails for attention, I tested my theory and allowed my back to relax into hers the tiniest bit. She pushed against me before jerking forward.

The most uncomfortably hilarious minute later, her back bumped into mine with a surprising degree of force.

"Logan, I swear, if you're laughing right now, I will cut your head off and feed it to the bears for a snack."

I rolled over onto my back. "You kiss your mother with that mouth?"

"Logan."

"Easy with the bear talk, alright? You keep this up, maybe I'll let you get eaten."

She spun around, her shoulder landing on top of mine as she did so. "You'll *let* me get eaten? Instead of what—*saving* me?" She scoffed. "We both know I can run a lot faster than you."

"Maybe, but I'm stronger."

Her eyebrows lifted, and I thought I detected the slightest hint of laughter lurking on her face before it was gone. "So, what do you do with all that strength when a bear attacks you?"

"Fight him."

"Great. While you fight him, I'll be running away. Much faster than you." She elbowed my arm. "Stop laughing."

"Stop being a baby. You need to eat something so we can have this out. You're scarier than a bear right now."

"I don't want to talk to you right now. I need to cool off without you annoying me. I'm too…something."

"Not angry, though, right?"

"Nope."

"That's good news."

"Good night, Fabio. Don't come crawling to me if a bear does come."

"Ditto. Sweet dreams, Princess."

31

TESSA

If I lay very still, I could make out the smell of Logan's peanut butter sandwich lingering in the air, tantalizing my taste buds. Along with probably all the bears within a ten-mile radius. I would have clawed his eyes out for that sandwich if it had taken him any longer to eat. I probably would have felt better if I had eaten something, but then Logan would have made me talk, and I didn't feel like talking yet. Acting like a wounded toddler seemed a much better option.

I needed to sort a few things out in my mind.

My therapist would tell me I was masking my hurt with anger.

She would be right.

Anger, rejection, and frustration were coursing through my veins, but hurt is what fed the flame. How could I have a conversation tonight when my emotions were all over the place? It was my fault. I knew we had a bet on the line. I knew we had agreed we could both date other people. I knew all of this, but I let one important stupid emotion into the equation.

Hope.

I had begun to hope. Hope that things were different. That *he* was different. Hope that I could be that girl—the *chosen* one who would be enough to make a man want to change his ways. He had seemed sincere. Things between us had felt real to me. Up until Jen. And I hated that he could still almost make me laugh in this stupid tent when I felt so gutted.

I sighed and moved to lie on my back, my shoulder brushing against Logan, who was sleeping peacefully on his back. I fully intended to edge away and turn again to my side until I felt how warm he was. Any dream I had of sleeping in this tent had gone away about the time my feet began to glaciate. Every piece of warm clothing I had packed was on my body, my sleeping bag was zipped around my chin, and my teeth were still chattering. I pulled my phone from my sweatshirt pocket and checked the time. 2 am.

Logan's heat began inching its way across my shoulder, warming me the smallest fraction. A girl could lean into that so easily. His breathing was slow and even. He probably wouldn't even know if I stole a bit of his body heat.

No.

Maybe I could stamp my icy feet over his legs. Kill two birds with one stone—part heat, part revenge.

No. He would definitely get the wrong idea.

Just the arm then, for a minute. Ever so slightly, I rolled over to face him, careful not to jostle him. It was almost pitch black in the tent, but I could make out his long shape lying so close to me. His right arm was flung across his face, his left leg completely out of his bag, and he was still an oven. I would kill for that kind of body heating system.

I wriggled my toes inside my socks to make sure they were still working properly, then inched my right foot closer to his leg. I got as close to his foot as I could and let it sit there, praying some heat would transfer, but I was not close enough. My hands clenched with irrational irritability. Or perhaps it was rational. I was tired. Starving. A little twitchy. And I had a big target for my anger.

Yes, anger.

Earlier I had tried to place the blame for Logan's behavior on myself. For letting myself hope, for getting involved in the first place. Maybe there was some truth to that, but Logan definitely shared the blame. He had kissed me multiple times, told me things, looked at me…that way. No. Right now, I was a lot of emotions, but first and foremost, I was most definitely angry at him.

Looks like we were going with revenge.

Yanking my sock off, I stamped my right foot on Logan's leg, almost sighing with relief at the immediate contact of heat.

Logan jerked awake, swearing and sitting up in confusion. In his movement, my foot fell off of his leg. I put it back.

His eyes adjusted to the dark, taking my outline in. "What are you doing?"

"Just thought you'd be interested to know I'm about to die from hypothermia."

"You're cold?"

"Yes."

"Did you pack extra clothes?"

"I'm wearing everything I've got, and I'm still freezing."

He took a couple of deep breaths before he got up and unzipped his sleeping bag all the way, rolled me over, and laid it down beneath us. He unzipped my bag and motioned for me to climb in beside him. There was only a brief hesitation before I joined him. I had zero shame about burrowing my head in his chest and tangling my feet in his legs.

He seethed in a ragged breath at *my* touch. I let out a sigh of relief at *his* touch.

"How are you even alive right now?"

"Want to hear how low I've fallen?"

He grunted a noise that I took as a yes.

"First, I'm here." I motioned my hand at myself draped all over him like sunscreen. "And second, I'm almost cold enough that I'm contemplating shoving my hand into your armpit." There was a deep chuckle before he covered his hand over mine on his chest. The relief of sharing Logan's body heat was immediate. I did not, however, let that cloud my head.

Logan began moving his thumb across my frozen hand laying on his chest. I yanked it away.

"Don't do that."

"Why?"

"Because this isn't a fun cuddle. It's survival. It doesn't mean anything."

"Maybe rubbing your hand is for extra warmth. Friction."

"It didn't feel like that was your goal. Let me be clear, you're a giant heating pad to me right now. Nothing more."

"That doesn't seem fair."

"You being a walking furnace and sleeping halfway out of your sleeping bag while I'm a human popsicle doesn't seem fair either."

He grabbed my hand and placed it back on his chest, covering it once again. This time with less *friction*. "It's all that running. I told you it would kill you someday."

I elbowed him in the side, feeling both satisfied and hollow at the grunt exiting his mouth.

I AWOKE FEELING cozy but on high alert.

Here were the stats: It was still dark outside. I was using Logan as a human body pillow. I was rolled onto my side, my left leg tangled into his legs, and my hand was still pocketed under his hand. I had finally thawed out enough to sleep. Except, now I was awake again.

Something had woken me.

I waited, my body tense, for the sound to come again.

A grunt outside had me gripping Logan's shirt at his chest. We were going to die. There was a bear outside, and we were going to be on the news for getting ripped out of our sleeping bag and torn to shreds.

My chest was pumping, but I sat still, tried not to smell like food, and listened intently for another noise. Maybe it was a deer passing through?

Did deer grunt?

No. Something big was definitely moving out there. And chewing. It sounded like something was sniffing and eating the grass while meandering closer toward us.

I shook Logan awake, and he moaned softly. I threw my hand over his mouth and leaned in close to his ear, whispering the most terrifying words ever uttered from my mouth. "There's something out there."

The only sudden movement he made was a long stretch before releasing a sigh. I pushed against him. "Did you hear me?"

"Yeah. Do you know what it is?"

Why wasn't he freaking out?

"I only have bear thoughts in my head right now. It's grunting and eating and moving closer to us. Do something." My mouth pressed against his ear as I spoke.

"Like what?"

"Use your strength and fight him."

He breathed out a chuckle, though I noticed he wasn't moving. At all. "It's probably just an elk or something."

"Or something," I repeated ominously.

We lay still, our bodies tensed, waiting for more movement. And then movement came. The side of the tent near our feet pushed inward in the distinct shape of a nose. Another grunt ensued.

Every swear word I could think of ran silently through my head as I scrambled to sit up, Logan following suit.

I had always tried to give the appearance of being tough. Strong. Sarcastic. Witty. All the things that made up who I was. I liked that image. I didn't want to be the girl hopping up and down on her knees in a tent, holding Logan's body in front of me as a human shield, but there I was. I had always heard you never knew what kind of person you were until a problem was in front of you. Turns out, I was the kind of person who would sacrifice my friends. Or…whatever Logan was.

The outline of the nose retracted from our tent, as the sounds of grunting and eating continued.

To his credit, Logan didn't remove himself from my death grip but, instead, calmly turned his head toward me, holding something in his hand. "I missed a sandwich."

"What? How did you do that?"

"It was dark. I grabbed all the food I could see. It was hidden between our sleeping bags. Why didn't *you* just eat?"

Curse me and my stubbornness which led me to both starve all night and attract the wildlife.

"I wasn't hungry."

He sighed. "Well, I'm pretty sure that's what it's here for."

It.

Such a terrifying word in the wrong context.

"Who's *it*? Do you know what it is?"

I resisted the urge to scream when the nose pushed the tent forward again, this time from the front flap, and instead, attached myself to Logan's back like a starfish to a rock.

Logan swallowed and pointed in front of him. "Yup. That thing right there."

I slid off his back, trying to gather some wits. "Should we throw him the sandwich?"

"How?"

"You open the flap and toss it outside so he'll go after it."

"Why am I in charge of feeding the bear? It's your sandwich."

"You brought it."

"You didn't eat it."

"You're the strong one, remember? I'm just the runner."

The nose disappeared again. A moment later, it came from the other side. It had almost completely circled our tent, trying to find our food. Presumably, it was only a matter of time before it used its claws.

Logan let out a low growl under his breath. His body tensed as he watched the thing remove its nose before he crawled toward the front of the tent. He dropped to his stomach when the creature poked through again. In a flash of movement as fluid as it was jerky, Logan unwrapped the sandwich, unzipped a few inches of the tent, and flung it outside into the darkness before zipping the tent back up and scooting toward me.

We huddled together in the middle of the tent, listening as the animal grunted and sniffed. Ever so slowly, we heard the sounds move off in the direction where the sandwich had landed. Logan crept again to the tent flap, unzipped it slowly, and peered out into the night. From behind me, the tent again pushed abruptly inward. My focus had been zeroed in on Logan, so I hadn't heard anything behind me. I gasped and flung myself toward him.

"What are you doing?" Logan whispered.

"He's behind us."

"No, he's not. He's right there," Logan whispered, motioning for me to look through the peephole. "It's a moose."

A noise behind us had us both turning around as what looked like a hoof stepped onto the side wall, squishing the nylon tent into the ground.

Logan pushed me to the side as another hoof came down, this time on Logan's pillow.

"There's two of them," Logan whispered in my ear, as we heard the animal move away from the tent.

I grabbed his arm and squeezed. "Aren't moose mean?"

He didn't answer, but there was no need. More grunting and clashing ensued nearby. I dug my fingernails into Logan's arm, but I didn't think he noticed. He peeked out of the flap again and ducked immediately, pushing us both backward as something veered close to our tent.

"What's going on? What's that noise?" I asked, squished underneath his body.

"They're fighting," he hissed. "It's their antlers clashing together. We've got to get out of here. We're gonna get trampled."

The shuffling and grunting grew closer and panic exploded into my nervous system. All I could think about was the hoof stepping onto Logan's pillow and it made me want to run as far away as I could. I made it as far as the zipper before Logan caught the back of my shirt and pulled me into him. He held my body, breathing heavily as the moose pushed against the front of our tent. The clash of their antlers sent a jolt of hysteria clambering up my chest.

After a moment, Logan looked through the flap again and started fumbling around the tent. "They're by the tree. Now's our chance. Get your shoes on. We gotta go."

"Where?" I yanked on my shoes in record time.

"I saw a tree stand a ways up the trail. Grab your phone, we'll need the light."

My hands were shaking as I did what he asked. I wasn't sure I knew what a tree stand was, but it sounded safer than a nylon tent. I pressed against his back as he looked once more out of the tent.

"Alright, let's go."

Slowly, he unzipped the tent, the sound about as subtle as a bomb explosion to my ears. The moon glistened off the shadows, but I didn't need much light to see the fighting animals five yards away from me as I exited the tent. They were huge.

Logan crawled out first, reaching behind him to grab my hand. We crept quietly around our tent, heading in the opposite direction of where the moose were pitted against each other, now only about three feet away. We could see well enough that I didn't turn on my phone's flashlight. My knowledge of moose was limited, to say the least, and I had no idea how they might react to a sudden flash of light in the darkness. They were at a standstill, their antlers locked together in a push-and-pull battle, as we rounded our tent, carefully keeping our eyes on the animals. Twigs snapped beneath our feet when we edged out into the clearing. Suddenly, one of the moose charged forward against the other, pushing him backward toward Logan and me. Logan's grip on my hand tightened as we both took off running blindly into the night.

All was going well, running along in a dark forest, until I tripped on an overgrown root and went down.

32

LOGAN

I felt Tessa fall. Her hand tightened while her body pulled mine back. I stopped, reaching down to help her.

Tessa swore at my hurried attempt to help her stand up. She went limp again, hopping on one foot.

"What's wrong?" I asked, the terrifying sound of clashing antlers ten yards behind us.

"My ankle. I think I twisted it."

The moose crashed against a tree. The forest floor shook at the sheer force of the blow. We had to get out of here.

"Can you walk?"

"Yeah."

She stepped one foot forward and almost went down again before I grabbed her arm, stopping her fall. She yanked it out of my grip and tried again. I clenched my fists tight in an effort to remain calm when there were two bull moose fighting it out in the dark only yards behind us.

When she almost fell at her second attempt, I ignored her mild threats and picked her up in my arms, moving up the trail and away from the powerful animals. I walked us not toward the hot spring, but up the trail, higher into the mountains. The first time Tessa had been changing in my tent, I had taken myself on a little walk up the hill to keep my mind in line and had discovered an abandoned hunter's tree stand. With our limited options, I figured that was the best place for us to crash for the rest of the night.

The stubborn woman refused to relax into my hold, so you can imagine how much more difficult it was to move what seemed like an angry, unbending tree down a darkened trail in the woods. If Tessa was grateful to me for finding us a safe place to hide out for the rest of the night, she didn't allude to that fact.

The tree stand was nothing but a metal ladder nailed to a tree, leading to a metal landing pad, maybe five feet wide. It was a simple place for a hunter to wait out his prey—or for a couple of miserable campers to escape two battling moose. Tessa climbed up first, a slow climb with an ankle she couldn't put any weight on. Finally, we both reached the top.

She scooted over to make room for me. With the thicket of trees between us and the moose, we could no longer see them or their movement, but I could still pick out the sounds of their fight. I wondered how our little tent had fared.

Once we were in the uncomfortable safety of our metal tree, my heart rate slowed. Our adrenaline rush was over. I scooted backward and leaned against the tree trunk. Tessa sat rigid beside me and looked very much like she could pass out from exhaustion any second.

"Should we call a truce for the night?" I asked.

"Hmm?" she mumbled, her head wobbling.

"A truce," I said gently, placing my hand softly on her shoulder and gently pulling her back against me. "You can yell at me tomorrow. But you need to sleep right now."

Her resistance lasted all of two seconds, and then she was curled up on the stand, her head on my lap.

"I am still so mad at you," she mumbled as she scooted backward against me like a kitten searching for warmth.

I wrapped my arms around her, trying to give her any heat I could. "I know."

She was asleep in fifteen seconds.

I<small>T WAS</small> strange for me to think this scene was romantic. Tessa shifted in her sleep, and I immediately cuddled her closer, my hand on her head, soft shushing noises escaping my mouth.

The metal tree stand dug into my tailbone. I hadn't felt my butt in an hour and a half. Earlier, a bird, lit only by moonlight, had attempted a shot at my head twice from his position above me in the tree. I flipped it the bird of my people. Tessa had a large, jagged scratch on her leg, near her twisted ankle. With all that, I shouldn't have felt anything but misery and guilt. The usual suspects.

I looked back down at her face, currently splayed out on my lap.

Tessa had the windpipe of my ninety-year-old grandpa. And it was adorable. She was furious at me right now—hated my guts, according to her 5 a.m. sleep-induced chatter. But all I wanted to do was pull her up against my chest and cuddle her like a newborn kitten. A kitten who got cranky when she was not fed on time. Or when she was on her period. Or when she found out just how much of an idiot I was. She was vulnerable in ways I wanted to be. She made me want to do better. Be better. Even fighting with her was unlike anything I'd ever experienced—in the best way possible. I could imagine us in our old age together, sending out zingers to each other with sly grins and exasperated huffs, all the while pinching butts before making each other laugh about something.

I pulled her more firmly onto my lap to make her more comfortable. She moaned and muttered softly in her sleep. Maybe I'd carve our initials into this tree. Our tree. I thought of that fish Jake had pulled out of the water. For years, there had been a pit growing in the bottom of my stomach, weighing me down. It was gone now. Replaced by something lighter. Something that breathed a lot like hope. I had no more shifting emotions. My thoughts were clear. All traces of doubt were gone. I knew exactly what I wanted. It would be a battle to get it back, but I was willing to fight for it. For her.

I sighed, rubbing my face with my hands—grateful Tessa slept onward, unaware of my emotions that seemed to want to leak from my eyes.

It was that damn sunrise.

How could I feel anything but amazing? Light was bursting through the trees. A new day was beginning. Sun rays were dancing off the leaves all around me. The air was crisp. A girl was in my arms. Not just *a* girl, but *th*—

Anyway...the sunrise. We had survived the night. The moose had scampered off not long after Tessa fell asleep. At least, I didn't hear them any longer. I had never been a morning person, but here I was, in a tree, with a beautiful woman in my arms, chainsaw-massacring the woods with her snoring, and I felt like I could spout poetry. And in case you didn't get the impression, I am not a poetry guy.

Too bad we hadn't had that talk yet, because she would have loved this sunrise.

———

TESSA SEETHED AS I wound half of my shirt around the cut on her calf after assessing the damage. Dried blood stained her ankle from her fall, but the bleeding had stopped. I was taking precautions and putting pressure on it for our journey back down the mountain. She was exhausted and wobbly, and her taking another tumble down the mountainside wasn't completely out of the question.

"Sorry," I mumbled.

Tessa woke up at 6 a.m., got off my lap, and refused to touch me— until I had to help her get down from the tree stand. It would have been much faster to carry her toward our tent, but she refused the offer, instead choosing to lean heavily on me, hopping on one leg and stopping to rest every ten feet. Our tent had been undisturbed. Other than the smooshed grass around it, there were no clues that we had almost been trampled last night. Even the rogue sandwich hadn't been touched, unless you counted a hoof print smashed into the edge. Nature was fascinating that way.

"You want to know what's funny?" Tessa asked, pulling me back to the present. She was sitting on a rock just off the trail while I knelt before her, trying to wrap her leg. She looked at me with an expression on her face somewhere between deep loathing and utter exhaustion. If I hadn't known the activities the previous night had held, I probably would have thought she was drunk. Her speech was slurred slightly, and her green eyes were wild, her hair plastered to her cheeks in clumps. The high ponytail she had gone to bed with had long since disappeared.

I looked at her but said nothing.

"I was going to marry Logan 2.0." She laughed without humor.

I continued wrapping the wound. This was headed somewhere I didn't want to go, and I refused to accelerate the process.

"Logan 2.0 was a big deal at his high school, too—he played sports, everybody liked him, had lots of girls after him." Another laugh blurted from her lips and sent chills down my back. "I think, deep down, I just convinced myself that if I couldn't'thave the Logan I really wanted, maybe Logan 2.0 would be fine. You see, Logans are a dime a dozen. Interchangeable. Except, I called him Tyler." She watched me until I finally looked at her.

By this time, I had finished my pathetic attempt at binding her wound, so I grabbed her hands, pulling her up gently. She balked at the movement. The moment she was standing on her own, she pulled away from me, favoring her leg with a limp.

"Can you walk?"

"Yes." Her chin lifted upward, eyes full of determination.

"It's about two miles down a steep trail. Are you sure?"

"Yes," she hissed again.

I held my arm out to her impatiently, her biting words causing my movements to be abrupt and callous. I reminded myself to be gentler. She was exhausted. That's what it was. She definitely didn't hate my guts. She brushed past my arm and limped down the trail.

I closed my eyes and took a deep breath, digging down deep for the patience I would need for the rest of this hike. Ahead of me, Tessa stumbled, her left leg giving out as she fell forward on her knees. When I reached her side, she was sitting back on her haunches, her hands dirty from catching her fall. She stared at them before slowly wiping them on her clothes. She was breathing heavily and looking like a bomb ready to explode at any second.

"Tess."

She didn't look at me. I reached down and gripped her under her armpit, attempting to pull her into a standing position once more. She leaned forward and yanked her arm from my reach.

"Tessa," I growled. This woman would be the death of me. "You might not like me very much right now, but I'm the only way you're getting down this mountain. You know it, and I know it. So. Let. Me. Help. You."

This time, when I reached down to help her, she didn't jerk away, but she didn't look at me either. Once I got her standing, I immediately put my arm around her, my fingers clasping her below her armpit, holding her up. She fit just right in my arms. Perfect, actually. Of course, that was a really unfortunate thought to have when the lady wanted me dead. We shuffled down the hill for a time. It was torture. At first, Tessa kept her hand fisted at my side, but eventually, her hand loosened, and she clutched at my shirt. We looked like we had just survived a zombie apocalypse. All I needed was a crossbow slung around my shoulders. And *that* was the fantasy that got me through the next two minutes of torturous silence.

Until she spoke again.

"You know, I've had this massive crush on you my whole life. And now, I don't even want you. It's funny how life works, isn't it?" More laughter that wasn't funny. "You'd just flirty flirt with all your girl-friends on the side. Never really commit. Dream about the old glory days. Same old, same old."

"Alright, you know what? I just realized something." I pulled us to a stop and moved her in front of me, forcing her eyes to meet mine. "I almost married Tessa 2.0. Blonde. Hot. Stubborn. Competitive to a fault. But in the end, I wasn't good enough for her. No matter what I did to try and prove myself, my job wasn't enough. My ambitions weren't enough. My personality wasn't enough. *I* wasn't enough. I'm not perfect. I never said I was. Yeah, I dated a lot of girls, but I never once cheated on anybody, alright? Not once. If you're going to lump me in with that jackass you almost married, at least you should know that about me."

She pulled away, and her lame foot immediately twisted, causing her to stumble. I caught her arm before she clattered to the ground. Frustration exploded inside of me. In one swift movement, I pulled her backpack off of her back, tossed it around my shoulder and lifted her off the ground and into my arms. As a reflex, her arm came around my shoulder, bringing her body and face close enough to nestle into my neck. Immediately, I reacted to her closeness. The warmth of her body contrasted with her icy stares, even as she nestled closer. Her soft curves sank into me. Heated puffs of air hit my neck. I ground my teeth in aggravation, my chest breathing heavily. We walked this way for a few minutes. My arms were burning, holding her and her pack, but I didn't want to let go. Everything was in my arms right now, and even though, at the moment, everything felt more like a hissing cat, it was still nice to hold onto it.

A sniffle broke into my trance. At my glance, she hid into my shirt, covering her face with her hand at my chest.

"Don't look at me," she whispered.

"Tessa." My words and my feet stopped there, waiting for her to speak to me. I wasn't taking another step until she did.

"Tessa," I said again. "I'm sorry."

"You terrify me." The words were a whisper. Maybe I wasn't supposed to hear.

But I did.

More than that. I heard what she didn't say. Those words broke open the barred window to my heart. All these years, I had dated every woman I could never bring home to my mom. I dated all the girls who were expendable to me. Safe from me because I knew I was never at risk of falling. Of failing. Of not living up to expectations. Of putting my heart out there again and watching it get smashed into dust. Tessa was the kind of woman you fell for. The kind you imagined your children to look like. The kind that struck terror into the hearts of men who were already scared witless.

The kind that could destroy me.

She looked at me then, her tears leaving streaks down her dirt-covered face. Her green eyes were softened...resigned. The fight was beginning to leave her. That should have been that. I would have kept carrying her down the mountain until my screaming muscles ached for a rest. Maybe we would have kept spitting out verbal jabs along the way, testing and trying each other before going our separate ways at the end of the week.

But our eyes clung a moment too long.

And then another moment.

And another.

My feet stayed planted. Her breathing grew ragged. My eyes found her parted lips. Waiting for me. And then I was done. At my limit. A man holding everything in his arms could only take so much.

And she was definitely my everything. That much I knew for certain. I didn't deserve her, but I wanted her. I wanted to be good enough for her. Dropping her feet to the ground, I kept her wrapped tightly in my arms. Closing the distance, I let my forehead fall against hers.

For as much as she was barbs and nettles, her lips were soft and pliable. Welcoming. She let out a soft gasp as my mouth covered hers. For the longest time, we stood together, locked in a simple embrace while our mouths held close. Touching and tasting, each of us giving a little bit more in the exchange. A little more opening, a little more tasting, a little more pressure until we were finally one.

33

TESSA

I tried to gain control of my slippery emotions, which was hard to do with his lips trailing across my cheek, his hand in my hair, and his arm pulling me snug against him. He felt so good. He was everything I wanted. He had been so close to being mine, but he wasn't. And still I kissed him, even as my heart was breaking. I pulled away from him and out of his arms.

We shouldn't have kissed. I was still so confused. The only thing I knew was that I was half-delirious in my exhaustion, and even though Logan might have saved our lives last night, I still couldn't let go of the betrayal I felt toward him.

He moved beside me quickly, reaching a hand out to grasp my elbow. But I didn't want him to be nice anymore. It pushed too hard against the wall I had built.

"Just stop," I said, flinching as I said the words—the war in my heart spilling out of my lips.

Pulling my arm out of Logan's grasp, I took my backpack from him and lifted my foot gingerly, beginning my slow descent down the trail, hobbling like an old woman.

"Tess," Logan's voice called behind me. "Let's talk."

I kept walking, head held high.

"You want to know what's terrifying, Tess?" His voice was louder. "You're not the kind of girl a guy can go on a date with and be done. You're not casual-dating material."

"What? What do you think I've been doing the past twelve months?"

"Hiding out. Same as me."

"Hiding out? Excuse me, but I don't have flavors of the week. I don't even have flavors of the year!" *Great. Yes. You tell him, Tess.* "Or was it a day for you? I don't even know."

"Yeah, and then they're done. It's the same thing you're doing. Hiding out. You just took a different approach. But you came along and scared the living crap out of me because you're NOT that. You're the girl you take home to meet your family."

"I already know your family."

"Even worse. There's history. You're best friends with my sister. If we ever broke up, they'd kick me out and keep you."

"Is this an apology? If so, you suck."

"It's not an apology."

"Great. I'll see you down the mountain."

"Tessa…"

I ignored him and hobbled off, my chin up and my dignity restored with each swear word I muttered when my foot made contact with the ground.

"Tessa, I swear…"

I kept walking. I was all heart and heat and fire coming out in tiny indignant gasps. We weren't anything. Nothing had been defined, but I had let my stupid heart get attached to him. Re-attached. My face twisted in ugly formations, trying to keep the tears at bay. The pathway before me became blurry.

"I'm so freaking in love with you, Tess."

His voice rang out, strong and clear, and it made me stop, though I didn't turn back to look at him.

"I thought I was in love once before. In fact, I was sure of it. The thought of Valerie saying no wasn't even an option. And then she did. She didn't just say no; she ripped apart everything I had imagined for my life. And I never really recovered from that. And the way I feel about you blows Val out of the water. That terrifies me. It makes me want to pretend I don't feel that way at all so you can't say no. It makes me make a stupid, rash decision to ask out another girl I don't care about to try and push you away before you can do it to me."

His voice had turned softer, gentle, with an ache in the tone that had me turning around to face him. We stood facing each other on the trail, fifteen feet apart.

"I'm sorry I asked out Jen. If I could go back to that second of self-doubt, I would punch myself in the face." Regret and remorse etched into his face as he continued, "I don't want any other girl, Tess. Just you. And if I scare you, just know you have the power to absolutely wreck me."

I blinked, and a tiny tear rolled down my face. I wiped it away. Logan stared at me with his intense eyes, as if watching for any sign to make a move. I wasn't sure what sign to give him. My mind wanted to sing out to the moon, but my heart was feeling too fragile to form a note. I decided to settle in on the one fact that changed everything for me.

"Did you say you loved me?"

He nodded.

I nodded, pursing my lips as I let the words wash over me again. And then again. And again. Until the feeling in my heart and the heat from my belly pooled together in my eyes.

Logan took a few cautious steps toward me. When I didn't move away, he took a few more. When he was standing before me, I shrugged, my emotions too attached to my sleeve to speak. He reached out and tugged at the arms of my sweatshirt tied across my waist, pulling me that last foot closer. I landed softly against his chest, and his arms wrapped around me, squeezing me into him. We stayed that way for several minutes, cocooned in the coziest of hugs.

"I'm so sorry," he whispered in my hair, sending tingles throughout my body.

I smiled against his chest. "I know. Me too."

He started to speak but stopped until he seemed to gather his thoughts and began again, softly. "For a really long time, it was just easier to push people away so I wouldn't get hurt. I had myself convinced that I didn't need anybody. And then *you* happened. I thought this bet would be easy. I had so many excuses for why we would never work."

"Like what?" I asked, feeling snug in his arms.

"You were jailbait." He smiled when I glared at him. His words rolled off of his tongue in a tender rush. "Kelsey's best friend. Untouchable. Too pretty. Too perfect. You name the excuse, and I thought it. I didn't want to hurt you, and I thought that, by keeping everything light and by pushing you away, I could save you from me. But come to find out, you were the one saving me."

As if he couldn't hold himself back any longer, he leaned down and kissed me. His lips brushed against mine, light as a feather. Sweet. Almost as if he were afraid he would break me.

I pulled back. "I'm sorry I overreacted about Jen. And I'm sorry I didn't talk this out with you last night, but I just…couldn't."

He interrupted before I could say more. "You didn't overreact. I almost blew this whole thing with you over someone that meant nothing to me. But I'm done being scared of you. I promise I'm going to face you like a man from now on."

I laughed softly.

"Besides," he added with a heated gleam growing in his eyes. "After our kiss in the hot springs, it was probably for the best that we went to bed mad. Your dad showed me his gun collection the other day. I wasn't sure if it was a warning or just guy stuff, but it painted a pretty good visual of what's expected of me."

My cheeks warmed while I smiled up at him. Then we were lost to kisses once more.

A pair of hikers walked past us with curious looks, effectively ruining the moment. After they passed, Logan pressed his forehead against mine.

"I've got a proposition for you, Jailbait."

"What is it?"

"Want to go double or nothing?"

I furrowed my brow. "What do you mean? With Jake's bet?"

"No. Jake is officially out of our relationship." He laughed. "With us. I've been thinking. We've both been hurt before and...hiding out." He smiled down at me. "But I'm ready to go all in again. With you."

I bit my lip, but it did nothing to stop the smile from spreading across my face. He moved to kiss me, but I pulled back. "Wait, what are my odds?"

He grinned. "Best I've ever seen. Should we seal it with a kiss?" He moved toward me, but just before his lips touched mine, he stopped himself. "Hold up, Jailbait."

I tried to reach his lips in outrage, but he kept himself just out of reach. "What?"

"I'm gonna need some insurance first." His eyes narrowed playfully on mine. "I bared my soul to you, and I wanna make sure you feel the same as you did ten years ago."

Laughter bubbled out of my throat even as I shook my head in disbelief at the sweet vulnerability on his face. I cupped his cheek with my hand. "I loved you then, and I love you still."

A smile lit his face at my confession, and I drew his face down to mine.

THE TREK back down the mountain included a lot of breaks for Logan because he insisted on carrying me on his back the last half of the trail. My ankle had swollen up like a balloon ready to burst. We looked terrible. I needed food. The granola bar I had eaten this morning had long since worn off, especially since I was on empty from the night before. People could survive on love for only so long. I might be in love with Logan, but I would eat him if I had to.

Thankfully, a few early-morning hikers took one pitiful look at us and gave us some of their protein bars and offered to help get us down the mountain. We took their food but not their help. The protein bar revived me, and we eventually found our way back to Logan's truck and were now lounging on the porch swing at my house, tired and dirty but not wanting to trade each other in for sleep just yet.

"So, correct me if I'm wrong, but did your fruit stand move a lot closer to the porch in the last few weeks?" Logan asked.

"Hmm?" I asked innocently.

"You heard me."

"It was all part of Jake's and my plan to get under your skin."

"I knew it."

"When did you decide you liked me?" I asked, suddenly curious to dive deep into Logan's version of the summer.

"This whole summer was like a Tessa drip in my IV. I tried so hard not to let you in, but I couldn't stop it. But I think I knew you were special when you went Rambo on Camille at the grocery store."

I elbowed him while he laughed. "You'll never let me live that down, will you?"

"Never." He was silent before he added softly, "I could have had your dad's porch finished in about three days."

I lifted my head from his shoulder and stared at him.

Three days.

Three. Days.

He had taken nearly three months.

Granted, it was an hour at a time, but visions of him sanding wood lazily on the porch while we joked and teased and flung mild insults back and forth came to my mind. I fed him treats and handed him tools. We had created a comfortable rhythm that I had grown to love.

"You were always the best part of my day," he said, smiling and brushing a strand of hair off my face. "And don't worry, I only charged your dad for three days of work. I think he was on to me."

His dark lashes hid soft eyes that watched as I snuggled into him. We stayed that way for some time, my leg throbbing and my stomach growling.

His fingers moved lightly across my arm. "When did things change for you?"

I smiled into his chest. "The second we shook hands on the bet, I was already having doubts. I thought I'd be fine if I went along with your plan to keep things shallow. But then I couldn't stand it. You were so annoying about it. So, I spent the rest of my time trying to figure out ways to get you to open up to me."

He laughed. "Saboteur."

I squinted up at him. "What did I tell you about quoting *The Office*?"

His fingers traced my lips, a smile on his face. "My evil plan worked."

His lips brushed my forehead, and I wondered if anybody had ever felt as in love as I did at this moment.

"Jake is going to rub this in for the rest of our lives," I said. Another thought came to me as we sat there, effectively squashing the mood. "When are you moving back to Boise?"

A shadow came over his face. "I don't know yet. I have… I have a few ideas I'm thinking on, but I'm not sure."

There were still so many questions we didn't have answers to. So many things still up in the air. Logan was two weeks away from going back to his home and life in Boise. Not that we couldn't still date, but I had gotten used to seeing him every day. It would be hard to give that up now, but I would if I had to. He was finally mine, and he was worth the wait.

34

TESSA

O n Monday, Logan was busy at the office, installing his cabinets and doing the finish work. Mom had joined me at the orchard, keeping me company on a particularly slow day. A pack of butterflies had moved into my stomach since I woke up. Tonight, we were meeting with Jake about the truck. I felt solid in our relationship. Granted, it had been going strong for exactly forty-eight hours now, but admitting things to a third party was going to be interesting. Especially a third party who had perfected an all-knowing, annoying grin. And one who would never let us live this down.

Mom came from the greenhouse, carrying a small box loaded with strawberries we had picked that morning. She was down to only using a cane when she walked.

"You'll be back to running 10Ks in no time," I said, patting her knee.

"I will," she said.

I turned to look at her. "Wow, you're optimistic today."

"I decided I'm going to get past this and heal. It's time to go back to doing everything I want to do. I've heard so many horror stories about knee replacements, but I'm determined not to be one of them."

"Good for you. And good job not being a terrible patient. You'll get better because you listened and did what I told you to do. That always helps."

My phone buzzed with a text from Logan, showing me the cabinets he'd just installed. After proudly showing the picture to my mom, I typed back a message to him, full of gushy embarrassing love stuff I couldn't hold back if I tried.

"I'm glad Logan finally admitted to being in love with you." She kicked my toe gently.

I lifted my head to look at her. "What do you mean?"

"Honey, that boy has been gone on you for months. He just didn't know what to do about it. Did you know your dad never told him to re-paint the porch railings?"

No. I didn't.

I was enjoying a quiet glow until Mom poked my arm. "Are you excited to see your new office?"

"Yeah."

The heat from her blatant stare singed my cheek until I turned and looked at her. "What?"

"And how are you feeling about your career choice in Eugene with Logan in Boise?"

"About as good as I felt about my career choice three semesters in."

"What?"

Here it was. It wasn't admitting it to Nate yet, but talking it over with my mom seemed like a decent start. "Honestly, Mom, I'm not sure that physical therapy is the right career for me. I thought I would like it, but unless screaming into a pillow after every session is normal, I don't seem to."

I bravely held eye contact with her and was startled when she began to laugh.

"Why are you laughing?"

"Tess, I always thought it was a strange choice of career for you ever since you went for it, but you were so determined. I don't know if it was pressure from Nate that made you do it, but for some reason, I always wondered about you."

"Wait, what?"

"You have a lot of strengths, Tessa Robbins, but patience for people isn't necessarily one of them."

"I was patient with you!" I protested.

"You were great," she said firmly. "But I assume that was more because I'm your mother, and I have many of your tendencies myself. We're goers and doers, and we like results. Some people are casual doers. And that's fine. They're probably great at something else that we're terrible at. The world turns because everybody is different. But I always wondered why you didn't become a chef or baker or something."

"I've thought about it, but I wanted a job with some stability. And hearing Nate always talk about it made it sound like something I could do. And then I didn't want to disappoint you and Dad. You spent all that money to put me through school. I'm not going to just throw it away."

"Don't worry about us, Tess. We'd much rather see you enjoy your career than stick with something you hate."

"I know, and I love that. But I think I've decided what I'm going to do."

"What's that?"

"I'm gonna stick it out—at least for a while longer. I chose this career. I gave Nate my word. And I'm going to give it my all for a while. I'm going to learn from Nate because he's got to be the best in the business. And I'm going to work on building up a gig on the side."

My mom smiled. "Bakery?"

"Yeah. I think I could easily do more with Chad once he sees a difference in his sales." I rolled my eyes as I continued, "But with selling stuff at the fruit stand, I've had some inquiries about making a couple birthday cakes and treats for a wedding reception."

"That's a pretty good start for a side gig."

The rumble of a familiar Ford pulled into the driveway. My mom chatted with Logan for a few minutes before excusing herself and walking back to the house. Logan took her chair and immediately pulled me onto his lap.

"How come we didn't just go full-blown into cuddles and make outs when we started this thing this summer?" Logan asked.

"Hmm," I said, snuggling into his chest. "If I remember right, I think one of us was a big fat chicken."

Logan began tickling my side. I squealed and tried to get away, but he held me tight. Finally, he released me only to kiss the top of my head, sending tingles down my spine. "That big fat chicken was a big fat idiot. The solution was *always* more kissing. My bad."

We were sitting opposite each other with our hands to ourselves by the time the other truck showed up. This time, the truck was big and black and beefy—the kind of truck you heard before you saw it. The paint gleamed, and the windows were tinted. It looked like it was freshly washed. There was no squeak of the door when Jake opened it.

"Game face, Jailbait," Logan said, and we stood up and went to greet Jake.

He was all smiles as he stood next to the truck, arms folded, studying us.

"Looks like you survived the camping trip. Barely." He nodded toward my bandaged leg.

He was looking at us expectantly, but Logan and I held strong. We stared back at him casually.

"Yeah, it was alright," I said, looking up at Logan.

He shrugged. "If you're into nature and hot blondes."

Jake's eyes narrowed. "Oh, I think you're into hot blondes."

"Okay, hi. My name's Tessa."

Jake looked at me innocently. "And how about you, Tess? How'd you sleep?"

Although everything had worked out better than I could have imagined, I was still miffed at the audacity he had to steal my tent. There may have been an imperceptible nostril flare before I tamed my natural reaction into something more wholesome. "Good."

We were giving him nothing, and I didn't think he was really buying it, but a glimmer of doubt crossed his face.

He cleared his throat. "Well, the time has come." He jingled the keys toward us. "What will it be? Love or truck?"

Logan folded his arms and moved forward, eyeing the truck in mild disdain. "What kind of gas mileage does this thing get?"

Jake shrugged, a hint of amusement on his face. "I've never bothered to check since I was planning to blow it up."

"It's probably terrible," Logan said, peering into the passenger side window. "And the color is terrible. Does it have to be so shiny? It wouldn't last a day on a construction site."

"I agree. It needs to be taken out and shot."

"It's too high, too." He turned to look at me. "Hey, Tessa Robbins. That's your name, right? Could you come here for a sec? I need to make sure a woman can actually climb in this thing."

I hobbled toward Logan, barely keeping the smile from my face as I made a sorry attempt to get into the truck. "Yeah, see. That's not going to work."

Jake was grinning by this point. "Do you want to fire it up and try driving it? I can give you both a boost."

Logan bit his lip. He was putting on a good show, but I knew there was nothing he'd love better than to take a drive in that truck.

"Yeah," I said. "Let's test drive it really quick."

The boys looked at me in surprise.

"I'm serious," I said.

Jake held the keys out to me, but before I could grab them, Logan knocked them out of my reach. We all watched as they clattered to the ground.

"We don't need to test drive it."

"Because..." Jake was watching us carefully, trying to rein in the beam of light wanting to escape from him.

"Because I fell in love with the only girl in the world I would want more than your dumb truck."

Logan ignored Jake's excited shouts and ribbing and pulled me into his arms. I came easily and snuggled into that perfect spot, somewhere between his chest and neck. And he held me tight.

The epic fallout of this bet would last the rest of our lives. At every gathering that included Jake, he would remind us of this moment. He would insist that we name a kid after him, and we probably would just to get him off our backs. But even that wouldn't work. He would be relentless.

And we would love it.

Because we only had appreciation for Jake Evans. A love as deep as any sibling could boast. And as Logan kissed my cheek and whispered his love for me in my ear, I knew he felt the same.

I only hoped that we could one day, if needed, return the favor.

35

LOGAN

The cabinets were in place. My guys were installing the hardware and touching up paint. We had flooring in. We were so close to calling a wrap on this project. I should have been more excited —the crew had killed it. Working in Eugene and being hands-on with almost every aspect of the build had breathed new life inside me. There'd been fewer hold-ups on the project because we didn't have to schedule too many outside subs. I got to build the cabinets, and help my dad, and be here with Tessa. The thought of moving back to Boise was killing me. Tessa had ruined me for the better. I thought about her constantly, which I guess was no different than earlier this summer, but now I didn't *have* to stop.

I was sitting in The Grub Shack, waiting for Nate, who had asked me to meet him for lunch. My mind was a whirl of activity as to why he would want to meet with just me. Tessa and I had informed both of our families that we were dating, and the most common reaction was a hearty slap on the back as well as an eye roll. Jake spent much of his time on the farm trying to find me alone so he could rub in his victory again. I didn't even mind. I owed that kid a debt of gratitude, and I'd let him have his hay day—at least for a little while longer.

The door of the restaurant opened, and Nate strode inside, the building seeming to shrink at his impressive presence. I stood to shake his hand, and when we were both seated again, he folded his arms on the table and studied me.

"So, you and my sister, huh?"

I shifted uncomfortably. I was a grown man. Nate shouldn't have had the power to intimidate me, but the fact that he was Tessa's brother and his biceps were, in fact, bigger than my head caused me to sit up a little straighter when I answered him.

"Yup."

His eyes pierced into mine. "You're not even going to ask my permission?"

What the...?

At my deer-in-the-headlights look, his face broke out into a smile. "I'm kidding. I'm happy for you guys. But I do feel like I have to say the obligatory...if you hurt her, I will kill you."

I fingered the straw wrapper on the table, breathing easier. "Don't worry about me. I'm all in. At this point, I'm more worried about Tessa realizing she doesn't want me."

He huffed out a sound of amusement. "Do you know anything about her scrapbook?"

"No."

A small grin slipped on his face. "You should ask her about it sometime. But don't do it when I'm around. Point being, I don't think you have anything to worry about."

Chad sidled up next to us, looking impatient. "What do you guys want? Or are you here for the free water?"

"Hot dog and fries for me," Nate said automatically. Apparently, he'd been here before. I was about to order the same thing when a familiar voice called out from the back.

"No!"

We turned to see Tessa come through the doorway from the back kitchen, an apron around her waist and a wide smile.

"Try the meatloaf sandwich. I've been giving Chad pointers. You guys can be our guinea pigs."

Chad sighed and tilted his head toward the ceiling with his eyes closed, looking as though he were gathering patience.

I had never once had or ever wanted to eat a meatloaf sandwich, but I immediately agreed. Tessa beamed in my direction, which made me want to eat meatloaf sandwiches every day for the rest of my life.

Nate wrinkled his nose in distaste. "Hot dog and fries for me still. I'm your brother, not your boyfriend."

"Chicken."

She came to our table and sat next to me, our hands finding their way to each other while Chad grunted and stalked back behind the counter.

"What are you doing here?" I asked. I knew she'd been taking her desserts to Chad for the last month, and it seemed to be going well for her, but I didn't know she was giving him cooking advice. Poor Chad.

"I came to drop off some desserts, and he was right in the middle of making the meatloaf, so I invited myself to keep him company."

I grinned. "I'll bet he's excited to have you."

"He's smiled twice already, and I've only been here an hour. I've got him eating out of my hand. What are you guys doing here?" She looked back and forth from me to Nate.

Nate answered, "I've got an idea I wanted to run by Logan."

Before she could respond, Chad yelled from the back, "Are you here to help me or to gab with my customers?"

She beamed and squeezed my hand before releasing it. "I told you he loves me. Have fun, you two."

I was disconcerted to see Nate's intense gaze on me when she left.

"Meatloaf sandwich, huh? Maybe I don't have anything to worry about."

I breathed out a laugh. "You really don't."

He shifted in his seat. "Do you know what your plans are? You're moving back to Boise, right?"

My stomach clenched at the thought of leaving. "That's always been the plan. If there was another way, I'd stay in a heartbeat."

"You like it here?"

I knew what he was really asking me. Do I like Tessa enough to stay?

"Yeah. I do. In Boise, I'm on the computer and making calls, so I rarely get to do what I want, which is being on site and actually building. So, if you're asking me what I loved about being here, it's everything. Your sister, my job, my family, running my own crew, and having more of a hand in the building process."

He nodded, looking thoughtful. "I've been talking with Chase about a few investment ideas for Eugene. With the new potato factory moving in outside of Salmon, the town's seen quite a bit of growth, and I think there's more coming. There's talk about getting more of Main Street up and running again, putting in some new businesses, new buildings, revamping the old. Chase and I are thinking about bringing on another partner to help get us off the ground. Is that something you'd be interested in?"

I stared at him, dumbfounded. "Yeah. I would. What does that entail?"

Nate smiled. "We're still working on the details, but essentially, you would handle the on-site construction projects. If some of your crew wants to stick around here with you, that would be fine, but I don't think it'd be too hard to hire some local guys. Chase would be a financial investor. I would handle the business and marketing side of things."

Hearing what he was saying and believing the words out of his mouth were two different things. Surely there was a catch. Life didn't happen like this. The perfect job did not fall into your lap without a catch.

Nate continued, "I know you and Chase will have some things to talk through before you can officially say yes, but as it is now, he's on board with this idea—if you need a good reason to stick around."

At that moment, Tessa and Chad came through the swinging door connecting the back kitchen to the front bar and grill. Chad was pretending to not be thrilled she was there, and Tessa was talking a mile a minute about the correct way to cook a hamburger. She was carrying two plates piled high with food. Extra fries. They paused as she set the plates down so she could use her hands while she animatedly finished their discussion. Apparently, slapping some meat down on a grill with a little salt and pepper was not the only way to cook a hamburger. I'd noticed the past month of dating her that only two things got her that animated: food and me.

Man, I loved her.

I turned back to Nate. "I don't need a reason. But I do need a job. And if you think there's enough work around here to keep me busy, I'm definitely interested in talking this over. So far, it sounds perfect."

Nate grinned. "Good. I was hoping you'd say that. Meet with Chase sometime this week and figure out how you want to proceed, and then we'll all meet up and go over a few ideas."

I had a hard time keeping the smile from my face by the time Tessa and Chad brought our food out. I eyed the monstrosity on my plate with an air of careful importance. At first glance, the presentation of the dish was much better than earlier this summer. The meatloaf looked less sludge-like than before, the bread was from a local bakery in town and looked hearty enough to handle. A piece of parsley and a toothpick rounded out the display, along with an impressive pile of fries surrounding the entire sandwich.

Aware of my audience, I hefted the sandwich into my fingers and took a large bite. A subtle yet delicious beef flavor flooded into my mouth. I pulled the sandwich away to examine it.

"I don't detect a hint of badger anywhere in here."

Chad swore while Tessa lifted her hands triumphantly into the air.

"That's a certified mixture of beef and pork," she said proudly.

I took another bite and groaned. Perhaps the groan was for my girlfriend's sake—it was good, but it was still a meatloaf sandwich.

Tessa sat down next to me on the booth seat, the ripped plastic squeaking, and shifted to wrap her arms around my neck to kiss me. Nate promptly asked for a to-go box and said he'd be eating in his car, while Chad left, muttering something about biased customers.

Tessa broke away from me. "I'm taking my lunch break now, Chad."

"You're not getting paid for this. I don't care what you do," he called back.

Soon, we were all alone in the booth. Tessa stole a few fries off of my plate and took a bite of the sandwich, chewing carefully as if trying to decide what else it needed.

"You did good," I said, nudging her with my elbow.

She smiled at me. "Chad wants me to help him overhaul his entire menu this fall."

"Really? That's awesome."

"It will at least give me something to do while you're gone during the week."

I grinned at her. I had wanted to surprise her with the news, but I couldn't stand waiting another second. Soon, she was all over me again, this time with only a disgusted Chad as our witness.

"Here, eat some more fries, Jailbait. We've got to keep your hands busy or else Chad will kick us out."

"So, you're staying?"

"It looks that way. I need to talk with Chase, and I'll be back and forth to Boise here and there. I've got a house that I either need to rent or sell."

Her brow furrowed slightly. "Are you really okay with moving back?"

"Oh yeah. Nate thinks there's a lot of potential growth for this town, and if all goes well, the possibilities are endless. And I'll be in charge of my own crew, which means I can do things my way. I guess the first thing would be to hire an assistant who can handle emails and phone calls for me. You interested?"

She laughed, tucking her hair behind her ear. "After the foosball table, I'm pretty sure I'd kill you if I had to work with you. Besides, I'm interested to see where things go with helping Chad out. I love being here."

"Really?"

"Maybe The Grub Shack's the perfect place to start on your quest to spruce up Main Street." She leaned into my shoulder, stealing more fries off of my plate.

My eyes narrowed. "You've taken most of my fries, but you've only eaten one bite of the sandwich. Something seems off."

She wrinkled her nose. "Eh. It's better than it was, but it's still a meatloaf sandwich."

"Any dessert?"

"Chocolate cake."

"Yours?"

"Yup."

"Now there's something that can make a man want to move to Eugene."

Her eyes narrowed while her hands found their way around my neck. "You had better be meaning me and not the cake, right?"

"Hmmm...it's definitely the cake. But the lemon bars are a nice bonus."

Before she could say anything else, I kissed her. The booth was not a place meant for make-outs, but I did the best I could, sliding the table away from us to give me enough room to pull her onto my lap.

Chad kicked us out a few minutes later.

We took our chocolate cake to go.

EPILOGUE

Tessa

Whistles and shouts filled the little white church in Eugene. White roses and flower petals were strewn all around the aisle. Dusty looked handsome in his black suit and matching cowboy hat. He wore a sweet and contented smile as he kissed his bride, who stood blushing in white satin. Lucy's dark hair curled loosely around her shoulders. Her eyes were big behind her dark glasses and pert nose, and my heart wanted to burst for my friend who had found such a lovely girl to marry.

After a luncheon, the crowd gathered at Dusty's parents' home for a reception. When we arrived at their backyard decked out in white string lights and complete with a moveable wooden dance floor, Logan and I made our way to the bride and groom's table.

"Congrats, man." Logan stuck out his hand toward Dusty, which he ignored, pulling Logan in for a hug.

"You up next?" Dusty asked Logan impishly, glancing over at me.

Logan grinned. "I'm still trying to convince her to keep dating me."

I ignored him and gave Lucy a hug.

"I'm so happy for you two."

She beamed, fixing her veil. "Thank you. Thanks for coming and for the desserts. I'm just praying I get a chance to eat some of them today."

I laughed. "Logan and I stashed a container full of everything in Dusty's truck."

Her eyes widened. "Bless you."

A crowd had gathered behind us, waiting to speak to the bride and groom, so I scooted Logan out of my way to hug Dusty before we left them to their guests.

"Have you heard anything from your parents?" I asked as we made our way to the treat table filled with two large chocolate cakes, cookies, brownies, and raspberry-lemon bars I had been hired to make for the reception.

"Nothing yet. You? They'd probably let you know before me."

"Kelsey was supposed to be giving me real-time updates, but she had to leave her phone with Cade, and for some reason, he's not texting every thirty seconds like I asked him to."

"I can't imagine why."

Logan had loaded his plate full of raspberry-lemon bars. He would have added more, but I stopped him. "I made you your own special plate, Logan Marten. Don't eat all of these. It's bad for business."

Since the summer and my stint baking for Chad's restaurant, word had begun to spread around Eugene. I had enough steady business coming in that I was able to drop down to part time at Willow Creek Physical Therapy. And that was enough for me. I realized that I didn't hate physical therapy; I actually enjoyed working with Nate. But I found that I was the sort of person who needed a creative outlet in the form of baking. I had been saving for a down payment to move into my own house by next spring. My parents had been great, but I would be twenty-five in another week, and I needed my space. Logan had been helping me with the house hunt, and we'd found a modest fixer-upper just outside of town that had everything we—I mean, *I* was looking for.

I wasn't sure where Logan was at with the whole marriage thing. We certainly acted like we would get married one day, but we never spoke about it directly. With Logan's past and mine, I hadn't wanted to broach the subject just yet, but with us talking about fixing up the house and the changes we would make, I couldn't help but wonder just where he was at in his head.

We spent the next while laughing and catching up with old friends. Logan was resistant when I pulled him toward the dance floor outlined by the glow of white twinkle lights, but when he recognized the tune of a familiar song we had slow-danced to earlier this summer, a soft smile played on his lips while his hand on my waist pulled me closer.

"Maybe I should tell the DJ to add my favorite Nelly songs to this playlist," he whispered. "To liven things up."

"Shhh," I laughed, placing my fingers on his lips, which he promptly kissed. "'Dirt' is my favorite song."

"Mine too."

We were interrupted a minute later by Jake and his girlfriend, Miranda, who danced up next to us. It was my third time meeting her, and I was hoping that the third time was a charm. Judging by the way her lip curled up in a fake smile when she looked at me, I seriously doubted that would be the case. I wasn't sure what it was about her, but something nettled me. I kept waiting for Jake to tell us they broke up, but they had been going strong for the past few months.

"You lovebirds heard anything?" Jake asked. He never ceased to call us lovebirds. His own personal reminder of his orchestrating our relationship.

Logan released me to check his phone.

"I just got a message from my mom." Logan read us the message. "The twins are here. Two boys. Kelsey's doing great. Babies are healthy. Cade is on cloud nine. No names yet."

I squealed, immediately pulling my phone out of my pocket and finding a row of pictures of a happy couple holding crying babies with red cheeks and dark hair. Tears leaked out of my eyes as I studied them before showing Logan and Jake. I politely held the phone out to

Miranda, to which she leaned forward, trading her disinterested gaze for a polite nod before tugging on Jake's arm.

"We better get going, Jake. My friends are meeting us for dinner at six." She began pulling Jake off the dance floor before he stopped, looking back at us.

"Wait, no names yet?"

"Not yet," Logan said.

"Ugh, text me when you know. I've never been a favorite uncle before."

He waved to us before being dragged away and out of his best friend's wedding reception early.

"I don't like that," I told Logan, who was also staring after them.

"Me neither. But I can't pinpoint exactly what's wrong—besides the fact that he thinks *he's* going to be the favorite uncle."

We helped close the reception down, staying late and talking with old friends before helping clean up and take down tables. We arrived back at my home sometime after my parents had already gone to bed. Dropping onto the porch swing, we sat quietly, holding hands and sighing deeply.

I sat up suddenly. "What time is it? I'm going to call her."

He wrapped an arm around my shoulder and pulled me back down against him. "Don't call her. It's late. Let her sleep. We can talk to her tomorrow."

I leaned my head on Logan's shoulder and closed my eyes. Kelsey had babies. Dusty was married. I was dating Logan Marten, and it was going really well. I was waiting for the ball to drop. There were too many good things going on. Certainly this streak couldn't last. Could it?

Logan leaned to one side, digging around in his pocket. "I've been meaning to talk to you about something, Jailbait."

I refused to let myself panic at words like that because he only called me Jailbait when he was going to tease me about something.

"Yeah?"

He pulled a wrinkled piece of paper about the size of a notecard out of his pocket and held it out in front of me. Laughter sprang out of me.

"You really kept it?"

"I really did. I thought you could put it in your scrapbook."

I almost didn't realize what he said. The way it rolled off his tongue was so easy and natural. And then I gasped, horrified. "I'm going to kill Nate."

His eyes were dancing. "I just need to know…what kind of pictures do you have in that thing? You didn't have a camera in the laundry room, did you?"

My cheeks burned while I hid behind my hands, trying to block out his face, brimming with laughter.

He tugged my hands down and pulled me back against his chest. "Don't worry, Jailbait, I happen to find your embarrassing ways adorable."

Holding the card in front of me, he let me read my love note from fifteen years earlier.

Dear Logan,

I hereby pledge my undying love
and devotion to you. Forever.
I pledge to marry you if you ever
ask me. (You just need to show
me this note and I will.)

Forever yours,
Tessa Robbins

"I'D LIKE to cash in this coupon." Logan's voice was low and soft and promptly erased any desire to laugh. My breath caught in my throat, and the hair on my arms and neck stood at attention, charged.

Logan stood from the swing, turned, and knelt on one knee in front of me. He grasped my hands and met my gaze, his steady eyes glistening.

"Will you marry me, Tess? I love you. You're the best thing that's ever happened to me."

Before he could finish, I flung my arms around his neck. "Yes! Yes, yes, yes." My tears came next before I could get out another word. Warm fingers wiped them from my cheeks.

"I also hereby pledge my love and devotion to you," he whispered.

A laugh bubbled out of my throat. He pulled me from the swing and into his arms, where I kissed him for a long time.

DEAR DIARY,

I'm marrying Logan Marten. Just like we planned.
XOXO
P.S. He loves me.

AUTHOR'S NOTES

Years ago, somebody asked my Grandpa how he raised such a good family. "It's easy," he said. "Just marry a good woman and get out of her way." This sweet sentiment has always stuck with me, and I was so happy when those words came back to me while writing a pivotal moment in Logan's transformation. My Grandma passed away a few weeks before the release of this book, and I am so happy to have this little tribute to her. She *was* a good woman, and I miss her every day.

Growing up, the neighboring farmer next to my family would host a fugitive game every so often. As you can imagine, it was always a highlight of our summers. The game felt very much like how I wrote it in this story, lots of running, dirt, and hiding, except with much less action in the ditch. Haha!

When I was around 13 or 14, I made a scrapbook dedicated to my teenage heartthrob, Leonardo DiCaprio. This was in his sexy hair days of Romeo and Juliet and Titanic. I bought every magazine that had his face on it, a pair of scissors, some glue, and buried it and my shame deep in the recesses of my closet. I loved the idea of Tessa doing something similar. I hadn't thought about that scrapbook in years, and when I tried to find it, it was nowhere to be found. So now I'm just left hoping I had destroyed it long ago and had forgotten.

In Idaho, most of us call soda *pop.* And we eat our fries with something called *fry sauce*—which is a mixture of ketchup and mayonnaise and a few seasonings. Now, I'm not biased at all, but dipping in fry sauce is actually the MOST correct way to eat fries. Haha! I mentioned *fry sauce* in this book, but I decided to refer to Margo's Diet Pepsi as a *soda* to make it more fitting for a wider audience, but just know that it killed me a little bit inside to call it that.

I hope you enjoyed this book. Thank you so much for reading!

THANK YOU

Did you miss Dusty's story? This sweet novella has forced proximity, very sexy cowboy, a sweet and anxious heroine, a snowstorm, cute grandparents, and a whole lot of flirtatious teasing! Buy it HERE!

Thank you so much for reading! There are so many great book options out there. I appreciate your time reading mine.

Reviews are so critical for an author. If you feel so inclined, you can find my books on Amazon, Goodreads, and Bookbub.

ALSO BY CINDY STEEL

ABOUT CINDY

Cindy Steel was raised on a dairy farm in Idaho. She grew up singing country songs at the top of her lungs and learning to solve all of life's problems while milking cows and driving tractors—rewriting happy endings every time. She married a cute Idaho boy and is the proud mother of two wild and sweet twin boys and a sweet baby girl. Which means she is also now a collector of bugs, sticks, rocks, and slobbery kisses. She loves making breakfast, baking, photography, reading a good book, and staying up way past her bedtime to craft stories that will hopefully make you smile.

She loves to connect and get to know her readers! She is the most active on Instagram at @authorcindysteel, and her newsletter, but can occasionally be found on Facebook at Author Cindy Steel, and her website at www.cindysteel.com.

Made in United States
North Haven, CT
26 May 2025

69203216R00173